Accidental Hitman

A.W. Wilson

Copyright © 2011 A.W. Wilson

All rights reserved.

The moral right of the copyright holder has been asserted

This book is a work of fiction. Names, characters, businesses, organisations, places and events are either the product of the author's imagination or are used fictitiously. Any resemblance to actual persons, living or dead, events or locales is entirely coincidental.

awwilson.com

Printed and bound by Amazon

ISBN: 9781726628198

For all the people who bought this book in its original format and bothered to tell me what they thought.

It meant an awful lot.

One

The first person I ever killed was my best friend. His name was Paul, I forget his surname. I didn't mean to do it. We were just unlucky. Or rather, *he* was unlucky. His girlfriend Susie was there too. She watched it happen. We were in the stream at the bottom of Paul's garden, all of us in welly-boots. There was a rope and a tyre hanging from a tree branch that stuck out over the water. We would swing on that for a while then we'd wander about in the stream and find stuff. Finding stuff was great. That day I found an old milk bottle. I filled it with water and threw it high into the air. I waited for a big splash but instead there was just a loud hollow crack as it connected with Paul's head. The bottle remained intact, but Paul's skull fared less well. He was floating, face up, in less than a foot of water with red cloud billowing around him. We could see that he was dead straight away, like someone had flicked a switch that turned him from a person into a corpse.

Susie and I just gawped at our fallen friend. Our child-minds had no idea of what to do in this situation. Paul and Susie had only got together two days before. They had broken their French-kiss virginity in that very stream. I thought it was disgusting to put your tongue in someone else's mouth (little did I realise that once I hit puberty I would spend almost all my time trying to get girls to let me do just that) but Paul insisted he liked it. I was sure he was just saying that to please Susie, but now we would never know for sure.

It was Susie who suggested the cover story; she was canny for a nine-year-old. I was still in shock when she said we couldn't admit I'd done it because I'd be put in a home. She was probably wrong, I doubt I would have been taken away; it was an accident after all, but I would probably have been forced to sit through hours of counselling and therapy, which would have been bad enough, so she was on the right lines. In all honesty I was more concerned about what his parents were going to say. It would have been terribly embarrassing. The previous summer I had accidentally knocked over a vase in Paul's house while we played hide and seek. His mum was livid; she sent me home and wouldn't let me round there for weeks. If she could get so het-up about something as trivial as a smashed vase then her reaction to me smashing her son's cranium would have been unthinkable.

So we told the adults that Paul had slipped and hit his head on a rock. He was floating right next to a big flat stone and that helped add weight to the story.

Susie kept our secret for the rest of her life. This is less impressive than it sounds. She died less than two years later on her eleventh birthday. Her mother took a group of us to a swimming pool as part of the celebration (a birthday celebration, not a celebration of her death, that hadn't happened yet). Nobody was looking; the other kids in our group were doing handstands in the shallow end. Susie and I were in the deep end having an underwater race. It wasn't hard to drown her. I waited until she had been under for some time and then came from above and guided her downwards. She seemed strangely compliant, soundless and yielding.

I had to do it. I trusted Susie-the-child to keep her promise, but I knew she would eventually become Susie-the-adult, and in the adult world different rules applied. A bond between children seems very strong at the time but I knew enough about the world of grown-ups to realise that secrets never stayed secret, not in the long run. Susie would eventually have boyfriends, and probably a husband with whom she would share her life. She wouldn't be able to keep something like that to herself forever. I wouldn't have been sent away for causing the accident of Paul's death, but knew that if it ever did come out, even years later, then I'd be on the end of a perverting-the-course-of-justice or even a manslaughter charge. It was a shame, she was my friend, and it was her birthday for Christ's sake, but it was a good opportunity and one not to be missed. Her mother didn't celebrate her daughter's death.

It seemed that my actions had brought me to the attention of the Grim Reaper, and that he wanted to play a bigger part in my life. I became surrounded by death; immersed in it. My extended family was large, but it was to get smaller. Some relation or other was always popping their clogs. I got used to death but never got used to funerals. In that grief-stricken, uncompromising atmosphere I get seized by an overpowering urge to laugh. I don't know why. Perhaps I have some form of very specific disorder that causes my body and mind to show me up when I'm expected to act with sombre reverence. I can get away with it when somebody close to me has died because it looks like I'm crying; really sobbing. It's when it's a more distant relative that it becomes a problem.

We are all instinctively aware of the hierarchy of grief at funerals: The close family and friends are devastated. The partners of the close family and friends feel grief in empathy for their bereaved loved ones. Then there are those who are there out of duty, who had a mere acquaintance with the

deceased but would feel rude if they didn't put in an appearance; they are sympathetic to all those involved but don't feel any personal anguish, and in most cases are bored within a few minutes. If I have a fit of the giggles when I'm in this outer circle there's no way of pretending it's anything else; it's obvious it's not grief that's making my shoulders shake, I'm clearly just pissing myself. Nobody ever says anything though.

Vicars sometimes wear microphones at funerals. Their words of comfort boom from speakers throughout the church. That kills me.

Worse than the funeral is the wake, which in theory is a good idea, a more fitting farewell than the stuffy formality of the funeral ceremony. It's a chance for friends and relatives to properly celebrate the life of the deceased, with the grief numbed by familiar company, a good flow of alcohol and a common ground:

"Do you remember when he…?"

"I never saw him laugh as much as that time when..."

"He loved that car, I remember when…"

Unfortunately, most wakes don't turn out this way. Obviously, I expect them to be sad occasions, but they always seem to be so *miserable*. The shameful fact is that most dear-departed are sent off by mourners who are wallowing in disappointment at the sorry sandwich selection, and the piss-poor array of cheap, warm cans of lager. Worst of all is the conversation; small talk about recently discovered inexpensive mobile phone tariffs, and directions back onto the ring road don't make a good soundtrack to a fond farewell.

The deaths around me weren't limited to my family; my colleagues also seemed to have a habit of, not shuffling, but leaping off this mortal coil. It wasn't that I had a dangerous job, well actually it was; I was a fireman. I lost three of my colleagues in one go when a gas tank exploded in a fire in a school kitchen. There weren't supposed to be any gas tanks in there, I had checked with the janitor before we cleared the lads to go in. It wasn't my fault; I had to go by his word. It wasn't my fault.

ACCIDENTAL HITMAN

I wasn't a fireman for long, it just wasn't for me. I was told before I joined up that firemen are supposed to get girls all the time, and that's true to some extent, but I quickly discovered that the girls who went for me because of my job weren't the most powerful hoses on the appliance, so it wasn't a huge benefit. It was the hanging around that did it for me; waiting on call at the station for endless hours. I was rubbish at snooker and there really wasn't much else to do. Except self-abuse of course. Everyone seemed to be wanking. There were stacks of skin mags everywhere. The floor of our common-room looked like a scale model of an inner-city council development, covered as it was with high-rises of porn. I like a squeeze on the icing-bag as much as the next man but I prefer a bit of decorum, so I didn't appreciate the other lads disappearing into the toilet with their favourite centrefold under their arm, emerging a few minutes later with sticky hands and a slightly lower sense of self-esteem.

So I left the fire service, and I don't think they were too sad to lose me. I took a job as a groundskeeper looking after the parks and communal gardens of the town. I liked spending my days sitting on a mower in the sun. Only one colleague died during my six-month stint and no, it wasn't me, I didn't mow him to death. Apparently his bladder exploded. It wasn't that he really needed to go either; he'd literally just been. I mowed round him a few times before I realised. I thought he was pissing around. I suppose he was. Kind of.

I should introduce myself, although it's difficult because I've changed so much, including my name. To keep it simple, I'll introduce you to the person I was when all this began. His name was Tom White. He lived alone, which he found worked best for him and for the whole of womankind too. What do you need to know about him? There's not much to know really, he was an average guy, well, slightly below average as I, he,

5

came to understand – a tad below par. He was thirty-one years old and lived in Brighton. He liked the sea air. His mother always used to pretend to be proud of him; his father didn't even bother to pretend. He never sees his parents any more.

We came to a mutual understanding one Christmas Day. I, the far from prodigal son, had returned to the family home to do my festive duty. It was mid-afternoon and I was wearing a party hat, trying not to fart and succeeding only in belching repeatedly instead. The television was off because we were 'having a family Christmas, not staring at the idiot box' (my dad's favourite term). We were bored out of our minds. We could think of nothing to say to each other. All I could think of was the fact that I was missing the Bond movie, and I didn't even like Bond, especially Sean Connery. Roger Moore was loads better despite what everyone says. Anyway, it could have been George fucking Lazenby for all I knew because I couldn't watch it. Instead I had to sit and endure the tedium of my parents' company. We sat and looked at each other, sighed and looked at each other again. This had been going on for hours.

But then something happened, something unexpected and beautiful. A power beyond my control forced me to speak. It was completely involuntary, but it was to be an epochal moment. My lips were moving and out came these words: "Do you actually enjoy my company?"

"You're my son." Mum's reply.

"Yes, I know that, and I know millions of sons are sitting with millions of parents at this very moment, and none of them really know what to say to each other, and all of them, not just the sons but the parents too, would be happier if they were doing their own thing, instead of searching in vain for some common conversational ground."

My dad spoke. "And daughters."

"I disagree, dad. Girls seem to like blathering on to their

mothers about pointless nonsense."

"Good point son." That was the most enthusiastic response I had ever had from my father, and the first and last time he ever called me son.

Mum. "What are you trying to say Tom?"

"I was just thinking perhaps it would be better for all of us if I…left?" Neither of them said anything.

We had never communicated so effectively.

So that was that. I drove home. I have to confess that I had long left the drink-driving limit in the dust, I'd been drinking sherry at eleven am for Christ's sake, but I drove home anyway. My father was from the old school of drinkers who think the risk of drink-driving is getting caught and fined - not killing oneself or others, while my mother exercised her mother's right to remain blissfully unaware of obvious facts like her son driving sixty miles whilst completely tanked up on wine, beer, advocaat and the aforementioned sherry. I had to pull over on the dual-carriageway to have a piss, looking over my shoulder all the while for a police car. Despite the distraction it was a piss of victory, the piss of a champion. I had effectively divorced my parents.

Everyone was a winner. They had gained as much as I had. If I wasn't their son they wouldn't want to spend any time with me. It wasn't like I was great company or anything. I didn't see it as fair on my mum to have to go out of her way to be nice to me just because my head once split her open, so now she was free. And so was I.

Two

I left the world of civic gardening and took a position as a domestic orderly in what in name was a hospital but in reality was more a state-funded care home for the mentally ill. It was soon after taking this job that my life was to be plucked out from under me and twisted beyond all recognition.

The year was 2001. We weren't living in domes on the moon like in the casual promises made by the TV of my childhood. The internet had already taken root to the extent that nobody seemed to remember life before it. Mobile phones had yet to become smart and 'social network' meant a group of friends.

It all stemmed from my aversion to confrontation; I found arguments of any kind horribly embarrassing. Even if I won the argument then I would find the other person's apology unbearable and would invariably find myself apologising for having caused a scene. Unfortunately I couldn't bear to be too meek either; if I didn't speak up for myself then I felt I was selling myself short. It was a tug-of-war, with my palms burning at both ends of the rope.

When my next-door neighbour became a noise pollutant I had to act. He had never given me any problems before but when his girlfriend moved out he seemed to hit an early mid-life crisis. In a desperate bid for popularity and to lure eligible girls to his home he started throwing parties. He had four in the first two months after the break up, not excessive but not ideal for me. I tried to be reasonable; I didn't knock on his door and complain, instead I just waited until I happened to see him next, and politely asked him if he wouldn't mind keeping the noise down late at night. He was surprisingly good about it, he was a flood of apologies and said he hadn't realised he'd been so noisy. The following week he had another party, and this one was even louder. There was no way I was going to go round there whilst the party was in full swing; I wasn't prepared to play the no-fun neighbour and run the gauntlet through his pissed-up, drugged-up guests. So I spent a night trying to convince myself that the thumping beat that shook pictures from the walls could actually be used to hypnotic effect and help me sleep. I failed. It was a night of despair, but my spirits rose when my neighbour came to see me the following morning and lavished me with remorse. He said it had got out of hand, and that he felt terrible about being such a bad neighbour. He promised it wouldn't happen again and apologised once more. I apologised too. I have no idea why.

Within a month he was having parties three nights a week.

Life became unbearable. The house-shuddering beats were bad enough, but the music wasn't the worst part. Far more annoying was the sound of voices; shouting, laughing and screaming. I was furious that they could enjoy themselves so much whilst knowing they were making my life a misery. As the party nights grew more frequent and the guests more noisy, I started to become convinced that their laughter was aimed at me, that they were celebrating my desolation. I visualised their faces and created a whole cast of characters at which to aim my fury. In my sleep-deprived psyche my rage grew and mutated. I became a twisted monster, like Grendel, the mythical beast who hated the sound of music and dancing.

I tried earplugs but that was no good. They were uncomfortable, and I resented having to stick things in my ears at night just because the dick who lived next door didn't give a shit about anybody else.

In the mornings I would often find empty beer bottles outside my house that had been dropped by the guests as they left. At first it annoyed me that they could be so thoughtless, but eventually, as with the laughter, it began to feel personal, as if, even on their way out, they couldn't resist sticking a middle finger up at me.

I could have gone to the local council; there are useful laws against noise nuisance, but I would have had to keep a log of my neighbour's misdemeanours, and there would have been the possibility of going to court, which would all be hassle, and more importantly, would be one confrontation after another. It was Hobson's choice really. I had to kill him. My neighbour, not Hobson.

Some would argue that the act of killing somebody is confrontational in itself, but I say otherwise. The biggest problem with confronting someone is seeing them afterwards and having to relive the awkwardness. This, of course, is not a problem with murder; once you've made somebody dead then seeing them again becomes less of a prospect. I accept that if you are killing someone face to face - and of course there are other ways - then there is bound to be a moment of self-consciousness, a moment when you will look to the victim like something of a psychopath, but that's nothing compared to having a full-blown argument; losing your temper and then having your mind replay a vision of your own big red shouting face every time you see that person again.

My neighbour's mid-life crisis was to be an end-of-life crisis. I had to make plans. I had to think on it for a while. It was, after all, the first killing I had actually planned (Paul's killing was of course an accident and Susie's was a moment of opportunism). The build-up was nerve-wracking but strangely intoxicating. It was like solving a logic problem from the back of a Sunday supplement. There was so much I had to get right, so many factors to consider. I lived in the middle of a terrace with a row of identical houses opposite. There were windows everywhere. It would take just one person to glance out and see me going next door and I would be undone. It's amazing how much people will remember when the word 'murder' is used by a policeman at their door. At the back of the house was a three-storey block of flats overlooking the patios behind; more windows, more eyes.

I thought about doing it at night but that brought its own problems. Firstly, there would be no extra benefit of a cloak of darkness, the streetlights would see to that, and if I was seen outside in the middle of the night then it would be all the more memorable to a witness. A figure in daylight is just going about his business, after dark he's skulking. And how would I get in? Knock on the door at two in the morning? "I've come to kill you."

I had to think of something. I had to be prepared, that was the challenge. Slowly and carefully I formulated a plan.

It was shit.

I formulated another. Not so shit, but not good enough. The third was just silly, but the fourth plan, well that had something. No, it didn't, it was shit too. But the fifth. Oh, the fifth. They were all shit.

I had absolutely no idea how I was going to do this, or if I could do it at all. I needed inspiration. If I could think like a killer then surely a plan would formulate itself, but despite my two childhood slayings I wasn't entirely sure how killers were supposed to think. For seemingly no reason at all I remembered that I owned a balaclava that I had bought in preparation for a skiing holiday that I never got round to booking. It was up in the attic in a chest of ancient, unwearable clothes that I couldn't bring myself to throw away.

The black balaclava has a long tradition of violence and murder. If I couldn't yet think like a killer, I could at least dress like one.

I took a chair from downstairs, lugged it up the stairs and put it on the landing. I stood on it and hoisted myself into the loft. The balaclava was easy to find, that was a good start. I also found a pair of leather gloves that I thought would be handy. I was to find something else up there too, something far more useful, something I had never noticed before.

My attic hadn't been converted into a proper room; it was just as it was when the house was first built, except for having years' worth of my crap stacked in it. No flooring had been laid; you had to walk on the wooden joists that held the ceiling of the floor below. I don't know why they're called joists, it seems that if a wooden beam is on the ceiling then it's called a beam, but when it's on the floor it becomes a joist. Please don't write in with the answer. It wasn't an ideal place in which to be wandering around; a misplaced foot landing anywhere other than on a joist would have torn a hole in the ceiling below.

It was dark in there. Scary dark. The kind of darkness where shapes move and shadows lurk. How shadows lurk in darkness is a mystery to me, but they do, they lurk. There was some light coming in from the open entry hatchway in the floor, but precious little. I shone my torch around, peering at areas emancipated from the darkness by the dusty beam of light. This was partly out of curiosity; the attic is a seldom visited place so it was quite a nostalgia trail to see all the remnants of the past that I had dumped up there on the off-chance of needing them sometime in the future. All those things: a lamp, an ornament, a stereo, they all had a place in daily life. They were once new, picked out from a shop and purchased; objects of desire. Now they were in purgatory, waiting for their judgement: the hell of the tip or the heaven, the rebirth, of a charity shop. In the gloom of an attic, under the glow of a torch, these items seem to regain their old charm; a gloss forms beneath the dust and they look exciting again, but my advice is to leave them where they are. There's always a good reason why they are up there in the first place, and no attempt should be made to breathe life back into these relics. Their time has gone.

My other reason for sweeping the torch like a demented cinema-usher was blind fear. I was scared of the dark, still am, and I was quite literally chasing shadows. I don't know why I was hanging around; I'd found what I went up there for, so my work was done, but for some reason I stayed there, shining the torch round and round. From above I would have looked like a lighthouse.

I could see a stack of boxes, the most neatly ordered part of the space, and I realised it was my books. I had accumulated more than I had realised. Then the beam lengthened, as if it had hit a mirror at an angle, but it wasn't a reflection, it was a gap, a hole. In the bottom corner of the wall dividing my house from my neighbour's, some bricks - maybe a dozen, had toppled away from the wall and lay scattered between the joists. Perhaps this was shoddy workmanship on the part of the builders, or perhaps my neighbour or one of his predecessors had stored something big and heavy in his attic and it had been pushed against the bricks and dislodged them. Whatever the reason for the hole, I didn't care, as long as I could get through it. I knew my neighbour was already home that evening, so I would have to wait before investigating further.

I knew from the thunderous slamming of his door, that my neighbour arrived home from work about forty-five minutes after me, so I knew how much time I had available when I got home the next day. Once again, I climbed onto a chair, pushed up the hatch and wrestled my way up into the loft, cursing the fact that I had not installed one of those slide-down ladders. Once I was up I located the hole in the bricks with the beam of the torch then clambered across all the accumulated obstacles to get to it, wishing I could have been stealthier, more like Bond. I found that in reality the gap was much smaller than it looked from a few metres away, and it shrunk still further when I tried to get my bulk through. This was made even more difficult by the fact that I only had the joists to lie on while I attempted to wriggle my way through. It was dusty, and I got splinters all over my hands, but after a lengthy struggle I was in.

My neighbour's attic space didn't have flooring either, so I had to get myself upright and then pick my way across, avoiding boxes and an old bike that straddled several of the joists. I felt something clinging across my face, a spider's web. I hate spiders, and I hate the fact that they ooze sticky mucus out of their arseholes with which to catch other bugs. I clawed at my face, pulling off the invisible insect-afterbirth all the while hoping to God that the spider was long gone. I became convinced that unseen things were in my hair; mummified insect corpses or the spider itself, and I couldn't stop slapping at myself like some deranged flagellant.

Luckily the hatch in my neighbour's floor was in the same relative position as mine. The hatch in my attic was just a square of wood, cut to fit the gap but my neighbour's had hinges. "Hingey hatched tosser." I muttered out loud. The screws securing the handle on the other side of the hatch were long and poked through, which was another stroke of luck, giving me something to hold onto so I could open it from the inside. I opened it and lowered my head through the hatchway. The smell hit me; the smell of another person's house.

I defy anybody not to notice the smell of other people's houses. It's an unspecific smell, not necessarily bad, and of course it differs from home to home, person to person. It's the smell of choices, the end product of a matrix of decisions: what cleaning products to use and how often to use them, what food to cook, which deodorant, shampoo, pets, aftershave, type of flooring, soap, carpet. Infinite combinations. An infinite number of smells, one for each house. But I had no time for smelling as I peered down from the ceiling like some gravity-defying chad.

There was a cupboard beneath me; Lady Luck was positively snogging me by now. The cupboard would allow me both ease of entrance and more importantly, an easy escape. My mission for now was complete. I closed the hatch and dragged myself back through the hole in the bricks back to my space. I walked through another web as I stood up, and carried on like a man with a burning head.

A shower was needed, and a shower is a fine place to think. As I washed my hair, rinsed, repeated and repeated again I consolidated my plan. All I needed now was a gun. A knife would be no good. A knife requires some level of physical strength. There would be a chance he would be able to fight me off, there would be a scuffle, a disturbance, as the police witnesses would say, and I would have to keep stabbing away until I hit a major organ. No, stabbing was not for me. I considered arson while he slept but there would have been a chance of him waking up and escaping, and besides, these were terraced houses and I would be putting my own house at risk if I torched the place next door. It had to be a gun.

I didn't know how to get hold of a gun, and I didn't want to cruise the underworld and be seen asking where I could get one. I'd seen the cop shows, the first thing they do after a murder is match the bullet with a likely weapon and then ask their underworld spies to tell them who has been in the market for that weapon recently. You'd think that if the police could find out who was buying guns they would be a bit more proactive and try and prevent the buyer from using the weapon, rather than only asking for the information once a crime has been committed. It's all about results I suppose, there's no clear-up rate for a crime that hasn't yet happened.

The other reason for not wishing to 'cruise the underworld' was because I had no idea what that entailed.

So what would I do? How would I get a gun? I decided I'd have to take my chances and hope that the police didn't really have underworld spies. Hopefully some honour amongst thieves still existed, or at least amongst vendors of illicit firearms. But where was the underworld? Where did one find it? My only contact with criminal activity was my drug dealer. He would be as good a person as any to ask. It was quite a good guarantee of anonymity too; a drug dealer isn't ever going to want to speak to the police.

I put in an order for an ounce of hash and went round to see Phil, for that was my dealer's name. Phil was better than most dealers, he told me straight. Many dealers I'd experienced seemed to delight in wasting my time. It would be the same old routine: They would tell me that my order was arriving soon and that I should call in an hour, which I would do, only to be told that I should call again in two hours. When I called again I would be told to go round to the dealer's house. The drugs would never be there, and I would have to sit on a grubby beanbag struggling for conversation. After an hour or so I would go home with nothing. Phil was different; if he didn't have the stuff then he just told me he didn't have it. And when he did have it he'd let me know. He wasn't a saint by any means. In fact, he was a complete wanker, but at least he didn't waste my time.

I went to Phil's and was glad to find him alone. As with all drug dealers he had a handful of hangers-on who would sit around his lounge, playing on his games console and waiting for handouts, like a nest full of new-born chicks squawking for food. Perhaps Phil's hangers-on had found a new keeper. Apart from not having to endure their mumbled conversation and annoying habits, another benefit of the hangers-on being absent was that an armchair was free, and I didn't have to sit on the bean-bag. Phil was a small man, mousey haired and mean looking. He carried his size like a grudge, forever lashing out with barbed humour at those around him.

I followed the standard user-dealer protocol and skinned up with my own gear. While we shared the obligatory reefer, I popped the question.

"What do you need a piece for?" Phil had one of those mockney accents acquired through a diet of British gangster films. I nearly took the piss out of him for using the word "piece" but I didn't think it would help.

"A friend of a friend of a friend needs one. I just thought I'd ask. Don't worry if it's off your radar though." Phil laughed at me for using the phrase "off your radar."

"I can get you a gun. What sort does your friend's friend's friend need?"

"What have you got?"

"I haven't got anything, who do you think I am...?" His question tailed off as he couldn't think of the names of any famous arms dealers with which to complete his smart reply.

"Well, as I said, if it isn't your bag then I'll ask someone else."

"I didn't say I couldn't get one, I'm sure I can get one, I just need to know what kind."

"Something small, not like an Uzi or anything."

"Don't remember seeing too many Uzis round here. It's not Lebanon. I suppose you need bullets too?"

"I don't need anything, my friend's friend's friend will though."

"How many?"

"However they come, a small box please, or bag. However they come. A gunful will do."

"Okay, I'll bell some people and get a price."

"Cheers Phil."

"When are you two getting married by the way?"

"What?"

"You and that spliff, you've been together so long, I thought you was getting married." Drug dealer humour is always funny.

Phil didn't let me down. He sent me a text three days later asking me to come and listen to his new CD. This was our code and I'm sure it would have fooled any police-surveillance team monitoring our communication. Despite these amateurish tactics, the whole thing gave me a bit of a buzz if I'm honest. I had set the wheels of crime in motion. I was a player.

I was in Phil's lounge once more and I watched in awe as he actually skinned up with his own gear. He inhaled deeply to make his delivery more weighty. "I can get you one."

"What sort is it?"

"A pistol."

"What kind?"

"One that fires bullets."

I wasn't going to be silenced. "Is it one where you stack the bullets in a magazine in the handle or is it the other kind, a revolver?"

Phil just looked at me.

I looked at Phil.

Eventually he spoke. "I didn't get a brochure."

"Fair point."

"It's not cheap. Not with the bullets on top."

"How much?"

"Grand." It was such a big sum of money that my first

thought was that Phil was actually from Yorkshire and was expressing pleasure at something.

Then I realised. "A thousand pounds?"

"Yeah."

"Shit."

"Did you expect it to be less?"

"I don't know, I hadn't really thought about it. So how much without the bullets?"

"What do you mean?"

"You said it wouldn't be cheap, not with the bullets on top, so presumably for some reason the bullets make it loads more expensive. Perhaps I can get the bullets somewhere else more cheaply."

Phil gave me that look again but spoke straight away this time. "First, me saying 'what with the bullets on top' was just something I said, it didn't mean nothing. I didn't get an itemised breakdown, and secondly what do you mean, you'll get the bullets somewhere else, you going to shop around?"

"Oh. I see."

"Don't be a twat."

After leaving Phil's I realised I hadn't asked for a silencer but realised it was for the best; I'd got the distinct impression that the extra request wouldn't have gone down too well, and I wasn't sure if silencers really existed, or if that was just in spy thrillers. I withdrew the cash over a period of a week. This was my rather pathetic attempt to cover my tracks in case I became a suspect for this forthcoming murder and the police checked my bank details.

I picked up the gun from Phil and found that it was a revolver, a six-shooter. It felt strange holding it, especially as it was full of bullets. "To fire it you cock the hammer back and just pull the trigger." Phil was acting like he knew what he was talking about.

"Does it have a safety catch?"
"You don't get them on this type of gun."
"Oh."

I was now a gun owner. I was armed and dangerous. My neighbour was going to be toast. Worm food. I was going to fill him so full of holes that his own mother wouldn't recognise him, but she would be able to use him as a sponge.

I set a date for two weeks' time, and even gave my neighbour a get-out clause; if he didn't have any parties in that time then I would spare his life. I added the caveat that if he then proceeded to have another party in future then I would have to reconsider, after all, I wasn't going to get a refund on the gun.

He had three parties over the next two weeks and I saw him twice in that period, exchanging non-committal nods each time. I couldn't let other neighbours think I had an axe to grind with him, it would be the first thing the police would ask: "Did the victim have any enemies?" "Well, yes, the bloke next door to him hated his guts, said he was going to kill him." Case closed. I was careful; polite without drawing attention to myself. It's an odd thing to speak to a person whose life you are about to end. I almost wanted to warn him, tell him to go somewhere he's always wanted to go, try out a new sexual position, live his last days as if they were his… last. I considered suggesting he had a party, but of course that's what got us into this mess in the first place.

Three

The two weeks were up and everything was set. I got home from work and went straight upstairs. I laid out some clothes on the bed. They were clean but not too clean, just what I would normally change into when I got home. I kept my green hospital overalls on. They would go straight in the wash after I came back down from the loft; the smears of grime from slithering through the gap in the loft's brickwork would just look like the usual grubbiness from work, nothing suspicious about them going into the machine. I'd cleaned the gun the night before and had been fastidious to the point of insanity. I scrubbed it, rubbed it and polished every millimetre, every calibre. I took out the bullets and cleaned each one individually, just in case the guy who sold the gun to Phil had his prints on any of them. I wanted no trace at all.

I put on the gloves. They were black and tight fitting, principally to protect against fingerprints, and for that test I had heard of where you can tell if somebody has fired a gun recently. I didn't know how much protection the gloves would offer on that score, but it was worth a try. The bonus of the gloves was that they felt as if I looked the part. I was gloved up, just like a hitman in a movie. An expert, top man, the best. I had my own incidental music playing in my head: all light tapping on a snare drum and occasional bursts of trumpet. I put on the balaclava and tucked the gun in the pocket on the front of my overalls. I caught my reflection in the full-length mirror in the bedroom: Doctor Kildare joins the IRA. Not a good look. The balaclava was itchy.

I had decided not to use a chair to get into the attic. This would save me time after I had done the deed but meant it took me longer to get up there. I closed the bathroom door so I could use the doorknob as a step; not the most solid of footholds, but, with my fingertips clasped around the top of the doorframe like an indoor mountaineer, I eventually managed to drag myself up. Once I was in the attic I had to rest for a few moments to get over the exertion, but then I burst into action, skipping between the joists as if playing hopscotch.

Thankfully, my balaclava reduced the effect of the spiders' webs draping themselves over me as I made my way through the darkness. I pulled myself through the hole that divided the two attic spaces, feeling the hard metal of the gun digging into my belly. I opened the hatch and climbed down onto the cupboard below. I was absolutely shitting myself. Adrenalin was charging through my veins; I felt ready to run a marathon but also felt a crushing urge to curl up and pretend none of this was happening. I tried to work out how long I had before my neighbour got home. I was furious when I realised I wasn't wearing a watch. This was supposed to go like clockwork; the irony was obvious but of no help. I estimated about ten minutes until he arrived. What was I going to do for ten minutes? Read his diary?

I went to go downstairs but then noticed that my feet, dusty from the attic, had made a mark on the top of the cupboard. I hadn't planned for this. I wiped it with my sleeve, it did the trick. But what about the footprints I'd leave all the way down the stairs? What about the footprints I'd leave on my way back up the stairs? What about the footprints I'd leave on the cupboard when I climbed back up into the attic after it was done? It would be like leaving a trail of brightly coloured arrows all the way back into my house. I took off my shoes and placed them, upside down, on the cupboard. I brushed at the marks on the floor with my hand, they didn't clear completely but then I told myself not to be too fastidious; people do sometimes have stains on their carpets, and this carpet wasn't the cleanest. It was only the really obvious stuff that I needed to worry about. I stood back on the cupboard in my socks and placed my shoes up in the loft, again to save time, I would be in a hurry on the way back.

One more piece of preparation before going downstairs; I opened the bedroom door. It wasn't the bedroom, it was a cupboard. How come he had a cupboard there? My house didn't have that cupboard. "Cupboardy cunt," I muttered. The next door was the bedroom. It was messy. I doubted it was tidied often, what with all the parties. I took a pillow from the bed and tucked it under my arm.

I went downstairs. Where would I wait? I was panicking again. It was all different from my house in here. The stairs met a hallway running to the front door. To the left of the hallway there were two rooms, a lounge at the front of the house and a dining room at the back. In my house everything had been knocked through to make the whole downstairs open-plan except for the kitchen. Obviously my house was better. I opened the door to the lounge. It opened into the room and to the right. This was more luck; I didn't want to go fully into any of these rooms in case I could be seen through the window. The open door provided cover; I could stand just inside the room, unseen from the outside and allowing me to remain hidden from my neighbour until he came up the hall. It was uncomfortable though; I wanted to relax but had to keep myself upright concealed behind the door. I was farting terribly with the nerves, generating great gusts of the most unearthly stench. At one point I thought I had followed through and sullied my underwear, but I had to put that out of my mind. Hitmen don't worry about what their underwear's like, but then proper hitmen don't poo in their pants.

I took out the gun and held it in my right hand. With my left I held the pillow over the weapon, this would be my silencer.

The ridiculousness of the situation hit me. Here I was, shoeless, wearing gloves and a balaclava, with the smell of farts wafting around me. How much longer? He was taking forever, why didn't he come home? What was he doing? I nearly threw up when I finally heard the key in the door. It was horrible. He was home. I cocked the pistol. I was ready with my great big pillow of death.

Now this is the weird part:

It was just like in movies. As soon as I heard the door close I stepped out from my hidey-hole. He was looking for the loop inside his coat collar to hang it up when I appeared. He started to look up at me and I fired, keeping the pillow tightly over the gun. He died in a flurry of polyester. It seems like something out of a book, but the truth is that the bullet hit him straight between the eyes. I dropped the gun: Michael Corleone killing the Police Captain in the Godfather, and dropped the remains of the pillow without finding a cinematic reference. I hurried upstairs as light-footedly as possible, trying not to let the neighbours on the other side hear. I hadn't noticed the sound of the gunshot. It could have been deafening but I had no idea. It must have been deafening, a pillow can't make that much difference. I climbed on to the cupboard and swung myself back into the attic, picking up my shoes on the way. I gently closed the hatch, and for the final time I negotiated my way across the dark, cluttered space. I lay down and dragged myself through the gap in the wall, feeling some relief at being back on home territory but knowing I was far from safety yet.

Now was the difficult part. I sat on the edge of the exit to my loft with my legs dangling over the landing. I reached back and rested the wooden hatch that was propped behind me and pulled it so it rested on my shoulders. I braced my wrists on either side of me against the wooden edging and lowered myself down. I was out of shape since leaving the fire service, so I dropped quickly, and found myself hanging from the frame of the hatchway with my arms stretched above my head. The wooden board had fallen onto my knuckles.

That's when I saw the figure standing on the landing. I nearly screamed. It was Colin, my best friend, my only friend really. I felt sick.

"What the fuck's going on?" It was a fair question.

I let myself fall the few feet to the floor. The hatch dropped nicely into place. "I just put something in the loft."

"In a balaclava? In leather gloves?"

"It's cold up there."

"Tom, it's May. It's not cold. Did I hear a gunshot a minute ago?"

"Gunshot? You think you heard a gunshot? I didn't hear a gunshot. A gunshot you say? No, I think I would have noticed a gunshot."

He just looked at me with half a smile on his face.

I tried to turn the tables. "What are you doing here?"

"What are *you* doing here?"

"I live here." I was panting through the wool of the balaclava.

"I mean what are you doing?" Why are you in such a hurry? Why did I hear a gunshot?"

I took off the balaclava. My face was sticky with sweat. "Col, you're going to have to trust me, I need a few minutes. Can you do me a favour? Can you go and stand on the front step and look confused?"

"I am confused."

"Yes, I can imagine you would be. Look, you know those scenes in films when a strong friendship is tested?" I didn't give him time to answer. "Well this is one of those times, but not in a film, for real. I haven't got time to fuck around. We are friends, aren't we?"

"What's this about?"

"There's no time, are we friends?"

"Yes, we're friends."

"Wait a minute, how come you knew it was me? I was wearing a balaclava."

"It's your house and you're wearing your overalls."

"Fair enough. I'm going to tell you something and I'm trusting you not to, well, not to grass me up to the police."

Colin nodded.

"I can trust you?"

"Yes, of course you can trust me. What have you done?"

"I killed the bloke next door."

"The noisy neighbour?"

"He's made his last noise."

"Was it 'ugh'?"

"What?"

"His last noise, was it 'ugh'?"

"I don't know."

"Okay." He turned and headed for the stairs.

"Where are you going?"

"I'm going downstairs to stand on the front step and look confused. Although I'm not confused anymore."

"Don't you want to ask me anything?"

"You said there's no time. And you're right; the gun would have been heard all the way down the road. You need to do whatever it is you've planned to do, burn your clothes, bury the gun, all that stuff, before the police get here. You told me to stand outside and look confused which I think is a good idea, that's exactly what the neighbour, or the neighbour's guest would do. But come to think of it, why wouldn't you be standing outside looking confused too?"

I was having trouble taking in his matter-of-fact reaction but didn't have time to dwell on it. "Because I'd just got into the shower when I heard a loud bang."

"That figures. You'd best hurry up and get in the shower then."

"Could you chuck my stuff in the washing machine please?"

"Okay, where is it, oh, I see. Hurry up and take it off then."

"Thanks Col, you really are a mate, really. Jesus, you're a mate." I began taking off my overalls, starting with my trousers.

"You could at least turn round." Colin had put his hand over his eyes. I turned my back to him. "Oh no, that's worse. You don't need to change your socks by the way. I don't want to see you bending over."

I was now completely naked and handed a wincing Colin my bundle of clothes. "Why did you have to take off your boxer shorts?"

"I think I might have shit them."

"You scum! I'm holding a bundle of clothes with your shitty pants in?" He once again turned to go downstairs, then paused and looked back. "Where's the gun?"

"I left it next door."

"Like Al Pacino in the Godfather, in the restaurant after he's killed the Police Captain?"

"Exactly!"

"What about your skiing gear?" He motioned towards the balaclava and gloves on the floor.

"Shit. I meant to leave them in the loft. I've got to go back up there. Quick, give me a leg up."

"You're joking, aren't you? Your cock will be right in my face, or your shitty arse. Fuck that."

"Just do it." He sighed and linked his hands together, face up, and braced to take my weight. I put my hand on his shoulder, catching his eye as I did so. His face was an absolute picture, grim, determined, trying to ignore my nakedness. I nearly burst out laughing but managed to keep it in. The last thing I needed now was to get hysterical. I pushed myself up.

Colin started whisper-shouting. "It touched my face, it fucking touched my face! It's all moist, what's wrong with you? Are you incontinent or something? It's shaking, why is it shaking?" It was shaking because I was laughing uncontrollably, my whole body quivering. I had pushed the hatch up and was gripping the wood that surrounded the opening, but Colin was still taking most of my weight. I couldn't go any further because I was giggling too much. I glanced down and saw Colin's face again. His head was pulled back as far as it could go to avoid my dangling member, his eyes were closed and his mouth was shut tight. He was repulsed but was sniggering helplessly as my cock dabbed his upturned chin in time to my laughter. He spoke through his pursed mouth. "It's like a fish, a fucking eel. Why is it so wet you filthy bastard?"

Thankfully my fear of getting caught took over, and I exercised enough self-control to haul myself into the loft and quickly pushed the balaclava and gloves deep into the bag from which they had come. Colin had obviously been spurred into action too, because as I repeated the tricky procedure of lowering myself back onto the landing and replacing the hatch, I heard him opening the washing machine door. I had the quickest of showers but left it running hot and closed the door. I was nearly dressed when Colin appeared at my bedroom door. "Actually Tom, we should call the police. That's what an innocent neighbour would do. I'll call the police. Then I'll stand on the front porch."

"Yes. Yes. Do that. No. Wait. I'll do it. You just stand on

the front porch."

"Okay, here I go." He pulled a face. "Do I look confused?"

"No. You look like you've had my knob dabbed all over your face like a Bingo marker pen. I can almost see the festering residue collected in pockets on your skin, being absorbed into your pores."

"Fuck off fuck off fuck off." He ran from the room.

I finished dressing then went back into the bathroom. It was good and steamy, like somebody had been in there for ages. I turned the water off and closed the door, then ran downstairs into my lovely open-plan lounge diner, much nicer than next door. I called the police and reported what I had heard. I tried to sound embarrassed for bothering them, saying that it was probably nothing, but it did sound like a gunshot. The reason for putting on this act was because if I had been the innocent neighbour and been sure it was a gunshot, I would have called straight away, not waited ten minutes. I was aware that if I did end up in court the recording might be used as evidence, so I wanted to cover all the angles.

I joined Colin at the door and saw people milling around outside. Everybody was doing their best to look the most concerned, but Mrs. McCulloch, the nosey old crone from number two, won the prize for most anguished citizen. "I've called the police. They'll be on their way. Did anybody see anything?" There were unspecific murmurs in response.

Mrs. Farmer from number fifty piped up in her best official-sounding tone. "Now everybody be calm. We don't know anything has happened yet, all we know is that we heard a bang. I've called the fire brigade and an ambulance. They'll be on their way." The look she fired towards Mrs. McCulloch was way more deadly than the shot that had killed my neighbour.

Mrs. McCulloch stared at her nemesis but couldn't think of a retort. Instead she started hectoring people individually to find out if they saw anything, as if she were the investigating officer. Thanks to the two busybodies' efforts it was like a disaster movie outside within a few minutes. The street was completely blocked with vehicles and personnel from all the emergency services. I was surprised that nobody had called the coastguard. A group of four policemen and two paramedics stood outside the front door as a fireman broke down the door. I knew they wouldn't all be able to get inside because there was a corpse blocking the doorway, but it was good to see such cooperation between the three departments. As I had expected, only the fireman made it in, but he quickly came out again and waved the paramedics inside. For the next hour the threshold was crossed back and forth by police photographers, forensic investigators, more police, more paramedics and a couple more of the firemen for good measure. I was happy to note that I didn't see any of my old colleagues from my brief spell in the fire service.

I was a bit embarrassed to be standing out there with all the gossip merchants, but I wanted to look like one of them, so I had to act like them. Colin seemed to love it, having a real nose around as if he didn't already know what had happened. The most senior police officer addressed the growing crowd of onlookers.

"Please can I have your attention? Thank you. My name is Inspector Buckley. It appears there has been a shooting inside the premises of number twenty-five."

Colin whispered to me. "Why does he have to say it like that? 'Inside the premises.' He's such a copper." I shushed him. I was busy affecting my honest, open and shocked face for anyone who might be looking.

Buckley had continued. "We will need to talk to all of you. Please can you all return to your homes and wait for one of our officers to come and speak to you." This caused a murmur of excitement amongst the crowd. "I thank you for your cooperation in advance. We need as much information as we can get, and your contribution could prove to be vital in this case." More excited murmurings from the crowd. A female subordinate got his attention and whispered in his ear. He spoke again. "If you are not a resident of this street then please come and speak to WPC Brown here."

Colin's ears pricked up at this last statement and he tried to edge through the crowd. I caught hold of the back of his shirt before he could take a full step. "What are you doing?" I whispered.

"I'm not a resident of the street. I've got to talk to WPC Brown."

"They don't mean you. You can just wait with me at my place. They mean people who just happened to be passing."

"I think I should go and see her, she's a fox."

"No Colin." And more quietly and firmly I said. "I mean it."

Colin put his tongue away.

I presumed they were working outwards from the epicentre of the crime, because there was a knock on my door almost straight away. Inspector Buckley introduced himself and Constable Brown. I responded very well, and so did Colin. I was shocked. Colin was stunned. What had happened? Had anybody seen anything? No, neither of us had seen anything, and we hadn't heard anything apart from the gunshot. Colin had called round to my house to drop off some CDs (this part was true and answered my own what-the-fuck-was-he-doing-in-my-house question that I hadn't had time to ask properly. I had forgotten I'd given him a key when I went on holiday last year, so he could look after my goldfish, which he had killed by over feeding them).

Inspector Buckley asked if we thought my neighbour had had any enemies. I looked appalled. He wasn't a saint, but I couldn't think why anyone would want to kill him. I played up the scared angle. Was it safe? Were the police going to offer protection to the people in the street in case of further attacks? Was this now a danger zone? They looked around the house while I acted more than happy to help them with anything I could. I cringed when we walked under the hatch to the attic and I hoped to God they didn't ask to look up there. They didn't ask, in fact they didn't stay very long. I supposed they had a lot of people to call on. I must say I was slightly disappointed that they didn't test me more after I had gone to so much trouble meticulously planning the operation. I was ready to be asked what was in the wash when they heard the machine spinning, and I was poised to reply that I got splattered with dribble at work, but I didn't get the chance. Later, they came back and repeated the same questions almost word for word. I was never completely sure if they remembered that they had already called round.

After they had gone I nearly hugged Colin. "Good work mate, you really came through for me there."

I expected him to give me an earful about what I'd done but instead his answer was, "Have you got any beers?"

"Don't you want to ask me anything?"

"I thought you'd had enough of questions."

"How come you're being so considerate?"

"Well I pretty much know everything. I know your neighbour pissed you off, and you've told me you killed him. I saw you coming out of the loft so I guess there must be a way of getting into next door from there. I'm glad the police didn't want to look up there though."

"They may still want to. So you're not shocked or anything?"

"I was shocked to see your dick, that was horrible, but not really shocked that you killed him. I always knew you were a bit weird."

"A bit weird?"

"Yes, you're very passionate about things. You go on and on about them, but you're too scared to do anything about it. It looks like all that frustration built up and the result was one dead neighbour. It's like that Michael Douglas film, Watership Down."

"Falling Down."

"What did I say?" He smirked, making me realise he had been taking the piss. Then his face went serious. "I do have one question though."

"What's that?"

"Why the hell were you wearing a balaclava? It wasn't like he was going to see you again."

"I was taking precautions. Something might have happened. I might not have been able to kill him. Then he'd have seen me and I'd have been fucked."

"And you think that if for some reason you hadn't been able to kill him, like you dropped the gun or something, and he'd seen you, that he'd have let you get out again, without stopping you and making you take off the balaclava?"

"I would have overpowered him."

"And then disappeared into the loft? That would have foxed him. Or perhaps you would have gone out the front door. Do you think nobody would have challenged you as he chased you and shouted down the street at the running man wearing a balaclava in the summer?"

I didn't argue any longer.

I had a couple of other visits from Buckley over the next few weeks but he was clearly hopeless, and I was never under any threat. I was lucky; two independent witnesses saw people leaving the house soon after the gunshot was heard; one witness lived in the flats behind and saw a man leaving through the back door, while the other witness lived a few doors down and saw someone hurrying out the front of my neighbour's house shortly after the gunshot. I don't know where these visions came from, but I was grateful for them.

I was in the clear. Now I just had to hope that whoever bought my late neighbour's house would be as quiet as the grave.

Four

They say everybody can get away with one motiveless crime. My crime had had a motive, but nobody seemed to notice. I had mentioned the noisy parties to Inspector Buckley in case the neighbours on the other side, or anybody within a hundred yards of the noisy bastard's house, had mentioned them; otherwise it would have looked like I was hiding something. I said to Buckley that I didn't like the noise but had found that wearing earplugs in bed had solved the problem. Buckley had obviously never had noisy neighbours because he didn't consider it to be a motive for murder.

I had returned to the loft and placed stacks of boxes in front of the hole in the wall. It wouldn't have stood up to a thorough search but I was sure it wasn't going to come to that, and I didn't want to arouse suspicion by banging around too much in the attic while a murder investigation was going on, although there didn't seem to be much investigating going on.

I had seen a lot more of Colin since the murder. We both felt that his being in my house when the murder happened may well have looked suspicious, and we didn't know who might have been watching us, waiting for us to slip up. If we had stopped seeing each other people might have thought we had something to hide. Colin lived three streets away and made a point of calling at my house prior to us going to the pub so everyone got the message that we often got together, not just when people were being murdered.

I liked Colin because he wasn't annoying, or at least if he did annoy me then I could tell him so. Most people I meet drive me mad but I am unable to tell them so. I curse this convention. If somebody has spinach on their teeth it's socially acceptable to bring it to their attention, but if they are just plain irritating then it's frowned upon to let them know. Colin and I met at sixth-form College. His girlfriend at the time was on my course so I would often see Colin at the refectory or in the pub. After the girl dumped him because she thought he had slept with her best friend, Colin and I continued to see each other. He always pleaded his innocence but never gave me an explanation as to why the friend would have lied. Colin was shorter than me but was undeniably better looking and more confident. He kept his dark hair shaved all over and always seemed to be wearing brand new clothes. We had the kind of friendship where we didn't have to see each other very often to remain close. We both had our lives, and in the past we had gone for months without seeing one another, but had always found it easy to pick up exactly where we had left off.

Colin was similar to me in that he was constantly bitter about how his life had turned out but was too lazy to do anything about it. He hated his job but didn't have the skills or the inclination to try anything else. He was a surveyor for the Highways Agency. He travelled a lot with work but it was always to the most depressing places, places where bypasses were being built, Coventry, Daventry, Braintree. If it had an 'ee' sound at the end then Colin would be there, standing in the rain in a bright yellow jacket, peering through something that looked like a spirit level on a tripod. Even if it was sunny everywhere else, I was sure it rained wherever Colin was on location.

Colin was a good friend, but I would be lying if I said I didn't consider killing him because of what he had seen. I did trust him though, and more importantly it would stir up a hornet's nest of police interest if Colin was murdered, and maybe they would put someone in charge who, unlike Inspector Buckley, actually knew what they were doing. To be honest I probably wouldn't have killed him even if I was sure I could have got away with it. Apart from everything else, he had been a big help. I was grateful that he hadn't started screaming when he saw me dropping out of the loft like a murderous Milk Tray man, and when he was interviewed by the police he held it together brilliantly. After the shock of him catching me in the act subsided, a part of me was glad that he had found out because it meant I could talk to someone about it. I was sure that if I had been forced to keep something of that magnitude to myself I would have gone mad; probably developing a guilty Tourette's syndrome, causing me to shout "I killed him" in public places. Colin wasn't the type to have a heart-to-heart with, so our conversations about the murder didn't go into any real depth but it was better than nothing, and besides, the last thing I wanted to do was analyse the situation and get to the root of why I had taken another man's life so relatively lightly.

With Colin's help I had slipped through the police's rather loose net, but I hadn't fooled everybody. I was soon to find out that another organisation was onto me, one with a lot more power than the boys in blue.

It was six weeks after the killing and I was busy improving my home. When I killed my neighbour, I had noticed that his carpet, although a little dirty, had put mine to shame, so I was keeping up with the dead Joneses and having a new downstairs carpet fitted the next morning. I was having a shit old time. The thing about carpet is that it's everywhere. You don't realise until you need to lift up a carpet how much stuff is on the thing. I had to move the dining table, chairs, three piece suite, potted plants, TV and accompanying peripherals, stereo, CDs. I could carry on… Actually I will carry on: bookcase, standard lamp, scarily big pile of magazines that wobbled and lurched next to the sofa, coffee table. And those were just the things that were directly on the carpet. There was all the stuff on top of that stuff to consider, things that you don't even realise you need to put anywhere, things that just sit on top of things. Loose change, keys, smaller pot plants, remote controls, ornaments, the telephone, they all had to be moved.

But I'd done it. I had moved everything out and dumped it in the kitchen, creating a possessions monster that was busy savaging the kitchen appliances. I could hear the cooker crying and I just knew the fridge was going to piss itself with fear. It pissed itself at the best of times; puddles of fridge-piss were often seen oozing from beneath it, so this trauma was bound to push it over the edge. I closed the door on the mess that the kitchen had become. I didn't want to look in there again.

Then came the really bad part; taking up the old carpet. It was such a depressing chore. It was stuck down fast, I couldn't get any purchase anywhere around the edge and I couldn't get to my toolbox because it was in the utility cupboard in the kitchen, hemmed in by lounge refugees, so I had to force my fingers down next to the skirting board. I'm no mountaineer so the ends of my fingers aren't used to sustaining any kind of pressure. It really hurt. Eventually I negotiated out a loose flap and pulled. It started to come. It felt good for about nine seconds; it was coming up nicely, I drew breath to whistle like a seasoned tradesman, but then I saw the horror beneath. The carpet was so old that the rubber base had perished into an inexplicable amount of horrible rubber dust. I looked around and realised how big the carpet actually was, and how much of this dust must be under it. I was in a twist-pile hell.

I thanked myself for making some provision for the clear-up; I had a roll of bin bags, a broom and a dustpan and brush. I had a knife too, a big one, the sort that wouldn't be out of place strapped to Tarzan's leg. I cut the carpet into manageable strips, rolled each one up as tightly as I could and stuffed them into the bin bags. After all my trouble emptying the lounge it was now full of fat black bags. I made several trips out of the back door and piled the patio high with carpet remains. The dustmen were going to love me on Monday. It took me a while to sweep up, as I seemingly had to go over each part of the floor a dozen times to capture all the dust. But I did it, it was over. I was filthy and covered in sweat. And I was hungry. I rang for a Chinese then I went upstairs to have a shower. It was a lovely relief to go upstairs; everything up there was as it should be. There was carpet on the floor, no dust, and no piles of belongings. Okay, there was a big pile of stuff under my bed but that was normal. It didn't count.

I got undressed and lay on the bed. I didn't have the strength to get into the shower yet, so I gave it a few minutes…

I was awoken by the doorbell. The food had arrived. I threw on my dressing gown, the last Christmas gift I ever received from my parents, and a fine example of how little they knew their son. It was a poor imitation of a kimono; black and festooned with dragons. I ran downstairs with the silk clinging to my sweaty body. The doorbell rang again while I was taking my wallet out of my jacket. The delivery man had turned to leave when I answered the door. He looked at me as if I were a mutant. I realised I must have looked a right state; a sweaty, bleary-eyed mess. He took my tip without gratitude and was gone. The lounge was no longer fit for lounging in, but it would have felt weird eating food upstairs, so I sat on the lounge floor and ate the food straight from the cartons. It was lucky there were chopsticks in the bag, because I wouldn't have been able to get to the cutlery drawer. The dust that I had missed on the floor collected on the bare skin of my feet and legs. I was crap at using chopsticks, but I wanted to eat quickly so I could get some clothes on. I really was having a shit old time.

The doorbell rang. I could only imagine it was the delivery guy from the takeaway telling me he had forgotten my prawn crackers. It couldn't have been anybody else, nobody just turns up nowadays. It's not like when you're a kid and you just go round to your friends' houses and they're always ready to go. I tiptoed towards the edge of the bay window next to the front door, holding the thin fabric of my dressing gown over my privacy. I leaned towards the window, master of stealth, and peeped round from where the curtain on my side was gathered up. There were two men at the door. I didn't recognise them. They certainly weren't the Chinese delivery man. The nearest was the shorter of the two, he was about five eight, had carefully parted blonde hair and was wearing a black roll neck jumper and dark trousers. The other man loomed over him, nearly a head taller. He looked like he would be starting his shift on the door of a club any time now. He also wore black but in contrast to his associate's carefully coiffured locks, he was completely bald. They both exuded menace.

I slipped, I bloody slipped and fell. The men turned as I flew across and down towards the hard, bare floor. In this situation there is an instinct above all others, above even that of protecting oneself. It is the instinct to keep one's dignity. It must be an evolutionary trait that humans have developed; I hit the floor, and with a superhuman shove I harnessed the momentum of my bounce and projected myself back up like I was a human spring. I still don't know how I did it.

I had to answer the door now. I thought there was a slight chance they might have seen me.

* * * * * * * * * * * * * *

"This is it, number twenty seven, doesn't look like much."

"And that's twenty five, the dead guy's place."

"Bit close to home, wasn't it? Shitting right on his own doorstep." I bet Frank's been waiting to use that line all the way over here. He rings the bell and we wait for a while. Quite a break, this one. Almost an evening off really. It's rare we get sent on a job to be nice to someone. The curtains move, and an eye appears at the window. It's like on those wildlife programmes where a whale comes past the camera and its eye fills up the whole screen.

"Is that a fucking ninja or something?" Frank and me are just staring, we can't believe what we've just seen. The bloke's in martial arts gear, some sort of kimono, he's thrown himself down on the floor and then just, like, flipped himself back up, like the film was rewound or something. Like an acrobat. Like a fucking ninja - just like Frank said. The curtain's fallen back into place. A few seconds, half a minute and the door opens. I relax my grip on my piece as he opens the door wide, that's a good sign, no surprises in store. Frank talks, I always let Frank talk. He's old school, likes the patter, I let him get on with it. "Tom White?"

"Yes, that's me." He's a strange one, intense. His feet are bare. He's just wearing this oriental robe. His hair's jet black and all over the place. Like Bruce Lee.

"Do you mind if we come in?" While Frank goes through the motions I look past White and into the room. It's completely bare, no furniture, nothing. It's just bare boards, not even sanded or polished. The only thing in the room is some Chinese food. He's eating his dinner sitting on bare floorboards with chopsticks. He's like a monk.

White is a statue, staring at us. "What's this about?"

"It's about the murder next door."

"You'd better come in then." That was easy. Frank normally has to say more than that to get us in. Maybe he's expecting us. We go inside but don't sit down, what with there being no furniture and all. White speaks again. "Have you found the murderer?"

"Oh no, we're not the police, you know that don't you?" Frank's trying his firm but friendly voice. White's face changes, not fright, he doesn't

seem the type to scare easy, recognition maybe. He's not Chinese but I bet he's one of them who commit their lives to enlightenment through fighting and killing. He's probably Shaolin or Samurai. I bet he's got a master somewhere who teaches him all the death-grips. Bet his master's about a hundred and seven, with a big long wispy beard that curls off his chin, and weird staring eyes.

"Who are you then?"

"My name's Frank, and this is Cheese."

"What did you say his name was?"

"Cheese."

"His name's Cheese?"

"Yeah."

"Cheese?"

"Yeah."

"Oh. I see."

Frank starts his pitch. "I know walls have ears and all, so I won't spell it out, but we know about you and you probably know all about us. Normally when we go on errands like this it's under different circumstances, but the reason for this one is to pass on a compliment."

"What sort of compliment?"

"A compliment on a job well done."

"I don't know what you're talking about. I think you've got the wrong person. I don't mean to be rude but as you can see I'm in the middle of my dinner, so if you don't mind excusing me, I'd like to get back to it."

Frank smiles, "Tom, come on man, let's not be like this, as I said, we mean you no harm, quite the opposite actually. The old man is grateful. That little toe-rag gets hit on the boss's birthday, it's beautiful. All he wants to know is who the gift was from, who gave you the job? The old man wants to show his gratitude."

White takes a deep breath then smiles back. "You definitely have got the wrong person. This is something I would never be involved with. I'm not going to ask for more details because I don't want to know. You gentlemen have obviously got your business, and good luck to you, but it's not a *business I'm involved in."*

Frank holds up his hands, trying to calm him down. "Tom, it's obvious you don't trust us. And why should you? You think we're gonna do the guy who gave you the job, not thank him."

"I don't know about any job or any old man. I'm telling you the truth. I'm just a bloke eating his dinner." *He's giving nothing away. He's good, definitely a pro. I see the sunlight reflecting off something in the corner, it's a knife, and it's fucking huge. Frank sees it too. White's taking no chances.*

"Perhaps this will jog your memory." Frank pulls out the clip of cash and holds it out to White, who just shakes his head. *Cool as you like.* "There's two grand there. It's yours, both to thank you for your part in the old man's birthday present, and as a reward for you letting us know who else he should be passing his thanks on to." White carries on saying nothing, just stands there. He shakes his head once more and stares straight back at Frank.

Frank pushes the wad towards White. "Two grand."

White steps back, like Frank's holding a poisonous snake in his face. "I know, you just said that. Listen, I really don't want to be rude and I'm sorry that you've wasted your time, but you really have got the wrong person. What makes you think I'm who you think I am anyway?"

"A friend of a friend of a friend told us." *Looked like something flickered on White's face but difficult to tell.*

"Who?"

"You're a player, you must know all this. When the hit went down we found out what kind of piece was used from our man inside the nick, then the usual feelers went out, to see who'd picked one up recently. Filth haven't got the resources we've got so they didn't get close, but you must know that already. Another thing we got from the man on the inside is how smooth the job was, accurate, quick and left the old bill without a clue. A classy piece of work, awesome was the word they used." *There's no mistaking the look of pride on White's face, however much he's trying to conceal it.*

"I don't know anything except that my food's going to be stone cold.

I'm not keeping anything from you, really. I'm trying to be polite and helpful, but I've got nothing to tell you. None of what you are saying is making any kind of sense to me. I'm sorry."

* * * * * * * * * * * * * * *

They left, they actually left. I couldn't believe it. I had never been so scared in my life, ever. I immediately started running through the encounter again in my head. I'd been careful not to touch my face while I was talking; one of those pop-psychology shows on television gave me that tip. Apparently when you aren't telling the truth you touch your face; subconsciously trying to stop the lie coming out. I had also kept eye contact; according to the bloke on the telly, when we're lying we look up to one side, retrieving information from the creative side of the brain; the side where we make lies up. I didn't know which side was the side where facts are stored, so I hadn't looked up at all. I'd just looked straight at them. I'd used the same techniques on the police too, but I had a feeling that these two were a lot harder to fool. Two words were lingering in the back of my mind, moving forwards, getting bigger. Now they filled my whole head: "The Mob."

I had just had gangsters in my house.

They were trying to thank me for killing my neighbour.

They offered me a wad of money.

One was called Cheese.

* * * * * * * * * * * * * * *

Frank's all worked up. "Come on Frank, calm down mate, you worry too much."

"I'm right to worry, we fucked up the job! All we had to do was go and thank him and give him a reward. And we couldn't even do that. Now we've got to tell the old man we haven't got a clue who gave him the birthday present."

"He's getting something better."

"Did I miss something? I don't think I missed anything."

"Come on Frank, settle, mate. We've got the old man a new man."

"We've got who what?"

"We've got a new man, for the old man."

"White? The ninja?"

"The boss has been moaning for years about not having another good man to trust. White's perfect, he's a total pro, you must have seen that."

"I wasn't disagreeing, Cheese, I thought he was the bollocks. He had us well sussed, probably could have killed us with his big toe."

"Or that fuck-off knife he made sure we could see. So you see what I'm saying? He's shit-hot."

"What about that move he pulled when he came to the window? That was something else."

"That was a warning shot across the bows. He was letting us know what he can do. And I'm sure there's plenty more in the locker."

Frank's more relaxed now. "So you think Stan's gonna think we're the bollocks for finding him a ninja?"

"No doubt, Frank, no doubt at all."

Five

As soon as Frank and Cheese had gone, I called Colin and insisted he come over. He came immediately, and I filled him in on what had just happened, in a rapid, panicked outpouring. Colin sat listening quietly. He finished rolling a reefer, lit it, took a big drag on it and handed it to me. "Tom, you need to calm down. I don't know why you're getting so worked up."

"Why shouldn't I be worked up? My secret's out, somebody's found me, and despite what that Frank bloke said about police resources, if the criminals can find me then so can the coppers."

"The police don't know what they're doing, that Inspector Buckley is rubbish. If they were going to find you they would have done by now."

"How did they find me?" I handed the joint back to Colin.

"The gangsters?" He took a lungful of smoke and spoke as he let it out, causing his voice to oscillate. "Your name's been linked with the gun, somebody must have been talking."

"The only person who knows I bought that gun, apart from you, is Phil the dealer."

"Maybe I was the nark."

"Don't joke about it, this is serious. It had to be Phil, they gave me a clue, they said they found out through a 'friend of a friend of a friend'. That's what I said to Phil when I bought the gun, but why would he squeal?"

"More importantly, why would you use a word like 'squeal'?

What are you, a gangster? One murder doesn't give you an excuse to talk like a twat."

"Okay, why would Phil tell tales on me?"

"Actually, you're right, squeal works better. But more to the point, why would Phil *not* squeal on you? It's not like you're close or have any loyalty to each other. He gives you drugs and you give him money, that's it. Your relationship with Phil is probably about as strong as mine with the newsagent near my house. Mr. Bhadressa gives me newspapers, milk and bread with the 'best before' tag removed, and I give him money. I wouldn't expect him to keep my secrets if some heavies from the Mob came to visit, so why would you expect anything different from Phil?"

"Okay, it's not his fault. I ought to kill him though."

Colin's faced blanched. "Are you joking?"

"No, not at all. I can understand why he gave my name to the gangsters, but logically, the only way to make sure he keeps quiet is to kill him."

"What about me? Is killing me the only way to make sure I keep quiet?"

"I trust you."

Colin was animated now. "And what if you didn't trust me? What if you thought I might tell someone, you'd kill me wouldn't you? You would, wouldn't you?"

"I know you're not going to tell anyone."

"But you'd kill me if you thought I would."

"No I wouldn't, I'd talk to you."

"And what if I didn't listen?"

"For fuck's sake Colin. I'm not going to kill you. I will never consider killing you." I emphasised the future tense so I wouldn't be lying.

"But you'd happily kill Phil?"

"Not happily, I wouldn't enjoy it, but I think it's the only option."

"Am I missing something here? I thought I knew you. Admittedly I could have been a little more shocked by you killing your neighbour, but I know what rage can do, and I know how annoying he was. But now you're talking like you've got the bug, like killing is an option to be considered in response to any kind of problem. Was this not a one-off? Are you now a serial killer?"

"I haven't got any bug, this *was* just a one-off, of course it was, but I'm now mixed up in something bigger than I've been in before. If I have to take even more drastic action to save myself then I will."

Colin leaned forward, waving away the joint I was holding out to him. "Think about it Tom. Phil lives round here, and if someone – oh go on then," he took the reefer from me - "If someone else round here gets murdered then it's bound to arouse suspicion. The police might think the murders are connected; especially when they find out Phil is a drug dealer. And it wouldn't be impossible for your dead neighbour to have been a customer of Phil's, after all he did like the odd party. If the police make a connection then you won't be able to move for squad cars. Your best bet is to leave it be. Don't kill any more people."

"You're right I suppose." I held up my bottle of beer. "To Phil, the big-mouthed cunt. May he live forever."

Colin clinked his bottle against mine. "Big-mouthed cunt. Forever."

"Okay, I'll stop worrying about the police finding out, you're right, they would have had me by now if they were going to. But what about the criminals? They weren't from round here. The one who did all the talking had a cockney accent, eastenders, obviously part of some organised group."

"Organised crime? Jesus." Colin exhaled loudly.

"The problem I'm having is what to call them. The Mob? The Gang? And what about this 'old man' they were talking about, the boss? When they mentioned him, I had an image in my head of some big fat guy who spends all day sitting by the pool of his mansion, stroking a cat and having a telephone brought out to him on a cushion whenever an important call comes in."

"It's too cold over here to sit by the pool."

"It's been nice recently."

"You're right, we're having a good summer, and apparently we've got an anti-cyclone coming from the Sahara or somewhere, it's going to be warm until nearly October."

"How the fuck do you know that?"

"I was in a bus queue with some old dears."

"Anyway, if I can drag us back to the matter in hand, I have no reason to trust this Frank guy, if that's even his real name, or Cheese, so why should I believe that the boss wants to reward me? It would be an obvious cover story; pretend you want to thank the killer so he admits to doing it, then bump him off. It must be an old trick in gangland circles. Maybe my neighbour was actually a friend of theirs and the boss wants vengeance. If I'd taken the money I reckon I would have been signing my own death warrant."

"Is there really such a thing as a death warrant?"

"What do you mean?"

"I mean, you hear it said a lot in films and stuff, but is there really such a thing? Does a judge really issue a death warrant on people?"

"Does it matter?"

"It does if you get one."

"I don't know, but I might have narrowly avoided getting one, can we move on?"

"I suppose so, but I take your point. Your neighbour might

even have been a made guy."

"A full member of the family, like in Goodfellas? Do you think they do that over here?"

"Everyone's copying the Yanks these days."

We decided to watch Goodfellas.

I couldn't tell Colin, but despite all the fears I'm ashamed to say that my main emotion was excitement, with pride running a close second. This wasn't my first killing, or even my first murder, but it made me see myself and my life differently. Was I playing with the big boys now? I'd clearly been noticed by some very dangerous people. After Frank and Cheese's visit I became constantly aware that I had joined some twilight club as I went through what now seemed to be the trivialities of normal life. I was bursting with my new status, but I wasn't able to tell anybody. When people at work commented on the weather, I had to choke down the response: "yes, you could be right, it has clouded over a bit, but more importantly, I killed a man, shot him right between the eyes. All those in the know are calling it the perfect job. Waddyathinkaboutthat? Eh? Eh? What do you think? You're impressed aren't you? Impressed and scared. I am the Gun King, and all must bow before me." And I had to stop myself from finishing by throwing my head right back, like a superhero in a cartoon, and laughing heartily, making sure the actual word 'ha' was clearly audible.

I had never felt like this. It was the first time I had ever felt passionate about anything other than sex. It took me some time to work out what the feeling was. It was a calling. I had found my vocation.

Or so I thought.

* * * * * * * * * * * * * *

Stan Costanza's not known for his patience, and when we get to his office he's not looking friendly. Not that he ever looks friendly. He's short and nearly as bald as me, so he doesn't look like much, but you can tell straight away he's not to be fucked with. You wouldn't start on him even if you didn't know who he was.

"So, what have you got for me fellers?"

I let Frank do the talking. "He's not budging boss, he won't let on who paid him for the job."

"Did you offer him the money?"

"Yes boss, we offered it to him, but he didn't want it."

Costanza doesn't seem too pissed. "Should have expected it really. He's not daft, I wouldn't believe that story."

"It was true wasn't it?"

"It was gospel Frank, but I still wouldn't believe it, would you? Say you'd taken a bloke out and a couple of heavies came to see you, saying their boss wanted to thank the bloke who paid for it. Would you tell them his name?"

"Fuck, no."

"Too fucking right you wouldn't, you'd expect them to put a bullet in your face the second after you'd told them."

"I don't think that's why he didn't tell us boss."

"No?"

"No. I don't think he was scared of us. We could've had his balls in a vice and he wouldn't have told us. He's one of them ones with the eastern mystical influences."

"What's he talking about Cheese?"

I shrug. Frank glares at me. "Cheers Cheese. Listen boss, I know I'm not explaining this very well but I'm not shitting you. If you were there you'd know what I mean, Cheese was there but for some reason he's taken another vow of fucking silence. Look boss, he had no furniture, nothing. He was sitting cross legged on the floor in a kimono, eating noodles with chopsticks, and he had this look."

"A look?"

"Yeah, in his eyes." Frank looks at me again. I've got nothing.

Stan's not impressed. "So you're telling me that because he's wearing pyjamas and eating a takeaway, and because he's got some kind of squint, that he must be good at knocking people off?"

"No boss, it's not just that, there was this move he pulled."

"Did it get on top?"

"No, it didn't kick off or nothing, but when me and Cheese were at the door, he saw us through the side window and pulled this move."

"What move? Jesus, who are we dealing with here, Michael Flatley or Michael Jackson?"

"It was like he flew."

"He flew?" The boss looks at me. I nod.

"Hallelujah, at last, Cheese has backed me up. I'll level with you boss. You know I wouldn't shit you about something like this. If I didn't think this bloke was something special do you think I'd waste your time and risk looking stupid by spinning you a fairy story? I hope you know me better than that."

Costanza shrugged. "I think Tony Visconti knew you better."

"Boss….Stan, that's ancient history, you know that. I'm your man, we both are. We never sided against you."

"Not that I could prove."

"Have we ever let you down?"

"I honestly don't know Frank."

"Jesus boss, what do I have to do?"

Frank's about to snap so I jump in. "Frank's telling the truth Stan. Even if you don't believe our opinion of what this bloke's like, the word on his last job should be enough. They're calling it the perfect hit. He left nothing for the police and it was like he injected the bullet between the guy's eyes. Like surgery they say."

"So, what are you suggesting, gentlemen?"

Frank looks relieved, "I think you could use him boss. You're always saying you could do with some more muscle, more firepower. This bloke could be your own fucking splinter cell."

"And what about my birthday present?"

"Sorry?"

"We still don't know who took out that piece of shit that defiled my angel. I still want to say thank you."

"Well you never know boss, if this Tom White bloke starts working for you he might tell you in a while."

"Not if he's as much of a pro as you say he is."

"Maybe he won't then."

"Alright Frank, I've pissed you off enough for one day. Go on then, we'll give this bloke a go, see what he's made of. I've got just the job for him."

When we're out of Stan's office Frank starts letting off steam. "That fucker needs to watch what he says sometimes. He'll get it one day."

"Let it go, Frank. For now anyway."

"Maybe you're right. So what do you think of the job Stan's got for the new bloke?"

Frank holds up the envelope Costanza gave him. "The Clarke job? From what I've seen of Tom White he won't have a problem. Clarke's a pussycat."

"It's me you're talking to Frank, we both know he's not a pussycat, he's proper hard."

"You're right, but I still think White can handle him."

"Why doesn't the boss use us for this kind of thing?"

"He's never said, Cheese, I reckon it's because we're too well known, he doesn't want us being recognised. And I don't think it's the old bill he's worried about. I reckon he's making some moves."

"Against another Mob?"

"Could be, Cheese. You know what he's like, he's never happy with his lot. He had it cushy before, but it wasn't enough, he just had to be the boss. Tony Visconti paid the price for that."

"You think he'd be stupid enough to start a war?"

"We'll see, Cheese, but I don't want to be caught cold if he does. I've been in this game too long to commit suicide for a scumbag like Stan Costanza."

* * * * * * * * * * * * * * * *

When I next saw Frank and Cheese it was in my local pub. The Pilgrim was an old-fashioned place. Much to the regulars' satisfaction it had seen off a series of takeover bids from the big chains and retained its original identity and character. It could be pretty rough but it was close and I fancied the arse off two of the barmaids, and a further two when I had had a few chasers between pints. It was noon on Saturday and I was standing at the bar talking to Laura; my favourite barmaid in the world. I was halfway through my second pint when Frank and Cheese came in. They greeted me like an old friend, at least Frank did, Cheese just nodded and did his best to smile. Frank, in trainers, jeans and a red hooded sweatshirt looked more casual than before. Cheese was the same as he had been the last time, still the big bald undertaker.

"How's it going Tom? I'm glad we bumped into you."

"Been going well thanks Frank. It's good to see you." That should have been a lie. It wasn't good to see them; I was scared. But part of me wasn't lying. I wanted more of this life.

"What can I get you?" Frank spoke like we were old friends.

I played it as cool as I could. "Cheers Frank," I downed what was left of my pint and put the empty glass on the bar. I was trying to act innocently in front of Laura as she served us. I knew she would have questions about these men, not out of any particular curiosity but because there was nothing else to talk about, and because they looked like the world they represented; they had the stink of violence. I managed to steer them to a vacant table as far from the bar as possible.

"We've got a job for you." Frank was obviously done with the preamble. He put a fat brown envelope on the table in front of me.

I stared at it. "Oh."

"That's right, don't take it yet, you don't need to look at it now. Sorry mate, you know the score, it's not like I'm talking to a novice." The envelope was getting a bit wet from a puddle of beer on the table.

"It's getting a bit wet." That was the first time I had heard Cheese speak. I looked at him in surprise. He didn't move so I picked up the envelope and held it in front of me like a sprinter with a relay baton, but a sitting-down sprinter, in the pub, with a slightly damp envelope instead of a baton.

Frank had been looking at Cheese since he spoke, looking neither puzzled nor angry, but strangely sad; as if he was feeling a great loss. His look changed when he had a handful of peanuts. He smiled with his full mouth, as if getting into character. "Dry roasted are the business. Anyway, as I say, you're not a novice so you know we can't just do this handover and fuck off. We're mates having a few beers. So we'd better have a few beers. Get them in Cheese." Silently, Cheese stood up and went to the bar.

There seemed to have been no question of whether I would take the 'job' or not, and I still didn't know what was required of me. "So, Frank, about the job."

"Walls have them Tom, walls have them. If I can be frank, and I always am, I'm surprised at you, you know better than to use careless talk."

I felt myself glowing red, as if I had been scolded by a teacher at primary school. "I'm not a pro, I'm just a normal bloke. I'm not a face in the underworld, you've made a mistake. I killed the cunt next door because he was a noisy bastard, and I was too scared to actually have it out with him about it. I'm a coward, a coward who sneaks around and catches people off guard. I know what's in this envelope, it's information about someone you want me to kill. Well I'm not doing it. I'm off. Enjoy your nuts." Of course I didn't actually say any of that. I just looked at him.

"One thing though Tom, there's no fee mentioned in what I've given you, so…." Frank wrote a number on a beer mat. 10k. "It's the standard rate. Half up front."

So that was it. I had become a hitman. Just like that.

Cheese came back with the drinks. As the beers went down I managed to put out of my mind the full extent of what I was expected to do for the money and was able to enjoy myself. Frank and Cheese were surprisingly pleasant company with a wider spread of interests than I would have given them credit for. I learnt that they both loved fishing but were divided by the fact that Frank preferred freshwater, coarse, while Cheese was a sea man, or semen as Frank pronounced it. This well-used line was given extra comedy by the fact that Cheese had once again regressed into his silent world and could only hold up his fist in response. The beers were going down quickly, and I went to the bar to get my round.

"So, who are your friends Tom?" The delicious Laura was serving me and had commenced her grilling. She was constantly fighting a crusade against fashion and wore the most bizarre clothes. They were baggy and shapeless, but if she was attempting to mask her beauty then she had failed miserably. She tended to wear her hair up while she was working, but she could have put a dead badger on her head for all I noticed because I couldn't take my eyes off her mouth. She had the most amazing lips I had ever seen. I've got a thing about lips. It's almost an obsession. Laura tended to leave hers slightly parted, and her breath would make them move just a little. It was like my own private porn film. All I could think of was what those lips were capable of. I wanted her so much I felt nauseous. Never has the term 'sick to the stomach' held so much resonance. Laura had no idea of the power she wielded. Or maybe she did.

It was time to furnish Laura with an answer to her question, despite what was really in my head. "I only know one of them. "He's the older brother of a guy I used to be mates with when I was a kid. He used to beat me up a lot, but he's stopped doing that now."

"The bald guy?"

"No, the other one, I don't think I would still be alive if Che-, that guy had beaten me up."

"What did you call him?"

"I'm not sure what his name is to be honest, it's a bit embarrassing. Frank, the blonde one, introduced us but I didn't quite catch what he said. Don't you hate it when that happens?"

"It's never happened to me, if I don't hear the first time then I ask the person to repeat it."

"What?"

"I ask the person to…. Oh, you're hilarious Tom."

"I am, aren't I? But what if you don't hear them the second time? It's awful asking someone to repeat themselves after the second time, and the third is just impossible."

"It's more embarrassing having to pretend to know their name. What about if the person who introduced you goes to the bar or the toilet, leaving you on your own with Mr. X, and then what if someone you know comes along, perhaps someone who works behind the bar, comes along and says hello? Then you've got to introduce the X man and you can't. Now that would be awkward."

"Don't even think of doing that."

"It wasn't a threat, I'm a nice girl."

"I bet you're not, I bet you're filthy."

"Sorry?"

"Nothing, just thinking aloud." I picked up the three pints, squeezing them together so they didn't slip out of my hands.

When I got back to the table I gestured for Frank to come close, so we wouldn't be heard. "Who am I working for? Who's the boss, who's the old man?" I was failing miserably to sound streetwise.

"Can't tell you Tom, not allowed. It's not difficult to guess though, just think big. The big man. Not the fat man, the big man."

That meant nothing. I smiled knowingly.

Frank returned the smile. "You've got it."

I didn't have it.

Six

I was glad to be home, not because I didn't want to be in the pub but because I was itching to open the envelope, but now I was back something was stopping me. I put the envelope on the coffee table. The lounge was looking nice now, the new carpet was a cheap one, but it did the trick, it had looked awful before. This was no time for a carpet inspection. I couldn't put it off any longer. I had to open the envelope. I nudged it around the table a bit. This was really pushing the envelope. I thought about my conversation with Laura and, looking back, it seemed like she was being a little bit flirty. Or perhaps she was just being friendly. It must be tough for attractive girls; if they are friendly to a man then he thinks he's got a chance and the whole friendship thing goes straight out of the window. From that moment on the man carefully plans every move, with the eventual aim of getting her into bed. If the attractive girl isn't friendly, then she quickly gets a reputation for being aloof. I'm glad I'm not an attractive girl, it seems like it would be quite a chore, despite the obvious benefits.

This prevaricating was getting me nowhere. The envelope remained on the table: a thriller in manilla.

Then.

I'd opened it.

It was all in twenty-pound notes - I did some quick mental arithmetic - two hundred and fifty of them. I put the bundle to my ear and ran my thumb down the edge as if I was counting them by sound alone. It didn't work very well, firstly because I didn't know how to do it, and secondly because they were used notes, and most were crumpled.

I was happy with the hard cash but disappointed with the rest of the envelope's contents. I'm not sure what I was expecting but I was disappointed anyway. I had wanted to be James Bond. I had wanted a professionally produced dossier with a picture of both the sexy female Russian agent I would be making contact with, and the thick-set diamond dealer who would be my target. And I wanted a first-class airline ticket to Cairo and directions to the most exclusive casino in the city.

But what I got was a piece of paper torn out of a ring-bound pad. The writing was in green felt tip. It said: '18 Steven Street, SW1. Alone on Thursday evenings between 7 and 10. Faulkner Clarke. Swap code.' It looked like the work of a child. There was a passport-sized picture pinned to the note of a man with a thin face, a bad moustache and a big bald patch. Who was this man, this Faulkner Clarke? Why did someone want him dead? What did 'swap code' mean? How was I going to kill another person? This was madness, I couldn't do this. I had let those two thugs believe I was capable of what they were proposing instead of just running for the hills. Accepting the envelope not only put me in a position where I was going to have to kill a stranger, it was also a tacit confession to the murder of my neighbour. I couldn't believe how stupid I'd been. I blamed the beer.

My head was split down the middle. On the one hand I was disappointed that the world of murder-to-order was not as glamorous as I had hoped, and on the other I was beating myself up for getting involved in it at all. I looked at the note again and despite the fact that it looked as if it could have been left for the milkman I found it intriguing, particularly the last two words, 'swap code'. Maybe I wasn't meant to actually kill the guy, maybe I was just supposed to swap something with him, some code, like a spy. That was nonsense. Why did James Bond keep cropping up? Frank and Cheese weren't into espionage; they were into violence and taking things from people and selling things that people shouldn't really be buying.

'Search returned 0 matches'. I clicked 'refresh', as if it would work this time.

'Search returned 0 matches'. Well that was the end of that then. There was no Steven Street in SW1, or anywhere in London for that matter. I tried the other spelling of Stephen, it didn't work either.

I stared at the screen for a while, as if it might suddenly admit to having made a mistake and show me the street after all. That didn't happen. I decided to try a more analogue approach, a London A to Z but I really couldn't be bothered to go and buy one, even for something as important as this. Nobody wants to buy something to use just once, unless it's a cigarette or a condom. I wondered if I could have claimed the A to Z on expenses, perhaps Frank had some kind of form to be completed and sent to the Mob's Accounting Department. Did he have the authority to sign off £7.99?

What didn't really occur to my more than slightly drunk mind was that if there was a Steven or Stephen Street in London then it wouldn't be limited to an A to Z, I would have found it online. Instead it dawned on me that I did have an A to Z. It was another badly judged Christmas gift from a relative, my crazy grandmother this time. I hadn't thrown it away because I have an aversion to throwing out books. It is something of a pathology for me, I simply can't bring myself to get rid of them. I've managed to contain my disorder in more recent years, but back then I was at my hoarding peak. I kept my best books on display, to hand, just in case I needed them at short notice, even though I never did, because I had already read all of them, and I rarely read a book twice. Why read the same book again when there are so many others to try? If I was honest I would admit that I kept my most highbrow books on display to impress guests. The books that didn't make the grade for my bookshelves went in a cupboard in the spare room or in the loft. I was sure the A to Z was in the loft, and as I was still feeling a bit pissed from the pub the prospect of going up there didn't seem too bad an idea. So to the loft I went.

You know the method of entry, all straining sinew and legs kicking out uselessly. I grunted my way up then realised the enormity of my task. Although I had stacked the boxes of books fairly neatly, there was no indexing system, so I had no idea which books were in which boxes. I wished I had been more organised as I knelt on the dusty joists and looked at the pile of boxes as high as the Hoover Dam. Staring at the task wasn't going to complete it any quicker but it was all I could do.

"Do you want a hand?" I jumped out of my skin. My knee slipped off the joist. There was a crunch as it dented the plasterboard below and I started to topple forward, breaking my fall by throwing out a hand and hanging on to one of the book-boxes that threatened to bring the whole stack down, but fortunately relented. I remained in that prone position for a few moments despite what felt like the head of a nail digging into my knee. I didn't want to look round, why would I want to look round? I was alone, in the dark attic of the house that I lived in by myself. I was certain I had no visitors: I wasn't having an attic party. I heard the voice again. "Tom?"

I recognised it on the second time of asking. "Colin." The relief was clear in my voice. "What the fuck are you doing in here? You scared the shit out of me. Are you stalking me or something? Stop letting yourself into my house."

"Calm down, you said you wanted me to come over."

"Did I?" I pulled my left knee out of the plasterboard and

shuffled round. Colin was nowhere to be seen.

His head appeared through the open hatch. He had obviously not got a proper hold the last time and had just pulled himself back up again. He heaved his body into the loft. "Yes, you sent me a text. It said 'come over'. I thought you might have been in trouble. I knocked but there was no answer, so I let myself in. I couldn't find you then I saw the chair on the landing. How come you're always in the loft when I come round? Are you on your way to kill the neighbours on the other side? And why is there a shitload of money on the coffee table?"

"Be careful where you tread, you can only stand on the joists otherwise you'll go through." I didn't remember sending a text but I was willing to believe that I had. I was in a bit of a state about the appearance of Frank and Cheese so I may well have sent a sneaky text while I was in the pub toilet, at the bar or even on my way home.

"You're pissed aren't you? How much have you had?" Colin had clambered over to me.

"Just a few. Listen, thanks for coming over, something's happened, those blokes came to see me again."

"Cheese and thingy?"

"And Frank, yes."

"Are you okay? What did they want?"

"I'm fine, just a bit pissed. They still seem to think I'm an actual real hitman. Apparently I did quite a job next door." I couldn't hide the pride in my voice as I said this.

"So you're the talk of the underworld. Congratulations. How come they gave you the money though? Did you tell them the truth, that nobody paid for their boss's birthday present and that you were acting alone?"

"Erm. No. Not exactly."

"What did you do? Tom, what did you do?"

"Can you help me get this box out?" Surprisingly he did help me. He lifted the two boxes that were on top of the one I wanted, allowing me to open it. There was the A to Z, right on top. That sort of thing never happened but I wasn't going to knock it. "Got it, cheers. Let's go downstairs, I'm sure it's haunted up here."

We were in the lounge. Colin was holding the wad of twenties and reading Frank's vague instructions. He looked up at me. "Okay, if you won't tell me what you've done, or agreed to do I'll ask another question. Why do you need an A to Z?"

"I need to find an address."

"What address Tom? Where are you going? You're doing it aren't you? You're letting them believe you're a hitman and they've given you a job. You're going to kill again aren't you?"

"Kind of."

"I'm in."

"I thought you were going to have a go at me."

"I'm in."

"I heard you, the first time, but I didn't ask you to be in on it."

"I don't care. I'm in." He folded his arms like a petulant child.

"Fuck off."

"You need me Tom. You needed me last time and you'll need me again."

"You didn't do anything last time. All you did was stand outside looking confused."

"I was cool under pressure."

"You were, I have to give you that, I thought you'd go apeshit when I told you what had happened but you took it well. Don't get me wrong, I really appreciate you sticking by me on that one but I don't think we're about to go into some kind of murder partnership."

"Okay, not partners, but I can be your right-hand man."

"What's in it for you?"

"I'm bored Tom. I hate my job, my life. I want to do something exciting. This could be it."

"To be honest mate, whilst I'm sure your contribution would be worthwhile, I don't think it would be worth giving up half the money for."

"I'll do it for thirty percent."

"Why?"

"Because I realise this is your thing and I'm stepping on your toes, so I'm happy to take a lower cut. Think about it Tom. Killing the guy next door is one thing, but do you really think you're going to be able to go up to London on your own and kill some bloke you've never even met? Someone who could easily be a really hard criminal? You're going to need some help. How much is there here by the way?"

"Five grand, with another five coming when it's done. But I think it's a non-starter, the place probably doesn't even exist. Steven Street doesn't sound right."

"Let's have a look then shall we?" Colin opened up the index of the A to Z. "No, you're right. There's no Steven Street." He picked up Frank's note again and then turned back to the A to Z eagerly. He smiled. "You need my help."

"Well it doesn't look like I'm doing it anyway, I don't know where it is."

"Exactly, you need me to tell you where it is."

"You know where it is?"

"Absolutely." He handed me the sheet of paper. "Read it again."

I read the note aloud. "18 Steven Street, SW1. Alone on Thursday evenings between 7 and 10. Faulkner Clarke. Swap code."

"It's obvious!"

"Tell me then."

"Work it out dumb-arse." Colin had become painfully smug.

"What is there to work out? Just tell me where it is."

"Only if you ask me to help you." He was starting to piss me off.

"I don't want you to help me."

"Oh yes you do. You need to know where the place is, otherwise all those mobsters are going to think you're a total tit, and they'll lose patience and shoot you in the face or something. Come on, ask me."

I gave in, not just about the directions, about everything. Colin was right, there was no way I was going to go to London alone and take some stranger on. "You can come along and help if you want."

"No, that won't do, you have to ask me properly."

"Forget it then."

He looked disappointed that I wasn't going to give him the satisfaction of begging, but he knew not to push it. "Okay, I'll tell you, I'm in though yes?"

"You're in."

"Right. It's not Steven Street."

"It says Steven Street."

"There's no Steven Street."

"I know there's no fucking Steven Street!"

Colin was loving this. "You're going to kick yourself in a second. You see the phrase 'swap code' there?"

"Yes, I don't know what it means. Do I have to take something, some code to swap with someone?"

"You're not a spy! It's not telling you to swap some code. It's referring to the note. They've used a code, swap code."

"How do you know what that is?"

"I don't, well I didn't until I looked at it, but it's obvious. Only an idiot wouldn't be able to work it out."

It came to me. He was right, it was obvious. "Fuck, it's not Faulkner Clarke in Steven Street. It's Steven Clarke and he lives at 18 Faulkner Street. I knew I'd work it out."

"You didn't work it out, don't try and pretend you did. I told you."

"Whatever." I wanted to get on with it. "That's the easy part over. Now, this thing about him being home on Thursday evenings, surely we can't bank on that. Nobody is so predictable that he is guaranteed to be home between seven and ten on a certain day. He might decide he wants to go out."

"I see your point but it's all we've got. Today's Monday, we need to decide if we are going to do the full job this Thursday or just go and check out the place so we're prepared for next week."

"Why are you so keen to do this?" I asked.

He shrugged. "Why not?"

"Do you think we're expected to do it this Thursday? Is there some kind of time limit?"

"I don't know, you're the hitman."

"I'm not a hitman."

"You've been given ten grand to kill a man. You got a better term for it?"

"Well if I'm a hitman what are you? The Hitman's Apprentice?"

"Yes, I like that." He looked satisfied.

"Right, we need to focus."

He looked offended. "I'm focused."

"Okay. We'll have three hours. We should be able to case the joint and make our move in that time. We shouldn't need two visits."

"Oh dear. Oh dear." Colin shook his head.

"What?"

He imitated my voice, quite well actually, "*Case the joint.*" His own voice came back "Why are you talking like that?"

"I'm a hitman remember?"

"I'll hit *you* if you keep talking like that. We can't just go there on Thursday night and do it. We should go tonight or tomorrow and see where the place is, how we get in, all that stuff."

"You mean case the joint?" Colin was about to respond but I interrupted. "Fuck fuck fuck fuck."

"What?"

"I don't have a gun."

"Shit. You dropped it next door didn't you? I forgot."

"Why did I drop it?" I was furious with myself.

"You did the right thing. You didn't have time to hide a gun after doing your neighbour."

"Actually I did, I could have just left it in a drawer and the coppers wouldn't have found it."

"You weren't to know they'd be so rubbish."

"We're going to have to go to Phil."

Colin sat up. "Big mouth? Is that wise?"

"Can you think of anything else?"

"I guess not. And I suppose it's not that risky. At least he didn't talk to the police."

"We can't be sure of that."

"Tom, if he'd gone to the police you would have been arrested by now."

"You're right. He's not going to go to the police. He's a drug dealer."

"He can't do you any more harm even if he does talk again. Apparently your name's already known in the underworld so it won't make any difference."

I sent a text to Phil.

Seven

Colin left, I told him it was best that I dealt with Phil on my own, explaining that having someone else around would only make Phil nervous. Despite having agreed to let Colin help out on the hit, I still wanted to keep control of the process. He was less a partner and more a hired hand.

While I was waiting for Phil to respond to my text, I trawled the internet to check up on silencers. I was glad to find that they actually existed and surprised to discover that they could be bought for almost any type of handgun. I was even more surprised to find the vast amount of American websites cheerfully selling literally thousands of different types of weapons. The product descriptions were something to behold; "This silencer reduces the sound of a pistol shot to that of a book being slammed. The sound carries a lot less and is not recognisable as a shot. In a busy city it will go unnoticed." I knew guns were legal in America, but I had thought that they would have to be sold under the banner of hunting, and use in a 'busy city' didn't seem to fall into that bracket. The only legal use for a gun in a city would be self-defence, but that didn't warrant a need to reduce and disguise the sound of the shot. It was, of course, hypocritical for me to pour scorn on the American gun laws as I sat waiting for my dealer to call so I could buy my next weapon.

Obviously, I couldn't order from any of these sites as I doubted they shipped internationally, and I wouldn't have had the appropriate licence, but my research gave me the confidence to ask Phil for a silencer now I knew they existed. Having one would make my job a whole lot easier.

I got a text from Phil saying he would meet me in the Pilgrim. This was a turn up. He never conducted business in public.

When I got to the pub Phil was already there, talking to Laura at the bar. I couldn't work out if they knew each other or not. I hadn't seen Phil in the Pilgrim before, although he lived nearby. As I got closer he saw me. "Tom! Great to see you mate, you're looking good. What are you drinking?"

I was confused. Phil never acted like this, and drug-dealers never buy drinks for their customers. I looked at Laura, "The usual please Laura." I could tell from her face she was as baffled as I was. It was obvious she knew who Phil was - she probably scored from him herself – and it was obvious she had never seen him acting like this before. Then I realised what was going on. He was scared. He saw me in a different light now he knew I was a killer, and he probably knew I had worked out that he had been shouting my name from the rooftops. He wanted me to meet him in a public place in case I had plans to shoot him. Marvellous.

I took advantage, "Do you want one Laura?"

Laura smiled, she had it sussed. "That would be lovely. I'll have a brandy, a large one." Phil didn't flinch. I was impressed by his performance. He paid for the drinks then steered me to an out of the way table. He spoke very quietly. "So what are you after?"

I decided to talk his language. "I need another piece." Okay I admit it, I enjoyed talking like that.

Phil maintained his poker face. "I see."

"Well can you get me one?"

"What type do you want?"

"The same as before, and I need it before Thursday."

He opened his mouth as if to protest then closed it again quickly. Could it really be that he thought I was dangerous? I could think of no other explanation for his behaviour. "I'll see what I can do."

"And I need a silencer for it too."

He frowned. "I'll see what I can do."

We didn't talk much after that. Phil became very focussed on his pint. It seemed that he was keen to finish it and get out. As he left I shouted after him that it was my round, but he didn't seem to hear me. I got more drinks for myself and Laura. She was still in a large brandy mood.

"You seem to have acquired some very interesting friends Tom."

It was great when she spoke to me. It meant I could watch those lips of hers up close. I hadn't heard a word she had said. "Sorry Laura, what was that?"

"Where were you? How could you not have heard me? I'm right here." She paused until she realised I wasn't going to answer. "I said you seem to be keeping new and exciting company."

"What, Phil?"

"For starters, yes. He's not exactly a social butterfly, is he? He seems to be very keen to be in your good books."

"Do you know him?"

"I've seen him around."

"I don't know what to tell you."

"I expect you'll tell me nothing. But it's not just Phil is it? There were those others in here with you the other day."

"What are you trying to say?"

"They looked unsavoury too."

I bellowed an awful false laugh in her direction. "Are you talking about Frank? He's not unsavoury. He's a friend of my cousin."

"That's not what you said at the time." I wasn't enjoying this grilling but I had to love those lips.

"I never said Frank was unsavoury."

"You said you were friends with his little brother." I took a swallow of beer. She was still looking at me intently. Another swallow. "What are you up to?" Despite the tone of the conversation it was great to have her full attention. She wasn't pulling a pint and she wasn't drying any glasses, she was just talking to me. Her shoulders had dropped and her face was open, concerned. She was wearing a white T-shirt, very loose and in need of ironing. I had never seen her look so beautiful.

I have always thought it a terrible cliché that women are attracted to danger, but Laura had never given me so much attention. I am sure it wasn't on a conscious level, she wasn't openly excited by violence, or criminals, but, like Phil, she seemed to be seeing me in a new light.

Phil was back within the hour. I was taken aback by this concierge-like service. He led me to the table we had vacated earlier, which in my opinion made us look more suspicious than we needed to. We sat down and he spoke quietly. "I'll have it on Wednesday evening."

"That'll do." Colin and I still hadn't decided whether to go up a couple of days before and 'case the joint'. This made our minds up for us.

"But not the silencer, I can't get that for another week."

"That's no good."

"That's the way it is. You can't just buy any old one and stick it on the barrel. It has to be the right one for the right kind of gun. If you want to cancel then that's fine."

I relented. "Alright, that'll have to do. I suppose the silencer can wait. I'll come and pick up the gun on Wednesday night, when's the best time?"

"No, my place is no good. We'll meet somewhere else, somewhere outside."

"That's a bit unnecessary Phil, what do you want to do, meet in a car park?"

He sounded very jittery. "That's as good a place as any."

"You watch too much telly Phil. It would be far less suspicious if I just came to your house."

"Don't take this the wrong way Tom, but I'd rather you didn't come to mine. You know what I mean?"

"Okay, come to mine then."

Phil raised his hands as if to placate me in advance. "Tom, I can't come to your place with a gun, right next door to that guy who…." he paused "…who was murdered."

He had obviously stopped himself from saying "Who *you* murdered," and I thought about taking offence but there was no point. I thought I'd have some fun instead. "Was someone murdered then?"

His eyes widened. "I…I think someone might have been."

"Do the police know who did it?"

"I don't think so."

I leaned closer to him. I could feel his breath on my face, he'd been eating garlic but I didn't pull away. I kept up my fearsome persona. "Do they have any leads? Any information at all?"

He leaned back so I leaned closer. He finally spoke. "No, I don't think they've got any leads."

One more just to make sure. "So nobody's told them anything?"

He spoke quickly this time. "No Tom, nobody's told them anything. Nobody knows anything." I detected the slightest whimper in his voice.

I stopped there because I didn't want to overdo it. I just wanted him scared enough to keep his mouth shut, not so scared that he feared for his life and went to the police anyway for his own protection.

I decided we would meet in the shopping mall in the centre of town. It was open late on a Wednesday. We would browse the mall looking like shopping buddies, probably looking quite gay. We would both have several shopping bags and I would, like any good shopping partner, hold Phil's bags while he tried on a new piece of clothing, then I would simply give him back one less bag when he had finished, keeping the one containing the gun. It reeked of overkill but if he wanted to play the big drama then that's what we would do.

The moment we had settled it, Phil was off out the door again. He was in quite a rush these days. I took our empty glasses back to the bar, regretting it immediately because it gave Laura a chance to make a comment. "You two seem very close. I thought you were going to kiss at one point."

"We're crazy about each other."

"Come on Tom, why won't you tell me what you're up to?"

"I'm not up to anything, and I don't mean to be rude but it's not like you and me are best mates or anything is it? You work here and I'm a customer, we don't have the right to know each other's business." She looked really hurt. "I didn't quite mean that the way it sounded, but you know what I mean, do you tell me any of your secrets?"

She perked up a little. "Are you saying you have secrets?"

"No. Well yes, of course I have secrets, but not bad secrets, evil secrets. Nothing to do with meeting a few mates in the pub."

She rested her slender forearms on the bar and smiled, her immaculate teeth glowing white between her wonderful red lips. "Tell me a secret then. A nice one."

"I'm in love with you."

She smiled, "That's a good one."

"Now tell me one of yours."

"I'm in love with you too." My heart leapt instinctively even though I knew she was joking. If only I had been too.

On Wednesday evening I headed into town to meet Phil, my new shopping buddy. I didn't hate shopping like many other men but I didn't do it very often. We met outside the main entrance to the mall and I couldn't help but laugh when I saw him. It wasn't his clothes or hair - it was what he was holding. I had made the effort to go along with the plan of bringing dummy items for that 'just out shopping' look. I was laden with bags daubed with retail logos, whereas Phil had two carrier bags from Tesco, each containing one small object. I didn't have to look hard to see the gun. It wasn't boxed, just loose in the bag. The barrel and handle were clearly visible through the thin polythene.

"What are you doing?" I was trying to say it quietly but was laughing at the same time and it came out in an effeminate hiss. The scowl on Phil's face was only adding to the comedy value.

"What's so funny?" He looked ready to punch me. Me laughing at him had obviously made him forget to treat me with kid gloves, or maybe he'd realised I just wasn't that scary after all.

"We're supposed to look like we're in the middle of a shopping trip. Is there a Tesco's in this mall?"

"I didn't have any other bags."

"You can see what's in there you know." I was hissing again.

"Fuck." He tried to cover the plastic shrouded pistol with the non-gun bag and looked around nervously. He wasn't a happy shopper. "They have plain-clothes coppers in these places to check for shoplifters, there'd better not be any round here."

He was starting to panic. I looked around, felt fairly certain that nobody was watching us, and snatched both bags off him. I stuffed them into the biggest one of my own and handed him two different bags. "Come on" I said. "And for Christ's sake relax." Phil seemed to feel more comfortable now he didn't have the gun. We wandered aimlessly through the mall in silence. Finally I spoke, "You know, we don't really need to shop anymore, not now we've made the exchange"

"We haven't made an exchange. An exchange is when something passes one way and something else passes the other." His nerve had definitely returned.

"I didn't realise I had to pay you." He studied my face for a while, looking for traces of a smile. I couldn't keep a straight face for long. "Funny aren't I? Actually I don't have the cash on me. I didn't think it would be wise to have the money and the gun on us in case we got caught. I've got it at home though"

"That sounds reasonable I suppose. When can I get it off you?"

"I can see you in the Pilgrim later if you want."

"That's a good plan. It means I'll get to see that Laura bird. I reckon if you gave her a good scrub she'd be pretty tasty."

I stopped walking and grabbed his arm. "Don't ever talk about her like that." I was surprised by the level of my anger. My measured tone seemed to make the command sound more threatening.

"Sorry mate, I didn't think." He looked scared again.

When I was back at home I made a cup of tea and sat down to inspect my new toy. As I picked up the gun I realised that tea didn't do the situation justice, so I poured it down the sink and fixed myself a scotch and water. I couldn't stand the taste of whisky, still can't, but it seemed to fit the moment. The gun was the same basic shape as the previous one – which presumably was bagged and tagged in the local police station – but it had a better look and feel to it. It was blacker and sleeker and felt weightier, meatier. I definitely wouldn't be dropping this one at the next crime scene. This would be my weapon, part of my persona. I felt I ought to give it a name then realised how ridiculous that was. After a few glasses of whisky, I decided it wasn't ridiculous at all. I'm sure the first entry in The Hitman's Handbook is: "a good hitman always names his gun."

It had to be a girl's name, guns and ships always have girls' names. Actually, ships don't always have girls' names; they have names like "Invincible' and "Endurance." Perhaps that's just warships. I tried to remember the name of the ferry that had taken me from Newhaven to Dieppe on a school trip when I was seven, the only boat I had been on. It was called 'Le Something', something French, but not a girl's name. So maybe I could give my gun a man's name. I brainstormed men's names. Geoff, Peter, Wilberforce. No good. Steve. Rubbish. It would have to be a girl's name after all. Carol, Philippa, Lucy. Laura Laura Laura Laura Laura. That was easier than I had expected.

I had been rubbing the barrel with a cloth as I pondered names and now it gleamed. "You're all nice and clean aren't you Laura? Yesh yoo are! Yesh yoo are!" I kissed Laura, leaving a bit of dribble on her sight. I apologised and wiped her clean.

I had to think of somewhere to hide her. If killing was to be my trade then I needed somewhere that was both accessible and secret. I couldn't think of anything. I felt a bit sick after all the whisky and gun-kissing and this wasn't helping. I considered the attic, but quickly rejected it. I was sick of the attic, it was scary up there. I needed advice from the Hitman's Manual. I vowed to write the Hitman's Manual as soon as I knew the first thing about being a hitman. After lengthy thought I formulated a plan. For some reason I remembered a situation a few years ago with an ex-girlfriend. I was at her parents' house for dinner and her father was exceeding his own exceptional standards in dullness. He was explaining how only a small part of the casing of a hi-fi system was taken up by the workings of the unit. I was less than fascinated at the time and was surprised I even remembered, but for some reason it came back to me. Even back then, hi-fi systems had started getting smaller, but I hadn't upgraded mine for some time so it was a fair size. I opened the back of my amplifier and there was ample room for Laura. I felt bad putting her in such a confined space but then remembered she was just a gun after all.

The whisky was wearing off.

Phil and I had the briefest of meetings at the pub later. Laura was at the bar, eyeing me suspiciously throughout, but I managed to hand over the cash without her seeing. Phil left just as quickly as he had before, and I felt I should stick around to make at least a token effort to look like I wasn't engaged in clandestine activities. The only person I knew in there was Laura, so I went to say hello, just being friendly, not because I was in love with her. No sir.

I wasn't an expert on women's couture but it appeared that she had made something of a departure from her normal anti-fashion look. Her clothes looked new and while still looking casual, they more clearly defined her excellent figure. She had been to the hairdresser's too; her blonde hair was styled, roughly parted on the right and eased down over the side of her face, just covering the corner of her left eye. She was also wearing make-up. It was subtle around the eyes and cheekbones but her lipstick was striking. It was a deep crimson, a strong look for someone who usually shunned such decoration. It made her lips look even fuller, even more sensual than before. I hadn't thought that was possible.

Eight

It was late afternoon on the day of the Clarke job and I was standing in my hallway trying to stop the myriad thoughts churning around in my head, and the lunch churning in my stomach. I hadn't been able to face dinner. I was waiting for Colin. Actually I wasn't officially waiting as he wasn't late yet. My thoughts tugged in opposite directions; I wanted time to pass quickly so this night would be over, but I also wanted to put off doing what I had to do for as long as possible. Unless the space-time continuum chose to explode tonight I couldn't have it both ways.

Colin arrived. We could have met at the station but I insisted that he come to mine so he could check I didn't forget anything. I wanted him to earn his money. He was wearing jeans and a blue T-shirt, suitably nondescript. I went through my checks again, feeling for the bulge of the gun in the inside pocket of my jacket. It was there of course, I had only checked it two minutes before. The jacket was a light waterproof, which was perfect, not just in terms of comfort, but also providing enough cover for my concealed weapon without looking suspiciously heavy for the warm weather. I checked myself in the mirror to make sure the bulge wasn't obvious.

"Don't flatter yourself mate, no-one can see your bulge." I had hoped Colin would be in a more serious mood. "We off then?"

"Wait a minute, I need to go through my checklist."

"Bugger that, all we need is a map, a gun and your…" he paused and came looming up to me with his arms raised, a caricature of a vampire… "woooooh - killer instinct!"

"It might be a joke to you but this is a big deal for me."

"I know it's a big deal but we've both got our own way of dealing with it." He looked at my bag. "How long are you staying Tom, a few days?"

"I just want to be prepared."

"I imagined hitmen to be exciting and devil-may-care."

Colin's conversation wasn't helping my nerves.

On the way to the station I tried to appeal to his better nature. "Listen Colin, we don't want to draw attention to ourselves on the train, so can you…?" I couldn't' think of a polite way of putting it.

"You mean 'shut the fuck up'?"

"No. I. Erm. Just. Well, yes. Would that be okay?"

We paid for the tickets with cash so as not to leave a credit card trail; I was in a cautious mood. The train wasn't busy and there were only two other people in our carriage, seated separately from each other. The journey would take over an hour. I couldn't bear it. I just wanted to get this whole thing over with. I hoped this nagging feeling in my gut would recede with each further job. If I felt this level of stress each time then I would surely be dead from a heart attack within weeks. One feeling I did enjoy was the weight of the gun against my chest. I was packing heat and it felt good. As soon as I thought this I was glad Colin couldn't read my mind. He would have ripped the piss out of me. He sat opposite me looking very impatient.

We arrived at London Victoria soon after six. The whole station seemed to groan with the weight of the rush-hour commuters. We joined the throng on the escalator down into the catacombs of the tube. Posters on the wall told me of the delights of the latest West End shows and ways for me to get cheaper travel insurance. Colin seemed to have acquired a marker-pen and was drawing a moustache and glasses on the image of the young girl's face on each Les Miserables poster. He was disappointed that the escalator moved so quickly as he wanted time to do a proper job.

The tube was packed. Those of us who were standing swayed as one with the train's movements. We were like coral, multiple organisms merged into one great mass of life. It was almost spiritual. At least it would have been if we weren't all hot and sticky and miserable and wanting to kill everybody around us. Colin was like a bored child. He had no room to move and yet he wouldn't keep still. He couldn't settle on which of the plastic balls hanging from the ceiling he wanted to hold. There were three within his range and he flitted between them like a bumble bee on a bunch of flowers. Other hands were clasping the sweaty balls, but this didn't bother Colin. I was sure if the train had been empty he would have been swinging up and down the carriage like a monkey. I chose not to tell him to stop because I knew he would only tolerate a certain number of whinges from me, and I wanted to save my allocation in case I needed the firepower later.

It was a huge relief to get off the stinking tube and up onto the cool pavement. It didn't take us long to find Faulkner Street, which was wide and lined with two-storey houses, unusual for this area where three or four storey houses, mostly turned into flats, were the norm. Steven Clarke obviously wasn't short of a few bob. It was further relief to find that Colin had started behaving himself and wasn't drawing attention to us.

It was just after half-past-six when we approached the address and I realised it was a mistake allowing so much time for the journey. The instructions said that the target would be in the house after seven so we couldn't stand outside before then in case he saw us on his way home. There was a good chance that he was already in the house but we couldn't tell either way. All we knew was that he was expected to be home alone between seven and ten. At least I thought it was that time. I pulled out Frank's note to check and received a slap on the ear for my trouble.

"What are you doing Tom?"

"I'm checking when he's supposed to be in the house."

He took the paper off me and screwed it into a tight ball. "Eat it."

"What?"

"What were you thinking? You're meant to be a pro. You don't bring the instructions with you. What if you got caught? Do you think having murder instructions on you as well as the gun would help your case? Now fucking eat it."

As I munched away on the ball of paper I realised this was a major development. Colin was in the zone. He wanted to do this right. He was on the team.

We had to get away from the house at least until we were sure our target wasn't going to wander past us. I attempted to communicate this to Colin but the noises I made through my mouthful of paper were nothing like English. Fortunately he had the same thought and we started walking.

"Where can we go?" I asked him when I had made my final papery swallow. "We don't want to be seen out here and we can't go to a pub. After it's done the coppers will visit all the local pubs asking if anyone suspicious was around on the night of the murder. We look suspicious, we must look suspicious. What the fuck are we doing here?" My voice was almost a squeal.

Colin spoke slowly and deliberately. "Tom, calm down. Listen to me. You're starting to panic. Recognise it and take control of it. It's doing you no good. We're walking along the street, just walking, nobody's paying us any attention and nobody will remember us afterwards." His voice was strangely soothing. His tone was different from normal; it was much deeper and more melodic. "Keep on walking, we're just walking. Breathe slow."

I became aware of my crazy-paced breathing and slowed it down as Colin had instructed. This was a side to him I hadn't seen. After a few measured breaths my breathing was back to normal and I no longer wanted to run as fast as I could to get out of there. "I think I'm okay now, sorry about that." I was starting to see the value of having Colin around. He continued his ponderous hypnotic delivery. "They-won't-think-we're-suspicious." Now he slowed his voice down even more, like a vinyl record on the wrong speed, mocking himself. "Because-our-clothes-are-nnnnn…" he couldn't keep his expression sombre any longer, "…nondescript!" He clamped his hand over his mouth so as not to make a scene and I did the same. Neither of us knew why we found this so funny but we were almost crying with laughter as we rounded the corner, nearly walking into someone coming the other way.

Colin managed to contain his mirth. He spoke quietly and quickly. "Keep walking, don't look back."

"Why?" I didn't need an answer. "It was him wasn't it?" I didn't think I had noticed the face of the man who just passed us but now I thought about it, I realised I had noticed it, and it was definitely Steven Clarke. He was bigger than I had anticipated, his narrow face looking out of scale with his broad body. Unlike in the picture that Frank had given me there was no moustache, but it was definitely the same man.

"It was him. I think we should go." Colin's voice was starting to sound like mine was a few minutes earlier, hissy and panicky.

"What do you mean, 'go'?"

"I think we should leave, go home. Now we know he definitely gets back to his house for seven, so we can work with that. The best thing to do would be to come here next week half an hour early and do what you did with your neighbour. We break into the house and when he comes in we…"

"Take him out?"

Colin seemed pleased, "exactly."

"I'm sorry but I can't go through this all again, I can't go home and wait for a week, it would drive me crazy."

Colin shrugged. He seemed to have contained himself again. "Okay, you're the boss. What's the plan?"

"I don't know."

"I thought you might say that."

"Can we get round the back?" This wasn't a plan, just something different to say. Something other than, 'what are we going to do now?'

"I think we can, they're all semis. They've each got a path down the side into the back garden, south-facing, very sought after. Whether he's got a good lock on his gate or not is another matter."

I carried on as if this was my plan all along. "How about this then? We create a diversion at the front of the house then while he's distracted we get in through the back. When he comes back in we kill him."

"How do we create a diversion? Are you going to run around naked?"

"You're not giving it a chance."

"Okay, I'll give it a chance. Here goes." He went silent for a while, looking like he was concentrating.

"Is that your giving-it-a-chance face or are you holding in a fart?"

"I don't hold farts in, you know that." I did know that, he was disgusting when he got going, and so proud of his work.

He thought for a while before speaking again. "Ok. I've given it a chance, and I've added value to it, made it plausible. I've thought of your diversion."

My hopes lifted but then I realised he was probably going to do some stupid joke. "What is it then?"

"We order loads of takeaways for his address, pizza, Chinese, Indian, and taxis too, we order loads of cabs. He'll be furious, and go out and give them all an earful, or at least he'll be checking out of his front window every few minutes to see what's going on. While he's doing it we sneak round the back."

I was impressed. "That's brilliant."

"Well let's do it then. Don't use your mobile, think about the police investigation afterwards. We've got to use a call box and put the sleeve of your jacket over your finger when you dial." Colin's businesslike nature was now verging on bossy, but at least he wasn't messing around. We walked a couple of streets away and found two telephone boxes back to back. We called directory enquiries a dozen times each and then put our lists together. There was some overlap, so we ended up with the numbers of thirteen takeaways and five cab firms. We got busy and started ordering. Some of them wanted our telephone number before they would take the order, so we gave the number of the call box, hoping they wouldn't check. We placed bigger orders with the first few restaurants so they would take longer to prepare, and wouldn't arrive at Clarke's place before we had time to get into position. We asked the cabs to get there around eight, knowing that none of them would arrive exactly on time. Some would be early, some would be late and if I knew cabs, some wouldn't turn up at all.

The frenzy of activity had calmed my nerves, replacing them with a kind of excitement. My lips were dry, my palms were sticky and I felt nauseous, but I was resolved to channel this energy, or whatever it was, into getting the job done.

"It's not the best time of year to do this, we could do with it being dark." I was still marvelling at Colin's change in character, he really meant business. He was right, we were completely exposed as we approached the house but we had no choice. We couldn't delay because the front of the house was going to be like a Hong Kong bazaar soon, and our chance would be gone.

"We've just got to go for it," I replied.

So we went for it. After a cursory glance at the windows to see if Clarke was looking out - there was no time to check if any neighbours were looking - we hurried up the driveway and reached the gate to the left of the house which led up a path into the garden. Clarke obviously wasn't concerned about home security because – thank God and the Buddha and all the prophets – there was just one bolt on the other side of the gate and it was right at the top, easy.

"Do you think anyone saw us?" I whispered when the gate was closed behind us and we were in a narrow alley between the left-hand side of the building and the house next door. I could see through to the garden at the end.

"I'm pretty sure Clarke wasn't looking, and I reckon apathy will stop anyone else raising the alarm."

"What do you mean?"

"People don't want to get involved. If you lived next door, or opposite, would you say anything if you saw two blokes go into Clarke's garden? You'd be too worried about looking stupid in case it was a couple of workmen, or some mates of his. Far fewer crimes would be committed if people weren't so worried about making fools of themselves." This statement seemed hugely profound coming from Colin's usually insincere mouth. I was happy to take his word for it because we had no other option but to continue.

We walked slowly up the side alley and peeked around the edge of the house into the garden. It was bigger than I had expected, about fifty feet to the end and twenty feet wide. It was mostly lawn, very well kept, with a scattering of garden furniture and no sign of a barbecue. Clarke obviously valued his privacy because there was a row of trees at the end of the garden and high hedges on either side. This was perfect for a couple of interlopers like Colin and me.

We now had to stay out of sight while we waited for chaos to descend on the front of the house. We retreated further back up the side path in case Clarke looked out of his back window. We were checking our watches every few seconds. Then we heard a sound.

"Was that the back door opening?" Colin was whispering so quietly that I could barely hear him. I nodded, feeling horribly sick. We heard the door close and then another sound. The pattering of tiny feet. We crept back up the alley and peered around the side wall of the house, our heads stacked on top of each other like a two-sevenths of Penelope Pitstop's Anthill Mob.

It was a dog, a chocolate Labrador. It had curled out a turd on the lawn but was still assuming the position. Judging by the size of the brown snake coiled beneath it, I couldn't believe that there was more to come. But more there was. I watched in awe as a fresh turtle-head saw daylight for the first time then dropped to join its fallen comrade.

Colin had dropped back into the alley, doubled up with laughter, mostly silent but with the odd muffled squeal sneaking from behind his fingers that were clasped tightly over his mouth. The dog looked my way, as if it was embarrassed. Its eyebrows twitched as it finished, and it shuffled forward leaving the pile behind. Then it just sat there and looked at me. Colin was as far from the garden as he could be without opening the gate we had previously entered. He was absolutely killing himself but I was deadly serious. I knew Steven Clarke was about to open the back door to let his empty dog back in, and it would be a matter of seconds before the dog led him to us. There was only one thing I could do. I took the gun out of my inside pocket and cocked the hammer. I was no longer nervous, I was ready. Colin was no use anymore, and it was probably better that way. If I were to discuss this with him I might have talked myself out of it. So I kept the gun hidden from Colin's view as I leaned round the corner, not that he could see through his tears anyway.

I felt calm and powerful. I wouldn't wait in the shadows to take a pot shot, I would go for it. The dog's eyes stayed fixed on me as I stepped out from the side passage and edged my way along the back of the house until I was right next to the back door, attempting to melt into the wall. For nearly a minute the dog and I stared at each other; the animal on its haunches, and me squashed flat against the wall. It was like a duel, except I don't remember Lee Van Cleef having a steaming pile of excrement behind him when he was engaged in a shoot-out with Clint Eastwood. Then the door opened.

"Tyson!"

Tyson didn't move. He just stood and stared. I no longer felt calm or powerful. My hands were shaking so much I was lucky I didn't shoot myself.

"Tyson, come on boy!" I heard the sound of hands patting legs, the universal gesture to summon a dog. Tyson still didn't move. With Clarke in the doorway and me trying to flatten myself against the wall, we were standing so close together that it must have looked to Clarke as if the dog was looking back at him, not at an intruder in his garden.

"Come on Tyson, good boy, wanna biscuit?" He was certainly nice to his dog. I hoped this didn't mean he was a nice person. I didn't want to kill a nice person. I glanced to my left and saw Colin peering round from the alley, his look of hilarity replaced with one of complete astonishment. I looked away. It was going to happen soon and I had to be ready.

And then it did happen. With the kind of affectionate sigh normally associated with a parent trying in vain to get his toddler to eat his dinner, Clarke stepped out into the garden. As he cleared the open door I took one step towards him, put the gun to his head and fired.

This happened in less than a second and I'm sure he knew absolutely nothing about it. He was dead by the time he hit the ground and I felt horrible, for Tyson mostly. I would rather he had barked at me with fury but all he did was trot to the body of his fallen master and start licking the part of his face that wasn't covered in blood and pieces of brain.

When I had killed my neighbour I didn't see the grief I had caused his loved ones. In this case the loved one was just a dog but it served to exemplify the consequences of my actions. Tyson represented every grieving family member, every friend, every lover. In fact the grief seemed all the more desperate *because* he was just a dog, because he couldn't speak, because he was a pet, because he was totally dependent on his now dead owner. It could have gone either way, I could have reacted to the overpowering guilt by turning my back on my new career, or I could allow my heart to become hard, calloused like a guitar player's fingers. I chose the latter.

But before I did that I ran like fucking hell. The gun would have been heard all round this quiet leafy glade, and there was an armada of taxis and pizza-delivery scooters on its way, just in case there was any doubt that something untoward was going on here. And I wondered why we'd come up with that ridiculous plan. Colin had pulled himself together and we ran down the garden and vaulted the back fence in unison, landing stride for stride in the garden of the house beyond. There was no time to be cautious and check if anyone was around; we just had to get out of there. We ran down the side of the house and unlatched the gate - the owners of this house, like the late Mr. Clarke, also had no idea about home security. We ran out across the front lawn and into the street beyond. When we had rounded the corner of the road - heading in the opposite direction to Faulkner Street - we slowed to a walk.

As we headed for the tube station we managed to look as surprised as any bystander would be by the horde of squad cars making its way towards Faulkner Street. By the time we reached the entrance to the Underground our breathing had returned to normal. We heard a helicopter somewhere overhead and ducked into the tube station. "What the fuck happened?" Colin had obviously been waiting until we had got a good distance away from the crime scene before starting his inquiry. "What about the plan?"

"The plan was messed up. I had to improvise."

"You could have waited down the alley like me, he wouldn't have seen us and we wouldn't have had to go on a flying tour of the neighbourhood gardens. We could have finished the job as planned then left through the front when all the cabs and pizza delivery boys had gone."

"There was every chance the dog would have alerted him."

"Alerted him? What are you, a copper? What are you talking like that for?"

I sighed wearily. "The dog would have barked, run round to where we were, humped our legs, whatever. Anyway, the only reason you stayed out of sight wasn't because of any plan, it was because you were pissing yourself too much to do anything else."

A broad smile broke out on his face. "It was funny though wasn't it? Did you ever see so much shit? I thought it was having big brown puppies!"

"It's not right to joke about it."

"Fuck off, it was hilarious. And you needed a stepladder to reach the guy's head, but you did it. You blew his head off on tiptoes!"

"I don't want to think about it. It broke my heart when the dog started licking his dead face."

"So you don't feel bad about blowing some stranger's brain out but you feel bad about a dog?"

I ignored his question. "Well thanks for your help, you really came through for me there, having someone rolling around laughing was just what I needed."

"I fancy a pizza. Do you know any delivery places round here?"

Three days later an envelope fell through my letterbox. It contained five thousand pounds.

Nine

I had completed my first contract kill and knew I would never be the same again. The most immediate change was that I seemed to have lost the ability to cope with the mind crushing boredom of my job in the hospital for the mentally challenged. I had never been in doubt that it was anything but sheer drudgery, but I had successfully employed certain tricks for retaining my sanity in the workplace. Unfortunately, these methods no longer seemed effective. Before today, a stolen coffee break was like sipping the divine ambrosia with the Gods, a mid-afternoon wank was like an hour with the Pharaoh's finest concubine, but now I could see these activities for what they actually were: ten minutes in the cleaning cupboard.

My job entailed cleaning the wards, day rooms, kitchens and offices, and washing up after the patients had their meals and tea and coffee at mid-morning and mid-afternoon respectively. It would be unfair to say it was wall-to-wall boredom but the parts that weren't tedious were deeply unpleasant instead. The hospital was split into two parts. One side was for the elderly who had lost their faculties through dementia, the other was for the younger patients who hadn't had any marbles to lose in the first place. I would start at one end of the building and make my way across, dusting, wiping and mopping as I went. Most of the patients were in their day-rooms while I was cleaning the wards and I would clean the day rooms while they took their meals, so I didn't see many of them often. One or two of them did hang around the ward while I was in there though. The only positive part of the job was being able to say "it was bedlam" whenever anybody asked me how my day was.

Many of the staff had developed a persona with which to deal with the patients. They would adopt a hearty ebullient tone, not patronising, just making the patient feel that they were the centre of attention, and mostly the patients were extremely responsive. I couldn't do it, I felt too self-conscious, I don't know why - the staff wouldn't think anything bad of me and the patients certainly weren't going to take the piss - but for some reason I was unable to. So my communications with the patients were restricted to grunts. They probably thought I was in a worse state than they were.

It was clear the staff enriched the lives of their charges and I often felt pity for those with similar conditions a hundred years ago or more, without any kind of real care or warmth. It was rare to see one of the staff take their frustrations out on the patients, even those nurses who were known to be miserable or bitchy, but the patients weren't treated like royalty either. Sometimes the distinction between human and animal became blurred. I often encountered one particular patient, probably the most afflicted in the place. She was, like many of the others, physically as well as mentally handicapped and her name was Rosie. The staff had their routine of getting the patients up, bathing them, feeding them and making their beds, amongst a million other things. The million other things included taking Rosie to 'the sluice', a room housing large sinks, sterile washing facilities, stocks of rubber gloves, polythene aprons and the like. This was the room you wanted to be in if chemical warfare broke out, it was the room where I would refill my mop bucket and rinse my cloths. And it was the room in which they put Rosie to empty her bowels.

I would know before seeing her if Rosie was in the sluice because the smell would engulf me like mustard gas while I was in the corridor outside. I would take a deep breath and step round the corner and into the room. Despite my efforts to look elsewhere, the first thing I would invariably see would be her vagina. She would be naked from the waist down and the clothes on her upper body would have ridden up as she squirmed on the commode. From the stench it was clear she had finished her business and was ready to be washed and dressed, but she would just be left while the staff attended to their other duties. A few times I approached the nurses on duty and told them that I thought Rosie was finished and ready to return to the ward or day room, but they shrugged it off as a joke, as if I was just offended by the smell. I won't pretend I didn't find both the smell and the sight downright disgusting, but my motivation was that she at least deserved some shred of dignity regardless of the state of her mental health. I suppose it was easy for me to say this, I just did a bit of cleaning and washing up.

Now I had taken less than gainful employment in the services of whoever Frank and Cheese represented – "the big man, not the fat man," which still meant nothing to me - I was tempted to just leave my job in the hospital but I felt this would be a bad move for two reasons. Firstly, I hadn't fully embarked on my new career; I had only completed one job so far. Secondly, I thought that having a steady job would be good cover if I was going to make a life out of killing people. Nobody would suspect me of being a highly paid contract killer while I was doing a horrible job in a horrible place. It might raise questions if I lived a life of apparent leisure.

The domestic staff at the hospital were not held in high regard by the nurses, and the other domestics weren't held in high regard by me. This meant that my lunchtimes weren't very sociable affairs. The hospital was quite a hefty bus ride out of town so I was forced to stay on the premises and try and make the best out of a sandwich and a newspaper. I was glad the nurses didn't want to talk to me. I wanted no part in their tiresome drivelling about their favourite soap operas and how well or badly they had slept the night before. They didn't exchange conversation - they just waited for a gap in the speech of whoever was talking so they could pitch in with their own view, their own story, their own shit.

Once, against my nature I wrote the word 'cunts' on a piece of paper in marker pen and left it in the middle of the large table they all shared for lunch. I was sitting nearby when the first one arrived. He looked at it then looked around. He was helpless without his gang. Then the others turned up and they whispered and looked in my direction. I stared back at them, surprised by my own boldness. None of them challenged me on it.

On the Monday after the murder of Steven Clarke I got a text from Phil telling me to meet him in the pub in an hour and I knew he must have got hold of the silencer. When I got there I was pleased to find that Laura wasn't working, which meant she wouldn't see me having yet another clandestine meeting with Phil. There were only a handful of customers and we sat in the corner where we wouldn't be disturbed and could talk freely. "You didn't want to go through the shopping rigmarole again then Phil?"

"No, fuck that." He wasn't up for conversation, and clearly wasn't scared of me anymore. "Here." He handed me a bag containing a small box, it was surprisingly heavy. "Do you know how to fit it?"

"It just screws on the barrel doesn't it?"

"No, this isn't Hollywood. They fit differently on revolvers, this one clamps right over the barrel. It looks clumsy but does the trick, so I'm told. One problem is that it has to be slid forward if you want to reload, so if you're going to be in a gunfight at the OK Corral then you want to take it off first."

"You're getting to be quite the arms dealer aren't you Phil?" I could picture Phil basking in the grubby glory of his new sideline to his hangers-on. Just as he had seen me in a different light after my entry into violent crime, he now saw himself as a big fish, and one not to be messed with.

"Keep your voice down."

"What do I owe you?"

"Three hundred." We sat and finished our drinks while I, after checking nobody was looking, took that amount from my wallet. I had brought five hundred with me so I was well within budget. When we stood up to leave we shook hands, passing the fifteen tightly rolled notes between us.

At lunchtime the next day, I was in the canteen when my phone bleeped to herald the arrival of a voicemail. This was strange because the phone had been in my pocket all morning and it was set to vibrate so I should have noticed any calls. Even stranger was the message itself. It was from a woman. "Hi, this is a message for Thomas White. Hi Thomas, my name is Stephanie." The voice was very distinctive, crisp and proper, very home counties, but dead sexy. "You don't know me but I feel as if I know you. God, this is coming out wrong, it sounds like I'm on the pull. Anyway, I need to meet up with you. What's today? Tuesday, can we meet on Thursday in the Karma Bar. Eight o'clock? Good. Thanks. See you then." The number was withheld so there was no way of getting back to her to confirm. I wasn't sure if she knew this. Either she was very confident and knew I would keep the date, or she was as forgetful and disorganised as I was. I was pondering over whether it was a good idea to go and meet this woman, but all along I knew full well I was going to be there. If the message had been from a man then it would have been different. But it wasn't, it was from a woman.

I hate sitting alone in bars. I feel as if everybody is looking at me. I constantly watch the door to make it obvious I'm waiting for someone. Another trick is to frequently check my phone, looking puzzled, as if it's inconceivable that not only am I alone, but also that nobody is calling me to tell me when they are going to arrive. While I sat there waiting – it was twenty past eight now - I started questioning what I was playing at. It was more than likely this had something to do with the criminal element I had recently hooked up with, and that should have been enough to warn me off, but unfortunately my dick saw things differently, and as my dick was a major shareholder in Tom's Brain Plc, it easily had sufficient majority to get the motion carried - the Jap's eye had it.

The Karma Bar had just been refurbished. The previous decor had been wood city: bare floorboards, beech panelled bar and walls. It had been a little too woody. Now the theme was chrome and it was like sitting under the bonnet of one of those big souped-up American cars. The bar itself was chrome, with chrome tubing running above it, the optics, taps and shelves were chrome. There were raised walkways flanked with chrome handrails in case the customers needed to support themselves on the twenty-foot journey out of the bar or to the toilets. It looked a bit too chromey for my liking. It could have done with something more down to earth, perhaps some wood panelling would have done the trick.

It was a fairly busy night and I was feeling more and more self-conscious. Then an angel walked into the bar and a quiet hell broke loose.

Everybody in the place was looking at her. Groups of men were just gawking soundlessly, their drunken bravado trickling away like piss from a weak prostate. Men who were with their wives or girlfriends were doing everything they could to keep their eyes on their partners, but their furtive glances were laying heavy foundations for massive arguments either imminently or later on in the discomfort of their own homes.

She was amazing, and she was looking straight at me, but I knew that couldn't be the case. Women like that didn't even see me. It was crazy to even engage the notion that she was facing my way, walking my way, approaching me. Her eyes were locked into mine and I stared right back, not in that suave film star way but like a rabbit in headlights. Powerful, bright, beautiful, sensual, seductive headlights. I was a moth to her flame. That sounds romantic but really moths are horrible, they're clumsy and hairy and, if you get up close you can see just how nasty they are to look at. And as for their light bulb antics... I once read that the reason moths fly towards bright lights is because they think it's the moon. That makes no sense at all. Firstly, how would anyone know that? Did a researcher once interrupt a moth while it was banging its nasty mothy snout against a hot light bulb and ask what it was up to? The next question is why? Why would they want to fly towards the moon? Moths are insects, all they care about is finding food and reproducing. There's no food on the moon, apart from the cheese obviously. Even if we, for argument's sake, accepted that moths are in fact under the illusion that every bright light they see is the moon, and they make a moth-line for it, how come none of them get it right and actually fly to the real moon? Maybe they do. Maybe there's an army of moths on the moon. There should be a movie. Attack of the Cheesy Moon Moths. I'd be the star. I'd be Mothman, the product of an illicit liaison between the Queen of the Moths and the Man in the Moon. I'd be like a moth, but human size, and not look like an insect with weird eyes and feelers and a proboscis. In fact I'd just have wings. But not with that powder on them that moths have that causes them to die if it becomes dislodged. That's just silly.

So I was a moth and I was staring and my jaw was dropping on the floor and she was like nothing I had ever seen. I remember thinking that she must assume that men always have their jaws on the floor in the same way that the Queen thinks that everywhere smells of fresh paint. And I was still staring back, still a rabbit caught in her cheese, or something. I couldn't think anymore, I was just looking at her face. Those lips and those eyes and the cheekbones and her forehead and chin and I wanted to take it all in but I couldn't, so my eyes just raced around her face. Just in case I missed something. She was right up close to me now and she spoke.

To me.

"Tom White? Thomas?"

She was speaking to me. How did she know me? I didn't know her, I would have remembered. Perhaps she was somebody I went to school with, somebody plain and unmemorable who had somehow blossomed into the most desirable woman in the world. It was time to reply. First I frowned. Then I smiled, trying to keep the smile detached enough for me retain some semblance of cool. "Yes, that's me." I had become aware of my awkward posture; half turned round on the stool with my feet gripping the legs to keep me there. I slid off, and as I did so the back of my shirt caught the edge of the seat and rode up, exposing my hairy belly. "That's me, Tom, hi." I never say 'hi'. I sounded like a dick.

She extended her hand. Not extended like a robot, not like Inspector Gadget, she just held it out. She proffered it. "Hi. I'm Stephanie."

I nearly kissed her hand, not because I was aching to kiss her, which of course I was, but because I was Bogart, because this had to be a movie scene; the eyes locking across the crowded bar, the beautiful confident sophisticated woman. But I wasn't Bogart. "I don't mean to appear rude but I don't think I know you."

Predictably her voice was like sweet music. "That's not rude, that's true. You don't know me."

"Good." I paused. "Erm…not good that I don't know you, good that I wasn't being rude." I was having trouble closing my mouth when I finished speaking. I would describe her but there is no need. Just mix up your top five all time beautiful women, taking the best features of each and then you will be getting close. Her beauty was such that the specifics of what she looked like - hair colour, nose size, shape of chin - were not important, what mattered was that she looked awesome. In case I haven't already mentioned her mouth, it was astonishing.

She spoke again. "I want to be honest up front. I don't want to pretend this is anything it isn't. I'm not coming on to you." I could clearly hear the sound of my heart breaking. "I'm here because somebody asked me to come and speak to you."

"Of course, that happens to me all the time. Mysterious unknown figures are always sending stunningly beautiful women to send me messages in bars." She didn't respond. "So who is the mysterious unknown figure that sent you?" It was only then that I realised how shocked she looked. Shocked and speechless would be the best description. "What's wrong?"

She rested her hand on her chest, a theatrical gesture, but she did it absently. "That was a lovely thing to say."

"What?"

"What you said about being sent messages in bars."

"What did I say?"

"I'm not going to repeat it, I'd sound really arrogant."

I realised what she was talking about. "Don't you get called stunningly beautiful all the time?"

She looked embarrassed, the sexiest blush I had ever seen.

"Nobody has ever called me that before."

"Please don't take this as a poor chat-up line but that's just ridiculous. I don't believe you for a second." Could it be that she didn't know it? I had always assumed that beautiful women carried their looks as they would a leg or an arm; something that's a part of them that they are very familiar with, something they know is always there. I'm not suggesting that I thought all good-looking women had a high opinion of themselves, just that it would be difficult not to notice if you went through life being adored by every member of the opposite sex. Could it be they are just as insecure as the rest of us?

"I don't know what to say." She looked flattered and embarrassed. It was weird. She seemed almost accessible.

"Would you like a drink?" She accepted my offer and we went to sit at a recently vacated corner table. I knew that every man in the place wanted to tear my head off with jealousy and I loved it.

"So what was the message you had for me? And why are we meeting in a bar? Why couldn't you have told me on the phone? And why couldn't the person with the message have sent it himself, or herself?" I realised I was going overboard with the questions.

She looked offended, and it didn't sit right on her. In my experience women like this didn't have feelings; they were made of ice, smooth, soft wonderful ice. "Would you rather I'd told you on the phone and we hadn't met?"

"No, I'm glad we met, not that I know anything about you, but I can't pretend it isn't fantastic just to be sitting with you, smelling you, wanting to touch you, wanting to taste you." Actually, I didn't say the last ten words of that sentence, but that's what I would have said if I was being completely honest with her. Christ, I hope I didn't say them.

"You seem nice too Thomas, but obviously I know there's

another side to you, although I'm not judging you, God no. Sorry, it sounds like I'm being negative, I'm just being realistic. That's why I'm here in fact, because of your… skills."

"My skills?"

"Yes."

"Oh." I was really hoping she was going to be more specific. My skills included gardening, cleaning up after the mentally challenged and killing. I was crestfallen that she was here on an errand, as a messenger but obviously I knew deep down that a beautiful stranger would never arrange to meet me with the intention of having sex with me, there was always going to be another reason. I was disappointed but being with a beautiful woman was better than not being with a beautiful woman.

"So which of my skills are you interested in?" I couldn't think of anything impressive to say and I wanted to find out how much she knew about me.

"I thought you'd gone to sleep, you've been gazing into space for ages."

"Have I?"

"Indeed you have."

"Do you mind if I say the word 'fuck'?"

"No, you go ahead."

"Fuck. Oh, seems pointless now."

She smiled, it seemed genuine but I cringed anyway. "Back to your question Thomas, the business I'm interested in is your waste disposal service."

With hindsight it's blindingly obvious that she was referring to me being a hitman, but at the time her statement seemed ambiguous. I had been a gardener until very recently and had disposed of a lot of waste, cleared out ponds, levelled slopes, cut back bushes. It all had to go somewhere. "So you've got some excess foliage you want cleared?"

She smiled, confused, beautiful. "You could say that. Did you say that? 'Foliage'?"

I nodded earnestly. "Foliage, it's nice if you keep it in check but if you let it run wild then you've got all manner of problems."

"So you can cut it back can you?"

"I can indeed"

"Are you actually talking about foliage?"

"I thought I would"

"Why?"

"Dunno."

"You kill people for money don't you?"

"Are you a policewoman?"

"No. I work for a criminal, a gang boss, for want of a better term."

"Really? Do you know Cheese?"

She smiled. "Yes, I do know him. We're colleagues. And Frank too."

"We shouldn't be having this conversation in such a public place, should we?"

"Nobody can hear us, it's a busy bar and everyone's talking, we're fine." Bugger, she saw through my attempt to get her to go somewhere 'more private'.

I thought I would play the game. "I don't know what you're talking about."

"About it being a busy bar?"

"No, the other thing."

"You don't know what a gang boss is? It's the boss of a gang."

"Stop it. You know what I mean."

"Okay Thomas, you can play the game if you want."

"Good. So you need some gardening done?"

"Stop it Thomas."

"Listen to us. We're like an old married couple."

"No we're not."

"Oh." I clearly didn't have a chance with her, this was just professional as she had pointed out, but I knew there would always be a part of me trying to get inside her underwear as long as I knew her. I wondered how long that would be. I wondered about her underwear. I imagined her panties clinging to her body, with her most delicate, sensitive area tucked inside. I imagined what it would taste like and decided it would taste amazing. We men hold strange double standards when it comes to giving oral sex. Going down on an attractive woman is of course a pleasure, but there is nothing more repellent than the nether regions of someone you don't fancy. We suddenly become aware of all the unhygienic implications of the deed. There would be nothing unhygienic about going down on Stephanie, it would be a delight.

Stephanie interrupted my thoughts. "Are you listening to me?"

"Are you talking?"

"Well, no, but you could at least give me your attention and stop thinking about licking my clitoris."

I'm glad I hadn't just taken a sip of my drink because I would have spat it out in amazement. "What did you say?"

"I said you looked like you were thinking mischievously."

"Did you really say that? You weren't more… specific?"

"What are you talking about?"

"Nothing." Oh god. What had become of me?

She dismissed the topic by yawning and stretching her arms above her head. She didn't bother to cover her mouth. She was all lips and flesh and I wanted her so much. Every tiny gesture was driving me insane. "So anyway, can you help me?" She asked, not having a clue what she was doing to me.

"Help you with what?" I sounded breathless, like I had been

caught masturbating.

"Will you kill someone for my boss?"

"I'm confused. If I'm already working for your boss why do you need to come and ask me?"

Stephanie smiled again. "It's complicated. I won't go into too much detail but when you are in a powerful position you take steps to ensure you retain that power. It's common practice in this business to have different chains of command so not every move you make is known by everyone in your organisation. You're a professional, Thomas, so you'll understand that complete discretion is needed from you. If we start a working relationship, and I hope we do, you must never tell Frank and Cheese what we talk about, or even that we talk at all, and I wouldn't expect you to tell me anything about your dealings with them. That would be unprofessional and would put me in a dangerous position." She leaned forward, her smile taking on a whole new twist. "And it would put you in an even more dangerous position. So, let's keep it quiet shall we?"

"Okay." I stammered.

"Right, that's it then. I'm going to give you a number to use in extreme emergencies, and I mean extreme. You should never need to call me on it, but it's there if you need it. She read out the number and I tapped it into my phone. "Don't put my name in the address book on your phone though, put something else."

"Like what?"

"A different name, it doesn't matter, anything. Monica, save me under Monica."

* * * * * * * * * * * * * *

"I'm still not convinced I should trust you, Steph." Joe Barrett's words are undermined by the way he is looking at me. But despite what he's saying I know I have him. My mother taught me how to use my beauty,

and my father taught me how to keep its power in check.

Joe is a big man, and sure in his own mind that every woman he meets craves every inch of his ample proportions. I stroke the back of his neck with a fingertip. His flesh is leathery, and the coiled ends of his grey hair scratch my skin like wire wool, but I mask my disgust and keep the movement slow and seductive. "You're right to be cautious Joe, but all I can offer you is the truth. We don't have time for anything else. You know I have to steal these moments to be with you." He twitches with pleasure and my stomach lurches.

"Has Costanza really got you on such a short chain?"

"Please don't make me go through it again Joe, it's too painful. All I care about is getting away from him, and you're the only person who can make that happen."

"Is that all you see me as, someone to get you out of a tight spot?"

I pull my hand away from his neck, feigning offence. "That's such a cruel thing to say. You know how I feel about you."

He takes my hand. "Why don't you show me?"

I bring my face as close to his as I can stand, close enough to feel his hot breath, and I fake my most doleful expression. "We've been through this Joe. Regardless of how I feel about Stan I'm not going to cheat on him. I don't want to get that sort of reputation. And it's not just that, I want to keep this horrible time with him separate from what we have. In the future, when we're together properly, I want to be able to erase this whole time out of my mind, and that will be impossible if there are good memories of us mixed in with the bad memories of Stan. That might not make sense to you but it's important to me." It's an appalling cover story but the alternative doesn't bear thinking about.

He says nothing but holds me close to him, his belly oozing around me like I'm leaning on a beanbag. My face instinctively curls into a grimace as my cheek comes into contact with his. I know he must have felt it so I stage a bout of crying, screwing my eyes up tight in the hope of squeezing a few tears out. He tries to ease me away so he can look into my eyes and say something reassuring but I hold on tightly. I raise my hand to my face, bringing it into contact with my tongue to make it wet then wipe the moisture under my eyes as if I'm wiping the tears off. It's completely ineffectual and it strikes me how ridiculous my actions are. I hope the shudders of my silent laughter feel to him like I'm sobbing in the most wretched way. It turns out my crocodile-spit tears are pointless because he shows surprising patience for such a self-obsessed oaf and continues to hold me without trying to look at my face. This allows enough time for my tears to have dried, if there had in fact been any.

I break our embrace and smile at him. "I'm sorry Joe, I shouldn't be such a baby, I told myself I wouldn't let him get to me like this. Can we change the subject?"

Joe looks perplexed. "What do you want to talk about?"

"You not trusting me about this new guy."

"I do trust you. I just have to be careful. You understand." *I have to admire my own work.* "So this mystery man."

"Tom White."

"He's on board is he?"

"He's on your team Joe."

"Is he really as good as everyone's saying?"

"There's only ever been one better."

"Who's that?"

"You must know who I mean Joe."

"Who?" *His face illuminates as he waits for the compliment.*

"You, of course." *He's visibly bristling with pride. This is too easy.*

* * * * * * * * * * * * * * *

"What do you think Costanza?" *I watch as John 'the Plate' Khan gets right close to Stan, his lips drawn back to show his narrow gums and his yellow teeth.*

"I think you're wasting my time." *I knew Stan wasn't going to go for it. He's not going to stand back and let some Paki 'borrow' a chunk of his patch, and even if he did agree, there's no way he'd do business with someone who obviously can't stand him. You've got to stand Stan.*

"You might want to think again, Costanza."

"Stop using my fucking name." Stan told me he'd been working on a catch phrase, this must be it. As he says it he stands and flicks his wrist. The blade flies across the table hitting Khan in the throat, no, not the throat, Jesus, it's stuck in his chin. This shouldn't happen, Stan doesn't miss. It's nasty, like Khan's tried to shave with a scalpel. There's too much blood, how come he's got an artery in his chin? Christ, the claret's pouring out of Khan's lips. The blade must have gone up into his mouth from underneath and cut his tongue. I've seen some bad business in my time and this has got to be up there with the messiest. Every time Khan tries to shout his words make less sense. His two minders are real slow. They're just staring at Khan and watching the blood spew down his front. So I make the move. I get my blade out and sweep my arm round to take out the throat of Khan's first guy. He goes down like a sack of shit. The other one's trying to move but Stan's straight on him. I'm closer to Khan than Stan is so I lunge at him, sticking the blade hard into the side of his head and pulling it out again. That's enough to put him down but not enough to kill him, and it makes him fucking noisy. Stan's on top of the other guy, holding his head back. I wonder why he's not finished him, then remember that his blade's still in Khan's chin. Stan's smiling. He holds the guy long enough for me to make the cut.

Stan's laughing like a kid watching a cartoon. He leans over Khan, who's half sitting on the floor, gurgling and bleeding. His throat's blocked with clotted blood and that quietens him down a bit. Stan's still laughing. "I got his fucking chin, his fucking chin!" He gives me a nod. I can't get a good hold on his neck so I have to wipe as much blood off as I can with my sleeve before I can choke him. When he's done I start to step away but Stan makes a big show of clearing his throat. I look at him and he rubs his chin. The knife. Course. The handle's real slippery from all the blood so it's hard to get a good hold even after wiping it. I can see the metal in Khan's mouth. I stick my foot on his face and hook my fingers under the handle so I can get the right leverage. I feel all kinds of bones breaking then it pops out. I give it a more thorough wipe and hand it to Stan.

"Was that wise, Stan? Khan was on the up, he had a few connections."

"I wouldn't call Joe Barrett a connection - I'd call him a cunt. I want this message to reach him and the rest of those fuckers."

"What's the message exactly?"

"Same message as always Andy. Stan Costanza is a fucking psycho, don't mess."

Ten

There was activity in the house next door, the one I had made vacant. I had seen a man outside whose bad hair and awful suit meant he could only be an estate agent. Another giveaway was the fact that he was meeting people outside and showing them around the empty house clutching a clipboard. My heart sank. I had enjoyed the benefits of living in a virtual semi-detached and I wasn't looking forward to having company on that side again.

I didn't see any of the would-be buyers run out of the house shouting "you must be joking," so I presumed the agent wasn't being too honest about the reason for the sale.

It was only a few short weeks before 'For Sale' became 'Sold' and this made my heart sink even further. I was desperate to know what sort of neighbours I was going to have to endure. My chances of anybody meeting my narrow criteria for the perfect neighbour were low, but I tried to look on the bright side. As long as whoever moved in wasn't as noisy as the previous owner then I would survive. Or rather they would survive.

It was a very quick sale and the day arrived when they arrived. A one-child family; I had expected worse. I wasn't great at guessing kids' ages so I had her down as anything between three and six. The father, at least I presumed he was the father, looked to be in his forties. He was tall and completely bald, with an earring giving him a touch of gypsy. His wife was an absolute state, but then he was no oil painting. When I met them for the first time (rather than just peeping at them as they made trips back and forth to the removal van) I saw what it was that kept them together: poor eyesight.

They came and knocked on the door to welcome themselves to the neighbourhood, a bit forward for my liking but friendly enough I supposed. As I opened the door I was greeted by two sets of goggle-eyes. Both of them were wearing glasses with ludicrously thick lenses that magnified their eyes to comic-strip proportions. I had often wondered about this condition, thinking that if the lenses had a magnifying effect for the non-wearer then it followed that from the owner's point of view everything was reduced, like looking through the wrong end of a telescope. If so, then the condition these poor souls suffered from was neither long nor short sightedness but enormo-sight. Through their naked eyes they must have seen a giant world full of giant people and needed inch-thick pieces of glass to shrink things down to manageable size. But my neighbours proved this theory wrong. The wife was as fat as a hill, so if the husband had enormo-vision then she would, in his eyes, have been too gargantuan even for him to contemplate. I didn't know what world they were seeing but it couldn't have been one that included the two monstrosities that stood before me; Mr. and Mrs. Gagie. Andrew and Sue.

Normally it takes a while to be able to gauge someone's level of intelligence, after all it's difficult to reveal one's feeble-mindedness when making small talk; questions about the weather aren't particularly challenging, but when Mr. and Mrs. Gagie introduced themselves they may as well have had the word "stupid" written on their foreheads. Yet it wasn't their magnified eyes that projected this image, it was the way they carried themselves, the way they moved. They were like Thunderbird puppets, lifeless and clumsy. Their voices didn't help either. He spoke like he was a tourist addressing a goat-farmer on some deserted dirt track on a Greek Island; every word was slow and loud. I quickly realised that his ponderous delivery wasn't to allow the listener to understand *him* but more to do with the limit of his own understanding; he was talking down to *himself*. All this was set to an accent, which wasn't from any geographical region but formed of laziness. He simply did not have the inclination to form the words properly so they just oozed out of his mouth like a bad LSD hallucination.

'The wife' which I was to learn was all he ever referred to her as, hardly spoke at all, but I could tell from the odd noises she did make (odd in both senses: infrequent and strange) that she must have had a Bingo number for an IQ.

They may well have had bad hearing as well as bad eyesight, because they communicated by shouting. From the moment they arrived I could hear their conversations barked between rooms, punctuated with "huh?" and "wuh?"

And of course the daughter Gabrielle; the little fucking angel.

She looked like the ubiquitous scraggy kid in every post-apocalyptic, dystopic sci-fi movie, the one who has been surviving on scraps of raw meat whilst dodging the race of mutants who have inherited the earth. But the kid in the movies is always mute, only speaking at the happy ending when the warm-hearted heroine takes her as her own, whereas Gabrielle was a cacophony all by herself. When she was happy she squealed her delight like she was being killed with a saw. When she was miserable she screeched her disgust, which sounded pretty much the same.

My first thought was the obvious one, to take a little trip through the attic and send them off in the celestial removal van. But then I stopped and thought about the complications. Firstly it would be like Carthage in there. Multiple victims were not my style, and I didn't know if I could make that much mess. Another problem was that they were noisy enough going about their everyday business, so I anticipated an absolute racket if I started killing them in front of each other. Then I thought this could actually work in my favour. The whole street heard their screaming, shouting and general blundering around all the time, so a few more screeches wouldn't provoke suspicion. But of course there were the police to think about. I was sure they would take a bit more of an interest in me if there were more murders next door, and they would make a more thorough job of searching the premises for possible entry and exit points.

The awful truth sank in that killing my neighbour had been a complete waste of time. All that trouble and I was back where I started. The Gagies may not have had late night parties but they had their own ways of driving me crazy.

They weren't nasty people; they just had no consideration, no empathy. They only saw life from their perspective. When you live in a terraced house you quickly realise that most sounds above a certain level can be heard next door. You show consideration for your neighbours in small ways. You don't put the washing machine on last thing at night. You don't have the television excessively loud. You don't let your child scream itself to sleep every night. And you don't have a barbecue for every single meal.

I don't mind the idea of a barbecue; in theory it sounds good; sunshine, good company, good food, but it's never that simple. Firstly the company; the Gagies didn't have any, just themselves. Barbecues to them weren't a social activity, just another cooking option; an option they exercised almost daily during the remnants of that summer. Then there is the food, burnt on the outside, undercooked in the middle. Home cooked poison. The worst thing about barbecues is that people feel such an urge to have them that they'll overcome any obstacle in order to do so. It's as if they feel they are wasting the sunlight otherwise. My new neighbours didn't have a big garden; like mine it was just a tiny patio. You couldn't swing a gnat in there so a barbecue wasn't the most obvious choice for home entertainment, but that didn't bother them at all. They had the barbecue pushed up against the wall that divided my garden from theirs and the smoke would pour over like liquid, carrying the smell of incinerated meat.

The constant noise and the loathsome barbecues were bad enough, and his and her stained underwear forever crucified on their clothesline was bad too, but it was my personal encounters with Gabrielle, the devil-child which overshadowed everything. Society dictates that children are beyond criticism. They aren't fully developed, and their character can't be judged accurately so it's wrong to refer to them in certain terms. If I were to refer to Gabrielle as a cunt, for instance, I would be pilloried by anybody who heard me, but a cunt is exactly what she was; an irritating, selfish, opinionated cunt. I'm not suggesting I would have ever used that word in front of her, but in her absence I should be allowed to use the most appropriate word to describe her. The argument that children don't know any better doesn't hold water for me. A homicidal maniac doesn't know any better, but I wouldn't choose to spend my time with one. Gabrielle was a cunt of the highest order. I would be sitting on my patio enjoying the sunshine and the peace would be shattered by her screaming from the upstairs window next door, "Oi, mister oi oi oi up 'ere," like she was a badly written extra in a production of Oliver Twist. I would try to ignore her but it never worked, the cunt will always prosper. In the end I would be forced to engage with her to try and shut her up. She always wanted to come to my house, to watch my television, see what my kitchen looked like, or some other nonsense. I let her in a couple of times and she just rambled on about her friend Claire, who I later discovered was a poseable action figure with hair extensions (sold separately). I felt very conscious of the implications of having an unrelated child in the house and was keen to avoid having a mob of enraged residents marching on my home brandishing poorly spelled placards, so it made me more than a little uncomfortable.

I was furious with the parents. They had chosen to have a kid, not me. It shouldn't have been up to me to entertain their offspring just because they couldn't be arsed. She was a wild kid, almost feral. She was constantly dirty; on her face, her hands, even her arms. Her hair was blond and thick, and as big as a Tina Turner wig. It couldn't have been easy to maintain and judging by the slobbery of the parents I doubted it was washed very often. It must have had its own eco-system. There was probably a Japanese soldier still fighting the war in there.

I was effectively driven out of my own back yard. If it wasn't the devil-child it was Andrew. One evening I was moving that fortnight's bin bags from the outside cupboard when I heard a voice. "Peter." He obviously wasn't talking to me so I continued going about my business. Then I heard the voice again. "Peter!" It was louder this time. Then a third time, much louder and much closer. I turned and saw his fool-face peering at me over the wall. He didn't look impatient; he just had that vacant look in his undersea-monster eyes.

"Me?"

"Yes, Peter?"

"No, Tom." This was like Tarzan, but I was no Jane and he was more Cheetah the chimpanzee than Johnny Weissmuller.

Most people would have been embarrassed to have got someone's name wrong, but he didn't register anything. He just pressed on with what he was about to say to me, which was, "Gabrielle's lost a little red ball. You haven't seen it in your garden have you?" While he was asking, his planetarium-eyes scoured my ten square metres of 'garden' for traces of the ball. Why Gabrielle couldn't ask me herself I didn't know, she wasn't normally shy about hassling me. Also, I didn't know why Andrew, who normally ignored his daughter, was suddenly taking such an interest in her life. I told him I hadn't seen the ball.

The ball was in the very bin bag I was holding.

I had assumed Andrew and Sue would want nothing to do with me. We were very different people with different interests, and I thought that would be enough to keep us buffered. Unfortunately Andrew had other ideas. He seemed to have decided that the fact that we lived next door to each other was qualification enough for us to be friends even though he didn't even know my name. This imaginary friendship came into existence on the day he met Stephanie.

It was a Saturday, just before noon, that beautiful weekend time so valued by the childless and so envied by parents. I loved that part of the day and still do, a time when you are in no hurry to do anything, when you can stay in bed until lunchtime if you like, or all afternoon. You can eat last night's pizza leftovers for breakfast and watch back to back cartoons. This is the time that parents miss the most, even more than being able to go out and get drunk whenever they like, more even than being able to have sex in any room in the house, in any position, with any number of accessories. Parents don't get the joy of the Saturday drift where you make up what you are going to do with the day as you go along. Most men in couples are denied it too.

I'd been awake for half an hour. I'd pulled the curtains half-open and was enjoying the warm sunshine beaming in. The Gagies hadn't bothered me too much so far that day; the only sound I heard from next door was the snapping of garden sheers as Andrew trimmed his front hedge. He had finally got around to doing it before it engulfed the whole street.

I focused my attention on a mammoth weekend wank. The obvious fantasy was Stephanie, and the scenario wasn't difficult to picture; she had met me on a professional basis but now couldn't get me out of her mind, finding my hitman status alluring. Drawn to my dangerous persona she turns up out of the blue and insists on taking me to bed. But then… nothing. I couldn't take it any further, I couldn't get any stimulation; the mental images weren't connecting with the physical sensations. I could picture Stephanie perfectly, her perfect face, her perfect body, and I had no trouble imagining us indulging in some filthy and barely legal practices, but nothing happened. I may as well have been playing with an executive stress toy. I shook my head to clear my mind like an Etch-a-Sketch, then twiddled the knob and waited for the picture to appear.

It was Laura, her face and neck and arms and breasts and thighs and hair and fingers and toes. I was visualising her whole being, connecting with the physical and spiritual sensation of being with her, being immersed in her, loving her. I could smell and taste her. I came in less than a minute.

I lay breathless for a while with my navel full of semen and pondered what had just happened. It was so different from normal. Usually I would have lost all sexual desire and felt ashamed and seedy afterwards, but I was still experiencing the same feeling as I had when I was stimulating myself. It was because my fantasy wasn't driven by sex, but by a different desire, one I had not previously experienced. It hit me that the reason I hadn't been able to base my self-abuse on Stephanie was because of my feelings for Laura; I would have been fantasy-cheating on her. This was difficult for me to comprehend. As a test I pictured Stephanie in my head – and felt no arousal at all. This was to be expected because after an orgasm even the most beautiful woman, and Stephanie was just that, wouldn't provide any stimulation. But then I pictured Laura, and while I won't pretend I got wood straight away - I'm no superman after all - I did feel aroused. Perhaps my mind only had room for one obsession and had already set its sights on Laura, maybe because she was more accessible. Whatever the reason for this feeling, I decided to go with it.

I mopped myself up with some tissue and lay enjoying the sunshine through the window some more, revelling in my feelings for Laura. Then the doorbell rang. Despite knowing from experience that I couldn't get a clear view of the doorstep from my bedroom window, I tried and failed anyway. I put on my dressing gown and went downstairs, fully expecting it to be somebody trying to sell me something and wondering why I was bothering to answer the door. I opened it and there she was, Stephanie. She seemed to have harnessed the sun's rays and was positively glowing. The sun was behind her so her face should have been in shadow, but every feature was bright and clear, particularly her teeth. She was like a model in a magazine where the photograph has been airbrushed, touched up and made perfect, but she was here in the flesh, with no camera trickery.

She was wearing a white T-shirt and baggy jeans with trainers. Last time we met I would have placed her age at about twenty-six but in these clothes she looked younger. She was still astonishingly beautiful, but my epochal wank had built up a barrier against her. Never before had I found a woman attractive but still not wished to sleep with her. Admittedly I had recently had an orgasm, and it would take a while for me to get back to full speed, but I knew I was now immune to her. Not having experienced love before, this was a whole new area for me, but it felt emancipating to be free of sexual desire when talking to a woman as beautiful as this. When we last met she had had all the control because I was in awe of her. This time we were equals. I didn't even mind that I looked ridiculous in my dressing gown and enormous bed-hair, well perhaps just a little. I should add that despite my new found Ghandi-like self-control, if Stephanie had insisted we go to bed then I probably would still have taken her up on it. I'm not an idiot.

She looked at my dressing gown, "Well aren't you just full of eastern promise? Am I in time for breakfast?" She kissed me on the cheek and bounded past me into the hallway. I was still facing out of the front door and saw a pair of massive eyes quickly disappear out of view. The hedge trimming noises resumed.

I went into the kitchen to find Stephanie rifling through the fridge. She pulled a disgusted face and slammed the door. "You've got nothing for breakfast." I ignored her and set about making some coffee. "Shouldn't you wash your hands first?" She asked just before I took the cups off the shelf.

"Of course I've washed them." I reached up for the cups again, but Stephanie interrupted me once more.

"I'd really rather you washed your hands first."

"I just said I've washed them."

"I heard you come downstairs to answer the door, so you obviously just got out of bed. Am I supposed to believe that you got up, washed and then sat in your bedroom? Please wash your hands. You've probably been scratching your balls all morning."

"You can't just turn up uninvited at someone's house and start ordering them about."

"Okay I'll go then. See you." She kissed me again, on the other cheek this time, smiled at me and made for the door."

"Why did you come round anyway?"

"Doesn't matter." She said brightly.

"For Christ's sake, come back. I'll wash my hands." I turned the tap on full so it could be heard and shouted from the sink. "Hear that? I'm washing my hands."

"Actually you're not." She was back in the kitchen, right behind me. "You're just running the tap."

"I know that, I was just getting your attention, I'm washing them now." She stood and watched as I did so. "Am I allowed to make the coffee now?"

"That would be lovely Thomas."

Despite no longer being besotted with her physical attributes I was starting to feel a bit conscious of my body-smell, morning breath and the remains of my ejaculation forming a crust on my belly and genitals, so I left her with a cup of coffee and had a quick shower and cleaned my teeth. I returned about fifteen minutes later and she was browsing my bookshelves. She seemed impressed and I finally felt vindicated for my decision to hoard my books and keep the best ones on display. She turned to me. "You look better."

"So, what made you drop in today?"

"It's nice to see you too."

"Of course it's nice to see you, but you didn't just pop in to look at my books did you? You must have something to talk about, you know, following our previous conversation?"

"I came here to talk about one thing in particular, Thomas, but it's a lovely day. We have plenty of time to talk business. Let's go to the beach."

"We can't go to the beach now. It's Saturday lunchtime, it will be full of tossers from out of town. Tossers with kids, with barbecues, huge groups of tossers making their noise, playing their music, throwing their frisbees. Don't get me wrong, I love the beach, but the best time to go is later in the afternoon when most of the fuckers have gone home because they're too sunburnt and sick of their kids asking for ice-creams. Or they're too pissed and need to get out of the sun before they die of dehydration."

Stephanie pulled a face and clasped her hands together. "So, not the beach then, what shall we do instead? How about the garden, we can sit in the garden."

"But the neighbours…." She cut me off.

"You're not embarrassed of me are you Thomas?" She had come close to me and was wagging her finger playfully. She didn't even think about it but I could see the power in that gesture. That's the stuff of obsession, not a heaving cleavage, not a sexy outfit or even a full set of lips, it's cute little things like the playful wag of a finger. Luckily my love-block was on and I could see it objectively, otherwise I would have proposed to her there and then.

"It's not so much of a garden, more just a few feet of patio." I protested.

"That'll do, I wasn't expecting Chelsea flower show."

I didn't want to seem too much of a killjoy after my outburst about the beach, so I humoured her. I dusted off the garden chairs that had hardly been used since the evil brat had started bothering me. I hoped the appearance of a stranger would ward her off today, leaving Stephanie and me in peace.

It turned out that it wasn't Gabrielle that we had to worry about, it was Andrew. Andrew the lanky goggle-eyed freak. He must have seen us sitting outside because he decided to loiter in his garden without even attempting to think of a decent premise as to why he should be there. Stephanie noticed him intermittently peering over the wall at us while we lay in our recliners eating cheese and pickle sandwiches – the only half decent food I'd been able to rustle up. Stephanie pulled her chair closer to mine and leaned into me, "Your neighbour's weird."

The jam-jar eyes once again made a foray over the wall, like sunflowers in a high wind. I leaned towards Stephanie and we were now as close as lovers. She whispered, "do you know what he said to me while I was waiting for you to answer the door?"

"What did he say?"

"He said 'are you here to see Peter?'" Stephanie had managed to achieve the impossible. She had mimicked Andrew Gagie's voice perfectly while not raising her voice above a whisper.

"What did you say?" It was difficult to keep my voice low while laughing at the same time.

"I didn't say anything, what's it got to do with him? And who's Peter anyway?"

"He thinks my name's Peter."

"He looks like an idiot. Is he an idiot?"

"He is indeed an idiot. He's won prizes for it. And unfortunately he's an idiot who fancies your arse off." As if on cue, Gagie jack-in-the-boxed his way clear of the wall for a further glimpse of this woman who, it would appear to him, was apparently my new girlfriend. I could almost hear his screams of anguish. It must have been painful to see someone with such shocking beauty when he knew he had to spend the rest of his life having sex with that hound of a wife.

Stephanie's face was considerably less playful than a moment ago. "What are you talking about?"

"I didn't mean to offend you."

"Well you did."

"I wasn't taking the piss, I was just stating a fact." I was surprised she was getting so upset about this. "What's wrong?"

"I don't particularly like being told that some fruitcake fancies me."

"You must have got used to it."

"What makes you think he fancies me anyway?"

I wanted to scream at her that everybody fancied her, and

berate her for not being able to work it out, but I thought better of it. "Well, firstly there's the doorstep chat, or at least his best effort at a doorstep chat."

"That doesn't mean anything."

"Do you think he would have tried to make conversation if you had been a man? My mate Colin calls round all the time and never once has old bottle-top-face shown an interest in him. But even if we disregard the doorstep patter what about his behaviour at this very moment? He appears to be on some kind of trampoline." And again, as if he was following a script, Gagie's eyes appeared over the wall to snatch another image of Stephanie. "Who do you think he's looking at? It's definitely not me."

"It's not me either."

I put my hand on her arm, this was something I could never have done if I hadn't been cured of my desire for her. It would have felt too transparent, too obvious. "Listen Stephanie, why is this such a big deal?"

She squeezed my arm with her free hand, either as a friendly gesture or because it was time for me to move my hand. I moved my hand. "You're right Thomas, I don't know why I'm getting so worked up. He's your problem, not mine. You have to live next door to him."

"I'm glad we cleared that up, now could you do something for me?" Gagie's head loomed over once more.

"Probably, depends what it is."

"Could you stop calling me Thomas?"

"Probably not, sorry."

I was enjoying the afternoon but I knew the time would come sooner or later when we would have to get to the point. Stephanie seemed to have the same thought. "Shall we go inside so we can talk?" Much to the chagrin of my smitten neighbour we went back into the house. When we were inside,

Stephanie came straight out with it. "You know why I'm here. I've got the details of a job for you."

"You really don't seem like the type of person to be in this kind of business."

"Well think again, look at me as your HR rep."

"Will we have to do quarterly appraisals?"

"Now that's a thought. Anyway, here's what you need to know. The target's name is Damien Hunter, he lives in Soho."

"It's okay, just give me the information and I'll read it."

"I don't work that way Thomas, it's unprofessional to have things written down, too risky. Don't you agree?"

"Absolutely, I agree. I prefer not to have written instructions but some customers insist on it." I didn't think I was fooling her with my attempt at looking like a professional.

"Anyway, here goes. Damien Hunter, thirteen Garden Mews, London. It's near Tottenham Court Road. There's a specific day you need to be there, it's next Saturday evening. He's having a party and you're invited."

"How did you get me invited?"

"Well it's not exactly you who's invited but we have the name of someone who is on the guest list and we know he's not going. Your name for the evening will be John Statt. With two 't's.'"

"But surely I'll get found out straight away, unless I look just like this other guy."

"It's a fancy-dress party."

"You said that as if it makes it all okay."

"Well it does doesn't it?"

"Please tell me how."

"They won't know who you are because you'll have a costume on."

"I was worried that might be your argument."

"It makes sense to me."

"Well it doesn't to me, to keep my face hidden I'm going to have to go in something that covers my head, like a dog or something. We're not living in pre-revolutionary France where everyone holds little masks up over their eyes. The Pimpernel had it easy."

Stephanie squeezed my leg. "I don't know why we're even discussing this, I've done my bit. You're the hitman. You do yours."

"If you were my HR rep you'd take my grievance further."

"Would you like me to raise your grievance with my boss?" Before I could answer she spoke again. "I didn't think so."

"What time's the party?"

"It starts at eight but you might want to get there a little later so you can blend in easily. She kissed me on the cheek again and stood up. It's been nice Thomas, we should do this again."

"The non-professional side has been fun."

"Speaking of being professional, I forgot a couple of things. She rummaged in her handbag. "You'll need this." She gave me a small photograph. "Study it then burn it. And of course you'll need this." She gave me a fat brown envelope. "This is five. I'll deliver the other half when you've finished the job."

I glanced at the photograph. A blonde man who looked to be in his late twenties. All I could tell from the picture was that he had stupid hair, chiselled and combed into points. "Wait a minute, what if his head's covered?"

"He'll be wearing a wig - and false teeth too. He's going as Austin Powers."

"International Man of Mystery?"

She nodded and kissed me again. She used kisses like other people used smiles. "Bye Thomas."

Eleven

After Stephanie left I lay on the sofa thinking about what I had to do. I was to be carrying out my first professional solo hit. I had learnt from the Clarke job that whilst it's possible to prepare for these jobs, it's far from possible to account for every detail. Much of the operation needs to be improvised depending on how matters pan out, and that's the beauty of having a partner. This time around there was no way I could take Colin with me; it was risky enough as it was with me posing as an uninvited guest, so to bring Colin along would be asking for trouble, or asking for raised eyebrows at least. In fact I knew Colin was going to be away with work that weekend anyway, so I couldn't ask him even if I thought it was a good idea. I was going to miss him. Even though I came up with all the ideas and did all the work for the last job it was useful having Colin there because it was someone to bounce ideas off. This time I'd have no idea if my ideas were any good, or if they were just completely ridiculous, especially in the heat of the moment when I wouldn't know up from down.

On the plus side this gave me an opportunity to get closer to Laura. I could ask her to help me find a costume. It was a perfect no-risk scenario, women know more about that stuff; that's a given, so me asking her wouldn't look like I was trying to get her into bed, but merely seeking her assistance as a friend. Of course if the opportunity arose where I could steer the situation into something more then I'd seize it. Well probably not, I would probably miss the chance as always, but a missed chance is better than no chance at all. If she turned down my request to come shopping with me then my losses would be limited, technically I wouldn't have actually asked her on a date so it wouldn't be like a massive rejection if she said no.

I decided against asking her in the pub as that would have seemed like just another regular vying for her attention. I wanted my request to look innocuous but also wanted Laura to feel that I had thought of her first and had planned to ask her, rather than just mentioning it in passing as she handed me my beer. So I looked up the Pilgrim in the phone book and made the call.

"Hello?" It was Bob the landlord, he never answered the phone, he never did anything.

"Hello, is Laura there please?"

"She might be downstairs." He put the phone down.

I dialled again.

"Hello?" It was him again.

"Hello, is Laura there please?"

"Did you just call?"

"Yes."

"Did you not try downstairs?"

"What do you mean?"

"I said she'd be downstairs."

"Is there a different number for downstairs?" I was trying to keep my temper in check.

"No."

"Oh."

"So did you try downstairs?" He was either very drunk or very stupid.

"I don't know what you mean."

"You should try downstairs." He was drunk *and* stupid.

"How do I try downstairs?"

"Put the phone down and call again, someone down there should pick it up. Laura's working down there, she'll probably get it."

"Okay, thank you." I put the phone down and shouted at it. "You thick bastard." I dialled again.

"Hello." It was. It bloody was. It was him again. The stupid fat twat. I hung up and decided I would go to the pub after all, and there was no time like the present. I picked up my keys and wallet and hurried to the pub, slowing down before I got there so I wouldn't be out of breath when I reached my destination. The Pilgrim was packed when I got there, full of the post-beach crowd on the next leg of their all-day drinking sessions. Laura was rushed off her feet and it took me a while to catch her eye. Eventually she saw me and smiled. Her cheeks were flushed from the heat and stress and I wanted to make love to her right where she stood. She looked away before I had time to return the smile. I stood at the bar and got served by Kirsty, another barmaid who I didn't know as well as Laura. I didn't fancy Kirsty, well I did, but she had a boyfriend who often came and sprawled over the bar while she worked, so there was no point fancying her.

I stood at the bar with my pint, trying not to look like I was only there to see Laura. Luckily there was a tabloid Sunday supplement on the bar, so I feigned interest in the celebrity gossip for a while. Then I realised I was genuinely interested in the celebrity gossip and became engrossed enough not to notice Laura when she came and stood in front of me. "Are you meeting one of your dodgy friends?"

I looked up with a start, putting my hand over a picture of a television presenter caught with her tits out on the beach. "Hi Laura, how are you? No, I don't have any dodgy friends. I'm here to see you actually."

She smiled. "That's nice, what did you want to see me about?"

"I wanted to ask you something." I hadn't wanted to build the question up but now I had, it had become a big thing, a massive thing, a beast.

"Of course I'll marry you Tom."

I just stared at her.

She looked embarrassed. "Because of the other day? You loving me, me loving you."

I carried on looking at her.

"We were joking together the other day and now I've made another joke in the same vein and it's kind of spoiled because you have no memory and it wasn't really much of a joke anyway, not a laugh out loud joke, more just a playful remark and now because of you I've made a fool of myself."

I finally realised what she was talking about and laughed, hoping it would diffuse some of her embarrassment. "Sorry, I'm a twat, memory of a goldfish."

"Yes, well thanks for that." She was still wearing 'proper' clothes and make-up, and despite the fact that I had thought she was gorgeous in her anti-fashion garb, I couldn't deny that she looked even more stunning now. She leaned toward me and her cleavage hung between us, obvious but unmentionable, like the death of a child. "So, what did you want to ask me?"

"I need to find a costume for a fancy-dress party."

"And where do I come in?"

"I thought you could come with me and help me choose one."

"Like a date?"

"More like a trip into town."

"Shame, but it will have to do. When?" My heart leapt a little at her suggestion that she would like a full-blown date, but I couldn't rule out the likelihood that she was just teasing me.

I tried to look pleased, but not too pleased. "Good, tomorrow? What shift are you working?"

"I don't start until six so we can go any time."

"Shall we go fairly early to avoid the crowds? There's nothing worse than other shoppers. How about eleven?" My plan was to casually and seamlessly blend our shopping trip into a lunch date.

"If you can get up that early. Where do you want to meet?"

We arranged to meet at the main entrance to the mall, the same place as I had so recently met Phil. My life had changed in many ways, I had become a killer, I may well have been in love, and I was about to go to the shopping mall for the second time in just over two weeks.

I got there early. I wanted to see Laura approach. I wanted other people to see her seek me out, see her kiss me warmly. She was bang on time and looked glorious in a sleeveless blue top and three-quarter length khaki trousers. The late-summer sun had yet to complete its work in warming up the day, and I realised that I found the goose-bumps on her arms surprisingly erotic, but not as erotic as her lips. Once again I was bowled over by her pout. I had to think about something else or I wouldn't be able to communicate, or even think. Her hair looked freshly washed and blow-dried and I dared to flatter myself enough to think she had gone to some trouble to look her best for me. I may not have been the world's greatest or most experienced lover but I wasn't a fool. All the signs indicated that she liked me, at least as a friend and possibly as something more. I wasn't going to become one of those neurotic men in chick-flicks who can't see the most obvious signs of attraction and spend hours analysing every move a woman makes to find evidence either way.

She didn't kiss me.

Well that was a turn up. I had thought a kiss was a given,

and despite trying to stop myself thinking about her mouth, I was banking on feeling the soft warmth and delicious promise that the slightest touch of her lips would bring. Perhaps she didn't like me after all. Perhaps she just liked shopping and would go regardless of who asked her.

"I'm not late am I?"

"No, I've only just got here." I was going to tell her how nice she looked but her absent kiss put paid to that. I didn't want to expose myself so early on. She would have had me arrested.

"I hate doing that." She said as we turned to enter the mall.

"What?"

"Walking towards someone when they are standing still, it makes me feel really self-conscious."

"You felt self-conscious walking towards me?"

"Yes, it's difficult to know what expression to have on your face, and you become really aware of the way you're walking, it stops being natural. Do you know what I mean?"

"Actually I do. I've not thought about it before but you're right. You don't need to feel self-conscious though, you look fantastic." I had exposed myself.

"Fantastic's not the word I'd use but I'll take it, cheers." If we hadn't been walking I was certain she would have kissed me then.

"So where are we headed?" I asked.

"It's your shopping trip. I'm just along for the ride."

"No you're not. You're the brains behind this operation."

"Do you want a ready-made outfit, or do you want to get lots of little bits and make it up yourself?"

"Ready-made is easiest isn't it?"

"You're less likely to win the prize."

"What prize?"

"The prize for the best outfit, there's always a prize for the best outfit at a fancy-dress party."

"When did you last go to a fancy-dress party, when you were a kid?"

"Even with adults there's always a prize."

"Who decides it? Is there a panel of judges?"

"The host decides."

"I'm not fussed about winning the prize I just want to get an outfit."

"Are you being a grumpy pants?"

"No, really I'm not, it's not your fault I have to go to a fancy-dress party, I'm really grateful to you for giving me a hand. Any time I sound grumpy please take it as read that it's not directed at you."

"I've got a better idea, you stop being grumpy then we'll both be happy." I was about to agree to her terms when she spoke again. "Let's get cookies!" We were passing a cookie stand and the smell was irresistible. Laura was already at the counter harvesting the dinner plate sized biscuits. She looked up from her labour of love. "Do you like chocolate orange?"

"It doesn't really matter, you've got more than the pair of us can possibly eat, I'm sure there'll be something I like." I was certain that this scuppered my plans, there was no way she would still be hungry at lunchtime after all those cookies.

She stacked her armful of cookies on the counter, then turned to me and held my head to face her and looked into my eyes. "Here's the thing Tom, when I ask you a question could you not always try and think up the wittiest, most cynical answer? You really don't have to put on a show, in fact it's better if you don't"

Her face glowed with overwhelming beauty. I felt the urge to drop to my knees and tell her I'd do anything for her, that I would be there for her forever. "Sorry, I'll stop being an arse. I do like chocolate orange." She held her gaze expectantly, still holding my head, her fingers felt delicious. "I'm getting these by the way," I said at last. She looked satisfied and took her hands away.

"Bloody right you're getting them. You're taking me for lunch too." I mentally high-fived myself. "My services aren't cheap." She gathered up her booty of cookies and waited for me to finish paying. She handed me a cookie and led the way, as if we had decided where we were going. I decided to trust her and I was right to because in the time it took me to finish my cookie, which turned out not to be chocolate orange flavoured, we were outside a shop window with all kinds of masks, gowns, hats and the obligatory big fluffy dog costume. The shop was called 'Fancy That'.

I was about to comment on the poor quality of the name when I remembered Laura's warning, so instead I said, "This is exactly what we need, how did you know about this place?"

"I've done a bit of dressing up." She winked at me then took a slow bite of her cookie.

I can flirt. I'm good at flirting but for some reason this caught me out. It wasn't that I was stuck for a good response; it was that I was stuck for any kind of response at all, this was because my mind was playing out a bizarre tableau of erotically charged images. She was the old favourite first, a nurse, the crisp white of the uniform emphasising the impact of her red lips which would borrow even more colour from the red-cross motif. Still stating the obvious, my mind then put her in a French maid's outfit, ludicrously short and low-cut with the black silky material complementing the pale and silkier skin of her legs, arms and cleavage. Then I entered the realms of the truly exotic: Cleopatra. Laura in flowing robes, gold serpents entwined around her slender arms, outshining Elizabeth Taylor in the role. There were more images, many more, and they flashed through my brain like a flood: cheerleader, belly dancer, various superheroes – not all of them female, medieval wench, Vampira, pirate. Pirate?

"Shall we go in then?" Laura said while putting the cookies away. I didn't know if my reverie had been taking up real time or if my brain had processed all those images, and many more, in less than a second. Laura didn't give me any clues. We entered the shop.

We waved away the female shop assistant, who was eager to assist, and looked around. This was a well-stocked shop; they had pretty much anything you could think of, and anything they didn't have could have been fairly well approximated from a careful choice of the various hats, masks and other accessories that were on show: swords, stick-on facial hair and the like.

"How about this?" Laura was holding up a pair of red dungarees.

"You want me to go as a children's TV presenter from the seventies?"

"Fireman, it goes with this helmet and that jacket. You could wear the boots too but you could probably get away with wearing trainers, nobody will notice."

I couldn't tell her that I needed to have my face covered. "That's one to consider, what else?"

"Batman!" Laura slid a load of costumes along the rail of a display rack to reveal the outfit of the caped crusader. A one-piece affair with padded chest and shoulders. "What do you think?"

"Looks good, nice and easy, does it have a mask?" Laura had taken the costume off the rail and held it up to show that the mask was attached.

"Yes, that's the one, nice one Laura."

"You don't know anything about shopping do you? You can't just settle on the first thing you see."

"That was the second thing!"

"Same applies, keep on looking."

We kept on looking, or rather Laura did. She held up a number of costumes, Zorro, the Lone Ranger (which I considered for a while before ruling out that I couldn't really use it as cover for having a gun), The Pope, Willy Wonka. Eventually I couldn't distinguish between them. "It's got to be Batman, Laura."

"Batman's too obvious. Let's see." Laura had disappeared behind a rack of outfits, she let out a squeal. "You've got to see this!" She reappeared, proudly displaying a white jumpsuit encrusted with rhinestones. "And this!" She held the wig, which was more sideburns than anything else. "You've simply got to go as the King, there's no question about it!" Again, my face would be uncovered, I couldn't do it, but I didn't want to offend her, she seemed really excited about her choice. "And to top it off," she was at a display over by the counter. "Vegas shades." She held up a pair of enormous sunglasses.

I realised that I could probably get away with it, the shades would disguise my face just enough, and at a busy party nobody's checking too closely. I grinned at her. "Yes, you've got it. Elvis has entered the building."

"Something like that Tom. So are you renting or buying?"

"Renting, it's not like I'm going to need it again."

"Okay, so that's you sorted, now what about me?"

"What do you mean?" I was hoping she didn't mean what I thought she meant.

"I need an outfit for the party too."

"Oh."

"What does that mean?" She had her hands on her hips and studied me intently, waiting for a reply.

"What?"

"'Oh', what does 'oh' mean?"

"Nothing, what are you talking about?"

"It means I'm not invited doesn't it?"

"Did you think you were invited?"

"It would be a bit weird if you invited me to choose a costume for a party and didn't invite me to the party itself."

"Are you serious?"

"Why wouldn't I be serious?"

"Do you actually want to come?"

"It would be nice to be asked."

I tried to keep calm and stay out of any traps. "If you were asked would you come, or do you just want to be asked?"

"I might come, I don't know, I haven't been asked."

"Are you winding me up?"

Laura was smiling but this didn't help me tell if she was joking. I had seen her smiling when she was in the middle of an argument before, and this looked like a similar type of forced grin. The shop assistant's eagerness had been replaced with embarrassment; it wasn't a large shop but she was doing the best she could to pretend she couldn't hear our exchange. Laura didn't answer my question, instead she handed me the Elvis gear and turned to leave.

I spoke to her back. "I didn't think you'd want to come. I'd love you to come, really I would. I thought it would be a bit forward to ask you."

She turned, looking pensive, then satisfied. "I suppose you're right, it would have been a little bit forward, and I probably would have taken the piss."

"So there you go." I resigned myself to the fact that she had been playing a joke, trying to make me feel guilty for not asking her when she never expected to be asked.

"But I'd still like to come."

"Really?"

"Of course, really. Where is it?" The shop assistant was looking a lot more comfortable now.

"It's in London, Soho."

"Even better."

This was great, I was taking Laura to the party. She wouldn't know anybody there so she would have to stick with me all night. Excellent.

This was shit. I was taking Laura to the party. She wouldn't know anybody there so she would have to stick with me all night whilst I tried to murder someone. Awful.

I kicked myself for being so unprofessional. It was wrong to use my preparation for a job as a vehicle to get closer to Laura. Even just telling her about the party was a stupid thing to do, and now she was coming along. I wasn't going to the party to enjoy myself; I was going there to kill a man, the host in fact. It was going to be hard enough as it was without having Laura to worry about. I couldn't do this. "We'd best find you an outfit then." I tried not to sigh as I spoke.

"I've already found one." She went down an aisle, realised it was the wrong one, came back, realised it was the right one after all and went down it again. "Look away until I say," she called back to me.

I looked away, investigating the latex masks of the Royal Family. "Do you want a hand?" I asked, hearing the heaving and struggling going on behind me.

"No, stay there." The shop assistant had relaxed completely now and was looking at me excitedly, waiting for my reaction. This made me uncomfortable. It was like being in a restaurant on holiday on a Mediterranean island, ordering ice-cream for dessert and the waiter bringing a dish with flaming sparklers sticking out of it. You are expected to make a big show of your reaction. I hate that. And it was about to happen here. I had no doubt I would find Laura's outfit amusing, but I couldn't be expected to whoop and holler because that just wasn't me. But when Laura told me to turn round I realised I was wrong, I did have a big reaction. I absolutely pissed myself. She was dressed as Big Bird out of Sesame Street, bright yellow and well over six feet tall. There was a gap in the long neck of the outfit that she could see out of, although not well. She looked fantastic.

"That's fucking awesome." I quickly looked at the shop assistant. "Sorry for the language." She waved my apology away. "You're going to get very hot. Are you cool with that?"

"I hope that wasn't a joke Tom." It wasn't meant to be but I was happy to take credit for it. "It won't be too bad I'll just wear a bikini underneath." My mind went back to its erotic slide show.

So at least Laura's face would be covered but that didn't make the situation any more manageable, I was still fucked. Then there was the problem of getting to London dressed as Elvis. We would have to take our costumes with us and get changed somewhere. We'd also need to change back afterwards because I didn't want to be leaving the scene of a murder clad in rhinestones and novelty sideburns, accompanied by a giant Muppet.

Laura seemed to read my mind. Everyone seemed to be able to read my mind these days. "My cousin lives in Tottenham Court Road, I'm sure he'll let us get changed there. Then we can get a cab to the party. He'll probably let us stay over too." Whatever the problems caused by Laura's attendance of the party, which were legion, the possibility of spending the night with her was ample reward. Crazy property prices in that part of London meant space was at a premium, so the chances of her cousin having two spare rooms were rather slim. The most likely scenario was that we would share at least a room. She had to be interested in me otherwise she wouldn't have suggested that she come to the party in the first place. Nobody wants to go a party where they don't know anybody unless they have some other motivation, and I was her motivation. This was huge, enormous. But I still had to kill someone first, while dressed as Elvis, and with Big Bird as an unwitting sidekick.

The shop assistant convinced me that I needed some high platform boots to complete the look and I reserved the outfits for the following weekend, arranging to pick them up late on Saturday afternoon. We left the shop, seemingly heading for somewhere in particular. "You don't need to go to any more shops do you?" She asked.

It was twelve-thirty and the mall was filling up fast. It would soon be retail hell. "No, please let's get away from here."

"Good, it's time for lunch then."

My smile was enough of an answer for her and she led us out of the mall to a nearby pub. As we entered I asked her, "Isn't this a bit of a busman's holiday for you? I thought the last place you'd want to be is a pub."

"I've found I enjoy going to pubs more since I worked in one. It's nice to sit back and let others do the work."

We talked solidly for nearly two hours. Laura had stopped flirting so there wasn't any particular sexual frisson bubbling away, but we seemed to get on really well. She was interesting and seemed interested in me. She was doing a part-time university access course and was hoping to do a maths degree next year. She had had an epiphany sometime after leaving school and discovered a fascination with numbers and logic. I had to bend the truth about my life. In fact I had to strip away all the interesting stuff. I knew Laura knew there was more to me, and I was surprised she didn't continue questioning me about my 'unsavoury associations' as she called them. We touched on Phil briefly and she revealed that she bought grass from him occasionally but then the conversation moved on.

The prospect of spending the night with Laura the next weekend, and the fact that I was sitting there having lunch with her made my fears about getting her into the party fade. I told myself that nobody minds if a good-looking girl turns up at a party uninvited. The fact that Laura's outfit would ensure that nobody would know if she was good-looking or not - or even if she was a girl or not - seemed to escape me.

I wanted the lunch to go on for longer but Laura said she needed to do some study before work. I tried not to be disappointed.

Twelve

The cab reached Laura's flat at six. I saw her face appear briefly at the window and soon she was sitting beside me, having put her bag in the boot next to the costumes I had picked up from the shop earlier that day. She had declared "big bag for Big Bird" then slammed the boot lid shut. I had decided to savour this time with the girl of my dreams, despite my multiple fears about the evening ahead. I was missing Colin, I could have done with him tonight but I would have to be my own man. A hitman. I had to relax and enjoy myself with Laura and then find a way to carry out the job.

A couple of days before, I had fitted the silencer to the other Laura. It wasn't an easy process and I had all but given up several times as my despair got the better of me. I had been tempted to ring Colin, who was much more technically minded than me but, while I wasn't deliberately keeping this hit a secret from him, I didn't want to tell him just yet. I soldiered on and was rewarded when the silencer finally clicked into place. I had no way of telling if it would work or not. I probably could have found somewhere to test it, some deserted wasteland, but I didn't want to risk being caught so I decided to hope for the best. The silencer made Laura nose-heavy and I had to use a stronger grip to keep my aim up. I practiced until I could comfortably hold her in one hand without her muzzle pointing downwards.

The train was mostly empty and Laura and I sat opposite

each other. As the journey got underway I started feeling awkward. There was no way either of us could call this anything but a date and I couldn't think of how I was supposed to act on this non-date part of the evening. Normally a night out with a woman would be at a restaurant, bar or club where there are the distractions of food, drink, music and the rest of it, all helping to get a rapport going, but here we were sitting on the train looking at each other, neither of us knowing what to say. Shortly into the journey there was a flicker of hope, the refreshment trolley came wheeling towards us - a clattering oasis - and I bought some wine, gin and some cheesy biscuits, the name of which I thought fitted with the inflated buffet-trolley price; worthy of the Ritz.

We started drinking and while I was waiting for the alcohol to relax me and allow me to get on top of my dating game I continued to fret about whether this was a good idea. I couldn't think how we would be able to go from this nervous, polite exchange to being fun loving party-goers. I had visions of us standing in the corner of the room pretending we were having a good time while we toiled to think of something lively to discuss. Fortunately the alcohol dragged the situation out of the doldrums and made it bearable.

"I don't think you've told me whose party this is?" Laura asked.

"I don't really know the host, but I know a group of his friends. To be honest I'm a bit concerned they might not go after all and we'll be stuck there without knowing anyone."

"Why would they not turn up after inviting you?"

"They're a bit flaky, which is why I don't see them too much."

"It doesn't matter if we don't know anyone, we'll have fun anyway. Are you not going to eat those?"

"Are you coveting my crisps?"

"They're not crisps, they're cheesy snacks." She took them from me and polished off the bag.

"Why didn't you eat before you came out?"

"Sorry mum, I didn't have time. I didn't get home after my shift until well after five. Anyway, if the party turns out to be rubbish you can take me to a restaurant, then to a flash wine bar. In fact it would be a shame to be in London and spend all evening at a house party. We should try and go somewhere else too, even if the party's good."

This wasn't good, I wanted to get her drunk, kill Damien Hunter then get back to her cousin's place and persuade her to have sex with me. Going out to London's most eminent night spots would only eat the night away, reducing the time I had available to make my move.

"You want to go to a bar or a club dressed as Elvis and Big Bird?"

"Absolutely."

"You're so right." I resolved to fix this later.

We finished our drinks and I was tempted to hit the bottle of wine we had brought with us. I decided against it, realising that opening a tepid bottle of plonk wouldn't look very sophisticated, and we didn't have a corkscrew, so I couldn't have opened it. For a millisecond I considered trying to push the cork through with a pen before remembering the whole sophistication thing again.

We arrived in Victoria and I was reminded of the last time I was there with Colin. I was a commuter of death. Laura rang her cousin to tell him we would soon be at Tottenham Court Road tube station where he had agreed to meet us. The tube didn't take long and I was soon being introduced to Steve. He was very friendly but had the misfortune of having a top lip that curled upwards at one side giving him a permanent sneer. He was in his late twenties with badly receding hair that he wasn't managing very well. The non-bald bits; above his ears and across the back of his head, were thick and lustrous, serving only to emphasise the smoothness of the bald parts. If he had kept the sides and back well shorn then the baldness on the top would have blended in more and might even have looked deliberate. But Steve had different priorities from me; he simply wasn't bothered about his hair and just had a functional trim every month. He wasn't bothered about his body either. His frame had all the DNA of a thin person, but he had accumulated a layer of lazy-fat. His metabolism wanted to make him lean but he kept thwarting it by eating junk and leading a sedentary lifestyle, but he liked it that way. I would like to pretend I surmised all this just from looking at him, but Laura was to fill me in later.

Steve was testament to the notion that women don't always go for looks, because his girlfriend Wendy was lovely in both appearance and personality. She and Steve had been together since school and she had known Laura for years and seemed even closer to her than Steve was. They were nice people. They made us feel more than welcome, which cultivated a feeling of guilt in me that I hadn't invited them to the party. I didn't think they would have particularly wanted to go but I felt rude for not asking them. It was too late now anyway, they wouldn't be able to get an outfit in time, although at a push Steve could have dyed his hair green and gone as Coco the Clown.

Steve called out for pizza and I remembered mine and Colin's takeaway scheme outside Steven Clarke's house. This seemed to have become a motif for my murders. The Mozzarella Murderer. The Thin-and-Crispy Killer. As our chubby host and his wife fed us, plied us with beer and wine and rolled joints for us, I felt evil. I was using these people for my decidedly unpleasant ends. I was using Laura too in a way. I decided not to think about it and instead just to roll with the alcohol and marijuana. This worked a little too well and when it was time to leave I didn't want to go, not because of any fears of what was ahead, but because I was enjoying these people's company, and enjoying their sofa cushions even more. I squeezed and prodded surreptitiously, it felt like a sofa-bed to me. My hopes were high for the sleeping arrangements. It was a one-bedroom flat, I had made sure I found that out straight away, so unless Laura was expecting me to sleep in the bathroom my luck was in.

We had to get ready for the party. Laura recruited Steve's help and his hands felt soft and pudgy as he pulled me from my comfort zone. I was sent into the bathroom to change while Laura headed for the bedroom. I stood and looked in the mirror for a while before putting on my costume. I looked completely caned, no surprises there. I stared directly into my own eyes for ages until that scary thing happened and my reflection mutated into some twisted version of itself. My eyes grew larger, then smaller, and seemed to move much closer together. My lips gradually moved around my face, settling just beneath where they normally resided, but with more of a downward turn at the edges. My nose was just weird. I was enjoying the horror show but had to snap out of it. Damien Hunter wasn't going to murder himself.

I set about the transformation into Elvis Presley. The jumpsuit wasn't a perfect fit but at least it wasn't too small. I had never worn boots before. They were a couple of sizes too big for me but it was still difficult to get my foot past the heel. They had zips down the side and I had to undo them completely so I could get my feet in. The platform heels made it incredibly difficult to stand once I had them on. The upper parts of the boots billowed away from my shins and calves like wellies. I was reluctant to put the wig on, envisioning the collected germs of all the other party-goers who had worn it in the past, but at least it wasn't as itchy as I had anticipated. The last piece in the jigsaw was the massive sunglasses, and they topped off the look a treat. I now had to stoop to see in the bathroom mirror because of the height the boots lent me and I indulged myself with a curl of the lip, which actually made me look less like Elvis.

Now I needed to stash Laura. When I named my gun I hadn't been expecting the actual Laura to be with me when I used it, so to avoid confusion I decided to stage an impromptu renaming ceremony. It didn't take long to think of a new moniker. I silently declared that from now on she would be known as Monica. I was glad of the extra space in the legs of my boots and I hung on to the sink while I crouched and partly unzipped my right boot and slid Monica down. It was difficult getting the zip to close over the gun and attached silencer, but I managed it and struggled upright. I stepped back as far as I could from the mirror, so I could see if the gun-concealing boot passed muster. It looked okay; both boots looked equally bulky and I didn't think it likely that anybody would unzip one and look inside. Satisfied with the look, I practised removing Monica a few times so I could be sure I wasn't going to have any problems with her when the moment came.

I staggered out of the bathroom to much wolf whistling and laughter from Steve and Wendy. I cut a few Elvis poses and nearly fell over. How I was going to commit murder in these shoes was beyond me. It was mayhem when Laura emerged from the bedroom. She looked absolutely ridiculous. Fair play to her for that. A lot of people see fancy-dress parties as an opportunity to show off their physical assets. Laura's assets were plentiful but she was clearly of the mind that the more you know the less you need to show. She could have been any shape inside that creation. She could have been a man. She could have been a gorilla. But I knew she was wearing a bikini inside that giant yellow ball of fluff - the soft flesh of her thighs, stomach, back and shoulders was just a zip and a struggle away. The costume was designed for a taller person so the head flopped forward, adding extra comedy to her already ludicrous look. She turned to me, an action that wasn't easy; she could barely see out of the opening for her face and had to turn her whole body round to face me. "I'm sure it didn't fit this badly in the shop."

"What if you need a piss?" Steve asked. I thought he and Wendy were going to die laughing. Steve got the camera out and we posed for the obligatory snaps. We called a cab and were soon on our way to Garden Mews. The cabbie didn't bat an eyelid; presumably there were a lot of fancy-dress parties on his patch. While we made the short journey to the party, the full enormity of what was in store hit me. I had to walk on shoes like stilts into a house full of strangers. I had to convince everybody at the party, and the girl I was with, that I belonged there. I had to hope that whoever answered the door wasn't friends with John Statt, my chosen name for the evening. I had to hobble up to the host and kill him without anyone seeing. I had to… I had to stop thinking about it and hope for the best.

Many of my fears dissolved as we entered the party. The flat was packed with revellers, the majority of whom had gone to some effort with their costumes. Nobody was paying attention to who should or should not be there. If it hadn't been a fancy-dress party then I may have had more to worry about, but it's generally assumed that most gatecrashers are opportunists, and don't tend to go to the trouble of finding and wearing a silly costume, they just find another party. Elvis and Big Bird caused a bit of a stir as we walked in but I got the impression that many of the more impressive costumes had had a more rapturous reception. The few cheers and whistles aimed at our attire were like those from spectators behind the crush barriers of a marathon, but a long time after the leading pack has passed. I regarded those with better costumes with envious eyes and sought solace in the fact that those who had really gone to town had nothing else to fill their empty lives.

Still on the subject of envy; I took in Hunter's home. It was on the fourth floor of a Regency townhouse. The word 'flat' didn't do it justice, it was vast. The lofty ceilings had ornate plastering and the antique sash windows were almost floor length. It would have been worth a fortune anywhere but being in such a sought after locale must have made its value astronomical; I had clearly been watching too many property makeover shows for all this to occur to me. If I had lived in a place like this I wouldn't have messed it up by having a party in it, but then I didn't think I had enough friends to fill a party even a tenth of this size. We went into the lounge where the action seemed to be. There was a DJ in the corner letting himself down by attempting clever mixing when most people just wanted to hear the tunes. He was wearing a leopard skin off-the-shoulder leotard. "What has he come as?" I shouted in the direction of my best estimation of the location of Laura's ear. "A circus strongman?"

"No, he must be Tarzan." Her hand rested on my head as she spoke, and I was glad for the volume of the music forcing us to be so intimate. "The theme of the party is TV and Films."

"There's a theme?"

"What?"

"I didn't know there was a theme." I shouted louder. "We were lucky, what if we'd come as something different?"

"I'm glad you didn't know, I would have been a bit pissed off if you'd known and not told me."

"I didn't know."

"Did you hear what I just said?"

"No. Where's your ear? Oh, that's your chin, sorry." Laura

pulled the opening of her costume so her face was protruding out. Her hair was pulled back and the action caused the neck of the Big Bird to stand upright. "You look great." I said.

"Thanks, I'll try and take that as a compliment."

I looked around at the other guests and quickly saw the host and his girlfriend. I took an instant dislike to them both. They were easy to spot, dressed as Austin Powers and that woman in the third film. He didn't tire of shouting "Yeah baby!" in the ear of anybody within his vicinity and she obviously thought she had an amazing figure because her costume left nothing to the imagination. Unfortunately, she was right about the amazing figure, but I refused to acknowledge it, even to myself, not wanting to give her the satisfaction. Within a few minutes I was in a silent rage about the couple, and him in particular. I wanted to kill him, an irony that wasn't lost on me.

The revellers in the room were in clearly defined groups and I felt like a naturalist observing the social structure of a colony of apes. There was a clear hierarchy based around Damien Hunter and each of the groups seemed to have a champion; the one who knew Hunter the best in the group. The role of the champion was to ensure that their group was as close to the host-with-the-most as possible. The fortunes of each group waxed and waned as Hunter worked the room. Occasionally Hunter would become engaged in exchanges with champions from two different groups simultaneously, and I watched in anticipation, hoping the two rivals would attempt to win his favour by clashing heads like duelling rams. I was disappointed.

Laura and I fell prey to another couple who were friendly with some of Hunter's friends who wouldn't be arriving until much later. They introduced themselves as Mr. and Mrs. Thompson whilst thrusting their ring fingers in our faces.

"Are you guys married?" The husband did the talking.

Laura and I exchanged smiles, we spoke at once, "No."

"You should get married, it's such a great day." He looked at his wife with simpering eyes, "And a great life." They proceeded to tell us, as if we had shown any kind of interest, that this was their first anniversary, and filled us in on everything that had happened in the year so far, which as far as I could tell was nothing. They were dressed as Batman and Robin. He looked gay and she looked like a transvestite dressed as a man; I know that doesn't make sense but that's what she looked like. I shuddered to think how close I had been to coming dressed as Batman myself. It became clear that Mrs. Thompson (they did eventually tell us their first names but I had stopped listening by then) was brain dead and just agreed with everything her husband said. They weren't my kind of people, but on another level their presence was good; as long as Laura's costume restricted her hearing enough to stop her realising what a pair of idiots these two actually were, then they would occupy her enough for me to slip away and complete my mission. All I had to do now was to find a way of getting Hunter alone so I could take a shot at him. It was ten-thirty, the night was young. I had time.

"Nice place this, isn't it? I think that's why he's having a party, to show it off." Thompson was speaking and his wife was nodding. His received pronunciation sounded aristocratic, but he didn't have the look of money. It was difficult to tell in the Bat-cape though. Perhaps he was an English Bruce Wayne in real life. "Damien Hunter's not thirty yet and he's already a millionaire several times over. I've heard some rather nasty stories about how he made his fortune too." He paused and looked conspiratorial. "You're not close friends are you?"

I had suddenly become interested in this man's conversation. "No, we're friends of some friends, what's the deal then, where did his money come from?" Perhaps I would find out why Stephanie's boss wanted Hunter killed.

"What?" Said Laura, the bird-head had fallen in front of her face.

"Mr. Thompson is just about to tell us how our host managed to afford this place. He's a bit dodgy apparently."

Thompson seemed to think that I had addressed him in such formal terms as a continuation of his and his stupid wife's stupid "look at us we're married" non-joke, rather than because I hadn't paid attention when he told me his first name. "Well yes, dodgy is the word. His tax return says importer-exporter but that's not very specific. He's actually an arms dealer." He snorted a little nervous guffaw. "Actually, arms dealer sounds a bit grand, he doesn't trade in missiles and the like, but the smaller stuff, handguns, rifles, the odd sub-machine gun."

Externally I was nodding and smiling and looking as shocked as anyone would at such a juicy piece of gossip, but it didn't seem juicy to me, it made me feel sick. If he was a gun runner then it meant he would be taking precautions for his safety. Suddenly the clientele at the party looked very different as I started to see every fifth person as an armed bodyguard.

"I thought people who sold guns were East End hardmen and dodgy Scousers." I replied, trying to get a handle on how dangerous an individual Hunter was.

"Well I wouldn't know about that." That nervous giggle again. "He's from a decent enough background, not loaded stock, but not from the workhouse either. I don't think he's one of those old style criminals who dirties his hands."

"Yeah Baby!" Hunter was shouting again. He couldn't have heard our conversation but his words were well timed.

I had to test my theory about the bodyguards. I excused myself, saying I needed the bathroom. I walked close to Hunter, and as I did so I moved suddenly, as if reaching for a gun or a knife. Nobody moved, the party continued around me. I doubled back and made another pass, doing the same sudden move, but again no human shield appeared and I wasn't bundled to the floor. This gave me some confidence. I didn't know why I was so surprised and concerned to find out about Hunter's occupation; I doubted Stephanie's boss would have wanted him dead if he was a florist.

When I returned from my manoeuvres it was just Laura and the Thompson wife. Laura pulled my ear close to hers. "Okay Tom, what the fuck are we doing at an arms dealer's party?"

"I don't even know the guy. It was news to me too."

"Talking of knowing people, how come none of your friends are here, why are we at a party where we don't know anyone? And why are we talking to the most irritating married couple since Katie Price and Peter Andre? I want to get out of here." It should have been difficult to take Laura seriously in that outfit but somehow it wasn't.

"But you said it didn't matter if we didn't know anybody."

"That was before I knew we were at the Kray Brothers' extravaganza, and before Mr. and Mrs. Dreary cornered me." I was just trying to think of something to say when Mr. Thompson came to my rescue by returning with drinks. Laura leaned close to him and shouted. "Thanks Neil, but this has got to be our last because we're leaving soon." She had apparently learnt Mr. Thompson's first name.

It was now or never, I had to do it. There was no time for cleverly executed strategy; this was no longer about poise and preparation, just about action. I had to think on my platformed feet. I looked around the room seeking inspiration. I had noticed that someone dressed as Predator had taken off his headgear and left it on the floor against the wall while he tried to pull a girl on the dance floor. That was all I had; I would have to shoot Hunter in the middle of the crowded dance floor and hope that the silencer would do the trick and that the darkness of the room, coupled with the flashing lights, would cause enough confusion for me to get away unseen if anybody did hear the gunshot. The mask would provide extra cover. I turned to Laura and aimed my voice at her ear. "Laura, I think I saw one of my mates going into the next room, I'll just be a few minutes then we'll leave."

"Okay, but if you're not back in five minutes I'm going on my own."

I felt bad leaving Laura with Mr. and Mrs. Twat again but I had no choice. With the leather of my boots flapping I hurried past the abandoned Predator head and picked it up without breaking stride. Then I went out into the entrance hall and took a coat that looked like a good fit, from the pile on a chair near the door. It was lucky there had been some summer rain recently, or perhaps people wore coats to cover their embarrassing costumes on the way to the party. There was a huge queue for the toilet, so I ducked into one of the bedrooms looking for an en-suite bathroom in which to make my hurried preparations.

The first room was no good but I got lucky in the next, much bigger bedroom, which had an en-suite bigger than my own bathroom and was much more luxurious, but I didn't have time to admire the décor. I took off my wig and sunglasses and unzipped my boot and removed Monica, concealing her inside the wig, which I put on the sink counter. I put on the borrowed coat over my jumpsuit and pulled the Predator mask over my head. I could see better than I had hoped inside it but it stank of rubber and sweat. I picked up the sunglasses and the wig with the gun inside and turned to leave the room. Somebody opened the door, someone with huge yellow teeth, glasses and a brocade shirt. It was Damien Hunter. We stood just a foot apart.

I still can't understand the gut feeling I had at that point. There were two natural reactions that I could have had: Firstly,

I could have been shocked and startled to see him, and feared that I had been rumbled. The second natural reaction was elation, I could have been pleased that he was away from everyone and I now had an easy shot at him. But what I actually felt was embarrassed for the imposition; this was obviously his own bedroom, his own bathroom, out of bounds for the guests, and I was taking the liberty of being in there. Luckily my embarrassment wasn't overwhelming and it passed quickly. It was obvious why Hunter wanted the bathroom; he was holding a bag of coke and a twenty-pound note that he had rolled into a tube. He was briefly startled to see me but then quickly re-adopted his party persona. "Yeah baby!" His last words.

I had meant to shoot him in the face but obviously I hadn't practiced my grip well enough because the barrel toppled downwards under the weight of the silencer and Hunter's chest blew open. It wasn't a pretty sight and I gagged inside the latex mask. On the plus side the silencer worked a treat, although the 'peeyup' noise I had got used to from Bond films was more of a 'thock'; a book being slammed shut, just like the ad had said.

Although the gunshot wouldn't have been heard, I still had to move fast in case anyone came in; the host of a party is never alone for very long so somebody was bound to come and find him soon. I wrapped the gun back in the wig and held it to my chest, in the hope of covering the sticky pieces of Damien Hunter that were clinging to me. I clambered over the body and headed towards the bedroom door, finding it easier to move without Monica's bulk. As I opened the door I came face to face with Hunter's girlfriend, obviously on her way to do a few lines with her boyfriend. She didn't seem at all concerned to see a stranger in a strange rubber mask rushing out of her boyfriend's bedroom, but then it was a party, and judging by the size of the bag of coke Hunter was still holding in his cold, dead fingers, his girlfriend must have already been well out of it.

I didn't stop for conversation and rushed to the sanctuary of the dark and noisy lounge.

I could just make out Laura standing about thirty feet to my right. She was alone and I wouldn't have been surprised if she had simply told the Thompsons to fuck off judging by the mood she was in. I took advantage of her restricted view and went past her to an empty corner to tear off my secondary disguise. I buried the mask beneath the coat on the floor, knowing that Hunter's girlfriend would have found her lover and would be raising the alarm any second. I stuffed Monica back into my boot and put the wig and shades back on just as Hunter's girlfriend rushed into the room and turned on the lights. I approached Laura from behind and put my arm around her. Hunter's girlfriend reached the DJ and made him turn the music off.

The girlfriend was hysterical. "He's been shot. Fucking shot." She was screaming. Everybody asked her at once what she meant. "Damien's been shot. He's dead." She became the pied piper, leading most of the guests out of the lounge and towards her boyfriend's corpse.

Laura pushed her face out of the outfit as best she could and I could see she was crying. "Tom, what the fuck's happened?"

"The host, Austin Powers, someone's shot him. We've got to go." At that point we could hear increased shouts and screams, and I guessed that the posse had reached Hunter's body."

"Shit Tom Shit. I wish I could take this bloody costume off."

"Let's go."

"Shouldn't we wait for the police?"

"Somebody in here's got a gun. I'm not sticking around." I pulled her out of the door, she had no choice but to move with me or she would have fallen over. I was desperate to get outside before the police arrived but then thought that perhaps nobody had even called the police, everybody seemed to be screaming and grabbing hold of each other. I almost carried Laura down the stairs and we flagged a cab, Laura's giant costume standing out like a beacon for the driver. I took my wig and sunglasses off before we got inside.

"What happened?" Laura was still crying and all I could think of was that I hoped she wouldn't use my name in case the cab driver was interviewed by the police. He was bound to be interviewed. I was sure it was standard procedure to contact all the taxi firms and check if the drivers had picked up anybody nearby in cases like these. The costumes were a good disguise but could also work against us. I imagined the interview:

Policeman: "Did anybody you picked up in the vicinity of the murder stand out at all?"

Cabbie: "Well now you mention it I did pick up Elvis and Big Bird out of Sesame Street, they were right outside the place where it happened and looked like they were in a hurry."

Policeman: "The place where what happened?"

Cabbie: "The murder."

Policeman: "Murder, that's an interesting word to use. I didn't mention a murder. Why did you use the word murder? Constable Harris, did you mention a murder?"

Constable Harris: "No sir, I'm certain I haven't used that word."

Policeman: "This is an interesting coincidence don't you think? You had no way of knowing we were talking about murder and yet you did know. It's almost like you were there when it happened, almost like you were holding the gun."

Cabbie: "Don't talk soft, you did mention murder, you asked me to answer a few questions in relation to a murder, then just a minute ago you said 'in the vicinity of the murder'…"

Policeman: "Please check your notebook Hamilton. Anything there?"

Constable Harris: "Yes sir, it was the first thing you said when you sat down."

Cabbie: "Dickhead."

Perhaps I was colouring it a little, but our costumes would definitely draw attention to us.

I was putting on my best sympathetic show and consoling Laura, but inside my mind was in overdrive. I was tempted to ask the cabbie to drop us off a street or two away from Steve's flat to cover our trail, but there didn't seem to be any point. The streets were busy with people spilling out of bars so somebody would be bound to remember us. Also we were bound to be seen by somebody as we entered Steve and Wendy's building. If we took our costumes off it would have made us less memorable, although maybe not; Laura in a bikini in central London at midnight would be fairly memorable to most people. I decided that if it came to it, I could just say to the police that we didn't know anyone at the party and were bored, so we had left early.

My biggest problem was that I would have to prime Laura with this story for it to work, and any kind of obvious move to cover our tracks would make her suspicious. I hadn't forgotten our spat earlier, and Laura's question about me not knowing anyone at the party was a bit too near the mark for me. I was sure the murder of the host wasn't going to help matters much. I considered telling Laura the truth so we could concoct a watertight cover story if the police did trace us, but I only considered it briefly. In reality I hardly knew Laura, and however much she may have liked me so far, she was unlikely to show blind loyalty to me if she found out I was a killer.

A wave of panic washed over me as I realised Laura and I

had been calling each other by our real names in front of the Thompsons, and I was furious with myself for not having been more careful. To be fair, I'm not sure how I would have been able to suggest to Laura that we call each other by different names, but I couldn't believe I hadn't even thought of it. I consoled myself with the fact that we had only used first names which wouldn't give the police too much to go on, particularly as we lived in a whole different city.

We arrived at Steve's flat and I was grateful he had given us a spare key, as it meant we weren't exposed on the doorstep waiting for him to buzz us inside. I helped Laura up the stairs and when we were inside the flat she sent me into the lounge to get her bag of clothes then waddled into the bathroom. I had expected Steve and Wendy still to be up because we were home earlier than expected, but the lounge was empty. They had tidied up after our pizza, cannabis and beer frenzy earlier and folded out the sofa bed, giving the room a homely feel. The light was provided by a standard lamp in the corner. My heart leapt on seeing that there was just a double duvet and two pillows on the sofa-bed and I started analysing whether or not Laura had known about this. Perhaps Wendy had called her in the week to check the sleeping situation in advance, and Laura had okayed us sharing a duvet. My next thought was to marvel at my ability to think about my chances of sex when I had just killed a man and the object of my affections was extremely shaken and confused by the night's events. I had to remind myself that I was supposed to be feeling shaken up too, so I breathed very quickly to get my heart rate up. Killing Hunter had been an adrenaline-pumping experience for me, but it seemed a long time ago now. Focussing my brain on the options available to minimise getting caught had served to numb my panic receptors.

I stashed Monica in my bag, struggled my way out of the

boots and sat on the mattress, leaning on the back of the sofa bed. I was delighted to see the extent of Steve and Wendy's hospitality; there were four bottles of beer in an ice-bucket (the ice had all but melted but it still did the job), a bottle opener, a bowl of peanuts, an ashtray, a lighter and four smooth, well-made reefers. They were good people.

Laura had been ages in the bathroom and I walked onto the landing and listened at the door. I could hear the shower running. She must have been soaked in sweat in that costume so I could understand why she would have been keen to wash it all off. My cock immediately stiffened at the thought. At that moment the sound of the water stopped and I hurried back to the lounge. I was about to turn on the television but thought better of it in case there was a local news item covering Hunter's murder. I also didn't want Laura seeing me happily watching television in case she wondered why the night's events hadn't disturbed me. I couldn't read any of Steve and Wendy's magazines for the same reason so I just sat down and waited. There was nothing further I could do to guard against getting caught for what I had done, so I gave myself a rest from the subject and cleared it from my mind. I sat for a few minutes feeling a little bored then heard the bathroom door open.

Laura came back into the room and she looked so beautiful I wanted to cry. She was dressed for bed, wearing a baggy T-shirt that came half way down her thighs. There was a picture of a cartoon pig on the front, generic, not Disney or Warner Brothers. Her hair was damp and combed back from her face, which looked as if it had been carved from a slab of delight. Her legs were toned and smooth. Physically she looked amazing but there was more at work here; it was her vulnerability that shone. This was Laura with her guard down, not playing the dating game, not swapping chat and making jokes. This was the Laura I would see if we shared each other's lives. I felt a bit inappropriate in my jumpsuit.

"What happened Tom?" As Laura spoke she lay next to me on the sofa bed and rested her head on my lap.

I put my arm around her and whispered to her, stroking her hair with my free hand as I did so. "Shhh, it's okay, it'll be okay. Shhh, it's okay."

Laura's face turned upwards to face me. "I'm not a baby you know."

"Sorry."

Laura readjusted her position, moving off me and propping herself up on her arm. I mirrored her position. "Jesus, that was crazy" I said.

"So the host was killed, that arms dealer?"

"So they were saying, or screaming. I don't know what happened. I didn't see anyone with a gun, did you?"

"I could hardly see anything at all in that costume, why did you let me wear it? It was totally impractical."

"It looked the business."

"I'm glad it's off, it stinks." She flipped a stray hair that had fallen over her face, the movement caused me to see down the loose sleeve of her nightshirt; just the tiniest hint of flesh from her side or maybe her breast. I was aching to touch her but I knew it was too soon. I had to act shaken. Laura spoke again. "So that's all we know, just that someone got murdered. Jesus, what a night."

"What a night." I couldn't think of anything better to say.

"Tom, I'm sorry for getting so shitty earlier, I was just pissed off. It wasn't your fault. I was hot. I couldn't see anything. It was difficult to drink and I couldn't get rid of those imbeciles. Did you find your friends?"

"Sorry?"

"You said you saw your friends. Did you speak to them?"

I tried to cover my error. "It couldn't have been them, or if it was they left pretty quickly." I wanted to suck those words back in as soon as they came out.

"Before or after the guy got killed?" She must have read the look that shuddered across my face, so she quickly continued. "Joke."

My smile was a poor replica of the real thing. "I know!"

"Why were we at an arms dealer's party Tom?"

"I didn't know he was an arms dealer, he's not, wasn't, a real arms dealer, he didn't do missiles and shit, just guns."

"Another word for guns is arms, short for armaments." Her words made me realise how prescient I had been; when Frank had given me my first job I had, thinking of Bond, fantasised that my target was to be an arms dealer. Admittedly, Cairo had been my city of choice but I enjoyed the coincidence all the same.

"My mates that invited me out tonight buy and sell antiques, and I suppose people in that market branch out a bit."

"Are you saying that all antique's dealers are gun-runners?"

"No, but it's a shady world. I wouldn't think for a moment that my mates have anything to do with selling guns, but I'm sure there are people in their business who do."

Laura shuffled a little bit closer to me. I could smell the soap on her skin from the shower. "What are their names?"

"Who?"

"You keep referring to these mystery men as your mates, you never use their names. What are their names?"

I know it's not hard to make up names, there are hundreds after all, but for some reason I couldn't think of any that sounded convincing. I decided to take the bluffing initiative, if such a thing existed. "One is called Sheikh Kaboom Kaboom and the other I just know as Hair Trigger Harry."

She smiled briefly but wasn't going to drop it. "What are their names?"

"There are a few of them, but there are two that I know best." I settled for two of my classmates at school. "One's called Mark and the other's Laurence."

"Do they have surnames?"

"Banyard and Wootton respectively. Why the interrogation anyway?" I was trying to act casually, as if I wasn't terrified of what she had worked out.

"I'm still a bit concerned you know such dodgy characters, what about all that time you spent with Phil the dealer, and how weirdly nice he was to you, and those other blokes, the best friend of your cousin's brother in law's aunt's dog? And then there's his giant minder…"

I lay on my back. "You're not going to go through all that again are you? I buy my gear from Phil, you know that, and that other bloke was also a dealer, he and Phil don't see eye to eye."

"So I was right about the big guy, he was his minder."

"Yes he was, but they're not big time."

"Why were they talking to you?" Laura started to unzip my jumpsuit while keeping her eyes fixed on mine.

"I bought some stuff off them once. There was a time when Phil couldn't get pills for ages, you probably remember it."

"Yes I do, the whole town was dry."

"That's right, so I got some off Frank, he's a bit higher up the chain, sold bigger quantities, so a few of us chipped in to buy a load. I hadn't seen him since, until I bumped into him in the pub."

Laura had opened the zip to just below my belly and was running her finger down my chest. My erection had nowhere to hide, even beneath the bagginess of the ill-fitting outfit. Laura smiled. "Was he trying to strong-arm you into buying your gear off him?"

I stifled a gasp as her fingers reached my groin. "No, it wasn't like that, he wouldn't bother, I only buy for personal use so it's not worth his time. He just wanted me to tell Phil he was looking for him."

"And is that why Phil was so nice to you when you saw him next? Does he think you're in cahoots with this Frank guy?"

Her fingertips were stroking the underside of my balls. It was like being hypnotised. "I'm…. I can't. No talk."

Laura smiled with satisfaction. "Take off your Vegas gear," she whispered. I did so and went to kiss her but she gently pushed me back down so I was on my back and she was leaning over me. She slowly kissed her way down from my chest to my navel then back up again while she relentlessly stroked my million-dollar spot. My legs were stretched wide apart. I was giving myself to her completely. I thought my mind had already blown, but there was more to come. Her lips, the lips that I had dreamed about, the lips that were the basis of my most intense fantasies, were lowering towards my cock.

My body was out of control, I was trembling with anticipation and my cock was having spasms. I felt the warm wetness as she enveloped me with her lips and I had to try hard not to explode there and then. She closed her lips around the shaft and teased the top with her tongue. At that moment my whole world was her mouth. All my memories, all my ambitions, everything was in that mouth. I wanted to tell her all my secrets. I wanted to pour my soul into her. She started to move up and down on my cock while still teasing the end with her tongue, and my balls with her fingertips. I felt myself climbing the foothills towards a mountainous climax and had to force myself out of the stupor and gently ease her off. I pulled her T-shirt over her head and gasped when I saw her breasts, her stomach, her shoulders. She hooked her thumbs into the elastic of her panties and pulled them off.

I had come down from cloud nine and now had some semblance of control. "My turn." I whispered, knowing I sounded cheesy but enjoying it anyway. I eased her onto her back, repeating her technique and kissing my way down her body but dwelling for longer on her chest than she had on mine. One nipple was harder than the other so I focussed on the softer one, balancing the equation. I kissed around her navel while stroking her clitoris with the tip of my thumb. Laura brought her knees up and opened her legs wider, and I pushed my index finger inside her while rolling my thumb over the hood of her clitoris. Either Laura was an excellent actress or she was having quite a time, she was losing control just as I had. Her back arched up from the bed, she was almost convulsing. It was such an exhilarating feeling to be having that kind of effect on her, to be responsible for so much pleasure in someone so beautiful. My eyes scanned every millimetre of her flesh trying to take in her body's every delight while I kept my finger inside her. I started to kiss and lick her throbbing clitoris while moving my finger harder and faster. Her body started to buck beneath me and I did my best to hold her down onto the mattress so I could maintain the rhythm of my tongue and hand.

When I thought that Laura was ready to burst I entered her, and held myself fast inside her, gripping her shoulders and staring into her eyes. I could feel my cock twitching of its own accord inside her vaginal walls and she responded with low moans and twitches of her own. All the most profound thoughts in the world were flying through my head, but not one of them was tangible. This moment meant something special, something more than sex, and I wanted to put that into words but couldn't. Laura was looking back at me with a look of steadfast intensity that I knew mirrored my own.

After we had both come I was relieved that I hadn't managed to vocalise the intensity of the moment while we were in the throes of passion.

I would have sounded like a dick.

I had been deeply moved by the sex but now felt impatient, I wanted to ask her something, and knew I couldn't ask it so soon after the intensity of our union. I would have to wait. We cuddled until I became uncomfortable, then made spoons until Laura became uncomfortable, then we lay on our backs. Laura broke the silence. "Shall we have a reefer?"

"Oh God yes." I lit one up and opened two of the beers, wiping the wet bottles on my now discarded Elvis gear. I handed the joint to Laura and she inhaled deeply. It was a good time to say my piece. "Laura, would you mind if we didn't say anything about what happened at the party to anyone?"

"What do you mean?"

"If we went to the police then they'd want to know who invited us, and as I have said, my friends, Mark and Laurence aren't in the most above-board of businesses, so they wouldn't be too happy to get a visit from the cops. I don't see how we can help the police anyway, we didn't see anything, and it would just be hassle for us."

"Is it your friends who wouldn't want a visit from the police, or do you mean you, Tom?"

"What do you mean?"

"Your next-door neighbour was killed in his house, shot in the head. Now you've been to a party and the host gets shot, possibly in the head, I don't know. I'm not saying it's suspicious but I'm sure there would be plenty of people who would be. The police for example."

"I hadn't thought of that."

"That's bollocks Tom, of course you've thought of it." She handed me the joint and I sucked on it like a baby at a teat.

"Honestly Laura I hadn't. What are you trying to say anyway?"

"I'm not trying to say anything except that it's a bit weird. If you had said you wanted to hush this up because you didn't want the police thinking you killed your neighbour, or this Hunter bloke, then it would make sense, but you don't even seem to have considered either of those things."

"Well now you mention it I don't want them to think that."

"Of course you don't, so just be honest about it."

"It's not just that, it's still true about Mark and Laurence."

"Yes, Mark and Laurence, of course, your good mates. Can I borrow your phone?" She took it before I could respond and started scrolling through the list of names and numbers stored in the memory. "That's weird, no Mark and no Laurence."

"Yes, that is weird."

"Yes. And it's also weird that in all the time we've spent together, you've not once mentioned your neighbour being killed. If my neighbour had been murdered I'd talk of little else for weeks."

"I don't like to talk about it. It's not a nice thing. I keep thinking it could have been me." I played it just right, not too much pathos but enough to make me look convincing.

"Sorry Tom, I didn't mean to bring it up, I didn't realise you felt like that."

"It's been difficult to feel any different."

"I'm sorry, I really am."

I looked into her eyes, choosing to play a risky card. "Do you think I've been killing people?"

"Of course I don't, but I think you're involved in something. I'm not going to pry because it's not my business, but after what we just did, I think it might start becoming my business. All I'm asking is that you try and get out of whatever it is you're mixed up in. And if you can't, then talk to me, I might be able to help."

"Okay. It's a deal."

She held out her hand and I gave her the joint. She smiled.

"I thought we were shaking on the deal! Don't worry, give it to me anyway."

I had questions of my own. "So when you said 'it might start becoming my business' did you mean what I thought you meant?"

"Well I don't sleep with just anybody, I normally think there's somewhere to go with it first."

"Like…" I couldn't think of a word, and I was horribly embarrassed.

"Like boyfriend and girlfriend? Is that what you're trying to say Tom?" She was smiling mischievously.

"Is there a way of putting it that doesn't sound childish?"

"No, I don't think there is."

"So, are you going to answer me then?"

"You're asking if we're boyfriend and girlfriend?"

"I suppose I am." I was glad the room was in semi-darkness so my crimson face didn't show.

"I suppose we might be." That was good enough for me. She handed the joint back to me and I put it in the ashtray and kissed her on those wonderful lips; lips that were now mine.

We made love again and lay in a pool of satisfaction once more, and once more I had to wait to say what was on my mind. Eventually I came out with it. "So we're not telling Steve and Wendy about what happened then?"

"I thought we were just not telling the police."

"I think it would be easier if we kept it to ourselves."

"Okay, but what if they see it on the local news? Or on the national news for that matter."

"We'll say we left before it happened."

"Okay, but only if you agree to keep something else to yourself."

"What?"

"Us."

"Why?" I assumed she was ashamed of me and didn't want anybody to know she was seeing me. The sentiment was obvious in my voice.

"It's not because I'm embarrassed to be with you, it's just that the pub is full of gossip, and I don't want to be the centre of it. Let's just wait until we're sure about things."

"I thought we were sure."

"We're nearly sure, Tom. It's nothing to worry about. Can you just do this for me?"

"Okay, fair enough, it's a deal." This time we did shake hands.

"I really need to sleep now, goodnight." She kissed me and rolled over and fell asleep almost immediately. I stayed awake and smoked myself into oblivion.

Thirteen

"I can't believe you didn't tell me anything about this. I thought we were partners." It was the Monday after Damien Hunter's deathday party, and Colin was far from happy. His movements were animated and I was worried he was going to spill his coffee on my nice new carpet.

"You wouldn't have been able to make it anyway. You were in Newbury painting new lines under a flyover."

"I wasn't in Newbury. I was in Grimsby."

"Well there you go then, that's even further away. You definitely couldn't have come. I knew you couldn't, so I didn't bother asking." I waved my arm to indicate the debate was now closed.

"We could have done it another night."

"That's exactly why I didn't mention it, I knew you'd try and make us reschedule and I knew that wasn't possible. The orders were very specific. It had to be at the party."

"I could have got out of Grimsby."

"Have you ever been able to get out of Grimsby before?"

"No." He looked crestfallen, like I had just thrown his ice-cream cone into the gravel.

"Listen Colin, I didn't mean to leave you out, it was nothing personal. You can come on the next one."

"I know I can come on the next one, we're partners. It's not your choice to make."

"I have to stop you there mate. We're not actually partners.

You just came along with me once, like an assistant. I'm the one who's done all the killing."

"Are you saying I didn't contribute anything last time?"

"All I'm saying is that these are my gigs, I'm the one who got into this. If it's going to be like this every time I decide to go without you, then let's just break up this partnership - as you call it - right now."

Colin went silent and turned away from me. Just when I thought he had dropped the subject he turned to me and spoke. "I'll pull the trigger next time."

"What?"

"I'll do it, I'll pull my weight, make the hit."

"Why?"

"Because I want to do this thing Tom. I hate my life, I want to do something different."

"So you see it as a lifestyle choice?"

"And you don't?" He had me there.

I tried to change the subject. "What have you done with your cash from the Clarke job?"

"Under the mattress, I'm scared to spend it."

"I don't think you should worry too much, the murder was miles away. Nobody's going to be onto us down here."

"Whatever. I still think I should have got more."

"I don't want to go over this again. You agreed to thirty percent so you got thirty percent."

"Two thousand seven hundred is not thirty percent of ten thousand." He rested the coffee cup on the arm of the sofa, it didn't look steady.

"I had to buy the gun."

"I think you should have just paid for it out of your cut."

"I know what you think, you've told me enough times. So what are you going to use in the next hit? You going to garrotte the guy?"

Colin was silent for a while before he spoke. "I'll shoot him."

"What with, a water pistol? You'll be needing Monica, and that proves I was right to use the communal pot to buy her with."

"Monica? Didn't you call it something else, Dora or something?"

"It was never Dora, why would I call my gun Dora? It was Laura, and now she's Monica because I'm seeing someone called Laura and it would have been confusing."

"It's that your way of telling me you've pulled?"

"Kind of."

He slapped me on the back, a bit harder than I thought was called for. "Nice one mate, I knew you'd manage to hide your sausage again one day." I was going to pick him up on his choice of phrase but I knew if I objected I would be forced to say something along the lines of: 'it isn't like that, it's more than that', and Colin wasn't the best person to have that sort of conversation with. I think that's why our friendship had lasted so long; we tended to keep to the shallow end in the swimming pool of conversation. "Wait a minute, it's not Laura from the Pilgrim is it, the one you're crazy about?"

I didn't know what expression to have on my face, I was excited and wanted to show it, but not to Colin. I just blushed and looked at the floor. "Yes, that Laura."

"Nice one mate. She's alright. I wouldn't have known what to say if you'd pulled a pig. I could have lied and said she was nice, but you would have known I was lying, and I would have known that you knew I was lying."

"How do I know you're not lying now?"

"Because everyone knows that Laura from the Pilgrim isn't a pig. She used to have a funny taste in clothes but she seems to have got over that – hey – that's nothing to do with you is it?

Surely she hasn't been scrubbing herself up to win your affections?"

"I think that's a coincidence." I was glad we had got off the subject of the allocation of blood money. This was another reason I felt so comfortable with Colin. We could argue like cat and dog but then be fine again, he didn't hold a grudge, he just said what was on his mind, be it positive or negative.

"I don't think this gossip is out yet, I was in the Pilgrim last night and Shelley and Lucy were working. They didn't say anything about it."

"We're keeping it quiet for that very reason."

"Whose idea was it to keep it secret? I bet it was hers. I don't blame her. I'd keep it quiet too if I'd shagged you."

"Fuck off."

"You still haven't told me the story of the party. What happened? How did you do it? I want all the details."

I had been dreading this. "Colin, I've got something to tell you and you're going to get pissed off. So I want to ask you please not to fly off the handle."

"Okay."

"Okay you won't fly off the handle?"

"Okay you can ask me not to."

"Consider yourself asked."

"Stop stalling Tom. Tell me the thing."

I waited for him to take a big swig of his coffee, thus lowering the amount of liquid in the cup and reducing the risk to my carpet. "Laura came with me to the party on Saturday."

"Damien Hunter's party?"

"Of course Damien Hunter's party, I wasn't doing a party crawl."

"Fuck, Tom. So you couldn't take me along but you could take her?"

I put my head in my hands theatrically. "For the love of

God, please not again. You weren't around you weren't around you weren't around. You were in Grimsby."

"So that's why you wanted to break the partnership? Because you've got a new glamorous assistant?" He punctuated his outburst with gestures with his right hand; the mug-holding hand. His coffee splashed onto the carpet.

"You knob." I went to the kitchen and got a wet sponge. I mopped up as much of the stain as I could then resumed our discussion. "Laura doesn't know anything about the murder."

"How could she not know? She was there wasn't she?"

"Well obviously she knows about the murder, she saw it happen, well, not completely, the outfit restricted her view."

"Who was she dressed as, Darth Vader?"

"Big Bird."

"Sounds glamorous. So she saw it happen but didn't know it was you. Did anyone else see it happen?"

"No, it was just me and him in his bathroom, he was about to do some charlie. Someone saw me coming out but I was wearing a mask."

"Who were you dressed as?"

"Elvis, but not when I made the hit, I had nicked part of someone else's costume." I drew a deep breath and then recounted the events of the party to Colin. He listened intently and saved his questions for the end.

"So this couple you stayed with…"

"Steve and Wendy."

"Yes, them, did you tell them? I mean about someone getting killed at the party, not that you did it."

"No, I told Laura I didn't want to tell anyone because of my friends getting into trouble."

"What friends?"

"The imaginary ones that invited me to the party, they're antique dealers so they're a bit dodgy and don't want the police sniffing around."

"Nice one, how did she take that?"

"She was fine about it."

"She sounds like a good'un, keep hold of her."

"I intend to."

Colin thought for a moment then spoke. "It's a bit of a risk though. The police are going to want to account for everyone at the party. They'll ask everyone they interview to give them a list of all the people they remember seeing. As it was a fancy-dress party it will be easier - Big Bird, Elvis - it's easier to remember costumes than real descriptions. They'll compile a definitive list from all the people they've spoken to, cross off the ones they've accounted for and anyone left will be their main suspects because they've not come forward."

"They'll have to find us first, and we're in a whole different city."

"Still risky."

"It's worth the risk, if I come forward and they ask for my address and it rings bells about the murder next door, then it's as good as a confession."

"What about the cab? The police are bound to get the taxi firms to tell them about any pick-ups from that area in that time, and they'll end up talking to the cabbie who picked you up. He won't have any trouble remembering Big Bird and Elvis. He'll tell them where he dropped you off and that'll lead them to Laura's cousin."

"I've thought about that too. Steve and Wendy won't tell them anything, they don't know anything."

"They'll tell them Laura's address."

"He'd nark his own cousin in?"

"He wouldn't think he was doing any harm, he wouldn't consider for a moment that you did it."

"If it comes to that then I'll say we left before anything

happened, so it won't look like we're hiding anything."

Colin shook his head. "This is a risky business."

I shouted. "I know it's a risky fucking business, did you think it was going to be anything else?"

"Okay, I see your point."

I forced myself to relax. "We've just got to stay calm and not do or say anything stupid."

"Are you saying I'm going to do something stupid?"

"Fuck off Colin, either one of us could do something stupid. We've just got to keep on top of it."

"So we're still partners?"

"Of course, especially as you're doing the dirty work next time."

There was a pause before Colin spoke again. "Tom, have you told any of your contacts about me? I mean, that I'm helping out?"

"No I haven't. I've thought about it but I'm not sure if I should or not."

"I'm not sure either."

"It's difficult to know what these people are expecting, or what they think is acceptable. I can't see why they would have a problem with it as long as the jobs get done, but I really don't know. They might think it's a security risk having someone else along, they might want to check everyone personally."

"It's a tough one."

"Why did you ask, did you want me to tell them?"

"No, not at all, I was just thinking aloud. Let's leave it for now and see how we go."

"Sounds good to me. I'll tell you what Colin, I'll give you forty percent from now on."

"Cheers mate." He slapped me too hard on the back again.

* * * * * * * * * * * * * * *

A lot of the fellers ask me how I've got the bollocks to deliver bad news to Stan Costanza. They all reckon they'd be too scared. These aren't schoolgirls I'm talking about, these are men, big men who've seen and done things most people couldn't imagine. Stan would love to hear that even his own men are scared of him, but they're wrong about him. He's a psycho, there's no doubt about that, but he's not daft. He's not going to waste a good man like me just because I've told him some bad news. It's never me who's fucked up, and even if it was, I think I'd have to fuck up pretty badly and pretty often for him to take me out. I'm valuable to him and he knows it. So I don't worry about giving him bad news. This messenger's not getting shot.

"What have you got for me Andy?" Stan knows something's up as soon as I enter the room. His office is basic. Stan's known as Stan Stalin, not just because he's so ruthless, but because he's known to like a bit of luxury, you know, the finer things. But the stories are wrong. Okay, so he does make a point of being seen in the best clubs and at the best tables in the best restaurants, and if he's staying out of town then he'll make sure he gets the best hotel room, but that's just public image. Everything Stan does is designed to send a message. He's like a great fighter, like Ali, he's all about the gamesmanship. And, like Ali, he does reckon that he's the greatest. And maybe he is.

"They got Hunter."

"What are they holding him on?"

"No Stan, not arrested, dead."

"Whacked?" Another thing about Stan's PR is that he likes people to believe he's old school, like from Sicily, proper mafia. His name is real but it's not Italian. His parents were Romanian, so really he shouldn't be Stalin, he should be that other one, the one with the big palace, Caucescu. But Stalin's easier to remember. "Was it Barrett?"

"I reckon."

"But we don't have proof?"

"No."

"Fuck proof. Proof's easy to bury. Proof's why I'm not inside. It had to be Barrett. I know how he works. He taught me everything he knew, which was fuck all, so I had to teach myself. If that fat fuck thinks Hunter was my only quartermaster then he's got more fat in his brain than his gut. Hunter was a little playboy, at least he wanted to be, and there's nothing worse than a wannabe waste of space. I was running out of patience with him, so Fat Joe's done me a favour. Get some flowers sent to Barrett, ten dozen roses, but bring me the card first, I want to sign it myself. My old mum always brought me up to say thank you."

I've worked for some big names but Costanza always pulls something different out of the bag. He's the real deal. When Stan took out Visconti nobody saw it coming, and it wasn't even like he was secretive about what he was going to do or nothing. In fact he was so loud about it that everyone thought Visconti had put him up to it as a bluff to the other bosses, like some kind of trap. But Visconti was never that sharp and Stan never bluffs. The rest is history. They call it the revolution.

Stan speaks again. "So how did they get him anyway? Did any of his muscle get done too?"

"He didn't have any. He had a party, Saturday night, open house, no protection."

Stan shakes his head. "Sounds like suicide to me. What the fuck is this world coming to?"

"And you won't believe this, it was fancy-dress."

Stan roars with laughter. "Fancy-dress? Did he get exterminated by a Dalek?" "What was he dressed as, Hunter I mean?"

"Austin Powers."

"Who? Never mind. Right, as well as the roses I want the name of Barrett's quartermaster, we'll do him when the time's right. We'll put that new guy on it, the one who got Clarke. And by the way, did we find out who paid for my birthday present yet?

"Not yet, Stan. I thought I'd leave him to settle in before I pushed him on it."

"Fair enough, you know what you're doing."

* * * * * * * * * * * * * * * *

"Who are they from, Geoff?" Joe's trying to keep his cool, like he gets sent a hundredweight of flowers every day, but he looks like a teenager on prom night, all of a flutter. I give him the envelope that came with the bunch and he reads it out loud. "To the fat fuck." He looks anything but happy but keeps on reading. "Thanks for getting rid of that little problem for me at the weekend. I'll let you know when I've got more work for you. Biggest kisses, Stan." Barrett looks like he's going to explode. He opens his mouth but instead of shouting he just says one word, and he says it real quiet. "Cunt."

If I had a different boss I might be getting scared right now. It isn't good for someone like Joe Barrett to be made into a mug, and I just saw him made a mug of by Stan Costanza. It's dangerous to Joe that I saw it, and it's pretty dangerous to me that I saw it. If it gets out, that is, if I tell anyone, then Costanza's rep will grow and Joe's will move in the other direction. It wouldn't be out of the question for him to put a bullet in my head right away, or arrange to have it done as soon as possible. But I don't think that's going to happen. It's not that Barrett is soft; he just hasn't thought of it. That's what separates Joe from the other players, Costanza in particular. From what I'm hearing, Costanza's got it all. He'll cut a man to pieces in front of his mother if he can benefit from doing it. But only if he benefits. And that's the difference. I've got to look for a new employer soon, I think Joe's fucked.

Joe takes out his Zippo. He holds out the card and sets fire to the corner.

* * * * * * * * * * * * * * * *

Laura came over at eleven-fifteen, after her shift at the Pilgrim. "Are you sure this isn't too late to be coming round Tom? I'm not just here for sex you know."

"The night is young. I don't need much sleep, it's not like my job's taxing." That was a lie. I hated being tired at work, it made it almost unbearable, but it was a fair price to pay to have Laura in my bed.

"Why don't you find another job?"

"I should really, I will do at some point I guess. How about you, do you like working at the Pilgrim?"

"Sometimes it's okay but mostly it's a nightmare."

"What makes you stay there?"

"The hours are good, well, not good, they're completely anti-social, but good for me. It means I can do my course."

"How's that going?"

"It's hard work, I'd got out of the habit of studying. I can do it but I find it hard to motivate myself. To be honest I'm not sure if I'll be able to do three years of college after this."

"Just see how it goes, I'm sure you'll get used to it."

"Maybe. So are you going to offer me a drink? And that thing on the table looks interesting. That spliff shaped thing that smells like marijuana

I got us some beers and sparked up the reefer. "Thanks for coming round. It's great to see you."

She kissed me long and slowly on the mouth. "Thanks Tom, it's great to see you too."

"It's weird this isn't it?" I thought I'd phrased that badly but she seemed to know what I meant.

"Yes, one minute we're making small talk in the pub and now here we are. What did you put in this? It's got a hell of a kick." She was all smiles and looked amazing.

"It's so I can get the truth out of you. How long have you known I liked you?"

She aped an amazed expression. "You like me? I'm flattered!"

"Stop that."

"I'm not very perceptive with that sort of thing, but Shelley used to make comments when we were both working. She said she could tell from the way you were looking at me."

"Or the fact that I couldn't take my eyes off you, did you not notice that?"

"I just thought you wanted me to get you another drink."

I was dying to ask her how long she had liked me, but it would have looked a little bit desperate to ask that sort of question outright. So I used underhand tactics. "Colin has been saying for a while that he could tell you liked me."

She looked surprised. "Has he now?"

"Yes."

She took another pull on the joint and passed it across. She said no more on the subject. My tactic had failed.

We were nicely relaxed when Laura decided to drop her bombshell. Presumably it wasn't a bombshell in her mind otherwise it would have been the first thing she said when she arrived. "I had a call from my cousin Steve tonight."

"Oh yes, how is he?" I still didn't know it was a bombshell at this stage.

"He's a bit worried, he saw a newspaper article, a news broadcast and had a visit from the police."

I tried to keep calm, "what about?"

"All about the same thing, the murder of a suspected arms dealer at a fancy-dress party in Soho. The police wanted to know if anyone dressed as Elvis or Big Bird had visited Steve's flat on the night of the twenty eighth of August. Apparently they're trying to account for all the guests, and they've got witnesses saying they saw some people fitting our description entering Steve's block that night."

I couldn't believe she was being so casual about it. I just wanted to run away, disappear, join the Foreign Legion, but instead I had to have this conversation without screaming. "So what did Steve and Wendy say?"

"Steve's had trouble with the police before, he lost his job a few years ago because he was done for dealing when all he had was an eighth of grass, it should have been classed as personal use and been a caution at best, but they took him to the cleaners. So he doesn't trust the police and didn't tell them anything."

"And what did you say to Steve?"

"I acted shocked and said that nothing had happened while we were there. I said I was glad Steve hadn't said anything to the police because your mates who invited us were a bit dodgy, not murderers but dodgy, and it might cause trouble for them."

"How was it left?"

"What do you mean?"

I tried not to let my panic show in my voice. "How did the police leave it? Are they coming back to see Steve again?"

"They were just following procedure and calling at every flat in the block."

There were a lot of flats in Steve's block. I felt the panic subside slightly. "I see."

She passed the reefer to me. "Steve didn't have much sympathy for the victim after reading that he was an arms dealer so I don't think he would say anything to the police even if we had done it. That'll probably be the end of it now."

I wished I shared her optimism.

Fourteen

It was Tuesday morning and getting out of a bed that contained Laura proved to be impossible, so I called in sick. I spent the morning trying to stop myself from being as soppy as hell but failed miserably. Colin had a stock piece of advice about romance. He would say that at the beginning of a relationship a man should rein in his urges to be over-affectionate, and make sure they spent time apart in those first fledgling weeks. The reason for this was to safeguard future enjoyment. Colin's theory was that after the honeymoon period the man is going to want some space again. He'll want to see his friends, play pool, go clubbing, stay home and watch television on his own. Basically he's going to want to start doing things without his new girlfriend. It's not that he will feel any less for the woman, just that he'll need a little variety back in his life. Colin theorised that if the man has kept some distance between them from the outset, then the transition will be seamless, whereas if he has spent the first few months spending every waking (and sleeping) moment with her then it's bound to be problematic to suddenly break the habit. "It's all about managing their expectations," he would say.

Colin was deadly serious about this piece of advice and I had often seen more than a glimmer of logic in it, but while I lay in bed with Laura it was impossible to even consider wanting any kind of space. I wanted the opposite of space; we were pushed right up together in bed and that still wasn't close enough. I could hear Colin's taunts in my head, 'sap', 'puppy dog', but I was helpless to feel any other way.

The reason I'd never had a strong relationship was my self-marketing. At the beginning of a relationship I was like a man possessed. I'd be the model partner; considerate, eager to please, and most importantly I made sure we were always doing something. There would always be an activity to look forward to, be it a trip to the cinema, a night at a club or a weekend away. I would put the effort in to make sure we constantly had something to talk about, something to experience, plan or review. As the months went on it would become impossible for me to keep up that level of effort and it wouldn't be long before the girl realised she had just been watching "Tom White – The Promotional Video" and was now seeing the real product. She would feel cheated, and at about the same time I would realise that it was only our busy schedule that was preventing me from seeing that she wasn't all I had cracked her up to be. We would drift along for a while because neither of us were guilty of anything bad enough to warrant the other dumping them (it's amazing how long people who don't even like each other anymore will stay together), but it would be inevitable that we would eventually crash and burn.

I knew exactly what I was guilty of, and yet I never learnt; I still fell head over heels and charged straight in, making them fall for a stylised image of myself, setting myself up to be something I could never live up to.

So as I lay there with Laura I made a note to myself that after this morning I would start to heed Colin's advice, after all, if I was to be a hitman then I was going to need some time alone. I also vowed to protect myself from myself. Laura liked me, that was clear, so I didn't have to sell her an idealised image of myself. I would be me, well not completely, I wouldn't burp and fart and pick my nose and wank in front of her, but I would present to her the real Tom White and just hope I was to her liking.

Obviously I'd have to leave out the professional killer part.

"I'm going to have to get up, I've got a class at twelve." Laura broke my heart with these words but I stopped myself from begging her to stay. "What's the time?" She continued. "Christ, is it half eleven?"

"No, it's ten past, I have the clock set fast as a safety measure."

"But don't you just translate the time in your head so when you see half past you really read ten past?"

"Yes."

"So there's absolutely no point doing it." She was right of course but I wasn't going to change my tried and tested practice, particularly as I was adhering to my new regime of showing her the real me.

It occurred to me that perhaps this part of me wasn't really worth saving. "You're right, I'll change it." I leaned over and held down the required buttons, watching the digital display speed through twenty three hours and forty minutes, like a vehicle in a TV show to indicate time passing between scenes.

"You don't have to change it on my account."

"I'm not. Shit." I had kept the button pressed too long, so I had to step through another twenty-three hours and fifty six minutes. It took me a while to realise that Laura was grinning to herself. "Right, because you find my misfortune so amusing, I'm not going to tell you the intricacies of my shower, so you'll have a glum old time in there and I'll stand in the doorway and laugh."

"It's just a shower, I'm sure I can work it out."

"Nobody can work any shower except their own, not without the proper directions from the keeper of the flow."

"Who's the keeper of the flow?"

"In this case it's me, but we are all keepers in our own domains. Without the esoteric wisdom held by the keeper, no other can feel the sacred comfort."

Laura climbed on top of me and I savoured the feeling of her skin on my own. Her hands cupped my face and she looked into my eyes, grinning. "You talk a whole load of shit don't you?"

"What about your cousin's shower? You were in there about an hour when we got back from the party, that's because the keeper of the flow, in this case Steve or Wendy, didn't impart his or her wisdom." Instead of answering me, Laura squeezed my cheeks and lips into comedy shapes.

After showing Laura how to use the shower (turn the cold tap on slightly, then the hot on full, then another quarter turn of the cold) I went downstairs to make coffee and toast. I would like to say that it was my strict relationship regime that stopped me from preparing a lavish feast for Laura, but really it was just the fact that she had to leave shortly that forced my hand.

She came downstairs just as I was buttering the toast, and I had to resist the urge to pull her close and ask her to confirm that I hadn't been dreaming, that she really had just spent the night with me and was willing to do it again. We ate a quick breakfast while Laura kept her eye on the kitchen clock, checking with me first that the time was in fact correct. She was just on her way to the door when the doorbell rang. She was closest so she opened it. There was Stephanie; confident, gorgeous Stephanie. This wasn't good.

"Is Thomas around?" She saw me behind Laura in the hallway. "Oh, hi Thomas."

"Hello Stephanie, Laura this is Stephanie, Stephanie, Laura." I tried to keep my tone bright and innocent, knowing what must have been going through Laura's mind on seeing such a beautiful woman arrive at my door. I wasn't sure which was worse; Laura thinking I was having sex with Stephanie, or Laura knowing the truth about why Stephanie was here. Laura smiled awkwardly at Stephanie and left without kissing me goodbye.

"I'll call you later" I shouted after her. She turned and looked at me without smiling then hurried on.

"She seems nice." Stephanie pushed past me into the house.

"I'm sure she'll say the same about you, what are you doing here?"

"I've got a job for you."

"Can't you let me know in advance when you're coming over?" I closed the door behind her and followed her into the lounge where we sat on opposite sofas. "How did you know I wouldn't be at work anyway?"

"I thought you only work at night." She was dressed smartly, a trouser suit and short sleeved white blouse. She had carefully placed the jacket on the cushion next to her.

"Well I don't, I work in a hospital."

"That's nice. Do you save as many lives as you end?"

"I'm not a doctor, I'm a domestic. I clean up after wheelies and dafties."

"That's not a very nice way of putting it."

"I'm not in a very nice mood, well I was; I was in a great mood. I just spent the night with the girl of my dreams, and then you turned up and made her think something's going on."

"Why would she think that?"

"Well you turn up at lunchtime, all bright and breezy and 'is Thomas there?'."

"So? You're allowed to have friends, aren't you? She seems like a smart girl, she wouldn't be threatened by little old me."

"Have you ever looked in a mirror?" I shook my head and changed the subject. "So what's this job then?"

"Why are you being so off with me?"

"Because of what I just said, in future can you please just let me know when you're going to be coming? Now I've got to make up some story to Laura about who you are and why you've come to see me."

"Okay, I see your point. I'll help you think of something."

"That would be good."

She sat with her hands clasped on her lap and gazed at the ceiling. She frowned then smiled at me.

"Any ideas?" I was sure she had thought of something.

"No, I'm afraid not."

I sighed. "Was that your thinking face?"

"Yes. It normally works."

"It didn't just then."

"No."

I decided to think of something later. "Do you want a coffee?"

"Yes please." She went back to frowning and looking at the ceiling.

When I came back with the coffee she looked satisfied. "I've got it. I've got the story."

"I'm all ears." I placed a cup in front of her.

"I'm seeing your friend Colin."

"How do you know Colin?"

"I don't, we're pretending."

"But I'm sure I've never mentioned him to you."

"Yes you have, how else would I know you had a friend called Colin?"

"Are you sure?"

"What else can I say? Why are you being so strange Thomas?"

"We've met twice and I'm sure I didn't mention Colin either of those times."

"I really don't know what to tell you Thomas. You did

mention him, obviously you mentioned him, otherwise how would I have known his name? Unless you think I'm stalking you, tapping your phone." She leaned over to the telephone and drummed her fingers on the white plastic. "Tapping, geddit?"

I ignored her joke. "I'm just being paranoid I suppose."

"It's okay, you probably didn't get much sleep, she seems like a nice girl." She accompanied her bawdy comment with an equally bawdy wink which I ignored.

"She is a nice girl, she's fantastic. So what's the rest of the story? You're seeing Colin, that's fine, but why were you calling round at my house?"

"I thought Colin would be in but he wasn't, so I popped in here to say hello."

"How do you know I live near Colin?"

"I guessed. You said that he calls round sometimes so I assumed he lived nearby."

"I'm still not remembering this conversation."

"Thomas, I'm not going to have this debate again, do you want my help or not?"

"Alright, we'll give that a go. Colin was out, so you popped in to see me. But of course he was out, he works every day."

"I thought he had said he was having the day off."

"But I should have been at work too."

"I doubt she's going to cross examine you, just say I've got a lot of friends who work nights and I got mixed up, say I'm a bit dizzy."

"Okay, it'll have to do. You popped in to see me, I happened to be here. We had a cup of coffee, you gave me the name of someone I had to murder and then you left, all very innocent."

"Absolutely."

"What if Laura and I become a proper item? That'll mean

she'll get to know Colin more and he'll have to pretend he's just broken up with you."

"Or we could still be together, we could all go out sometime."

"Why the hell would you want to put yourself in that situation? That would be like a bad sitcom. I think we'll just go with the break-up story if it comes to that."

She took a sip of coffee. "Right, that's settled. Can we get down to business now?"

"Everything okay with the last one?" I was keen to know how the Hunter job had been received but didn't want to seem desperate for praise, like a beginner.

"You mean you want the rest of the money?" She rummaged in her handbag and tossed a fat jiffy bag in my direction, nearly causing me to spill my coffee.

"Thanks. Last time it was a party, so where next? At the opera? While the target's receiving a knighthood? That would be a good one, I could grab the sword off the Queen and cut the bloke's head off."

Stephanie held her hand up as if stopping traffic, which she probably did just by walking down the street. "Hey, it's not my fault, I'm just the messenger, I don't set the targets, but now you mention it, you're not going to like this one either."

I put my mug onto the table and lay back on the sofa, rolling my eyes. "Oh Jesus. What is it?" Stephanie looked like she couldn't bring herself to say it for fear of laughing. "Come on, what do I have to do?"

She did her best to compose herself before speaking. "Paintball."

"Paint what?"

"Paintball, haven't you heard of it?"

"Of course I have, stag weekends, hen parties, a load of twats go into a field and shoot each other with balls of paint under the guidance of some wannabe drill instructor."

"You won't be firing paint."

"You want me to kill someone while they're having a paintball day?"

"Not some *one*, some *two*."

"What?"

"There are two targets. Brothers, twins in fact."

"You're joking, right? This is all a big joke."

"No joke Thomas. Your targets are Jasper and Max Calson, identical twins. I didn't think you'd like it but I think you'll like the rate. It's thirty for the pair. Fifteen now. She took out three more jiffy bags from her handbag, it was a big handbag, and placed them on the table like she was about to do a street corner sleight-of-hand trick. She saw the look on my face and leaned towards me. "I don't think you need to look after the wheelies and dafties anymore Thomas."

"I need more information than before. Last time you just told me the bloke's name and where the party was, then you ran out. I want a full discussion."

"That's fair enough." She leaned back with her arms above her head. Her breasts strained against her blouse. "I'm all yours, ask me whatever you want."

She told me almost everything I needed to know. The twins were having a birthday party. They were both going to be thirty. The event was going to be in some remote woodland in Hampshire. There would be thirty people at the party, and the way it worked was that they would split into two teams and take part in a number of different games with the twins as captains of opposing teams. This was an advantage in that they would be wearing captain's armbands, which would mean I would be able to spot them, otherwise they would be impossible to recognise beneath their overalls, protective masks and caps. The disadvantage of them being on rival teams was that they would be apart, making it difficult to do the double hit.

Stephanie's handbag was apparently bottomless because there were yet more things inside for her to give me. I noted she had broken her tradition of not having anything written down as she handed me a map and some photographs. "You'll have to destroy these once you've memorised the contents." She unfolded the map and placed it on the table, moving my mug out of the way. "The yellow area is the paintball site, it covers about fifty acres. Now, if you look at the line around the perimeter you'll see it's coloured differently in different places. The colour code indicates if there's a fence or not, and if there is, what it's made of. She traced the line with an elegant fingernail. This part is red, which means it's barbed wire, difficult to cross."

"Why would they go to so much trouble to keep people out? It's only a paintball site, not an army base."

"Gypsies. A lot of farmers in the area have had their land squatted so nobody round there is taking any risks." Her fingernail continued on its path. "The yellow part is a wooden fence, it's about six feet high, not impenetrable but not easy. Now this part here, where the line is dotted, that's just a ditch. It's difficult to get to that part by road so they haven't bothered with any real security, but the ditch would stop the caravans from getting in if they did get that far. That's where you should go in. It won't be particularly easy though, it'll be horribly overgrown so remember to wear lots of protective clothes. Which leads us to this." She picked up one of the photographs and placed it on top of the map. It was a man in green army fatigues.

"Is that one of the twins? I can't see his face under that mask."

"He's not a target, the picture's from the website of the paintball company. I just wanted you to know what they'll all be wearing. You should get something similar."

"Where am I going to get green overalls like that?"

"You really do whinge don't you Thomas? Go to an army surplus shop." She laid out two more photos.

I scanned the pictures. "So that's the twins, you didn't really need two photos, they're exactly the same."

She smiled for the first time in a while. "Yes you're right, that was a bit silly, but you get the picture."

"I think I do. I get to play soldiers."

"So that's everything you need to know."

"Not quite. There's one more thing."

She sat up, looking interested. "What's that?"

"Why is this contract out on these two? What have they done?"

She shook her head and sighed. "I don't know Thomas, honestly I don't. And if I did I wouldn't tell you. It's not necessary for either of us to know."

I didn't reply.

Stephanie slapped her suit-clad thighs. "Right, that's everything. Memorise all that stuff and then burn it okay?"

"Yes."

We were both standing now. She put her hand on my shoulder. "Okay, Thomas?"

I didn't know if she was confirming that I would burn the map and pictures, or if it was a more general question. "Of course I'm okay."

Fifteen

My head was reeling. The juxtaposition of the delights of spending the night with Laura, and the near impossibility of my next assignment was hard to bear. Then there was the fear of Laura wanting me to explain who Stephanie was and why she was visiting me. I wondered if Laura would call. I knew she would be in the pub later, but I didn't want a scene there. I thought about it for a while and decided that Laura was an intelligent girl, not the jealous type so I was sure she would understand, but then I remembered how astonishingly beautiful Stephanie was, enough to make even the most secure person feel a little shaky.

I called Colin and got his voicemail, he must have been in some godforsaken place measuring an adverse camber. I left a message telling him we needed to talk about a gig a week on Saturday. I was getting good at this code stuff.

As I had so much time on my hands I sorted out the money, separating it into two bundles, sixty-forty. I put my share inside the hi-fi unit, burying Monica in the process and put Colin's share in the back of my wardrobe upstairs; a temporary home until I saw him. As the money was now starting to roll in I started thinking in earnest about my job at the hospital and whether I should resign. My argument to myself that my nasty job was good cover for my real occupation was losing weight every day. I decided to decide tomorrow.

Now I was really bored. I had nothing to do. I made a sandwich and then, even though I had no sexual desire left after repeated bouts with Laura last night and this morning, I had a wank. It was difficult to finish the job but I managed to squeeze out a few drops, like the end of a well-used toothpaste tube. Boredom wanks always make me sore. I had a bath, allowing my violated penis to bob around in the warm water before it felt too pleasant, and I actually had to stop myself from wanking again. Then I got dressed and did the washing up.

I was still mulling over whether to call Laura, but sheer boredom made up my mind for me and I made the call. It went straight to voicemail and I left a stilted message, as I don't know how to leave any other kind of voicemail message. I had been tempted to apologise but technically there was nothing to apologise for. Okay, so a stunning woman had turned up at my house, but I hadn't done anything wrong. I decided there was no point worrying about it until I knew if Laura was upset or not.

A few minutes later there was a knock at the door. Perhaps Laura's class had finished early.

It was Frank and Cheese. Frank seemed pretty chuffed with himself. "Tom my boy, how've you been? It's been a long time."

"Hi Frank, Cheese. What brings you here?"

Cheese did his best to smile but it was more of a grimace really. Frank spoke. "Me and Cheese fancied some more sea air so we thought we'd pop down from the smoke and see you." He paused. "So, you going to let us in or what?"

I stood back and ushered them past me, looking around to see if any neighbours were looking before I closed the door. There didn't seem to be anyone watching; perhaps Stephanie was right and I was getting paranoid. It wasn't unreasonable of me to feel a little bit on edge, after all I was now living a completely unpredictable life where there was danger at every turn, but despite the drawbacks, life was a lot more interesting than it had been before.

I wished that Frank, Cheese and Stephanie's boss was better at co-ordinating his various 'chains of command'. I didn't like his representatives all turning up on the same day. I nearly voiced this thought but remembered that Stephanie had warned me not to mention my visits from her. I wondered what would have happened if Frank and Cheese had arrived when Stephanie was here, that would have made discretion difficult.

We went into the lounge and they remained standing, so I did the same. "So no more floorboards then Tom, you finally decided to embrace the trappings of western consumerism?"

"What's that Frank?"

"You've got carpet."

"Yes, I've got carpet." Then I realised what he was talking about, the last time they were here the room was completely bare because I was having the new carpet fitted. Surely he didn't think I lived like that all the time. I was about to ask when Frank launched into a monologue.

"Right, Tom. Everyone's happy with your last job, the Clarke job. I've been told to pass on the old man's compliments on that. We've got another contract for you, but the boss is still keen to know who it was who paid for the guy next door to be done in." He looked at my blank face for a moment. "Okay, you're not ready to tell me, I get it. The old man will just have to understand that. Sorry to have brought it up."

I maintained my blank face, glad that Frank had decided to answer his own question and not bother me with it anymore. I was still unsure who to trust. If I was completely comfortable with Frank and Cheese and their so-called 'old man' then I would happily tell them it was all a misunderstanding; that I killed my neighbour because he was annoying me and that I wasn't actually a hitman. However, a part of me was screaming that I shouldn't trust them, still fearing that the neighbour was one of their own and they were looking for revenge. I was sure I would be able to tell one way or another as time went on, but for now I wasn't taking any chances. I eventually spoke. "So what's the job?"

"Cheese, you got the envelope?"

I hadn't noticed but Cheese had a small rucksack over his shoulder. He opened it and slid out an A4 sized envelope. "Frank's given up using that stupid code, so you don't need to worry about that." It never failed to amaze me when Cheese spoke.

"I haven't given up, I just realised it wasn't necessary, it was never stupid though."

"Whatever you say Frank." Cheese grinned at me as best he could, amazing me again. "You'll be wanting this too." He pulled out a fat brown jiffy bag and handed it to me. I thought I could build a bunker with these things at this rate, and that perhaps I would need to.

"It's all there, you know the drill." Frank shrugged. "So that's that I suppose." He said this as if he was about to leave, but he didn't move. He just stood there looking slightly uncomfortable.

"Yes. That's that I suppose" I repeated.

They still didn't move. Frank looked decidedly awkward while Cheese stared at the floor.

"Do you want a cup of tea?"

Frank visibly relaxed, as if he was on the way to see a particularly dreary bedridden great aunt but had just been told she had passed away. He rubbed his hands. "That'd be great Tom. Is it okay to sit down?" Cheese looked enthusiastic too, or at least as enthusiastic as he could muster, and they both made themselves comfortable, with much "ah" ing and "ooh, it's good to take the weight off." Surely these hardened gangsters weren't just hanging around for tea and biscuits.

I tested the water. "I've got some gingernuts too if you want them."

Cheese rubbed his hands together and his attempts at a smile became more successful. Frank said, "we both like gingernuts Tom" and replicated Cheese's grin. I was baffled, were they really so pleased with my offer of tea and biscuits or was 'gingernuts' some hilarious double-entendre that was lost on me? They never said, and the longer they stayed the more I became aware that the situation was just as it seemed; that they did just want a chat and some light refreshment. I was bemused by this but also flattered that they valued my company so much. I wanted to take advantage and find out more about the Clarke job; why he was killed and who he was, but they didn't mention it again so I chose not to.

After an hour I started to get restless. It was nearly five and Laura would have finished her class. I didn't want them here if she called round; I had enough explaining to do already. So I was glad that she didn't come over, but I was aware that the longer she left it, the longer it meant she was ignoring the message I had left on her phone.

Boredom drove me to ask them a question that felt risky as soon as it left my lips. "Do you do what I do?"

Frank sat up. "Why do you ask?"

"I'm interested, obviously the old man has fellers like you, who are doing the day to day stuff, and he gets you to come to me for certain jobs. I wondered if there was an overlap."

"There's an overlap." There was finality about Cheese's statement. The conversation was over.

They left soon after, not piqued at my question but more because it brought them back to reality; tea and chat weren't part of their lives.

After they had gone I wearily opened the thin envelope. It was just as amateur as the last one they had given me, but as Cheese had pointed out, there was no use of 'swap code' this time. The name of the target was Mark Smith and in the photograph he was wearing a suit and tie. He didn't look like a thug; he looked like he sold insurance. Maybe somebody had got fed up with him knocking on their door and decided to have him killed. The only writing on the note, apart from his name, said "8.10 East Croydon to London Bridge platform 4. Accident." All I could do was shake my head with despair.

I was at a hiatus with my two burning issues. I had to talk to Laura to make sure she was still keen, and that Stephanie's visit hadn't messed things up, and I had to speak to Colin about how the hell we were going to kill twin brothers while they were surrounded by their mates, and then kill a commuter on a busy rush hour station. I hated being at the mercy of other people, but here I was, unable to move forward without their input. This was the stage where any doubts were blown away about how much I needed Colin's assistance in my new profession, and I already knew how much I needed Laura for everything else.

I called Colin and left a message on his voicemail, I was sick of voicemail. Then, after hesitating, I called Laura again. She didn't answer. I didn't leave a message and instantly regretted calling, picturing the display on her mobile, "2 missed calls: Tom." It would make me look desperate, like I had something to cover up.

Colin called back within five minutes. "What's up Tom?"

"I've had a couple of visits. We've been given loads of money and two more jobs, well three actually. One's a double."

"I'll be there in ten minutes."

"Okay mate, oh, sorry to be an arse but if Laura calls then I might have to cut your visit short."

"Jesus Tom, have I taught you nothing?"

"No, it's not that, we just had a misunderstanding this morning and I think she's pissed off with me."

"My question stands."

"No Colin, I've listened to your advice, really I have. I'm not dropping everything for her. I just want to sort this thing out."

"Oh for fuck's sake, you're always the same. We'll talk when I get there. Actually, you come here. I always come to you." I started to protest but he hung up.

Now I had a quandary. I should tell Laura where I was going in case she came to mine while I was out, but if I called again and she didn't answer then that would be a third missed call on her mobile. With Colin's words still ringing in my ears I decided to take my chances and not call her. She had already ignored two messages from me so I wasn't going to chase her anymore. I decided to stop being the weaker party and start to assert myself. After all, I hadn't done anything wrong. Apart from all the murders.

I stuffed two of the envelopes of cash into my bag along with the photographs and information I had been given by Stephanie, Frank and Cheese. It was quite a collection. As I arrived at Colin's flat I remembered why I didn't go there very often. It was a grim little place above a convenience store. Colin always said this was very convenient, but he was only fooling himself. Just outside Colin's door on the communal stairway was his big yellow reflective jacket and helmet. Having already buzzed me in the front door Colin was waiting in the doorway to the flat. I stepped past his big yellow reflective jacket and helmet that he clearly just dumped inside the door when he got home from work. The spirit-level-on-a-tripod-thing added to the obstacle course of his hallway.

The flat smelt musty. There was a bin liner full of rubbish in the kitchen doorway. It hadn't been tied at the top so presumably it served as Colin's dustbin. He led me into the lounge and I sat down on an armchair that didn't match the sofa. It was one of those flats that feels freezing all year round and even though it was late summer, the fabric of the armchair felt cold and damp. The sun outside was kept at bay by the filthy windows, making it look like January. Colin sat on the sofa and started rolling a joint.

I couldn't hold my tongue. "Col, this place is horrible."

"This is how I like it."

I looked at a mug on the floor next to me and wondered what birthday the mould inside was about to reach. "Is this really how you like it? Honestly?"

"Yes, I'm not obsessed with hygiene like you."

"It's like on those reality TV shows where they follow the health inspectors around. I've seen them, they have real nut-jobs who can't bear to be parted from anything produced by their bodies. So their houses are full of their shit and piss all kept in bags."

"Fuck off" he said in a bored tone.

"Do you keep your own shit and piss in bags?"

"Fuck off."

"How about your spunk, do you keep your spunk in Petri dishes?"

"You're not getting any of this reefer if you don't shut up."

I focused on trying not to imagine the culture of bacteria oozing around the sofa and encompassing me into its domain. "So do you want to know about these jobs?"

He sparked up the reefer and inhaled, making his voice sound nasal. "Fuck yes. What have you got?"

"Well firstly I've got this for you." I opened my bag and pulled out the money, "There's ten grand here, I'll sort out the rest later." I threw the bulky envelopes onto the sofa next to him and he gave me the joint.

"You can come round more often." He opened one of the packages and grinned at the contents. "So what's coming up then?"

"There's all sorts coming up. You'll not believe what we've got to do. We've got three people to kill. Two at once."

"At once? What are we meant to do, bomb them?"

"Oh no mate. The two targets are having a paintball party. There'll be about thirty of their mates there."

"Fuck off."

"We're supposed to sneak onto the site and kill them, they're twin brothers. Look." I showed him the map and the photographs of the twins.

"Who's that?" Colin pointed at the picture Stephanie had given me from the paintball catalogue.

"That's what we've got to wear."

"Fuck off, this is ridiculous. I thought hitmen were just given a name, address and photograph. That's what happens in films. They don't get special requests. Go on then, what's the other job? Don't tell me, we've got to take out a ringmaster at a circus while he's… while he's mastering the ring."

"It's not that ridiculous but it's pretty ridiculous."

"Come on then, what is it?"

"We've got to kill this man, Mark Smith…" I put the photograph Frank had given me in front of Colin like I was doing a tarot reading. "…while he waits for the ten past eight train from East Croydon. We've got to make it look like an accident."

"a.m. or p.m.?"

"a.m."

That seemed to swing it for him. "Fuck it Tom, that's crazy. The station will be packed at that time, what are we meant to do, push him in front of the train?"

"I guess so. I think that's the accident part."

"Mind the fucking gap."

After a while and a few more joints Colin and I stopped our histrionics and discussed our tasks logically, trying to cover all possible eventualities. Colin was going to be working in Barnsley over the next few days and said he would visit an army surplus shop to get us some overalls. We decided that Barnsley was suitably far away for it to be difficult to tie the purchase to us if there were questions afterwards. He made me feel like a fool by pointing at the huge pile of notes in front of him when I warned him not to use a credit card and asked him if he had any cash to pay with.

We planned to make a reconnaissance mission to the paintball site on Saturday to make sure we would be able to find it the following weekend, and to see how we were going to get in. For the railway hit we decided we would get the train to East Croydon and see if Mark Smith had any habits that could work to our advantage, or as Colin put it "Let's hope he always stands near the edge of the platform so we can push him off easily." We agreed to go to East Croydon on Thursday and Friday Morning for reconnaissance, and then make the actual hit on the Monday. It was going to be a busy few days.

I left Colin's at about ten-thirty and realised I'd forgotten all about Laura. I checked my phone and saw that she had sent me a text message nearly an hour ago. It must have arrived when I was in Colin's grubby bathroom and had left the phone on the coffee table. I kicked myself for not checking it before now and wanted to kick Colin for not mentioning it; he must have heard it go off, he was sitting right near it. The message said to come and have a drink in the Pilgrim just before closing so I could walk her home. My heart leapt but experience told me not to be complacent. I had learned that women have a way of painting a certain picture, then tearing it down to reveal a dark image of wrath beneath. Her potential anger aside, it was perfect timing, I could go straight to the pub in time for that drink.

The Pilgrim was almost empty when I got there and Laura had her elbows propped on the bar with her chin resting in her hands. She was chatting to two men sitting on barstools, they looked like students.

A young couple sat at the table furthest away from the bar. They seemed to show quite an interest in me as I walked in, which, after the amount of gear I'd smoked with Colin, made me paranoid before I pointed out to myself that they had obviously just run out of things to say so every distraction had become a talking point. Laura beamed at me as I approached, and I could see an immediate change in the countenance of both the men talking to her. It felt good to be the alpha male for a moment.

Laura linked her arm with mine as we walked back to my house. It was a shamelessly couply gesture and I shamelessly enjoyed it.

"Did you get my messages today?" I was going to save the question until later but it just came flooding out.

"Yes." There was no tension in her voice.

"Oh."

"You think I'm upset because that woman turned up as I was leaving don't you?"

"I wanted to make sure you weren't."

"What would I have to be upset about?"

I didn't want to spell it out and point out Stephanie's obvious physical attributes. "I just thought you might have thought she was a girlfriend, more than a friend I mean."

"Tom, neither of us is a virgin. We've both got histories. I trust my own judgement well enough to know that I don't pick bastards. If you were a bastard then I might have some concerns about Miss World coming to your house, but I don't think you are a bastard, so even if you do have some history with her - and I'd be quite impressed if you did - I think you would have stopped any shenanigans after we got together. I also don't think you would have jumped into a bed with her that still had the imprint of my body in the mattress." Hearing her refer to her own body made me feel as horny as hell.

"That's good" I said. "I mean, you're absolutely right about it all."

"Who is she anyway?"

My defences rose, I suspected that Laura's previous monologue had all been a cover and now here we were with the real line of enquiry, but I decided to follow her example and trust my own judgement. Rather than go with the story Stephanie and I had concocted about her being Colin's lover, I opted for a more truthful answer. "She's a friend, I've known her for a while. We've never been romantically involved."

Laura feigned an upper-class voice "romantically involved?"

"Okay, it wasn't the best term to use. What do you want me to say?"

"You've never had sex with her, that's what you're trying to tell me."

"That's right."

"Okay."

I didn't waste any time getting Laura back into bed.

* * * * * * * * * * * * * * * *

"Why haven't you called me, Joe?" My voice is tearful, pathetic.

"Take it easy, love. You know I've been busy." I step up the snivelling. "But I've wanted to talk to you."

"Calm down, calm down, I've wanted to talk to you too." It's obvious that he's with at least one of his men. He's almost whispering. "I'm always thinking about you, babe, I just haven't had a chance. And when you're

with…. Him. It's hard to know when might be a good time."

"I can't take it anymore. This is too much. We should stop. You haven't got time for this. I shouldn't have put you in this position. Perhaps Stan is what I deserve."

"Don't ever say that!" He's not whispering anymore. "It's gonna be you and me. Don't ever talk that sort of shit again. You got it?"

"Is it really Joe? Is it going to be you and me?"

He pauses and I think I've overplayed the lovesick schoolgirl act but then finally he speaks, back to whispering again. "You are my whole world, and I'm gonna be yours. It's gonna be you and me."

"I hope so, Joe. I can't be with him much longer. I need to be with you." I hang up before he can hear me smiling.

Sixteen

So, this was the rat race. This was what the outside world looked like at this crazy hour. It was seven o'clock on Thursday morning. I reached Brighton station and couldn't believe the number of people up at this time of day. Colin was due to be here any time now, he'd taken some holiday and I was still pretending to be ill. There were people everywhere and they were all in a hurry. Politeness had no place in this netherworld; getting there was all that mattered. I queued to buy a newspaper before realising that queuing had been consigned to history in this strain of reality. People pushed past me, scattering coins on the counter. Even those without the right change charged to the front and fought for the attention of the newsagent. I was instantly affronted but then realised there was no malice in their actions. To them this wasn't rude at all, it was just getting by.

Colin was now officially late so I called him. The phone rang for a long time then went to voicemail. I didn't bother leaving a message. My phone rang almost straight away. It was Colin; my call must have woken him but not quickly enough for him to reach it. He was trying to put on his best awake-sounding voice. "I'm sorry mate, I messed up. I won't be able to make it on time now. I'll be there tomorrow."

"I know you'll fucking be here tomorrow. We've already arranged to come tomorrow. What are you playing at? Just sort it out Colin."

"You don't have to go today, we'll start tomorrow."

"I'm up now so I may as well go. We're not fucking around here." I hung up before he could answer. The fact that I had half expected this to happen made it even more infuriating. There was absolutely no reason for it; Colin was used to being up early for his job, so this shouldn't have been a problem. He was like this whenever we went anywhere, always late and unreliable. I had hoped it would be different for something as serious as this, and I kicked myself for being unrealistic. I regretted increasing his share of the proceeds.

I went to get a ticket from one of the machines and noted that, because the regular commuters all had season tickets, none of them used the machines, which meant this was one part of Early World where the social conventions of Normal World applied; people waited their turn and didn't try to force each other to go more quickly, although I would have liked to have shouted at the woman in front of me to hurry up, because she clearly had the brain of a pigeon. As I reached the ticket barrier I was dragged back into the laws of Early World: I stood back to let an elderly woman go ahead of me, and a commuter saw the space I had opened up and shoved his way through. I didn't cause a scene.

I was wearing smart trousers along with a shirt and tie to try and blend in with the commuter crowd. Brighton is a terminus station, so the London train was already at the platform. There was a collection of men in reflective jackets shooting the breeze at the driver's end of the platform, and a refreshment vendor waiting with his cart next to the first carriage. As I walked up the platform I soon realised my search for a seat was futile. The regular commuters all knew the score and arrived early enough to guarantee a seat, probably the same one every morning, amongst their travelling gang.

There were only a few minutes to go until the train was due to leave so I boarded about two-thirds of the way up. I was looking for the most comfortable place to stand when I saw it, like a mirage. An empty seat. I couldn't believe my eyes until my tunnel vision widened its focus and I could see why it was empty. It was because of the giant of a man sitting on the next seat, or rather sitting on both seats. I had been seduced by the glitter of fool's gold, but I was undeterred. I had paid the same fare as him for my journey, probably more, as his was a season and mine was a day return, so I didn't see why he should have two seats. He was sitting at the aisle, an old trick to force people to ask him to move if they wanted to sit there, relying on them being too embarrassed to ask such a big man to let them in, but I was determined to fight for my rights.

I realised that I was obviously getting over my fear of confrontation as I forced myself between the guy and the wall of the train. He made no attempt to free up any space for me even when I pressed my leg hard against the various parts of his body that encroached onto my territory.

I should point out here that I don't care what size or shape anyone is. It's nothing to do with me. But he was taking up my seat so it made it my business.

The battle raged. I managed to claim back an inch or so of space but it was a constant struggle to hold my ground. My troops were quicker and more manoeuvrable but his had the advantage of sheer weight of numbers, and his army was always going to win a war of attrition. A nervous cease-fire was declared, broken only by the occasional skirmish at the border.

And all the while he kept on staring straight ahead as if nothing was happening.

As the train started to move I was mortified to discover that the sounds of the engine, or motor or whatever, were insufficient to drown out the sound of his breathing. He badly needed to clear his throat but either he didn't notice or he chose not to. He just allowed the incoming and outgoing air to roll noisily back and forth over whatever goo was sitting in his windpipe. I had to accept that I was stuck with the soundtrack for the rest of the journey.

I insisted on reading my paper even though it was more trouble than it was worth; I couldn't open it comfortably because of my hemmed-in state but I wasn't going to be thwarted. There was a principle at stake. I had been through a lot to buy that paper so I was going to enjoy it. Well I wasn't going to enjoy it but I was at least going to read it.

On top of the discomfort of the heat of the packed carriage and being seated next to my silent nemesis, there was even more unpleasantness on board: a sniffer. I didn't see who it was but I guessed from the volume that it must have been a man. It was exactly seventeen seconds between each sniff; I know because I timed it. I wondered how anybody could have such little self-consciousness to be able to force snot up into his nose with that kind of force and frequency without realising that everybody around him wants to pull off that nose and stuff it back into the bleeding hole in the middle of his face. If I could hear it so loudly then God knew how bad it was for the people seated closer to him. As I sat there enduring the torture I wished I had taken up yoga and could mutter a mantra to myself to elevate me away from this Purgatory.

Thankfully it was only about forty minutes to East Croydon and after much pushing and shoving and panicking that perhaps I wasn't going to get through the crowd of passengers and would miss my stop, I alighted, as they say in the trade. I had about fifteen minutes before the train to London Bridge arrived, so I waited at the start of the platform and watched the walkway from the station concourse for Mark Smith to appear. As the flood of commuters swirled around me I realised the task of finding him was going to be difficult, and that I needed a better place to stand. Nobody had any qualms about shoving past me, and the combined effects of all the pushing was tantamount to assault. I stepped back and took up a vantage point away from the thoroughfare. I had memorised the photograph but it was still going to be difficult to spot Smith amongst so many faces. I saw and disregarded several candidates, and as time went on I started to worry that I had missed the real Mark Smith. Eventually he appeared. I was sure it was him. In fact I was sure he was wearing the same tie as he was in Frank's photograph.

My heart immediately started racing and I reminded myself this was a reconnaissance mission. I just wanted to get an idea about where he stood to wait for the train and if he was a creature of habit or not. This would tell me how difficult our job was going to be.

I followed Smith as he made his way along the platform, weaving his way through the melee of people, some coming towards him, some that he was overtaking, and some who were just standing in the way. There were only a few minutes left until the train was due, so I was surprised when he ducked into the platform café. There was a big queue inside and I was sure he had no chance of getting served and back out onto the platform in time to catch his train. I watched through the glass walls, amazed, as he walked straight to the front of the queue and addressed the girl behind the counter. She finished serving the person she was dealing with and then, astonishingly, she served Smith. A few people in the queue adopted peeved expressions, but nobody challenged him outright, and nobody berated the girl behind the counter for serving somebody so obviously out of turn. This was another insight into the altered reality of Early World. I was far from home.

Smith re-emerged from the café, cup in hand, he glanced at his watch, and I had to keep my wits about me to stay with him as he stepped up the pace. The edge of the platform was like a bar at the Glastonbury Festival, at least six-deep. I despaired; if this was what happened every morning then he was never going to be anywhere near the platform edge when a train passed, so the easy route; pushing him under the train, was going to be closed for engineering works. But I hadn't considered the full extent of his rudeness. He simply picked his spot and pushed his way through the crowd of people. I was dumbstruck but didn't hesitate. I had to follow in his wake quickly, like chasing an ambulance through a busy high street before the gap closed again. People muttered objections but I could tell their hearts weren't really in their protests.

Smith reached the front and I was right behind him, packed so tight that if I had chosen to lift my feet from the ground, the crush of commuters would have kept me upright. The announcement came over the speakers that the eight-ten to London Bridge would be arriving imminently. Smith was well past the yellow line of safety and his feet were almost hanging off the edge of the platform. It wasn't just him, the whole front row of the crowd of waiting commuters were teetering on the brink. We were not quite halfway up the platform as the train came in and although it was slowing, its brakes squealing with the strain, it was still travelling at a fair pace. I thought of Colin lying in his bed, probably wanking by now, and I thought of how unpleasant this morning had been. I didn't want to do it again, not tomorrow, not Monday, not ever, and I realised I wasn't going to get a better chance than this. If I am honest I had known I was going to do it as soon as I followed Smith through the throng to the edge of the platform. I got my hands ready, palms outwards and within millimetres of the small of Mark Smith's back. When the train was just a few yards away I shoved him as hard as I could. I thought he wasn't going to budge because of the crush at either side of him, but then he burst free, like squeezing a boil. His feet seemed rooted to the spot while his body toppled over. I took a step forward and flailed my arms as if I was trying to catch him, all the while shouting, 'Noooooooo' like in a TV drama.

Smith fell as good as head first towards the rails five feet below the edge of the platform but before he hit the ground the train connected and that was the last I saw of him before my view was blocked by the moving train. His screams told me it took him a few moments to die, that's not to say he was actually shouting "it's taking me a few moments to die," although I would have preferred that to the animal shrieks that howled over the screech of the train's wheels. From my assassin's point of view it couldn't have worked any better, but in reality it was horrible.

I played the shocked onlooker, which wasn't completely an act because I was genuinely dismayed and shaken by the results of my actions. I rushed up the platform, trying to catch up with what was left of Mark Smith. This was for two reasons; it was what a concerned citizen in a state of shock would do, and it also allowed me to break free of those who had been around me when I pushed him, just in case anybody saw what had happened through the crowds. The platform was chaos. People were trying to catch up with Smith just as I was pretending to do, while others were trying to get out of the way. Even if I had wanted to get to the front of the train I wouldn't have been able to, and I took the opportunity to step away from the crowd, pretending to be trying to call an ambulance on my mobile. I edged my way to the adjacent platform. A southbound train had pulled in and I fancied that I might be able to jump on it and it would take me back to Brighton; the perfect getaway, but that clearly wasn't going to happen. The guards on the southbound train had seen the carnage on the next platform and were busy blowing their whistles and generally rushing about. I was now pretending to talk on the phone, barking desperate pleas at the imaginary switchboard operator to send help. This was my cover for walking in the opposite direction to where Mark Smith's body was spread over sixty feet of railway line.

I repeated my dialogue, looping it for the fresh ears that I passed as I left the platform, and hurried up the walkway towards the station concourse. I happily endured the crush of people at the ticket barrier, blending in nicely. After about ten minutes I was onto the concourse and had slipped out of the station. I was exhilarated and disgusted with myself all at once, but my main motivation was not being caught. I knew I would have to wait a while before returning to the station as it would soon be crawling with coppers. I walked into the town centre and ordered some breakfast in a greasy spoon, trying to feign the look of somebody killing time before a job interview. Perhaps 'killing time' wasn't the best phrase to use.

I ate a disgusting breakfast accompanied by a chipped mug of tea, which bore the stains of a thousand previous servings. All the time I was eating I could hear the wail of police sirens, and each one sounded like Mark Smith's last scream. I attempted to read the newspaper that I had struggled with so much on the train, but I couldn't focus on the words. This was the worst I had felt so far after carrying out a murder, but at the same time I felt tremendous relief at having got the job out of the way. It was just after nine when I left the cafe. The crowds of commuters had all started work now so there was hardly anybody about. I was still angry with Colin but couldn't resist giving him the good news, so I called him. He answered much quicker this time. "Hi Tom, I'm sorry about earlier, mate."

"It's done."

"What?"

"It's done, I finished the job."

"But you were just meant to be checking it out."

"I know, but the opportunity was there and I had to take it." Colin had fallen silent. "What's the matter? I thought you'd be pleased."

"Why would I be pleased? We're meant to be partners. I knew you were pissed at me for oversleeping."

"That's paranoid bullshit. Yes, I was pissed at you, course I was, but I hadn't planned to do it there and then. But I had a chance, a perfect chance. So I made the most of it."

"I know you Tom. This is your way of teaching me a lesson."

"If you'd turned up like we planned then we wouldn't be having this argument."

"I knew it! So I suppose I won't be getting any of the money?"

"You didn't do anything."

"Fuck you, Tom." He hung up.

This was all I needed. I had put myself into a state of shock by throwing a man under twenty tons of screeching metal and I had just eaten a plate of lard. Now Colin was crying like a girl because he couldn't be arsed to get up on time.

I decided I would get back to the station at ten-thirty, that would be a reasonable time to allow for my imaginary interview, so I had nearly an hour and a half to kill. There was that word again. I didn't want to be seen wandering around for no reason so I decided to do some shopping. I rarely bought new clothes because I hated being amongst other shoppers, but the shops were empty now so I went on a spree. After I had bought a new pair of jeans and two shirts I realised that having armfuls of shopping undermined my cover story, so I amended it in my head to allow for post-interview shopping. Unfortunately this would add an hour to my departure time to allow for both activities.

I found the shopping trip quite a tonic; it felt good to free my mind from the horror of what I had done; the sight and sound of Mark Smith being pushed and pulled to death and focus instead on a shallow and essentially wasteful activity. Both my recent trips to the shopping mall in Brighton had been in preparation for murders. This was the first time I had been in ages where it was just for me to get things I wanted. I liked to pretend I wasn't a big consumer but once I got going I was as bad as the next man, or the next woman would be more accurate.

The town started to fill up as I shopped, and by the time I started my walk back the streets were fairly busy. When I reached the station I saw that a sign had been put up with "Accident, can you help?" printed at the top. I liked the word 'accident' but didn't like the handwritten text below. "If you have any information about the possible murder on platform 2 of this station on 1st. Sept please call this number." They must have run out of "There's been a murder" signs. There were two policemen near the ticket barrier and I wondered if they would normally be there or if they were part of the murder investigation. My thoughts were answered when they politely blocked my way and one addressed me. "Excuse me sir, can we ask you a few questions?"

"Of course, what about?"

"A man fell beneath the eight-ten London Bridge train, sir. The train was stopping but was moving at a speed in excess of thirty miles per hour when it made contact." I had to stifle a smile. Policeman-speak always made me laugh. This one sounded like a recorded announcement. "We are calling it a possible murder at the moment but it could still be an accident. We have no strong evidence either way but the man who died had some notable enemies."

"Jesus, that's awful." I shook my head and put my hand over my mouth theatrically. "Sorry for the language."

"That's okay sir, I understand, it's quite upsetting. We're just following procedure and asking anybody within the vicinity of the railway station for information about their journey."

I put on my concerned citizen face but I was in a state of blind panic. My hands gripped the handles of my shopping bags tightly. "Okay."

"Firstly can I ask you if you were on any of the platforms or the station concourse at the time that the eight-ten to London Bridge arrived on platform two?" This was copper-speak for "did you see the man get squashed by the train?"

"No, I arrived before that time and left the station."

"Could you please tell me if you are from this area sir?" I thought quickly. It was a risk to tell the truth but if I lied, and he then asked for identification, it would look suspicious. I decided to go with the truth. "I'm from Brighton."

"Could you tell me what the purpose of your visit to Croydon was today sir?"

"I had a job interview earlier."

"Can I ask who with?"

"Absolutely, it was with Dunholme Lambert Insurance, the office is just off the high street." I was grateful to myself for memorising an office building I had seen, but I was telepathically begging them not to check with the company that I had really been there.

"I know it," chipped in the other officer; the first time he had spoken. "It's the new building with the mirrored panelling. They used to have a place on the industrial estate."

The first policeman glared at his partner and interrupted. "And I see you've been shopping too."

"Yes, they as good as told me I got the job so I thought I would treat myself. I've been out of work for a couple of months so haven't been shopping for ages."

"Good for you" said the second officer, receiving another

glare for his trouble.

"So can I ask you what train you took from Brighton this morning?"

I thought about saying that I took an earlier train than I had, so I could distance myself from the time of Smith's death, but I didn't know the times of any earlier trains, so if I made one up and if this copper checked a timetable it would be obvious I was lying. "I got the seven-thirteen."

"That's quite early, what time was the interview?"

"Nine o'clock."

"So what time did you get to East Croydon?"

"About ten to eight."

"That's pretty early."

Adrenaline was charging through my veins. I felt faint. "You can't trust trains anymore, they get delayed and cancelled all the time and this interview was really important to me. I would rather have got there an hour early than a minute late."

"Good for you." The second officer again. A third glare from his partner.

"So what did you do in the time between arrival and the interview?"

I felt sick. I was sure I was going to hurl all over this copper's shiny black shoes. I glanced down. They were enormous, like deep sea diver's boots. "I went to get some breakfast. It was too early to eat when I left the house this morning."

"And where did you have breakfast sir?" I wanted to scream at him to stop calling me 'sir'. Policeman always have a way of making that term sound ironic and patronising, like a disgruntled waiter taking away a dirty fork.

"I think it was called Spike's café, it's quite near the Dunholme Lambert building." I attempted a relaxed smile. "I wouldn't recommend it though, I think the health inspectors will get them soon."

"I'll take your advice on board sir." Now he was just being an arsehole. His face had remained impassive throughout the exchange, apart from the glares at his more genial partner. I was amazed that neither of them was taking notes of our conversation. "Thank you for your time, sir, and if you think of anything else you might think is relevant then please contact the Croydon police station, directory enquiries will have the number." He was surely a candidate for the most patronising man of the year competition. I didn't need advice on how to get telephone numbers, but I was happy to tolerate him. My relief was overwhelming as they stood back to let me through, signalling the end of the interview.

"Good luck with the job," said the good cop as I passed.

The digital displays announced severe delays, but I was lucky. There was a train leaving for Brighton in ten minutes that should have left nearly half an hour before. It would be arriving on platform three, right next to where Mark Smith was spread like strawberry jam along the track. There was reflective tape running the length of the platform and numerous police officers in attendance. I was glad I had waited the extra time, because it must have been chaos for a long time after the murder on an already overcrowded station. I walked down the ramp to the platform and tried to keep a low profile as I didn't want to answer any more questions, but I wasn't overly surreptitious as I didn't want to appear evasive.

The journey home was a lot more bearable than on the way up. A woman in business attire sat opposite me and talked loudly on her mobile phone about Smith's death. She was complaining that his suicide had been extremely inconvenient for all the other folk who 'wanted to go on with their lives'. I marvelled at her petty-mindedness but liked her use of the word 'suicide'. Luckily she lost signal as we went through a tunnel and I didn't have to hear her piercing voice any longer. As we neared Brighton I hit a wall of tiredness, as if I had been awake for days. It was hard to believe that I had murdered Smith only that morning. It seemed like an age ago.

* * * * * * * * * * * * * * * *

Inspector Marcus Taylor enters the room. He doesn't look nervous, which isn't normal for one of Stan's guests. I do the introductions. "Inspector Taylor this is Mr. Costanza."

I'm surprised when the copper speaks first. "Thanks Andy. Pleased to meet you Mr. Costanza."

Stan shakes his hand firmly. "Good to meet you Inspector Taylor."

"Please call me Marcus."

"Marcus. Thanks for coming. I understand you've helped me out a lot in the past, I'm sorry I haven't met you before now."

"You've helped me too Mr. Costanza." He waits for Stan to say 'call me Stan' but Stan doesn't want to be called Stan, not by this copper. Taylor carries on. "And I understand why we haven't met before, we have to be discreet don't we?"

"Yes Marcus, yes we do. Now what have you got for me?"

"This is how it is. Everyone knows it had to be a murder even though all the witnesses say he barged his way through the crowd to get to the front and then just slipped. Apparently some bloke tried to save him but nobody's been able to find him. So it looks like an accident, but on a station at rush hour there's people everywhere and nobody can really see what's going on even if it's right under their nose. It's like trying to spot a pickpocket at Mardi Gras. Chief Inspector Lewisham's not an idiot. He knows Smith was killed to stop him testifying. He's under pressure to get tough on organised crime so he's not going to let up on this one. He's not the sort of bloke you want causing you trouble. He'll never believe it was an accident, even if Smith comes back from the grave and tells him personally that he slipped."

Stan gestures for Taylor to stop talking then thinks for a while. Taylor starts to sweat but Stan takes his time. Stan looks like he's about to speak but stops himself and thinks for a bit longer. He finally says something. "This is what we do. A witness is going to come forward, someone who was right there next to the accountant when he fell on the line. He clearly saw the guy who pushed him and he'll give your police sketch artist a very accurate description." *Taylor starts to interrupt with a question.* "Let me finish." *Frank doesn't bother shouting, the copper gets the picture.* "The description will be of a man called Shaun Read. I used to work with him but now he works for Joe Barrett. He's the fat fuck's best piece of muscle, only called in for the top jobs. We'll give your Chief Inspector a little puzzle to work out, and when he cracks it he'll think he's a genius. He'll recognise the description of Read and, if he knows his arse from a hole in the ground, he'll make the link with Barrett. Does he by the way?"

Taylor looks startled. "Does he what?"

Stan looks impatient. "Keep up. Does the Chief Inspector know his arse from a hole in the ground?"

Taylor wakes up. "Yes."

"Good. So your Chief Inspector will cleverly work out that Barrett is trying to frame me by taking out the key prosecution witness in a case against me. He'll think Barrett's not happy with the money laundering rap, and wants me to go down for murder. It's just the sort of thing that fat fuck would do too. I know for a fact that his man Read got in late last night and he's been in his house alone ever since. I make it my business to know shit like that. He won't wake up until this afternoon. He's got no alibi and even if the charge doesn't stick then it will at least throw some shit Barrett's way. He deserves it for trying to pin this murder on me."

"But Mr. Costanza, he didn't try and pin it on you."

Stan grabs Taylor's lapel and pulls him close with one hand while keeping the other in his pocket. "Yes he fucking did. From now on that's what you believe. That's what you know. Got it?"

"Yes Mr. Costanza."

"Good." *Stan lets go of Taylor with a shove.* "I think we're done here.*

It was good to finally meet you Marcus."

Inspector Taylor does his best to look relaxed. "It was good to meet you too Mr. Costanza."

"Give my love to that pretty wife of yours and those darling kids. They must have both started school by now."

Taylor's eyes widen as he reads between the lines. "Yes. School. Yes."

* * * * * * * * * * * * * * * *

It felt fantastic to get home, like returning from a long-haul flight but without the nightmare of unpacking and having to do laundry. I had a bath and fell asleep several times in thirty second bursts. I smoked a joint then got into bed, loving the feeling of sleep approaching.

When my mobile rang I glanced at the display and saw that it was Colin. I was tempted to turn it off but thought he might just come round anyway. I answered it, immediately wishing I hadn't, as I couldn't face an extension of our argument from earlier, but it wasn't an argument he wanted. "Jesus, Tom, have you seen any news programs today?"

"No, I've just got back."

"Smith's death under the train. It's all over the news. They're calling it a murder."

My heart sank. "I thought they might."

"There's more."

My dreams of imminent sleep dissolved. "Shall we stop talking about this over a mobile phone line? Come over."

"You come over here."

"I'm not coming to that shithole. I'm knackered. I got up at the crack of dawn while you had a lie in."

"I'll come over if you promise not to go on about that."

"Whatever, just get over here." I ended the call and thought about getting off my bed. The next thing I knew I was waking up to the doorbell ringing furiously. I hurried downstairs.

"Christ Tom what were you doing, having a wank? Or was it a shit?"

"I fell asleep. You've got a key anyway, you're not usually reluctant to let yourself in."

"You got all shitty about it so I didn't, and judging by the last couple of times, I don't know what I'll find if I do. You might have been burying your mum in the back garden or something."

We went to the kitchen and I put the kettle on. "So what's this other stuff about Smith's murder?"

Colin's face was grave. "I think I know who you're working for."

"You mean who *we* are working for."

"It wasn't us today, it was just you."

"I thought we weren't going to go on about this."

"I agreed we wouldn't talk about me not turning up, but I never said we wouldn't talk about you hogging the Smith hit for yourself."

"But the two things are connected. We can't talk about one without the other."

"Do you want to hear who we're working for or not?"

"You're the one who keeps burbling on about other stuff, just tell me."

"The guy who was murdered, Mark Smith, he was an accountant."

"Is that supposed to mean something to me?"

"Not yet."

"Well get on with it then."

"He used to work for a bloke called Stan Costanza. Have you heard of him?"

I thought for a while before replying. "The name sounds familiar but I couldn't say who he is."

"He's your boss."

"How do you know that?"

"Costanza is what the media like to call a crime overlord. He runs a London gang who deal with drugs, robbery, extortion, all that organised crime stuff. Costanza was about to stand trial for money laundering, apparently that's all the police could get him on."

"Like Al Capone?"

"No, not like Al Capone, he was done for tax evasion."

"Isn't that the same thing as money laundering?"

"No." Colin sounded authoritative, like he'd read up on the subject.

"But there's some overlap surely?"

"No." He sounded less convincing.

"You don't know do you?"

"No. Anyway, this Mark Smith, Costanza's ex-accountant, he was the key witness for the prosecution."

"Really?"

Colin seemed a lot happier with my response this time. "And now Mark Smith has fallen under a train. And the experts reckon they won't be able to make a case now."

"Wouldn't he have been under police protection?"

"I doubt the police thought he'd be murdered on a busy station at rush hour."

"But he was right at the edge of the platform. He was almost on the track already without any help from me." My voice had become a high-pitched screech.

"So what do you think?"

"I don't know what to think. I knew I was involved with organised crime but I thought I'd just be killing other criminals."

"You didn't really think that did you? You didn't think it was like all that shit that gets spouted about the Kray Brothers, about how they only killed their own?"

"No. I guess I didn't."

"Good, I didn't think you were an idiot. There's some good news by the way."

"I could do with some."

"Well, first off, they reckon that the CCTV footage hasn't given them any clues, platform was too crowded."

My first reaction was annoyance with myself for not having considered CCTV. Back then there weren't cameras on every corner like there are now, but there were still plenty about, and definitely at railway stations. My second reaction was of course, huge relief.

"And that's not everything, they've produced one of those police sketches of the guy who did it."

"Of me? Shit."

"Calm down. I said it was good news. The bloke in the picture is bald."

"That is good news."

"And get this, he's got a beard, a massive Rasputin beard."

I allowed myself to punch the air like I'd scored the winner in the cup final.

Seventeen

I was learning to compartmentalise my brain. I had somehow managed to put all my feelings of guilt and anguish over the things I had done, particularly the murder of an innocent accountant whose only crime was to try and tell the truth, into one dark part of my mind and close the lid on it. It was my own personal oubliette and I hoped the thoughts that were dragged screaming through its iron hatch would die in there, along with my fears of being caught by the police.

Colin and I had a 'clear the air' session on the Thursday evening and eventually resolved our differences about me doing the Smith job on my own, when I offered him a token percentage of the fee in exchange for a guarantee that he would stop treating the whole thing like we were playing soldiers and start being as responsible as I'd been forced to be. Unfortunately the next hit was going to be very much like playing soldiers so I hoped he wouldn't fall at the first hurdle. I was pleased to discover he had got the paintball overalls he had promised, along with caps and protective masks. He would have got himself a gun too but I didn't want to expose him to big-mouthed Phil, so I organised that myself. Phil said he would have us something by Tuesday. This gave us plenty of leeway before the hit a week on Saturday. Colin got another gold star when he told me he had managed to borrow a car for our scouting trip to the paintball site this coming Saturday. We both agreed that we needed to get there early so we could find somewhere to park and be in position near the perimeter before the site opened. I suggested seven o'clock, but Colin inexplicably insisted on an hour earlier. I wasn't sure if he was doing this just to prove he could be responsible, but I went along with it, fully expecting him to be at least half an hour late anyway.

I hadn't seen too much of Laura because she was having a busy time at college and was working extra shifts at the Pilgrim to cover for one of the other girls who was on holiday. Our enforced absence made it easier for me to keep myself in check, preventing me from making my usual mistakes and overplaying myself. We kept in touch though, talking frequently on the telephone and exchanging soppy texts. I was sure I was breaking at least some of Colin's relationship guidelines, but he would have been pleased to hear that I turned down Laura's request to meet for breakfast on Saturday in favour of our paintball reconnaissance mission, I would never tell Colin about it though; I didn't want to give him the satisfaction. I told Laura I had promised Colin I would help him look at some cars because he was thinking of buying one. I didn't like lying to her but it was the softest option. She agreed to come for dinner on Saturday evening then stay over and spend Sunday with me.

I would have been less shocked to have seen alien invaders landing outside my house than Colin pulling up at five-fifty-seven on Saturday morning, but it was definitely him. He was in his borrowed car, a silver-grey saloon which was nicely nondescript. I had prepared some food to take with us: sausage rolls, sandwiches, crisps and a couple of bottles of Coke, but now I felt embarrassed to bring it. Colin often likened me to his mother, saying I fussed too much, and I feared this would fuel further comments of this nature, but we were going to be stuck out in the arse-end of nowhere and I didn't want to get hungry, so I picked up my bag of provisions and left the house.

Colin, like me was dressed in black. It was obviously going to be another gloriously bright day, Colin was enjoying being behind the wheel and I just admired the scenery. We didn't talk much because we were both still half asleep, but we did eventually have a conversation when we stopped at a garage to get some petrol. After paying for the fuel and returning to the car he noticed my bag for the first time. "What have you got in there?"

"Provisions."

"Oh shit. I thought we were just checking it out today? You haven't brought your gun and overalls have you? I'm not getting my gun until Tuesday."

"It's not that. It's food."

"What food?"

"Sausage rolls and stuff."

"What, like a picnic?" He leaned across me and rummaged in the bag, pulling out a sandwich triumphantly. "It is a picnic! Have you got a flask? I bet you've got a flask."

"So you won't be wanting any food then?" I held the bag to my lap so he couldn't get anything from it and snatched the sandwich from his waving hand.

"I didn't say that."

"What did you say then?"

"I didn't say anything."

I held up the sandwich, "hmmm BLT, so you won't be wanting any BLT?"

"I didn't say anything."

"You were taking the piss. You said I'd brought a picnic."

Colin was eyeing the sandwich hungrily. "I said 'great, a picnic, nice one'."

"So you revoke all rights to taking the piss out of the fact that I brought a bag of food." I felt it was important to get the words right so the agreement could be carved in stone.

Colin made a show of putting his hand on his heart. "I hereby declare that I, Colin Parker, will not mock Mr. Thomas White for having brought what some could describe as a 'baby picnic' on a mission to plan a murder."

I shielded the food with my arms. "Fuck off, that's it. It's all going to be mine. I don't even want it all but I'm going to stuff it in until I feel really sick."

"What are you talking about? I took the oath didn't I?"

"You didn't do it properly."

"Yes I did."

"No you didn't, you called it a baby picnic."

"I'm sorry, it's not a baby picnic, I hereby declare and all that."

I gave him a sandwich.

"Thanks mum."

I punched his arm as hard as the confinement of the car allowed. He spent the next ten minutes scaring the shit out of me by driving one handed and eating his sandwich at the same time, and I was glad when he finished his food and could give his full attention to the business of driving. The roads were clear and we chewed up the miles quickly.

"We are now entering Hampshire," Colin read the sign we were passing. "This is it Tom, we're crossing a frontier, this is a new dawn, a new beginning."

"You're bored aren't you?"

"God yes. And my arm's still sore."

"Good." I pulled out my road atlas and the map Stephanie had given me.

"Weren't you meant to burn that?" Colin looked concerned.

"I'll burn it later, we're not actually killing anyone today so it's not much of a risk." I noticed Colin's glance. "And no, I'm not going to eat it."

We found the paintball site and drove past the entrance,

looking for a turning into the small road that ran near the west side of the site. A nature reserve backed onto the paintball land, and there was a small National Trust car park with a couple of cars in it already. This was ideal; I had been worried the car would look suspicious if we just parked it at the side of the road.

"Here goes then, let's go and learn our battleground." I was trying to be uplifting.

Colin was unmoved. "All in good time Tom. We need to eat at least two sausage rolls first." I was a bit peckish too so I didn't argue. We rushed down the food while trying to spot some wildlife in the expanse of nature reserve in front of us. Our stationary safari was unsuccessful. I waited patiently for Colin to finish his second sausage roll then we both washed the food down with some Coke. We were ready.

We locked the car and got our bearings on the map. "It's about a mile and a half from here," I said.

Colin didn't need to voice his opinion on this, his face said it all, but he spoke anyway. "A mile and a half, bugger that. That's miles." He didn't seem to understand why I found this funny.

We left the car park and crossed the road, then headed north-east across country where Stephanie's map said there was no fence at the site perimeter. It wasn't much fun. Despite the weather being good, the long grass was wet with dew and neither Colin nor I was wearing suitable footwear. Our canvas trainers were instantly soaked through and we felt thistles, and God knew what else, assaulting our ill-protected feet. After the first few hundred yards we approached some woodland and noted how exposed the path we had just taken had been. We looked back to see if there was another route that would provide more cover for when we had completed the hits and were making our escape, perhaps if we parked the car further up the road. Unfortunately we could see the road for miles, which indicated that the last stretch on the way back was going to be exposed however far around we went. We decided we'd have to lump it and take the risk. We entered the canopy of trees.

"I hope we're still going north-east." I knew I had no sense of direction.

"Hold on a minute." We stopped, and Colin rummaged in the inside pocket of his jacket. He pulled out a small flat object and stared at it. "Yes, this is the way."

"Is that a compass?"

"It is indeed. You've got to be prepared for all eventualities. I told you I could be responsible. Come on, admit it, you're impressed."

I couldn't deny it.

This was more fun, we were soldiers in the undergrowth. We had a compass. We were keeping low. Nasty pointy nature was still lacerating our feet though. We had been moving for nearly twenty minutes and I was starting to think we should be approaching the site by now. "Are you sure we're going the right way Col?"

Colin checked his compass, then his watch. "We should be nearly there. What's that up ahead?" He pointed at an area in front where there seemed to be a long clearing in the trees. "I think that's the ditch, we're nearly there." We negotiated our way through the remaining trees to get to the clearing, but then our hearts sank in unison. It was the ditch, we could see the ground drop away, but it was packed with dense undergrowth, gorse bushes and nettles.

I spoke first. "Impenetrable."

"Shit. We're just going to have to follow it along and hope it gets clearer at some point."

"It's probably like this all the way along."

"Have you got any better ideas?"

We headed north and followed the line of the ditch. After about five minutes we struck gold; a concrete pipe, about two yards wide traversing the ditch and burying itself into either side. The top of the pipe was about a foot below ground level and although it was overhung with brambles on either side, it looked like it could be crossed with only a little discomfort. Colin led the way and we quickly found that it was still a massive struggle to get across. We were practically crawling, hugging the curved top of the pipe like horizontal koalas. At one point Colin pushed an overhanging branch out of his way and when he had passed he let it spring back. I raised my head just in time for it to catch me across the face. He ignored my torrent of abuse.

We finally made it over the ditch and into the trees beyond. "So is this the site?" Colin asked. We could see that the woodland opened onto an expanse of land about thirty yards in front of us.

"It must be." We moved closer to the edge of the clearing and lay on the ground. The clearing was in a long strip, like a golf course, punctuated with the odd tree and mound of earth, presumably for hiding behind whilst playing army. We were near the left hand end of the strip. To the right it swept downwards then back up again where there was a building at the far end. The whole area was surrounded by woodland. Stephanie had said the site was fifty acres; the open area wasn't nearly that big so I assumed that it included at least some of the woodland. I pointed at the building, "That must be where they keep all the toy guns and overalls and stuff." Colin didn't answer me so I looked over at him. He was squinting into a pair of small binoculars. "Bloody hell mate you really have come prepared haven't you?"

Colin didn't look up. "If you fail to prepare you prepare to fail."

"Okay, well done on the binoculars and the compass but don't start being an arse."

"Sorry mate." He still hadn't looked up.

"Can I have a go?" I thought Colin would tell me to stick it, but he handed them over to me. I looked through and could see the same as before but a little bigger and slightly out of focus. I twiddled the knob between the lenses and it improved slightly but it was still better with the naked eye. "I don't think I'm doing it right Col."

"No, you're fine, they're rubbish." He took them off me and stuffed them into his jacket pocket.

We lay on the ground and stared for a while. "So what are we doing then?" I asked eventually.

"Fuck knows."

"Don't call me fuck nose."

We lay in silence for a while.

Colin spoke. "I've got spiny stuff in my socks."

"There's bits of tree in my hair."

It was nine-thirty and we were sure there would be a group of paintballers arriving soon. We decided to follow the edge of the clearing while remaining under the cover of the trees to try and get an idea of the layout of the site. After a while we heard voices but didn't see any people until we got about fifty feet away from the building at the top of the slope. We were behind some bracken, lying as close to the ground as we could. Our view was limited but it was more important to stay out of sight. There was a tall man with a beard standing just outside the door of the building and it was clear from his countenance that he ran the place. He was chatting to a group consisting of three teenagers and one older man, presumably the father of one of them. Another almost identical group walked into view; three teenage boys and a man. From the handshakes and congratulations it was easy to spot the birthday boy. Another carload arrived; a bigger car apparently; five more teenage boys and one girl. The man who accompanied them had the look of a people-carrier driver, and I guessed he had been just dying to get an opportunity to show off his giant vehicle to the fathers of his kid's friends.

Colin nudged me and gestured that we go further back into the woods. This wasn't easy to do without being seen and it took us some time before we were out of sight and able to talk freely. Colin spoke. "So what are we doing then? They're going to be ages before they start. Do you think we've got enough of an idea about the place? We know how to get in now. I'm not sure what else we can achieve by lurking in the woods."

I felt I should be pushing for us to stay but realised he was right. There wasn't much benefit in staying there. I was about to answer when Colin unzipped his flies and turned away from me. "What are you doing?" My voice was a high-pitched whisper.

"Having a piss, what does it look like?" I needed to go as well so I turned my back on him and did the same. We were like two duellers caught short long before the ten paces were up.

We made our way through the trees until we found our crossing point and shuffled painfully across. I couldn't wait to get home and have a bath. It felt like I had more thistle than foot in my trainers, and my hands and face were filthy. I pointed in one direction. "It's that way isn't it?"

Colin pointed in a different direction. "I think it's that way. Let's consult the compass shall we?"

"You just want to play with your new toy."

"Bloody right, how often do you get to use a compass for real? It's like being in the scouts again."

"You were never in the scouts were you?"

"No."

"Maybe if you had been you wouldn't be so excited about using a compass."

"Whatever." He had the compass on his palm and was trying to hold it still while squinting at the dial. "I was right." He pointed in the direction he had indicated a moment ago. "It's that way, my way." He started singing: "Start spreading the news, I'm leaving today…"

"That's not 'My Way', that's 'New York New York'. You're a penis."

We reached the edge of the woods and tried our best to look like hikers as we crossed the last open stretch and crossed the road to get to the car park. We were so glad to get to the car that we exchanged a high-five, something we had never done in all the time we had known each other. We sat sideways in the front seats with our legs sticking out of our respective doors and removed our shoes. We set about the laborious task of picking the prickles out of our socks. It was tempting to rush the job so we could get home more quickly, but we both knew how uncomfortable it would be if we didn't get as many of the tiny spines out as possible.

"We've learnt a lot today" Colin ventured. "We've found out where to park, where to cross the ditch, or the ravine as I'm going to call it from now on, and we know we should wear better shoes and bring spare socks."

"And we should dress more like walkers so we're less conspicuous on that open stretch."

"What do walkers dress like?"

"Badly, hiking boots, trousers tucked into big socks, functional anorak and normally a beard."

"We could get false beards." I couldn't tell if Colin was joking or not.

We ate the rest of the food I had brought, even though it

had gone a bit manky in the warm parked car, then started driving. "So how are things going with Laura?"

"Really well, although we haven't seen too much of each other as she's got loads of college work to do and she's working extra shifts."

"I'd work extra shifts to get away from you. Are you keeping yourself under control, you haven't proposed to her or anything?"

"Fuck off. I don't need to keep myself under control."

"You do and you know it." He was right and he knew he was, but I wasn't going to admit it.

"Shall we stop for breakfast?" I knew the mention of food would get Colin off the subject.

"That's the best idea you've had all day Thomas. I think there's a service station about twenty miles away. He spent the next twenty miles planning in surprising detail what he was going to have to eat.

Eighteen

It was two in the afternoon by the time Colin dropped me home. I smoked an enormous reefer then soaked in the bath for ages, trying to soothe my pin-cushion feet. Laura wasn't due for dinner until eight so I had the afternoon to myself, and chose to use it wisely by watching back-to-back Twilight Zone episodes on a dodgy digital channel. Suddenly it was after six and I had to leap into action and tidy the house and clear the backlog of washing up before she arrived. I had thought about cooking for Laura, but it wasn't really fair to her. She deserved something nice to eat so I opted for a take out. I rang her at seven-thirty to find out what she wanted so I could place the order in good time for her arrival. She chose Thai. When she arrived she was ten minutes late but looked even more gorgeous than I remembered so I forgave her tardiness immediately.

Laura smiled when she saw my dining table, which was candlelit and under a cloth for the first time ever. "This is nice. You shouldn't have gone to so much trouble."

"It was no trouble." This was true. It had been the vacuuming, dusting and the rest of the chores in preparation for this most regal of visits that had been troublesome, not throwing a piece of fabric over the table and lighting a few candles. I had some joints already rolled but we had to delay smoking any because the food arrived. I told her to choose a CD while I dished up in the kitchen. I had ordered a range of dishes so I would be sure Laura liked at least some of them, so it took me half a dozen trips back and forth to bring it all in, and the small dining table was eventually covered with an obscene amount of food. It turned out that Laura liked everything except some unidentifiable dish comprising mostly of batter that I couldn't remember ordering.

At the beginning of the meal I couldn't take my eyes off her mouth and couldn't wait to get her into bed, but as the food started piling up in my gut my sexual appetite receded. This made me better company than I would have been; it meant Laura could savour her dinner rather than being forced to wolf it down and dragged to bed. Laura talked the most, telling me about her week, about her insane sounding college tutor and the quirks of some of the stranger regulars at the Pilgrim.

After dinner I insisted that Laura sit on the sofa while I cleared away the remains of our banquet, like a nuclear war in a catering firm. She agreed surprisingly readily. I had my usual dilemma of whether or not to keep the leftovers to eat later, but past history told me it would only end up in the bin anyway, so I cut out the middleman, or the middle-fridge.

"Do you want some help?" Laura called from the lounge as I clattered and scraped in the kitchen.

"No, you're fine. You can start one of those reefers if you want."

"I'll wait for you."

The bin was nearly collapsing under its load. I rinsed the plates and cutlery and left them reasonably tidily by the sink, hoping I wouldn't be too depressed by the sight in the morning. I took a fresh bottle of wine from the fridge and went into the lounge where Laura was half laying on the sofa. She wasn't wearing any tights and her denim skirt had ridden up her legs exposing her thighs. She was wearing a sleeveless T-shirt and all that delicious flesh on show sent my libido back into orbit. Laura lit one of the joints and I watched her lips close around it. A few weeks ago it actually hurt to think of those lips because I never thought I would stand a chance. It was surprising how easy it now was to take her and her mouth for granted, so I vowed always to be grateful and to celebrate what I had. I topped up our glasses.

We had eaten a lot and now we smoked a lot and drank a lot, and all the while we were laughing a lot. Our time apart meant that the night felt more like a second or third date but without the pressure. It was a perfect evening topped by an amazing night in bed. After we had finished for the final time Laura dozed off and I watched her sleeping for ages, telling her how beautiful she was, hoping she couldn't hear me but then realising that I didn't really care if she did.

* * * * * * * * * * * * * * *

"You know you were always my father's number one don't you?"

"Nah, Frank was Tony's golden boy. He saw him like a son."

"He saw you both as sons Cheese."

"I guess that makes us brother and sister."

Steph laughs but I see what she's getting at. She's gorgeous, there's no getting round it, but I don't fancy her. I've known her since she was a baby. She was Tony Visconti's pride and joy. Most men in this business would be gutted not to have a son, but Tony was different, he was crazy about his little princess, proud as punch. He would be even more proud if he could see her now, all grown up. He was robbed of so much. Steph's beautiful, she's got brains, and she's completely set on getting her way. She's just like her old man, except for the looks. She got those from her mum.

"Have you had your talk with Frank yet?"

I swallow, like I'm a kid and the teacher's asking for my homework. "I can't find the right time."

"I don't know why you're putting it off. He's bound to go for the idea."

"I'm not worried that he won't go for the plan, I'm worried about

telling him so late in the day. Frank's pretty paranoid, he might think we had other plans for him at first but just happened to change our minds and decided to bring him in."

Steph looks shocked. *"Surely Frank knows you wouldn't do anything to harm him."*

"Yeah, deep down he knows. But he knows there are, what do you call them? Precedents. Look at Costanza and Barrett. They used to be best buddies when they worked for your dad but now they'd rip each other apart given half a chance."

"Stan and Joe are insane. They're nothing like you and Frank."

"As you know Steph, this game's all about instincts. Frank's have always been sharp and he's always on guard - he'll just see danger, not reason. When Stan and Joe turned on their own boss nobody saw it coming. That sort of thing just wasn't done, but they did it. It changed everything."

"Don't you think I know that? He was my father." Steph's eyes are welling up. *"I'm sorry, I'm not crying."* She wipes her eyes hard, like she's trying to force the tears back in. *"You said you were worried about telling him so late in the day. If that's the case then it doesn't make sense to delay any longer."* Steph talks posh, she's lost the cockney that the rest of us have got, but even though she's been living in America she hasn't picked up a Yank accent. Her Uncle Bobby insisted on an English nanny, poached from some fading aristo, and she was home-schooled, so her voice sounds like the World Service.

"I know that Steph, but I've got to do it at the right time."

"I'll tell him."

"No, no you can't. He'll definitely think we've been going behind his back if you bring it up. I'll do it."

"Do it soon."

"The thing is Steph, we have been going behind his back."

"Only because we had to, Frank doesn't think the time's right to go for Costanza. Now we've set things in motion he should be more easily persuaded."

"Okay I'll tell him next time I see him."

She relaxes. *"Good, thanks. So how about our young Mr. White then?"*

"You were right about him Steph, he's doing better than I thought he would. How many scalps has he got now?"

"Three."

"It seems like more."

She thinks for a while and counts on her fingers. *"Clarke and Smith for Costanza and Hunter for Barrett. And of course there was his neighbour but that doesn't really count. It's a shame about Smith."*

"The accountant?"

"Yes. He was a civilian. I had hoped Costanza would only use Tom for inside targets."

"You can't have been too hopeful. Stan's not choosy about who he takes out."

"I know, and I'm not going to feel too guilty about it. Smith was an innocent, unconnected man, but Stan would have got him with or without Tom."

"You know Stan's going to pin it on Barrett don't you?"

She grins. *"That's even better than I thought."*

"You've started rocking the applecart just like you said you would. I just hope White can dodge bullets. I kind of like the guy."

"So do I. There's something about him. I can't help but admire him. He doesn't seem very confident to speak to, but when you think about the hits he's pulled off, he must be a whole different person when he's working."

"Invisible."

Steph's eyes widen. *"Exactly! Invisible. How does he do it? He killed Hunter at Hunter's house surrounded by Hunter's party guests then walked onto a railway station at rush hour and pushed Smith in front of a train."*

"And nobody saw him. So what's next Steph?"

"I persuaded Joe that he should take out the Calsons, I said it would

hurt Costanza badly."

"The twins? Christ Steph that will hurt Stan. The Calsons have got the sticks sewn up. Take any poxy little town in the south with a drug problem and it's a given that the twins are running the show there for Stan."

"Exactly, it'll hit Stan hard but it'll hurt Joe more because Stan will throw everything at him."

"There's going to be a war."

"That's what I'm banking on." Steph's not looking at me anymore, she's lost in her thoughts.

* * * * * * * * * * * * * * *

"Joe, if you go for the Calsons it'll be war. It's that simple."

"Geoff, I know Costanza, he doesn't want a war, his operations are running smooth. A war would cost him too much."

"Listen, Joe. I may not have been best pals with Costanza like you were, but I know this, if you hit the Calsons it'll be like Pearl fucking Harbour. Costanza will come at you with everything he's got." Joe raises an eyebrow to acknowledge my use of the profanity. I don't normally swear at him.

"Stan doesn't want a war." His tone says I'm getting tiresome.

"How can you be so sure?"

"I," he hesitates. "I just know."

"It's that woman isn't it? Stephanie, she's told you Stan doesn't want a war."

"Don't fucking start Geoff." He bangs the table. "I asked for information and I got it. It doesn't matter who gave it to me."

"Why do you want to hit the Calsons anyway?"

"They're getting tighter with their territory. Our boys haven't got any room to move."

"We seemed to be doing fine the last time I checked."

"'Fine' isn't good enough, I want everything Costanza's got and I'm going to take it, piece by piece."

"You used to tell me that the first thing Tony Visconti ever taught you was that mixing business and pleasure was like mixing gin and whisky."

"Tony Visconti's dead."

"Yes, two of his rising stars felt they weren't rising fast enough."

"I don't need you to tell me what happened, Geoff."

"All I'm saying is you should be careful. Trust your own judgement, not someone else's. Not until you're sure they've got the same agenda as you."

"Are they more of Tony Visconti's words?"

"They're your words Joe."

"The order's been made. I couldn't change it even if I wanted to. I'd look weak."

* * * * * * * * * * * * * * *

I was on a raft in the middle of a pond, lying flat on my back. I felt physically comfortable, but with a growing sense of unease in my head. The raft started to rock, which I found irritating, and I looked up and saw my parents in the water at one side of the pond. My mother was dressed as a fairy princess, while my father was wearing one of those Victorian bathing costumes, the sort you see on old newsreel footage, with black and white hoops that covered his whole body. He had an ornate moustache that curled up at the corners, and his hair was parted at the centre and waxed down close to the scalp. They were standing about ten feet apart and throwing a beach ball to each other but each time the ball was thrown it would become as heavy as concrete whilst in mid-air and fall straight down into the water, causing an enormous splash. The ball would then become light again and one of my parents would retrieve it, take a few paces back then throw it again. This happened over and over, and the waves upsetting my raft grew bigger and more frequent.

"Tom, wake up, it's time for breakfast." I slipped off the

raft and into my bed. I opened my eyes and looked at Laura, who was gently rocking me and speaking softly, almost singing. "Time for breakfast time for breakfast."

"How long have you been doing that?"

"Quite a while actually, I was trying to be gentle so I didn't give you a rude awakening but you didn't seem to want to wake up, so I had to get quite rough by the end." She had showered and dressed and looked immaculate.

I yawned, taking care to cover my mouth because I was conscious of my morning breath especially as she smelt minty-fresh from the toothpaste. "Why did you wake me up?"

Laura grabbed my hand with both of hers and spoke quickly, affecting a child's voice. "I'm hungry I'm hungry, you need to take me out for breakfast."

I yawned again. "Can't we just have something here?" Colin would have been proud of me, this definitely wasn't overselling myself.

Laura maintained her playful voice. "No no no no, we need to go and get a slap up."

"I'm tired."

"I'll make you a cup of tea while you're in the shower." She left the room, leaving me no choice but to get up.

When I was dressed I went downstairs and saw that Laura had forgotten all about making me a cup of tea. I thought better of mentioning it, and we left the house and headed for the café round the corner. "Isn't this a bit public?" I said as we sat down. "I thought you didn't want to let anyone know we're together?"

"Oh, yes. Sorry I've told loads of people. You don't mind, do you?"

"I don't mind at all, it was your idea to keep it secret, I was just going along with it. What made you change your mind?"

"I just forgot. Why did I want to keep it secret again?"

"You didn't want anyone gossiping about us."

"I remember. Oh well, fuck 'em."

It was interesting to see the real Laura. When I had worshipped her from afar she exuded confidence and wisdom and now it was nice to see her making the same mistakes as everyone else, not because I wanted to belittle her but because it highlighted the fact that I was closer to her now. We both ordered a full English and sat in silence waiting for the food to arrive, our hunger being too great for conversation. The waiter, who was also the cook, placed our plates in front of us. They overflowed with food. The first few mouthfuls silenced our stomachs and we relaxed and started talking.

"What are your plans for the week?"

"I'm going to find a new job, I'm not going back to the hospital. I'll ring them on Monday. It's shit there."

"You seem to be okay for money." Her statement was innocent but an image of all the blood money hidden inside my hi-fi jumped into my mind. Soon there would be no more room for it all, even after giving Colin his share. I kept meaning to think about laundering the money, but I didn't really know what that entailed.

"The money from the hospital wasn't too bad and my outgoings aren't huge. The mortgage on the house is really low."

"Lucky you, you don't want to know how much my rent is."

The words "why don't you move in with me?" tried to jump out of my mouth but I kept them in.

"I wasn't hinting that I should move in with you by the way." She accompanied the statement with a nervous laugh.

Now I didn't know what to think. The fact that she was saying she wasn't hinting suggested that maybe she was. I now thought I should at least acknowledge her disguised request, if indeed it was that. "How long do you think couples should be going out before they live together?"

"I don't agree with living in sin, I think people should wait until they're married. In fact, I've been wanting to talk about us." She leaned forward.

I leaned back. "Are you saying we should get married?" I dreaded to think what expression I had on my face as I said this.

"No, well not yet anyway." She stirred her tea idly. "I just think we shouldn't have sex anymore, not until we do eventually get married."

I stared back at her as she continued to stir her tea. She raised her eyes, they were full of sorrow. She lowered her gaze again. I racked my brains to think of something to say. Spending the rest of my life with Laura was a fine prospect but my natural aversion to the words "marriage" and "shouldn't have sex" was throwing my head into an unpleasant spin. "Whatever you want," I said eventually, so quietly that I hoped she wouldn't even hear it. I wanted the benefit of having said 'the right thing' but didn't want to consent to her outrageous suggestion. Her head seemed to move involuntarily and I realised she was sobbing silently. I instantly felt bad about thinking such selfish thoughts and cupped her face and raised it towards me.

"Got you!" She was pissing herself.

Nineteen

On the Tuesday evening before the double hit on Max and Jasper Calson, I picked up Colin's new gun. Phil and I met in a pub (not the Pilgrim, Laura hadn't made any comments about my associations for a while and I wanted it to stay that way) and swapped bags. I had also ordered more bullets, and Phil had come up with the goods even though he had to get two different types for the different guns. Colin's new weapon looked impressive. It was more modern, like something out of a Hollywood shoot-em-up. I considered keeping it for myself rather than passing it on to Colin, but I didn't want to give him the opportunity to whinge about anything else and besides, there were Monica's feelings to consider.

"You building a collection then?" This was Phil's extremely witty and observant question. I considered shooting him in the foot just to keep him on his toes but then realised a foot wound was more likely to keep him off his toes. When he didn't get a response from me he moved on. "You didn't want a silencer did you?"

"Not at the moment, I'll give you a shout if I do."

"Right, let me know and I'll sort you out."

"Right."

"So how's it going Tom?"

I knew he wasn't just being friendly; he wanted to know what all this firepower was being used for.

"Is that the time? I must be off." I took a swig of my half-full pint and stood up. "Thanks Phil, see you soon."

Colin came over to mine and was chuffed to bits with his new toy, I'm sure if I hadn't given him a bollocking about acting as though this was all a game he would have asked me to re-enact scenes from Goodfellas with him. Instead he just bragged about how much better than Monica his gun was.

"Look at this fine piece of craftsmanship, sleek, modern. Not like the antique you carry around with you."

"Monica's not old."

Colin wasn't listening, he was gazing wistfully at his new weapon. "I'm going to call him Dave."

"You can't call it that, that's a shit name for a gun. It has to be a girl's name."

"Why?"

"Because that's the done thing."

"Bollocks, I'm calling it Dave, calling *him* Dave."

"Do what you like mate. You'll be the laughing stock at the Hitmen's Gala Dinner."

"I will do what I like. I think you should change Monica's name. You should give her something more suited to her advancing years, like Ada or Dot."

"Monica pisses on Dave."

"Only because she's so old. Her bladder muscles have given out."

"Fair enough, that was a good one, I'll give you that. So, what's the plan for Saturday, what time are we going to leave?"

"Do you want to go early again?" It was obvious from Colin's tone that he was trying to sound enthusiastic but really didn't want to get up at the crack of dawn again.

"I suppose it depends on what our plan is, when we're expecting to make our move."

"We don't have a plan do we Tom?"

"No."

"Right." He paused. "Do you think we should think of one?" He gazed absently down the sight of his gun.

"Careful, that's loaded. Yes, we should think of a plan."

He lowered the gun. "We need to think of a plan."

"Okay."

He looked at the floor then back to me, "Right."

"Okay."

"Right," he said.

We were silent for a moment and I absently started to roll a joint.

"No Tom, we can't smoke, we'll never think of a plan if we get caned."

I had to concede that he was right and put the drug paraphernalia down. "We'd better think of something quickly then. What have we got? We've got twins, it's their birthday and all their mates are there. We've snuck in through the back way, we've crossed a big concrete pipe and we're lying in the woods armed and ready."

"Me with Dave and you with Monica."

"Exactly. Armed to the teeth."

"Okay Tom, let's say we get there as early as we did when we checked the place out. We'd get in position near the building and wait an hour or so until the group started turning up, and they'd chat to the beardy guy who runs the place while they waited for the rest to turn up. Do you think we could take them out at that point?"

"I guess not, but Colin?"

"What?"

"I can see what you're doing, you're trying to make sure we don't have to get up really early again."

"Okay, you got me. But I'm right aren't I? There's no point in getting there too early, we're better off turning up when the game's in full swing. They'll be focussed on being toy soldiers and their guard will be down."

I didn't want to get up early either. "I suppose you're right, let's leave at nine then we'll be ready and lurking in the woods before lunchtime. We've got to accept that it's impossible to have a firm idea of what we're going to do without knowing where the targets are going to be. Really we should have stayed all day when we went last time, to see what kind of games they play and where we might get a good shot."

"Yes, we should have done, shame that." I knew Colin was thinking exactly the same as me; that there was no reason why we couldn't skip work and go to the site again before Saturday and watch another party for the whole day, so we would see everything that happened, and would know where the targets were likely to be. I also knew that we were both hoping that the other one wasn't going to suggest doing this, even though it was the right and professional thing to do.

Neither of us suggested it.

Colin quickly continued. "If we get there before lunch there might be an opportunity to get some shots in when they break for food, or otherwise we just wait for the right moment while they're playing soldiers, if there is a right moment."

"Can I make a reefer now?"

"Yes, Thomas you can."

I didn't see Laura until Thursday as we continued to take things slowly. I was relieved when she told me she would be seeing her friends after work on Friday evening and going clubbing. This meant she wouldn't be there when I left on Saturday morning, so I wouldn't have any trouble getting Monica from her hiding place and out of the house.

The weather had been lovely for ages, so I didn't expect the storm that arrived in the early hours of Saturday morning. My first thought was that it was a portent of bad things to come. It sounded like somebody was machine-gunning the windows with ball bearings. I didn't know how localised it was and if it was a similar story in Hampshire, but I decided to put off worrying about it until the morning. Unfortunately the storm was still raging when I woke up again at eight so I checked the weather on the internet. The whole of the south on the forecast map for that day had 'storms expected, massive gusts and heavy rain' plastered over it, and I wondered why they felt they needed to describe what a storm was. I checked a few other sites and they told a similar story, except one, which forecast bright sunshine.

I called Colin. He answered his phone quickly. "Morning Tom, you trying to get out of going out in this typhoon?"

"No, I just wanted to check you were still up for it." I tried not to let my hope of him cancelling show in my voice.

"I am indeed still up for it." My heart sank. "Were you expecting something different?"

"Do you think the Calsons' paintball party will still go ahead then?"

"I don't know Tom, but we've got to be there even if there's only a faint chance that the twins will be. If they turn up and we're not there then you'll get all sorts of grief from that Costanza guy."

"I'm hoping we'll never see Costanza, there seems to be quite a hierarchy between us and him."

"I still don't think we should take any chances. We can always come back if they don't show, then you can report back honestly to that bird that the targets simply weren't where they were supposed to be."

"Stephanie."

"Yeah, her. By the way, I'll bring you a decent coat, I've got a spare. It's awful out there."

"Thanks." I hung up. I was more nervous now than for any of the hits so far. I didn't feel like eating but I managed to force half a bowl of cereal down. Colin and I had agreed that it would be best not to put on the paintball gear until we got to Hampshire, as we thought we would look a tad suspicious if anybody saw us dressed like army cadets on the way there. I wore jogging bottoms so I could get changed easily at the other end, and put on a pair of old walking boots that I used to wear to rock festivals, 'stout' was the best word to describe them, and I knew they would offer more protection than my trainers had the week before. Colin arrived in his borrowed car and I double checked that I had Monica and spare bullets. I didn't bring the silencer as the weight of it affected my aim, and besides, Colin's weapon wasn't silenced and it was likely we would be firing together, so we'd be making a racket anyway. We had memorised the map and the photographs of the twins. I was travelling light, not risking more piss-taking from Colin by bringing a picnic. The wind caught the car door as I opened it, nearly ripping it off its hinges. It was a struggle to close. "Christ, it's nasty. Look at me, I'm soaked. How long was I outside? Less than 5 seconds? I should have worn a coat just for the few yards from my house to the car."

We started moving and Colin gestured to the back seat with a jerk of his head. "You'll dry out quickly enough, and once you're there you'll be protected from whatever the weather throws at you. Have a look at the pair of beauties I brought along."

I looked behind me. "You're joking, right?"

Colin took a good look at the road in front then turned his head right round to make sure the coats he'd brought were indeed on the back seat. I was relieved when he faced the road again. "What do you mean? They'll keep us dry and toasty. I thought you'd be grateful."

"Isn't there something about them that tells you they're not suitable for a premeditated murder?"

"What do you mean?"

"They're fluorescent yellow!"

He looked genuinely confused. "So?"

"So we may as well hold up a banner that says 'woo hoo! Over here'."

"Shit, you're right. Before you say it, yes I'm an idiot."

I wasn't going to let his admission spoil my fun. "You're a fucking idiot. What were you thinking?"

"I know, I've just said I'm an idiot."

"But you are, you're so much of an idiot. You've made being an idiot into an art form."

"You're a tiresome prick. Stop now, you've had your fun."

"I'm still having fun, it's not over. This one's going to run and run. Bright yellow fucking jackets, Jesus."

"What are we going to do? I can't go outside in this weather with just this jumper. We could be out there for hours."

"Haven't you got anything else at home?"

"Nothing that'll be any good in this weather, just my bomber jacket."

"We'll have to buy a couple of raincoats at the mall."

"Fuck that, the queue for parking will be huge, you know what it's like on a Saturday morning. Wait a minute, let's try here." He stopped the car outside a charity shop.

"You want me to wear some dead man's coat that probably won't even fit me?"

"Let's just have a quick look. It's got to be fate. We need coats and just as we were talking about it we reached this shop. And there's this parking space right outside. It's definitely fate. I'm a strong believer in fate."

"Since when?"

"Since just then, come on."

I braced myself to get wet again and jumped out of the car. In the few seconds it took us to get into the shop we were soaked.

"Good morning boys." There were two women behind the counter. I guessed their combined age to be around a hundred and ninety. The one who was speaking to us seemed to have blue make-up on her cheeks while the other one, who was silent and seemed to be gazing at the counter for no apparent reason, had her cheeks done in bright pink. I concluded that they had applied each other's.

"This probably won't be the only time you'll hear this request today," Colin spoke in a voice that I recalled him using on my mother on the few times he had met her, "but we need raincoats, do you have any?"

The silent women who I had thought was comatose suddenly burst into life, as if an air-raid siren had just gone off. "Yes, yes raincoats yes!" She barked, her head quivering like a Jack Russell. "Raincoats, yes." She froze and reverted to her catatonia. The other woman took over and pointed to a rack that was overflowing with coats. She cocked her head to one side and watched us approach the rail, beaming like a proud parent at a school sports day.

"What about this one?" Colin was holding a thick tweed overcoat that would have been too big for the two of us at once.

"Stop pissing about. Let's just get going as quickly as we can." I flicked my way along the rail and was surprised to find something that looked like it might fit. It was a light grey raincoat that appeared to be from the seventies. It had vast lapels and a belt at the waist. I put it on and it fitted perfectly. Colin started humming the theme from 'The Pink Panther'. "I don't really care what I look like. We're going to be in the middle of nowhere. At least it'll keep me dry."

"Alright grumpy pants, it's lovely, now let's have a look for me."

I nudged him. "She's still staring at us you know."

Colin had his back to the women and didn't turn round. "What about the other one?" He was whispering. "The raincoat shouter?"

"She's still dead."

Colin held up a coat. "How about this one, it's similar to yours."

He was holding what was obviously a woman's coat. It was plastic, almost transparent, grey in colour with an unmistakeable tinge of pink. The white plastic buttons were the size of saucers. It had a vinyl belt sporting a plastic buckle that matched the buttons. I looked at his eyes to work out if this was a joke. I wasn't sure it was. I didn't know how to respond, I just looked at him.

"Well what do you think? It'll do won't it?"

I carried on looking at his eyes and realised he was deadly serious. My instinct was to collapse with laughter, but I tried to control it. I needed him to buy this coat. I was already visualising him hiding in the woods dressed as his grandmother. It would simply have been the best thing ever. I lost it, my face cracked into a grin.

"What's funny?" Colin looked at the coat then back at me.

I'd almost blown it. I had to think fast. I let the smile continue and whispered, "she's still staring."

Colin glanced towards her and suppressed a laugh of his own. I'd done it. He'd bought my story and now he was going to buy the lady-coat.

We went back to the till and paid for our purchases, telling the woman to put the change in the collection jar. This prompted the response: "Really? Are you sure? Perhaps you could buy something else with the difference?"

"No, it's fine, really. We've got everything we need." As I spoke the coma-woman seemed to have another electric current passed through her, but this time she didn't speak. Instead she started pulling fervently at the slab of carrier bags on the counter, her fingers never quite making the right contact to strip the top one away. She was like a wind-up toy, waving her wrist in a repeated arc, swatting at the polythene. Her associate leant across and stripped a bag away, and the coma-woman became a petrified statue once more. "It's okay, we don't need bags thanks," I said, feeling awkward.

Colin gestured towards the downpour outside. "I think the coats will come in useful straight away." He had adopted his addressing-someone-older-than-fifty persona again.

The non coma-woman looked at the rain and back at Colin with a puzzled expression on her face. "You think they'll come in useful?"

Colin looked at me for assistance but I made it clear he was on his own on this one. He looked back at the woman. "Yes, I think they might." He shrugged his shoulders and put on his polite smile again.

"You think?" The woman still looked confused. Colin nodded towards the window again and looked back at her. She didn't break her gaze.

My feeling of embarrassment about looking rude was fading quickly. "Thanks for your help, bye." I started to make for the door.

"Yes. Thanks," Colin repeated, but the woman wasn't having any of it.

"Do you think they'll come in useful?" She leaned towards him, the puzzled expression giving way to a fierce questioning frown.

"Yes I do." Colin's voice was oscillating wildly. I was nearly out of the door but he was still stuck behind enemy lines. The woman continued to stare at his face, as if trying to draw a response to her nonsensical question out of the pores of his skin. "I think they'll come in useful." He didn't bother pointing at the scene outside again.

"Carrier bag!" Coma-woman screeched, and started slapping at the pile of polythene again.

That broke Colin's trance and he buried his feelings of embarrassment as I had done. "Bye, got to go!"

"It's raining very hard" the non coma-woman shouted.

"Bag!" was the last word we heard before the door closed behind us.

Colin was surprisingly unsettled by the events in the shop and I had to put his mind at rest while suppressing my intense joy that he had bought such a ridiculous coat.

He had filled up the fuel tank the previous evening so we didn't have to stop at any services on the way down. This was a cautious move to avoid anybody from the service stations near the crime scene giving a description to the police later. "Who do you think they'll get to play me on Crimewatch?" Colin asked.

"Nobody knows the names of the actors on Crimewatch."

"Yes, but this will be a special case, they'll get someone from the A-list to play me because I'm such a master criminal."

"A mistress criminal you mean? Your coat is ridiculous, you look like a penis. It's the funniest thing I've ever seen. It's a woman's coat, what were you thinking?" That's what I wanted to say but I had to contain it. What I actually said was, "We won't make Crimewatch." If I mocked him now there would be no way he'd wear it when we got there, and I needed him to wear it for a while so I could rip him apart to maximum effect. His coat wouldn't jeopardise the mission as we were going to be taking them off when we reached the actual site so we could blend in with the paintballers in our combat gear. This meant that I could comfortably enjoy the spectacle. It would be some comic relief from the more grisly purpose of the day.

* * * * * * * * * * * * * * * *

"Terry, it's Jasper. What you doing? Where are you?"
"It's still on?"
"What you talking about? It's only a bit of rain."
"It'll be muddy."
"For fuck's sake Tel, just get your arse down here."
"Is everyone else still up for it?"
"About half so far, the others have got their phones switched off, but I'll keep trying. You've got to come. Carl, Jez and Milt are banking on you for a lift."
"I don't know, Jasper. It looks pretty shitty out there."
"If you won't do it for me, do it for Max. You know how he gets."
"Is that a threat Jasp?"
"I'll see you down there."

* * * * * * * * * * * * * * * *

The windscreen wipers struggled manfully to fend off the sheets of water crashing down onto the glass and we were forced to drive much more slowly than we had the previous week. The rain showed no sign of abating as we entered Hampshire and seemed even worse by the time we passed the entrance to the paintball site. I had hoped to see the gates locked but they looked very much open and there were cars in the car park. I was gutted.

We passed the site and soon reached the nature reserve car park. It was empty of cars this time and I hoped this would work in our favour by minimising witnesses. Because of the Biblical rainfall outside we were unable to open the car doors to make room, so it took us ages to change into our combat fatigues. They had a handy pocket at the front, perfect for stashing Monica and Dave as well as our paintball goggles. I stifled a smile as Colin put on his old woman's coat and I thought I saw a slight flicker of doubt on his face as he fumbled with the massive plastic buttons and belt buckle.

We sat and stared out of the window.

"We have to go out there don't we?"

I didn't respond. I continued to stare out of the window.

"Come on, we've got to do this." He leaned over and opened my door and tried to push me out.

"Alright, stop pushing. I'm getting out."

We put on our caps, completing the look, and stepped out into the rain.

We could hardly see as we crossed the fields and it was a relief to reach the relative shelter of the woods. Colin's coat billowed in the wind and I thought his giant buttons were going to catch a gust and whisk him into the air. When we got to the ditch we could hear the sound of water running beneath the dense foliage. A layer of leaves clinging to the slippery wet surface of our pipe-bridge made crossing it hard work. We were both thoroughly miserable by the time we reached the other side.

It was around midday. We could hear voices; orders being shouted. The game was obviously in full swing so we had to be careful. We removed our coats, put on our goggles and made our way closer to the edge of the trees. We lay on the soggy ground at the edge of the woods where we could see the open part of the site slope away from us and back up at the far end. There was a red flag on a pole in the ground just in front of us and we could see a blue one near the building at the opposite end. With some relief I noted the rain had eased off considerably, but the damage had already been done, we were soaked.

Colin squinted into the distance. "How many people can you see?"

"Only three at the moment."

"I can only see two, where's the other one?"

The two that Colin could see were lying to our right and facing away from us, hiding behind a mound of earth. The one he couldn't spot was further across the field, crouched on our side of a tree. They looked poised for an oncoming attack and I presumed there were a lot more hunkered down in the trees, both to our right and across the clearing. I saw movement in the woods to the far side, revealing two more toy soldiers standing separately and peeking out from behind trees. I pointed them out to Colin. They all wore red sashes, like muddy Miss Worlds. There were no captains' armbands to be seen.

Colin pointed out some movement on the upward slope in the distance. There was an advance party of four blue-sashed men moving quickly towards us. They were spread out across the field and each one stopped when he reached some sort of cover, allowing his fellows to overtake him, then the process repeated. It was clearly an attempt at military strategy but it was pointless; if we could see them then so could the whole of the red team in front of us. It looked like fun though. More of the blue team came running behind, looking more gung-ho than those who had led the charge. The two at the vanguard of the attack were now three hundred yards away and were nearing the bottom of the valley, lying on the ground behind some bushes but clearly visible to us. Suddenly a red sash burst out of the trees to their left and started pumping paintballs in their general direction. His gun wasn't particularly accurate and the pellets flew past them. The blue sashes both turned and started shooting and it was obvious straight away that their guns were more precise. The third or fourth shot connected with the maverick red soldier's chest, 'killing' him, but that didn't stop the paint-thirsty blue invaders. It was like Sonny Corleone getting hit at the toll booth in Godfather; shot after shot rained into his technically lifeless body. The cry of "Fuck off you cunts" echoed across the battlefield. They finally stopped shooting and the dead soldier traipsed away towards the building at the far end. He cut a sorry figure on his long walk of shame, receiving a splatter of paint every time he passed another concealed member of the blue team, and raising his middle finger instinctively each time.

Colin and I thoroughly enjoyed the spectacle. The blues came closer and both sides suffered losses. There seemed to be two types of player: those who were apparently following some sort of plan, and those who wanted to be heroes, slipping round one of the flanks to appear as if out of nowhere in an attempt to take out two or three of the enemy at a time, just as the first casualty of this war had done. These glory hunters didn't last long but did take at least one of the opposition with them when they 'died'.

The red team seemed to have opted for guerrilla warfare and had made no obvious progress towards the flag at the opposite end. As the blues got closer we became more wary that we might be seen by one of the red team guarding the flag near us so we ducked low but kept our position.

The battle stepped up a gear and the blues continued their approach, despatching the red defenders but paying a heavy price. Then came the moment that changed the course of the war. Four of the blue attackers formed a line across the clearing about a hundred feet away from us, they had no cover at all but had probably realised that the guns only worked at close range. They knelt like musketeers in formation and a lone blue-sashed figure came from behind and ran between them. Colin and I both noticed that he was wearing an armband. It had to be a Calson, but there was no sign of the other twin. The blue musketeers stood and ran behind their captain, shooting at any red sashes who jumped out of the woods to defend their flag. More reds started emerging from the trees much further away, realising they had lost the tactical battle and were about to lose the war.

The blue-sashed Calson was clear and close to the flag. The red team needed a hero or the day would be lost, or at least this particular game would be. Their prayers were answered: A figure appeared from the woods near us and I swear a flash of sunshine appeared from a crack in the clouds to illuminate the red armband of the other Calson twin. I could almost hear a fanfare as red Calson ran to his flag and let fly with a torrent of shots in the direction of his brother who returned fire immediately. Both of them connected several times but their corpses didn't break stride and continued to run headlong towards each other. They chewed up the ground between them and collided in a heap. Their guns now forgotten they proceeded to beat the absolute shit out of each other.

Fights between siblings are something to behold; all normal ethical considerations are cast aside and pretty much anything goes. The Calsons were no exception, in fact they were worse. They both fought dirty, gripping each other's hair and using elbows and knees as well as the more conventional fists. It was lucky they were wearing goggles because I was sure that otherwise at least one would have lost an eye. If they always fought with such intensity then it was surprising they had lived as long as they had. It looked like we could save ourselves a job and just let them kill each other, but their friends were nearly upon them and looked ready to break it up, albeit cautiously. Without speaking Colin and I simultaneously withdrew our guns from the front of our overalls. "You take the blue armband," I whispered, and he nodded.

Colin held up three fingers and counted down, two, then one and we both leapt up and ran forward. Neither of us was a marksman and Colin had never fired a gun before, so we had to get fairly close before we started shooting. I emptied the six chambers of my gun into their furious bodies and Colin at least matched that volume and probably more with his higher capacity weapon. All but one of their friends stopped dead in shock and horror. The one exception was a giant of a man, who came at us from our right-hand side. Colin moved with Matrix-like speed, spinning to the right and shooting the man in the chest, dropping him to the ground immediately. The rest of the onlookers seemed more shocked by this than by the frenzied murder of the birthday boys and they all backed away, like a macabre game of grandma's footsteps. I was tugging on Colin's sleeve, itching to get out of there, but Colin addressed the assembly. "There are ten more of us in the woods. Anyone who follows gets what fatty just got." He pointed at the dead man who lay just yards from his feet.

We turned and ran, grabbing our coats as we passed and gaining the power of flight as we shot across the concrete pipe. We ran at full pelt through the woods and I had never felt so physically powerful. Adrenaline and fear were sending energy to my legs that I didn't know I had, and Colin matched my pace. It took us under ten minutes to reach the edge of the woods where we paused and looked across the open field towards where the car was parked, dreading the sight of police cars. There was none to be seen. I turned to Colin. "Shall we just go for it?"

He responded by breaking into a run across the field. I followed suit. We crossed the road and reached the car park, unzipping our overalls as we went. Colin unlocked the car and we pulled off our overalls which slid over our muddy shoes. We put on our dry trousers, bundled up the clothes we had removed and dumped them on the floor in front of the rear seat, pulling Colin's bright yellow reflective jackets over them. When we got to the main road we turned right instead of left to avoid the entrance to the paintball site and just kept driving. We were heading west, the opposite direction to Brighton but I wasn't about to complain. The speed and agility supplied by the adrenaline in my body had now given way to overwhelming nausea. I just wanted to be as far away from the scene of the crime as possible.

"How do you feel?" I broke the silence.

"Nothing. I feel nothing. I just killed at least one man, possibly two or three, and I feel nothing." It took me a moment to work out what he meant by the number of people he had killed. It was of course that we had been just firing into the pair of fighting men and we had no way of knowing which bullets had been fatal. There was no doubt about the third man though, he was definitely Colin's.

"Do you want to talk about it?"

"I'll say if I do."

"Ok."

We drove for thirty miles and were getting close to the town of Salisbury. Colin headed north when we hit the A road. "Do you know where we're going?" I asked weakly.

"I'm taking no chances, we're going to go in a massive loop round Andover and Basingstoke then we'll head east until we hit the M25 then go south to Brighton."

I thought my sense of unease would recede with each passing hour, but although my fear of us getting caught had subsided, the nagging in my gut that had started when Colin shot the bystander at the paintball site was threatening to consume me. I had chosen this life and had managed to reconcile myself with the obvious wrong doing of taking human lives for money, but now Colin was in as deep as I was. I felt guilty for dragging him down into my mess but more than that, the sight of Colin turning to effortlessly kill that onrushing onlooker served as a window into what I myself had become. It was a moment of clarity, where the mesh of lies I had told myself to allow me to justify my actions unravelled and I could see things in simple terms of good and bad. All the 'bad' boxes on the survey about my new way of life were ticked and I could no longer see a way to defend it. It wasn't the first time I had had one of these moments, and it certainly wouldn't be the last. I buried my feelings deep down so they would be harder to get to next time.

I had never seen Colin like this. He was silent and visibly nervous. He constantly checked the rear-view mirror, and if he accidentally caught my eye his face would twitch and he would avert his gaze. I was sure he wasn't worried about being caught, we were a long way from the crime scene, the roads were busy and there would be nothing to single out our car. The fear and confusion so apparent in him was because he was now face to face with a part of himself he didn't know existed. He had been party to me killing Steven Clarke and was less involved in the murder of my neighbour, but now he had actually pulled the trigger and been the sole reason for at least one man's death. Colin's demons were coming out to play.

As we entered the outskirts of Brighton, hungry, tired and freezing cold from being out in the rain for hours I realised I hadn't taken the piss out of Colin's old woman's coat.

It didn't seem very funny anymore.

* * * * * * * * * * * * * * *

"What the fuck happened Andy?" Stan's screaming. He's lost it completely.

"They got the twins."

"The Calsons? How the fuck? They're surrounded by muscle."

"Plenty of muscle but no shooters. They were playing paintball, the only guns were toy ones.

"What were they doing playing paintball?"

"Birthday. Birthdays. The twins."

"Another fucking party? What is it with these dickheads? Didn't they learn nothing from what happened to Hunter? We told them to be careful. We told them not to let their guard down. In fact we told them to put their fucking guard up. Tell me if we didn't Andy."

"We did, Stan."

"And some fucker comes along while they're playing toy soldiers and blows their fucking heads off."

"There were two of them, and it wasn't pretty. They came out the woods and unloaded. It was like Bonny and Clyde. They got Fry too."

"Who the fuck is Fry? Do I care about Fry?"

"Fry was the Calsons' top man. We've used him a few times for specialist jobs, dirty ones."

"Was he a target?"

"Don't think so, just got in the way. He made a move for the shooters but he wasn't armed so he bought it pretty quickly."

"So not only are my men stupid they're fucking suicidal too. Who else was at this toy soldiers' party?"

"Three more of our blokes were there, the others were just friends of the Calsons, not connected. Do you want the names of ours?"

"I haven't got time to remember names, just send Frank and Cheese round to beat some discipline into them. Tell Cheese to break a bone in each."

"I'll get on it Stan. So what about Barrett?"

"From now on, for every man we lose, Barrett loses three. Our man Tom White's going to be busy. If Barrett wants a war then I'll give him world war three, four and fucking five, the fat fuck."

Twenty

I didn't see Colin for the next week. I called him several times but he didn't answer or return my messages. Stephanie, after calling in advance to let me know she was coming, dropped the rest of the money round for the Calson job along with details of the next hit. She picked up on the vibe that I wasn't feeling particularly sociable and kept her visit professional and brief. I called Colin and spoke to his voicemail again. This time he called back. He asked me to go round to his flat and the tone of his voice made it clear that I shouldn't argue. Before I went over there I made sure I had calculated Colin's share of the money correctly. I didn't want to give him anything to argue about.

Colin hardly said a word as he let me in, and if my cargo had been less delicate I was sure he would have just taken it from me at the door and closed it in my face. Instead he grunted that we should go and sit down. He was obviously pissed. There was a bottle of single malt on the coffee table, it was half empty. Colin refilled his glass. He didn't offer me any.

"Come on Col why have you been avoiding me? What's going on? Just say whatever's on your mind."

He looked at me for a long time then dropped his gaze. "You don't want to know what's on my mind."

"For Christ's sake Colin, let's just nip this in the bud shall we? It's me you're talking to, Tom, your best mate, remember?"

"That's why I said you wouldn't want to know what's on my

mind. If I try and explain the fucked-up state I'm in you'll just tell me to stop being stupid, that I knew what I was getting into."

"That's bollocks, I understand what you're going through and I can help, I've been through it all myself."

"Exactly, Tom, in your eyes there's nothing I could experience that you haven't already sold souvenir mugs for. You're the one blazing a trail and I just tag along and play second fiddle."

"Where's all this come from?"

"It's come from you Tom, and me I suppose, I've always let you be how you are."

I knew if I said what I was thinking, which was that he'd had too much to drink and that this wasn't the best time to talk about the myriad problems he seemed to have with me, then his response would be something along the lines of: 'exactly, you won't even let me talk about it, you just want an excuse to shut me up'. So I tried to think of something else to say to stem this torrent of irrational resentment that had built up inside Colin's head. Nothing came to mind so I returned to my initial thought. "Colin, how much have you had to drink?"

"I dunno. A bit of whisky."

"Let's talk about this another time, I'm not saying I don't want to hear what you've got to say, I just think it's not the best time. What do you think mate?"

"You're so fucking patronising."

"Jesus, I can't win."

"*You* can't win? That's rich. You always win. You always have to keep control. You have to be the boss and pay me just that bit less so you can keep on top. I bet you couldn't stand it when I shot that bloke who tried to be a hero at the paintball site because it meant I'd done more than you. I knew you wouldn't give me any more of the money though."

"Is this about money?"

"It's about everything." He sat back and sighed, keeping his eyes fixed anywhere but on me.

I wasn't going to sit there and let him make me the bad guy. "Fuck you Colin. I'm not listening to this shit anymore. If you've got a problem then I'll talk to you but you're not making any sense. You're pissed out of your mind and talking total bollocks. Call me tomorrow when you can form a reasonable sentence and we'll talk. The one thing you've managed to make clear is that you think I'm a cunt, and it's also clear that you have done for some time, so I'm sure we'll have lots to talk about when you're good and ready. But for now I'll leave you to your whisky, so you can carry on playing out your big soap opera scene, you fucking drama queen."

"Fuck you Tom. You won't have to listen to my shit anymore, and I don't have to take your shit anymore. I'm…" he held up his glass and rotated it gently, studying the moving liquid, "dissolving this partnership, I'm breaking out on my own." He knocked back what was left in the glass, which was quite a lot, and winced.

"What are you talking about?"

"You're on your own now Thomas. Let's see how you get on without me."

"You don't want to do any more jobs?"

"Au contraire Thomas," he sat up and forced a smug grin on his red drunken face, "I will be doing more hits, plenty more, I'm just not going to be doing them with you. From now on it's just me and Dave."

"Who's Dave?"

"You can't even remember the name of my gun."

I laughed, not mockingly, I just couldn't help it. "Listen to yourself mate, you're being fucking stupid. Let's talk about this another time."

"There's nothing else to talk about, you've paid me my pitiful fee for services rendered, and I've found employment elsewhere. I'm handing in my notice, effective immediately." He poured himself some more whisky and knocked it back. He looked directly at me and belched loudly.

"I didn't employ you, it's not like that. We're mates helping each other out."

"Not any more we're not."

"So who are you working for?"

"I'm not at liberty to divulge that information." I knew full well he was deliberately trying to wind me up and I shouldn't have risen to it, but his drunken manner was making me want to punch his smug face.

Instead I shouted. "You're a fucking idiot Colin. To get offered a job you must have told somebody about what you've been doing, what *we've* been doing. Who've you been talking to?"

"I didn't tell anyone." His voice was slurring badly now. He went to pour more whisky but I pushed the glass away and it fell on the floor. It didn't smash but he was still tipping the bottle and whisky went all over the table. "Fuck off" he shouted.

"You did tell someone, now tell me who. I'm not fucking around."

"There's a bloke looking for good men. I'm a good man. I am, aren't I Tom?" His eyes filled with tears and I was grateful for the coffee table between us, otherwise I think he would have hugged me.

"Don't start getting soppy. Who's this bloke and how did he know to offer you anything?"

"Phil knows him."

I was beyond fury. "Phil? You told Phil? You fucking arsehole. Jesus." I leaned back and tried to relax and think straight, but my rage just got more intense. I stood up, rounded the table and punched Colin as hard as I could on the jaw. I've not got a knockout punch but I caught him pretty well. He burst into tears, swaying gently. I pulled him towards me and spoke in his ear. "If you've told him anything about me and it causes any kind of trouble I'll fucking kill you, and I mean kill you, I'll put a bullet in your stupid face. You got that?" I shoved him back onto the sofa. He didn't respond so I gathered him up again and slapped him. "Have you got that?"

"Yes. Fuck off." He broke away from me, pushed his face into the sofa cushions and sobbed like a baby.

* * * * * * * * * * * * * * * *

"We need new men, Joe. And this one comes recommended."

"Who's he recommended by?"

"A dealer down in Brighton."

"And why should I take the word of a druggie low-life?"

"Because he's got his ear to the ground."

"Too many people have their ear to the ground Geoff, there should be more people with their heads in the air, facing forward, using their fucking eyes." I can tell that Joe's furious but he's trying to keep it under wraps, keeping his anger up his sleeve to use later.

I continue my sales pitch. "He's done a few jobs helping out a full-timer and wants to break out on his own."

"What do we know about him?"

"That he can be useful, and we need useful people right now."

"How do we know we can trust him?"

"How do we know we can trust that woman?" I had planned to raise this issue with him, but not yet, and I hadn't meant it to come out so bluntly.

Joe smiles, as if he's unravelled a great mystery. "Now we're getting somewhere. What's your problem with Stephanie, Geoff, and why don't you just come right out and say it?"

"I've got no problem with Stephanie, Joe. What I have a problem with is the fact that we know absolutely nothing about her and yet she seems to be making most of the decisions around here."

Joe thumps his desk and leans towards me. "The only person who makes decisions around here is me, you got that?"

I've seen this routine a million times and it doesn't scare me. "Whatever you want to call it, Joe. We both know what I'm talking about."

"You're way out of line Geoff and I'll thank you to keep your fucking mouth shut about her in future. She's the only woman I've ever met who I can talk about my business with, who understands and actually has a credible opinion."

"That's what I'm worried about, Joe, how freely do you talk about the business, and how often does she offer this 'credible' opinion of hers?"

"You're pushing it Geoff, I'd stop while I still had a face if I were you."

"Let's stop fucking around Joe. She could be dangerous. We don't even know if her story about being Costanza's prisoner-girlfriend even checks out. Nobody's ever seen him out with her."

"Costanza never takes women out in public, not since Mariella got blown away. You know that."

"That's very convenient for Stephanie. I'm sure it wouldn't be hard to find out the truth, just get a few guys to ask a few questions in the right place and we could confirm or deny her story."

"That's not going to happen, Geoff. If any of our clumsy fuckers start asking questions it's bound to get to Costanza and it'll be dangerous for her if he knows something's up."

"Joe, I mean no offence here but if she cared about you as much as she says she does, then she'd leave Costanza right now."

"You really do want to be stopping talking now Geoff. She's got good reason to stick it out for a while, it's all planned out."

"When are you going to share those plans with the rest of us Joe?"

"Get the fuck out of my office."

* * * * * * * * * * * * * * * *

I simply didn't know what to do. It was dangerous for me to be Colin's enemy; he knew too much about me. I felt like a fool for being so open about everything and decided that from now on I would trust nobody. I couldn't understand Colin's anger towards me. I hadn't wanted to bring him in on the business but had done so as a favour to him. I had even increased his cut. All that stuff about me wanting to win all the time just made me sound like an egomaniac, and anyone who knew me could vouch that I was nothing of the sort. Unfortunately nobody knew me better than Colin.

My mobile rang. It was Colin. "Yes?" I said.

"We should talk."

"Yes we should. What the fuck are you playing at?"

"I said talk, not shout. I'm coming over." He hung up.

He arrived in ten minutes. His jaw was swollen and discoloured and, not wanting to give him the moral high ground, I resisted the urge to apologise. We sat in the lounge and looked at the floor for a while. Eventually I spoke. "So what's going on?"

"I went over the top the other night. I said some things I didn't mean."

"It sounded like you meant them from where I was sitting."

"I meant some of it but didn't mean it to come out like that."

"So you think I'm a control freak, an autocrat and a megalomaniac."

"I don't know what an autocrat is."

"Doesn't matter, you'd think I was one if you knew what it was."

"I don't think I really know what a megalomaniac is either."

"Same applies."

"Right."

"So what's all this about your new job?"

"Right, firstly Tom, you've got to understand that I haven't told anybody anything they didn't already know. It was just Phil."

"Phil's got a big mouth."

"And he's sold three guns to you in the last six weeks. He knows what's going on."

"But he didn't know any specifics about the jobs I've done."

"And he still doesn't, I didn't tell him anything like that."

"So what exactly did you tell him Colin? And why did you have to go to Phil anyway? Why did you bottle up all this anger and then just explode? We're mates, or at least we were, so why didn't you talk to me sooner?"

"I've always thought you were a bit bossy, you seem to want to mother everybody," I was tempted to interrupt but bit my tongue, I wanted to hear what he had to say and arguing would just delay it, "but I didn't think it was a real problem until we got into this. It's kind of my fault too because I practically begged you to let me come in on it, and this gave you the upper hand, you were in control from the start."

"But it wasn't about control Colin."

"Oh but it was Tom. It was all about control, but that still wouldn't have bothered me, it was when we killed those twins and that other guy."

"What about it?"

"I don't know, but it changed everything."

"I'm no psychologist but it's pretty obvious what's going on here. You're shaken up about what happened and it's manifesting itself as resentment towards me."

"You're right Tom you're no psychologist, so don't bother trying eh? Sorry, I didn't mean that. Whatever the reason for this resentment - as you call it - we can't be mates anymore. We've both said too much," he rubbed his swollen jaw, "and done too much."

"You're wrong Colin, we just had an argument, it was a big one, granted, but nothing that was said can't be taken back."

"You threatened to kill me."

"I was scared you'd turned on me and you were going to shout around some dangerous information. I didn't mean it. People say that all the time and nobody ever means it."

"Most other people aren't killers, Tom. You are, you did mean it and you know it."

"You can see why I got so wound up though can't you? I was worried that you'd got pissed up and dropped me in it. I don't want to get caught Colin."

"I don't clearly remember what I said to be honest, but I get the gist of it, and I assume you didn't like it, judging by the extra face I seem to have grown on my chin."

"Can we just forget about it all?"

"No Tom, we really can't."

"So you're just going to go off to some mate of Phil's and start up a hitman business?"

"That's all off, the guy didn't want me anymore."

"Why didn't you say that straight away?"

"You didn't give me a chance."

I found this statement very annoying, he could have told me if he'd wanted to, but had wanted to let me simmer for as long as possible. I choked back my anger as I didn't want to cause another scene. "So are you still going to be looking for work?"

"No, it was quite a relief when Phil told me his man couldn't use me. I've thought about it and don't think I could ever do that again really. I don't want to experience that feeling of having killed someone ever again. The worst part about it isn't the guilt about ending a man's life, it's the exhilaration. After I'd done it I got a buzz, and I hate myself for it. I don't want to be like that."

"I think you're right, unfortunately I'm too far in to get out now, but I can see why you're stopping." I was sure he was going to tell me I was being patronising again but he didn't. "So can we go back to being mates?" It felt weird talking like this to Colin, like I was trying to talk my way out of being dumped by a girlfriend.

"No." He spoke with a real finality. "Not for the foreseeable future."

"Why does it have to be like this Colin? Jesus, it was just one argument."

"It's more than that, Tom. I know I'm sounding like a girl and I'm sorry, but I don't know what else to say. I'll see you around."

I sat and stared into space for half an hour after he left. It didn't make any sense. Admittedly we'd had a huge slanging match and I had physically assaulted him, and there was the small matter of me threatening to kill him, but he had been a complete arsehole and fully deserved it. I could imagine him being angry with me but not to the point of severing all ties. There must have been more to it. He had disregarded my suggestion that he was moulding all his bad feeling about the paintball murders into resentment towards me, but I didn't think I was so far from the truth. However, if I tried to convince him it would push him further away; I had experienced that with women enough times. I would just have to accept that for the time being I would be the face of evil to Colin, and hope that sometime in the future he might come to his senses.

* * * * * * * * * * * * * *

Me and Frank are on our way out to the sticks to do Costanza's dirty work. We've stopped for lunch on the way. We're sitting in a pub garden overlooking a river. The pub's in the middle of nowhere. It's kid-friendly, with a big playground. It's not a pub, it's a fucking theme park. I'm trying to block out the noise of the screaming brats and I've chosen my seat carefully so I can't see any of them, just the river. I tell myself I'm in unspoilt countryside. It's the last knockings of summer and it'll be cold out here soon, but for now it's just right.

"I'm fucking starving," Frank says. "Where's my pie?"

"We only ordered five minutes ago. Give them a chance."

"What the fuck are we doing out here? Surely the old man's got someone else he can use, someone who doesn't have to travel so far. He needs more personnel."

"Or we need less of him." This isn't the best time to bring up the news about my contact with Steph but I've realised there won't ever be a good time so I'm just going to go for it.

"What?"

"We could do without Stan Costanza."

"What are you talking about?"

"You know what I'm talking about, Frank."

Frank looks around, like he's checking if anyone's listening to us, they aren't, it's just his instinct. He probably doesn't even know he's done it. "This again? Listen mate, you know I'm against Costanza as much as you are, and there'll be a time when he'll pay through the nose for what he did to Tony, but we've agreed to keep our heads down and wait 'til the time's right."

"And when do you think the time's going to be right Frank? Six weeks? Six months? Six years? The longer we wait the stronger he's going to get."

He takes a swig of his beer and gets foam on his top lip. "So, what do you suggest Cheese?"

"I'd suggest wiping your mouth." He wipes his mouth. "And I'd suggest you listen to what I've got to say, and not just jump straight in. I don't want you throwing one of your fits."

I've played this badly. He's got the look on his face that I've seen so many times. It's the one that says he's about to go psycho. "Actually, forget it Frank, this isn't the right time."

"When will be the right time Cheese? Six weeks? Six months? Six years?" He looks well chuffed to have repeated my words back to me.

"Another time, there's no point when you're being like this."

"Being like what? I'm calm aren't I?"

"I can see your eyes, Frank, there's no fucking way I'm talking to you now."

"Christ, you must have something pretty fucking bad to tell me otherwise you wouldn't be so scared. What are you scared of Cheese? Big man like you shouldn't be scared." I know he's trying to rile me. This is the side of Frank I can do without. He's a clever bloke but sometimes he just slips into the whole macho routine. I ignore him and take a swig of my pint. It tastes good, so I have some more.

We sit in silence for a while, Frank knows me and he knows I'm not going to take his bait so he's obviously planning another move. I'm stuck. He's not going to let me leave until I've said what I was going to tell him, and if I tell him he'll go off on one. The food arrives, this should buy me some time and it should calm Frank down a bit. Hopefully he won't be so quick to pounce once he's got a decent meal inside him.

We stuff down our food in silence. When we've finished I take a deep breath. "You've never let me down Frank and I'm grateful for that."

He looks up from his meal. "And you've never let me down. Is that what you want me to say?"

"It's true though ain't it? I never have."

He grudgingly agrees with a nod of his head.

I look at him and decide to go for it. "I've seen Steph."

He looks shocked. "Where? When?"

"She sends her best."

"Where is she? How long's it been?"

"Ten years."

"How is she?"

"She's great, really well."

Frank smiles for the first time in a long time. "How does she look? I bet she's a cracker."

"*Like an angel. She looks a bit older than she is, that's probably down to what she went through as a kid, but she's a stunner."*

"*Where's she been?"*

"*Bobby set her up in America, somewhere down south."*

"*I bet she's got a suntan and a half."*

"*She looks good."*

Frank's look of excitement slips away. "*How many times have you seen her?"*

"*A lot."*

"*And when were you going to tell me?"* He doesn't look as angry as he did before, but there's still time for him to lose it.

"*I'm telling you now."*

"*What are you telling me exactly?"*

"*She's going for Costanza. And I'm going to help her. And she, we, want you to help too."*

He sits back and sighs loudly. "*How old was she when she went away?"*

"*Eleven."*

"*So she's twenty one now, and you think a twenty one year old girl can go up against the biggest player in London?"*

"*Actually she's going up against the two biggest players, she wants Barrett too."*

"*I'm guessing you and her have got somewhere with whatever plan she's got. That's why you're nervous about telling me, you reckoned I'd think you were plotting against me."*

"*Exactly."*

"*Are you?"* He gets real close, stares at me.

"*Fuck no."*

"*So why didn't you tell me straight away, when she first came to you?"*

"*I knew you wouldn't want to make a move on Costanza, you'd have said it was impossible."*

He leans back, picking up his pint and taking another swig. "*Fair *point. Now tell me what's going on, and what daft scheme the two of you need me to salvage."*

I can't believe it. I thought this was going to be the end of everything. "Good to have you aboard Frank."

He smiles but his face quickly clouds over again. He leans forward once more. "One thing though Cheese."

"What's that?"

"Don't ever keep anything from me again. You understand me?"

"Yeah, fair enough."

"Oh, and just one more thing."

"What's that, Frank?"

"I'm going to need another one of these." *He grins and holds up his empty glass.*

When I come back with the beers I can see that his mind has been working overtime, but in a good way. He downs half straight away, then gets to work. "I need to know everything. What's the plan?"

"At the moment everything's going through the new guy, Tom White. He's doing hits for both Costanza and Barrett."

Frank's stunned. "White? Fuck off. Double crossing's not his style. He's straight down the line."

"He doesn't know what's going on. He's green to all the politics that go with this business."

"You make it sound like he's some dopey kid. He knows what he's doing when he goes on a job."

"Exactly, and that's why he's so good for us. We've got someone with all the talent, but easy to control. Steph's got him round her little finger."

"Steph sees him?"

"White believes that Steph is another of Stan's agents. She gives him jobs to do but they're really for Barrett."

"Steph works for Barrett?" *Frank's running out of shocked expressions.*

"More than that, Barrett's got it bad for her, and thinks she feels the same. She's convinced him that the bloke she's with keeps her pretty much *against her will, like a prisoner."*

Frank smiles and shakes his head. *"Don't tell me, don't fucking tell me, the other guy, the one who's keeping her against her will, it's Costanza ain't it?"*

"You're sharp Frank, I'll give you that."

Frank starts laughing proper loud, people start looking over. *"That's fucking priceless!"*

"It's a nice touch."

"Risky though, Steph's playing a dangerous game."

"She reckons she knows what she's doing

"It's all good shit, but why's she doing it? What's it all for?"

"Steph's controlling Joe. His judgement's all to cock because of how he feels about Steph and how much he hates Stan. You know that since the revolution Stan and Joe have left each other be for the most part, but now Steph's making it personal. She's guiding Joe's hand, gently persuading him to put contracts out on Stan's boys, the ones that Steph knows will make Stan hit back the hardest. If Joe doesn't make an order then Steph makes it anyway, and White carries it out. Steph wants chaos. She's trying to make things spiral out of control. Every time Stan retaliates for one of Joe's attacks she persuades Joe to hit back even harder. She's weakening both of them, softening them up for the final push."

"Final push? I suppose that's us is it?" Frank doesn't look scared, Frank doesn't get scared, he just knows how this is going to end, just like I do, in a bloody mess one way or another. *"So let me get this straight. Steph's got her very own double-agent, Tom White, but he doesn't know he's a double agent. She's started tit-for-tat killings to get Barrett and Costanza at each other's throats. She basically wants to start a war, and then we're going to steam in at the end and take out Costanza and Barrett."*

"That's it exactly."

"And then what?"

"What do you mean?"

"It'll leave a power vacuum. Who's going to take over?"

"According to Steph, Tony Visconti's wishes were to have us take over. This isn't business for her, this is strictly personal. She's carrying on her father's legacy."

Frank leans back and can't hide his pride. He finishes his pint. He's getting through them today. I'll have to drive the rest of the way. He looks out at the water. "This is huge. Do you really think we can do it?"

"Steph thinks we can, and I'm starting to believe her." Frank looks at his empty glass and I expect him to ask for another but instead he says we should get moving.

"What about today?" Frank says as we drive. "We've got to dish out punishment beatings for the Calson fuck-up, we've got to break bones."

"That's right."

"How about we recruit these blokes instead? We're going to need all the muscle we can get when it kicks off."

"We'll need to recruit but not yet, it's too soon. It's too dangerous to let anything out. We don't know who we can trust yet."

"So you're just going to do what Stan's ordered?"

"That's exactly what I'm going to do Frank. We're going to see these three blokes one by one, and we're going to hurt them, just like Costanza told us. He's never trusted us and I don't want to give him anything to go on." Frank looks at me with disgust even though he knows I'm right. I smile at him. "I'll tell you what, Frank. I'll let them choose which bone gets snapped."

Twenty-one

The next few weeks saw summer finally give in and let autumn take its turn. I did three hits, two for Stephanie and one for Frank and Cheese. There seemed to be a lot of killing to be done. Even though I had previously done hits without Colin, it felt strange knowing I couldn't turn to him if I needed to. In fact I couldn't turn to anybody. I couldn't show any kind of weakness to Frank and Cheese, they didn't seem the type to want to talk to another man about things like feelings of remorse and regret. I wasn't sure I could speak to Stephanie either; she seemed to flit between being a playful friend and a harsh boss. I wondered what her story was and why she was mixed up in such a seedy world. She had looks, charm and intelligence and gave the impression she could have made a success of whatever field she wanted, but instead she had chosen to arrange deaths for a gang boss; hiring gunmen like she was booking party caterers.

I still had Laura. Everything in that particular garden was rosy at least, although it was getting difficult to keep up the deception of what I did for a living, which as far as she could tell was nothing since I left my hospital job. It was also difficult to explain why Colin and I no longer communicated. I said he had been busy at work, and that I was glad because I was starting to find him a bit irritating, hoping this would throw her off the scent and prevent her asking in future. Laura thought it was a classic case of a man shutting out his friends to spend time with his new girlfriend, and she encouraged me to see him. I politely ignored her.

Laura and I set a stay-over limit of four nights a week. She had been in relationships that had burned out too quickly and wanted to make sure it didn't happen to us. I didn't admit to being a serial relationship burner-outer myself, and went along with her plans. I did want to see her more, but it was useful to have the space to organise and operate my nefarious activities. Whenever she did stay over it was always at mine, because she insisted her place was 'a shithole'. She often joked that she had another man living there who she saw for the remaining three nights a week, and in my darkest moments, normally if I woke up alone at some godforsaken hour, Laura's joke would crystallise into a hard fact in my sleep-deprived brain and would take some scraping out before I would be able to sleep again.

Laura was easy to love, but making her boyfriend feel secure wasn't her highest priority. She was unbelievably easy going and expected me to be the same. I was forced to bury my jealousy when she talked about the men she was friendly with in the pub, even though it was obvious from her stories that they were clearly trying to get into her knickers. On the few times I did try to make her aware of how men's minds worked she laughed and said that all men didn't think like me. It wasn't that I was genuinely concerned that she would be tempted to stray; it was more that I wanted the world to know that all that beauty belonged to me, that those lips belonged to me. I recalled how much I had fantasised about her before we got together and imagined the men in the pub having similar thoughts. I wanted to be able to force my way into their fantasies in all my pasty nakedness, so I could steal any eroticism and stake my claim on Laura. I know that sounds terrible, like I saw her as a possession, but it's the truth. If I had ever let on to Laura that I felt that way, her response would have been, "Why don't you just piss over me to mark your territory and be done with it?" Then she would collect all her belongings from my house and that would be that.

Without knowing it, Laura taught me to have a thicker skin, and just to be happy to be with someone like her. I gradually stopped picking at the weeping scab of insecurity and became a much more confident person all round.

I started doing at least two jobs a week, sometimes three, and killing had become second nature to me. The feelings of anguish and remorse that I had buried in the past stopped surfacing and the only thing I was concerned with was Laura finding out. As she and I got more serious I knew that talk of living together was inevitable, and I started to consider whether I would one day have to tell her about what I did for a living. In the meantime I had to come up with some explanation for my seemingly bottomless pit of money. I decided my cover story would be to own up to a lesser crime, a fictitious one. I told her I was a drug dealer. She didn't seem very surprised. "Why didn't you tell me before?"

"I'm sorry. I thought you might not be too impressed."

"I'm not. What are you dealing?"

"Not crack or heroin. Just pills, charlie and grass."

"How can you use the word 'just' in that sentence Tom?"

"You're right, but you know what I mean."

"I suppose so, but I don't know how I feel about you having lied to me all this time."

A bolt of fear shot through me. I was sure she was going to leave me. I opted not to insult her with excuses. "I'm sorry."

"Is that girl something to do with it?"

"What girl?" I knew exactly who she meant.

"Miss World?"

"Oh, Stephanie. Yes, she is part of it, but it was the truth that we've been friends for a while, I didn't lie about that."

"Am I supposed to be grateful for that?"

"No, I'm just trying to be honest, too late for that, I know. All I can say is I'm sorry."

"You are aren't you?"

"What?"

"You are sorry."

I wasn't sure what the purpose of this question was. "Yes. Yes I am."

The bottom line is that she eventually forgave me, but it was by no means the end of it, I had to go over long hours of discussion, with Laura bringing up things I'd told her, things that in the light of my confession, she now realised were lies. It was a grim ordeal, made worse by the fact that throughout my apologies and explanations, I was still lying. I was creating lies to cover up darker lies. I was grateful she had forgiven me but dreaded finally telling her the real truth. I knew when she found out she would replay my faux-confession in her head, watching a rerun of my sincere, apologetic face; the face of a liar. When that happened, I knew that however well I tried to convince her that my deception was for her own protection, it probably wouldn't be enough to keep her.

I now had to live the lie. I told her my illicit wares were stored in a secure place away from the house. She didn't want to know where this place was and that suited us both. In my story I shifted big quantities to dealers higher up the line rather than selling to the low level users; this was my reason for not being out selling all the time. It was ironic that instead of cutting deals with the drug barons I was killing people, probably for the same drug barons.

* * * * * * * * * * * * * * *

"Joe, this is madness. We can't afford this war. There's still time to pull out without anyone else getting killed."

"No chance, Geoff, we're in this for the long haul. I'm not pulling out of nothing."

"If we carry on the way we are, our own men are going to start questioning your motives." This is an edited version of the truth. The men are already questioning Joe's motives, but I'm not going to tell him that in case he does something stupid, like killing anyone who doubts his abilities.

"Who's questioning my motives? I want names."

"I didn't say anybody was yet Joe, but if things carry on the way they are then it's inevitable. Your men are behind you all the way, but you shouldn't test their loyalty by forcing them into a personal fight over a woman."

"You'd better watch your mouth Geoff."

"Joe, with all due respect, don't put me in this position. I'm your adviser, let me do my job. I have serious doubts about this woman."

"I know about your fucking doubts, Geoff and I've told you before you should keep them to yourself."

"Joe, we're in the shit. It's carnage out there, Costanza's kicking our arses, we're losing good men and the police are all over us. We're making too much noise."

"Costanza's losing good men too. Now you listen to me, Geoff. I don't know what the fuck your game is, but you can't keep trying to undermine me and make me look inadequate in public."

"I haven't said a word about you in public."

"Listen to me Crowley. I try to be a nice guy, but the truth is I'm a fucking nasty piece of shit. You know this business, so you know how things can turn out for those who don't do the right thing. Normally we use men who do things clean and quick, but as you know I've got other people, people I call on when I want a special job done, to sort out someone who's let me down. These guys aren't clean and they're not quick. They're fucking messy. And fucking slow."

I can't believe what I'm hearing. *"Are you threatening me?"*

"Take it how you want to."

* * * * * * * * * * * * * * *

"Give me the latest, Andy."

"We've been hitting Barrett hard Stan, but he's hitting back and it's starting to bite. We've still got money coming in from distribution but we're running on empty, we haven't got enough bodies. We're doing no protection at all 'cause it's too risky to have muscle in the open."

"When can we make a move on the fat fuck himself?"

"Barrett's taking no chances Stan. He's like Hitler in the bunker."

"Well he'd better take the cyanide pill soon, or I'm going to send some ferrets down his hole to flush him out. Tell me this Andy, what's he playing at? Why did he start this? He must know I'll never let him win."

"I thought you two had an agreement after the revolution."

"Revolution! Are they still calling it that? That agreement was shaky at best. The two of us had just stabbed our boss in the back, so our relationship wasn't exactly built on trust."

"I never thought Joe would come for you, he knows you too well, he knows you won't let him win."

"So why the fuck's he doing it Andy?"

"I don't know Stan, I really don't. It's like he's been possessed or something."

"You could be on to something there."

Twenty-two

* * * * * * * * * * * * * * * *

"Come." Whenever I enter Chief Inspector Lewisham's office he's always sitting bolt upright with his hands clasped in front of him. Today is no exception and I wonder if he spends all his time in this position or if he just strikes that pose when he hears a knock on the door. Lewisham is a hard man to please, but I think he'll be satisfied with my work today. "Chief Inspector, sir. We've got a couple of leads on the Hunter murder."

"Elvis and Big Bird?"

I open my notebook, more for effect really; I know what I'm going to say. "A witness has come forward from the building, the block of flats, where the taxi dropped them off." I look for a flicker of excitement in his eyes, but he remains steadfast. "The witness says he saw Elvis and Big Bird enter the flat across the hall from him, late on the evening of the twenty seventh of August."

"Why didn't he come forward before? We've been appealing in the press for weeks."

"He's been away sir." I check my notebook, for real this time, "he was looking after his sick mother in Essex."

"And how is she?"

"She didn't make it sir."

"Shame."

"Yes sir."

"The flat the neighbour saw them enter, what number was it?"

"Number eight sir."

"We spoke to the couple in number eight, a portly chap and a rather

fetching girl."

Lewisham's memory is legendary. *"That's right sir, a Mister Steve Robinson and a Miss Wendy Armitage."*

"They denied all knowledge."

"Exactly sir."

"They didn't seem like killers though, when you've been on the force as long as I have you develop a nose for these things." I suppress a smile at him using his catchphrase, made all the more amusing by his huge beak of a nose.

"I think you're right sir, they probably aren't the killers. Our calls to the fancy-dress shops in Greater London drew a blank, so I took the liberty of extending the scope to the whole of the south east." I wait for a word of praise but get none. *"We've found a shop in Brighton that rented out an Elvis and Big Bird outfit on the weekend of the Hunter murder."*

"Have you been to the shop?"

"Yesterday afternoon sir. The manager was kind enough to arrange for the assistant who served them to be there to speak to me. It was a man and a woman who hired the outfits, the man was in his late twenties to early thirties, while the girl was younger, in her mid-twenties at the most. The girl accompanied the man to choose the outfits on the Sunday prior to the murder, and he made two more visits alone, once to pick up the costumes on the day of the murder and then the following day to return them and claim his deposit."

"Did he pay by credit card?"

"Unfortunately not, all cash."

"Did we get any other description apart from their ages?"

"Absolutely. The girl serving the two of them on the Sunday before the murder had a long look at them, they were in the shop for some time and there were no other customers. The sketch artist is working with her right now."

"Do the descriptions match the couple in the flat, the portly one and the attractive girl?"

"No sir."

"Did he leave a name when he paid the deposit?"

"Just the first name of the man - Tom, but the assistant who served them says the girl was called Laura."

"How does she remember so well?"

"I asked the same thing sir, apparently it's because they were arguing and that made them stick in the assistant's mind."

"What were they arguing about?"

"She didn't remember sir."

Lewisham finally looks pleased. "Good work Sergeant. So what do we have now? We have all the party guests accounted for, except for Big Bird and Elvis. We have a witness who was dressed as a predator reporting that he lost his mask…"

I interrupt, "'The Predator' sir."

"That's what I said."

"No sir, you said 'a predator'. He was dressed as The Predator, or just Predator, it's a horror film where an alien is hunting humans. But he comes up against Arnold Schwarzenegger."

"Thank you for that lesson in cinema history Sergeant, may I continue?"

"Yes sir."

"That's very gracious of you. So, as I was saying, we have a witness who was dressed as," he pauses, "'The Predator', who lost his mask and found it later across the other side of the room to where he had left it, next to a jacket splashed with the victim's blood. This jacket belonged to another witness who claimed to have left it hanging near the front door and could not explain how it had moved to the room where the murder took place. We also have a third witness claiming to have seen a man changing from…" he pauses again, "…'The Predator' to Elvis after the murder took place, and we've got a very tedious couple, Mr. and Mrs. Thompson saying they spoke to Elvis and Big Bird at length at the party and that Elvis left their company shortly before the murder." He opens a drawer in his desk and takes out the file for the Hunter case. He hands it to me without opening it. "Please be so kind as to find the Thompsons' statement

and read out the names they used for Big Bird and Elvis."

I scan the document and quickly find the names. "Laura and Tom sir."

He smiles. "Laura and Tom, Tom and Laura. Big Bird and Elvis. I think we should pay another visit to that lovely girl and the portly chap who didn't remember Elvis and Big Bird entering their flat that night. Then I think we're going to get some sea air. Brighton's nice at this time of year."

"Yes sir."

* * * * * * * * * * * * * * * *

As soon as I saw Laura's face I knew it was bad news. "My cousin just rang."

"Steve?"

"He and Wendy just had another visit from the police."

My stomach churned. "What did they say?"

"They say they have reason to believe that Big Bird and Elvis entered their flat on the night of the party."

In other circumstances the example of copper-speak would have made me laugh but I was too scared to find anything funny at that moment. "What did Steve and Wendy say?"

"They said they didn't know anything about it."

"Good for them."

"There's more Tom."

"What?"

"They asked if the names Tom and Laura meant anything to them."

"Shit."

"Is there more to this than you're telling me?"

"You think I killed the guy?"

"Of course not, but since you told me what you did for a living I thought there might be more to the story."

"So you think I'm still lying to you?"

"Possibly, why not? Look, Tom, I'm not having a go at you. I fully expect you to keep things from me, you're a drug dealer so there'll be a lot of things you won't be able to tell me, and I'm glad you don't tell me, but this is different. My name has been used by the police in connection with a murder. I'm part of their investigation. They might find us and give us the third degree, so I want to know everything that's going on, so I know what I'm caught up in. I want to be prepared."

"They won't ask you any questions. They don't know where we live. Steve and Wendy have denied seeing us so how are they going to follow us down to Brighton? You're not caught up in anything."

"Okay, maybe the police won't question me but it's bad enough that Steve and Wendy had to be put on the spot like this. Quite frankly it's embarrassing."

"If I had known there was going to be anything untoward going on at the party I wouldn't have taken you."

"Tom, at first you weren't going to invite me to that party; I had to ask to come with you, and it turned out that if I hadn't come then you would have been on your own. It just seems a bit strange that you were willing to travel seventy miles to go to a party, dressed as Elvis Presley, knowing that there was a fair chance that you weren't going to know anybody there. Are you sure you had no other reason to be there?"

"Okay, I expected that I might arrange a bit of business with some guys I thought would be there, but it was nothing major and I could take it or leave it."

"And they weren't there so you had to leave it."

"Exactly."

"From now on I want you to tell me if we're going anywhere that's remotely connected to your business. I'm happy that you keep me in the dark about things that don't affect me, but if I become the slightest bit involved then I need to be warned."

"Of course. Sorry."

"Now give me back that reefer, you've had it ages."

* * * * * * * * * * * * * * * *

Frank and Steph have been getting on real well. Maybe a bit too well. I have to keep reminding myself that Frank would never fall for Tony Visconti's little girl; she's like a niece, a kid-sister even

We have to be careful when we all get together, even though it's been ten years since Stephanie 'died'. If word gets back to Stan that me and Frank have been seen with Tony Visconti's daughter, then that would be the end for all of us. Stan wouldn't hang around for explanations, he'd just assume the worst, and he'd be right to. The same goes for Joe.

If we stay out of sight we'll be okay. There's no reason for Stan or Joe to think for a second that Steph might be alive, and they probably don't even remember her if truth be told. She was in the car when the bomb went off, so she should have been killed along with her parents. She was trapped in the wreckage for four hours and was clinically dead when they finally cut her out. The doctors managed to get her heart going again. They called it a miracle. Frank and I had to work overtime to bury that miracle; we pulled a lot of strings and leaned on a lot of people to make sure the world, or anyone who cared at least, believed Tony Visconti's little girl had died. It helped that the tabloids picked up the story. The papers always pretend to be outraged by crime and violence but really they love it. It's juicy stuff to them, and their readers lap it up. A picture of Steph wearing a gap-toothed smile and a Hammers shirt, taken six months before she supposedly died was on the cover of every newspaper. The story would have been even bigger if anyone had bothered to find out the truth.

Even back then Stan was ruthless and paranoid, and it would have been too dangerous to let the world know Steph was alive. However harmless she was as an eleven-year-old orphan, Stan wouldn't risk letting her grow up into someone who fancied a bit of revenge, or even spill to the filth, not that she would have any evidence, but Stan wouldn't have taken any chances. He would have done the necessary. Joe was higher in the pecking order in Visconti's crew at the time but it was obvious Stan called the shots in that ugly little pairing. After the revolution they carved up Tony's empire between the two of them and went their separate ways. They've hardly spoken since.

We're in Steph's hotel room in West London, it's not the lap of luxury but it's no flea-infested knocking shop either. Her uncle Bobby is one of the few people who knows who she really is. Despite being Tony's brother he's not in the life, he chose a different path and made his wedge, a proper wedge, in property development over in the States. Steph said he was reluctant to go for revenge on his brother's killers; he's a religious man and believes God will deal with Costanza and Barrett, but Steph needed somebody to put up the money for her to stay in London to put her plans in place, and Bobby caved. When Steph wants something, especially from a man, she usually gets it.

I'm sitting on a chair in the hotel room and Frank is sprawled on the bed, looking a bit too cosy for my liking. Steph's standing up. "Do you want a coffee?" She asks.

"Are we ordering from room service?" Frank replies.

"I thought I'd use the kettle in here."

"In that case no thanks. I know a guy who used to be a roadie for a band who almost made it big. He said when they was on tour the drummer would shit in the kettle in every room he stayed in. I've never used a hotel kettle since."

Steph puts the kettle down. "Thanks Frank, that's a charming story. Shall we ring room service then?"

"Yeah, let's do that." Frank picks up the phone.

I turn to Frank. "I thought you said you don't trust hotel kettles. Room service coffee still comes from a kettle."

"Don't be stupid Cheese, nobody's going to shit in the one in the kitchen."

I know he's trying to make me look like an idiot in front of Steph but I bite my tongue. I don't want us to look like a couple of kids. "If you're calling room service get me a chicken sandwich. And it's your turn to pay."

Steph must have noticed the tension between me and Frank. "Let's forget about refreshments and just get down to business."

"Yeah, let's do that." Frank's quick to agree with her. "What's the latest on Barrett? Does he still think you've got the hots for him?"

"He thinks I'm in love with him. It's all going to plan."

"Do you…" Frank checks himself, "nothing."

Steph won't let it drop just like that. "Do I what, Frank?"

"Forget it, carry on. Tell me the latest."

"No Frank, you tell me. What were you going to say?"

Frank sees that Steph's not going to budge and gives in. "Okay, but don't take this the wrong way."

"How do I know what the right way to take it will be?"

"Let's just forget it." I can see Frank's digging a hole for himself.

"Just tell me, Frank."

Frank sits up on the bed, his hands on his lap, protecting his crown jewels in case Steph loses her temper. "Christ, you're not going to let it go are you? Okay, what I was going to say was do you have to, Jesus, how do I say this? Do you have to," he pauses again. I've never seen him so nervous about saying something, "You say he thinks you're in love with him, well, do you have to show him?"

"You mean do I have to suck his cock?" Frank looks at the floor and so do I. "Come on Frank, that's what you mean isn't it? You want to know if letting Joe Barrett fuck me is part of the plan. Is that what you think of me?" Her eyes are pure rage.

Frank raises his hands, trying to calm her down. "I wasn't saying that, Steph. Christ, I knew you'd take it the wrong way."

"Is there a right way to take it?"

I step in. "Steph, I'm sure Frank didn't mean nothing by it, I think what he meant was, is Barrett suspicious that you and him… don't… you know?"

Frank's quick to hang onto my explanation, like a hanged man pulling at the rope to save his neck from breaking. "Exactly, that's what I meant Steph. I wasn't suggesting nothing."

This seems to calm Steph down a bit, but her anger's still in her eyes. "Seeing as you're so interested, Frank, no, I don't have sex with Joe Barrett, and when I say sex I mean any kind of sexual contact. I've told him that I can't share his bed while I'm with Stan, because I need to keep them totally separate. I've told him that in the future, when Joe and I live happily ever after, I need to block out my time with Stan, and I won't be able to do that if Joe is part of that memory. I made it sound like it was very very important to me."

Frank has relaxed after Steph's attack. "And he believed you? Fuck me, he's easier than I thought."

"He'll believe anything I tell him."

"You sound almost proud of it." Frank's pushing his luck.

"I am proud of it. Would you rather I felt ashamed? I've got nothing to be ashamed of."

Frank doesn't give her what she wants this time, he just waves her away. I stick my oar in. "We both know you're doing a great job Steph. It takes guts to do what you're doing." I shoot a look at Frank.

Frank's slow to react but then he goes along with me, "yeah, it takes guts."

I carry on, "So what's the latest? What's he planning? Or what have you told him to plan?"

Steph's face says that Frank isn't off the hook forever but that we need to get on. She says, "He's going to go to war."

Frank almost falls off the bed. "Is he off his trolley? He knows he can't possibly win."

Steph smiles. "He doesn't know anything anymore Frank. And before you say it, yes I'm proud of that."

"How long?" I try to keep things moving.

"Soon. The whole situation has accelerated. Tom White is more of a success than we could have imagined. We picked a good man there."

Frank cuts her off. "What do you mean 'we' picked a good man? You didn't pick White, Costanza sent us round there because he killed the guy next door. Are you saying you set that up?"

I answer for Steph, "No Frank, even we're not that good. We were looking for someone to use in the middle, someone from the outside. White fell into our laps by doing his neighbour, so Steph made sure the rumours about this shit-hot kid reached Joe, who was more than grateful to have his services."

"Alright Cheese, do you think I'm deaf? You've explained all that to me before."

"So why did you fucking ask then?"

"Shall we move on?" Steph spares Frank's blushes by getting back on with her update. "Every time Joe gets hit he's hitting back much harder than even I hoped he would. I hardly have to persuade him what he should do, or give Tom White fake orders anymore. It's saving me a load of Uncle Bobby's money."

Frank interrupts. "Christ, I hadn't thought of that, so every time you get White to do a hit that Barrett didn't order it costs Bobby ten grand? Jesus, he must be doing alright across the pond."

"He's doing just fine Frank. But back to the point, Joe's living on blind fury and Stan's just reacting, reacting, reacting. The murder of the Calsons was the turning point and it's just snowballed since then. Some are saying the war's on now." She frowns. "I wish I had some coffee."

Frank speaks. "It's getting weird out there now, nobody knows who to trust, and nobody knows who they should be loyal to, everyone's trying to second guess who's going to come out on top."

Steph smiles. "You know Geoff Crowley, Barrett's right hand man?" We both nod. "He's been warning Barrett about me."

"Why didn't you say that before?" I ask. "What does he know? Is he on to us?"

"He's got no proof, but he's not a fool. He doesn't trust me. He thinks I have too much influence."

"Has Joe told you this?"

"He would never tell me directly. To let me hear the merest suggestion that I have any kind of influence over him would be to show weakness in

front of me, and he couldn't handle that."

"But surely it's his own men he should be worrying about looking weak in front of," says Frank. He looks at Steph and puts on his kid gloves. "No offence Steph, but being seen to take orders from a woman isn't going to send a good message to his personnel." Steph's eyes start to fill with rage again. Frank jumps in quick. "I'm not saying it's right Steph, just, well, that's the way it is. These men are old school, from a time when you couldn't be seen to be inferior to a woman."

That seems to put Steph's fire out. "Well, any kind of disharmony in the ranks can only be good for us, whatever the reason."

"Steph," I say, "I think you're in too close. With all the distrust that's going on a lot of Barrett's men are looking to feather their nests with the likely winner, they're all trying to get on Costanza's side. What if word gets out about what you've been saying to Joe? What if Costanza works out what's going on?"

Frank replies instead of Steph. "I don't think it's much of a problem. The situation's got so tense that Stan won't believe anyone from Joe's side, even if they look like they want to defect. He'll think Barrett's trying to fuck with him. Stan hardly trusts anyone at the best of times, and in wartime he only trusts himself."

Twenty-three

* * * * * * * * * * * * * * *

I'm driving Inspector Lewisham to Brighton. He seems to be in good spirits and I hope he's going to be more relaxed than he is normally. "So, Sergeant Milford, how's your wife these days? What's her name again?"

The fact that he remembers the tiniest detail of any case he's working on but has forgotten my wife's name proves he doesn't give a toss about me as a person. "Her name's Alice, and she's fine sir. She had our second child a few months ago."

"Oh yes, I seem to remember a collection going round at the station. Unfortunately I don't think I had any change that day."

"That's okay sir." *I don't try very hard to sound convincing.* "By the way sir, I'd rather you called me by my name, John."

"No Sergeant, that's not the way I do things. Now, this Inspector Buckley, what time are we meeting him?"

"Eleven-thirty."

"And how did you find him?"

"I called Brighton Station and asked for the Inspector in charge of the murder squad sir."

He looks at me, puzzled, then a look of realisation crosses his face and he speaks. "No, no Sergeant. I don't mean how did you find him I meant what did you think of him when you spoke to him?"

"I see sir. No offence sir, but please be more specific with your questions. You always taught me sir, that a policeman should always be specific with his questioning to avoid ambiguity. There's no place for ambiguity in an investigation sir, that's what you taught me sir." *I love playing the army cadet while I'm taking the piss out of him. I often wonder if he realises that every time I say 'sir' I mean 'twat'.*

He hesitates and decides not to react. "I take your point Sergeant. So what did you think of Inspector Buckley? Does he seem to be the sort of man who can help us?"

"I didn't form an opinion sir, you always taught me, sir, not to make snap judgements. I didn't speak to him for long sir so I'm waiting to see how he pans out. Sir." I can hardly remember anything about Buckley, I just asked him if he was free for a meeting about a murder investigation and we arranged a time.

Chief Inspector Lewisham doesn't speak for the rest of the journey.

We arrive in Brighton, the police station looks like a railway depot. There are the usual scumbags loitering about, mostly boy racers queuing to present their tax and insurance documents after being pulled over for speeding. There is nobody behind the window they are queuing at, and the line grows longer. We go to the front desk and Lewisham lets me do the talking. I'm sure it's because he likes to be announced, like a visiting dignitary at a royal banquet. "Good morning, I'm Sergeant John Milford and this is Chief Inspector Lewisham, we're from Scotland Yard."

The WPC at the desk looks at us as if we're no different from the yobs queuing with their speeding tickets. "You're from Lewisham." It sounds like a statement rather than a question.

"No, we're from Scotland Yard, this is Chief Inspector Lewisham. Although coincidentally I do live in Lewisham myself." I half-laugh as I say this and expect it to break the ice.

"So you are from Lewisham." Her face remains impassive.

Lewisham butts in, talking loudly. "We're from Scotland Yard and we're investigating a murder. We're here to see an Inspector Buckley. We have an appointment. Please tell Buckley we've arrived." She looks at him and, remaining silent, she turns and goes through a door. When she returns a minute or so later she doesn't look at either of us, making a point of becoming engrossed in some kind of register on the desk.

Lewisham's not having it. "It's been a long time since I manned the front desk but I'm sure that procedures don't indicate being objectionable to visitors from other forces." The WPC ignores him. *"Constable?"*

She looks up. *"Are you talking to me?"*

"Yes, of course."

She looks blankly at him. *"Can I take your name?"*

"It's Lewisham, as you well know, seeing as you have just gone back and told Inspector Buckley that I'm here to see him. You have asked him, haven't you?"

"Yes," she returns her attention to the register.

Lewisham prides himself on never losing his temper but the throbbing vein on his temple is a dead giveaway. I'm finding the woman offensive but I'm enjoying the spectacle. A male officer comes out of the door behind her and cuts short my private floor show.

"Chief Inspector Lewisham, I'm Buckley." He looks at me, *"And you must be Sergeant Milford."*

"Yes yes yes," bellows Lewisham.

"Won't you come through?" Buckley gently moves the WPC's register and lifts the hinged panel on the desk. *"Thank you Constable Brown."* WPC Brown looks at him as blankly as she had looked at us. She doesn't make any effort to get out of the way which hinders our progress as we make our way through.

Buckley leads us into his office. He's a tall man and looks to be in his late forties. His hair is short and black, a man of his age should have some grey by now and I wonder if he has dyed it. His face has the look that is so familiar to me; that of a senior officer, decades on the force. Adherence to procedure and constant suspicion of most of the people he encounters have chiselled and moulded his face. I know I'll have that look in ten years' time, maybe I'm already part of the way there.

Buckley moves a stack of papers from one of the chairs in front of his desk and indicates that we sit down, taking his own seat behind the desk. *"How can I help you?"*

Lewisham speaks. *"Thanks for your time Inspector Buckley. We're investigating the murder of a Damien Hunter of thirteen Garden Mews in central London."*

"The fancy-dress murder?"

"That's what the tabloids like to call it, yes." *Lewisham's voice is stern, bordering on snappy.*

"The victim was an arms dealer if I recall."

"He was an alleged arms dealer, and I know what you're thinking." *Lewisham pauses, Buckley doesn't make any move to indicate what he's thinking. "You're wondering why the Yard are going to so much trouble to catch the killer of a man who deserves everything he got."*

"That's not what I was thinking, Chief Inspector Lewisham, I was actually thinking whether the vending machine has been fixed yet so I could offer you both a coffee, after all, you must have had a long journey. But now you mention it, I do agree that this case wouldn't be my highest priority."

"Don't tell me how to do my job Inspector." He emphasises Buckley's rank, using the tone of his voice to highlight the prefix his own title enjoys.

"I most certainly was not telling you how to do your job, sir." I stifle a smile. Where I have always pronounced the word 'sir' as 'twat' when addressing Chief Inspector Lewisham, Buckley pronounces it 'cunt'. "I was merely responding to your statement, sir."

"Inspector Buckley," Lewisham's voice has lowered; he's trying a different tack, one that I've been on the receiving end of myself; he's going to try and patronise Buckley into submission. "I think every murder should be investigated with the same professionalism, the same vigour, the same determination..." he sounds like a newly inaugurated politician, "... regardless of the victim's standing in the community. We are not judges, we merely uphold the law, and the law of this land states very clearly that taking a person's life is the most serious of crimes. There is nothing in the statute books to indicate that an investigation should be any less thorough if the victim is rumoured to be involved in dubious activities. But apart from that Inspector, there are other factors to consider. Down here by the seaside you have plenty to deal with, but you don't share the problems that we have in the capital." Now he's pulling rank with geography. "A murder is a murder, but it can be so much more." He pauses to allow his

previous insults to sink in.

Buckley feigns boredom. "Get to the point Chief Inspector."

"We have reason to believe that if we find the killer in this case it will lead us to solve a number of other serious crimes in the city. We are seeing evidence of gang warfare and we need to take as many of the perpetrators out of circulation as possible. The two main players that we know of are a Stanley Costanza and a Joseph Barrett, heads of rival crime organisations. Any leads in this case could cause us to make huge inroads into the problem of organised crime in the capital; organised crime that I am sure has some influence out here in the provinces. In the light of this, Inspector, we are grateful for your kind assistance."

Buckley, already resigned to helping us, waits patiently for Lewisham to finish then responds slowly and carefully. "We in the city of Brighton and Hove are always happy to provide assistance to our colleagues in other regions. Now, how can I help? Which I think is what I said when I first sat down."

Lewisham ignores the jibe and gets to work. "From extensive interviews with witnesses who were at Damien Hunter's party the night he died, we have established a list of all the guests that were present, at least, we have a list of the costumes they were wearing. We have accounted for all but two of these guests. The remaining two were dressed as Elvis Presley and Big Bird, a character from the Muppets. Now…"

Buckley cuts him off, "Sesame Street."

Lewisham looks at him wearily. "Excuse me?"

"Big Bird was in Sesame Street, not the Muppets. I can see your confusion though, they were both Jim Henson." Buckley's tone is condescending rather than sarcastic.

"But you knew who I meant?"

"Of course, a bright yellow bird with a long neck."

"So what difference does it make?"

"Down here in the provinces we like to be as accurate about our facts as we can." Round two to Buckley.

Lewisham mutters under his breath before moving on. "Sergeant

Milford here has traced the rental of the outfits to a shop in Brighton town centre…"

"Fancy That," I say.

Lewisham puts his head in his hands. "What?"

"Sorry sir, I didn't mean to interrupt. I was letting Inspector Buckley know the name of the shop."

Buckley is grinning from ear to ear. "Thank you, Sergeant Milford. I know of the shop, although I haven't been there myself."

"Yes yes yes," snaps Lewisham. "Now, the assistant at the shop says it was a young man and woman who rented out the costumes and that their first names were Tom and Laura. These names match the statements of two witnesses who say they spoke to the couple at the party. This evidence could suggest that the couple are from London and merely went out of town to rent the outfits. However, we have a further witness placing Elvis and Big Bird at a flat near the scene of the murder later that night and the couple who live in the flat do not match the descriptions of the couple who rented the outfits. This suggests that they were merely staying the night, leading us to believe that they may actually be from the Brighton area." Lewisham finishes speaking and sits back, letting Buckley absorb his soliloquy.

Buckley jumps straight in. "Is it not possible, Chief Inspector, that they live in another town altogether, came here to rent the costumes, then went to London to carry out the murder?"

Lewisham looks wearier still. "Yes Inspector," he sighs, "it is possible that there is a third town, and of course they may be from London and merely visited the flat near the scene of the murder, but we can only follow the leads we have."

"Of course, Chief Inspector, I just wanted to make sure your investigation isn't too narrow." Buckley's face is smugness incarnate.

Lewisham again resists the bait. "What I would like from you, Inspector, is details of all your murder enquiries from the last twelve months. We need the names of all suspects and witnesses, along with details of the crime, suspected motive and the weapon used. We have ascertained that the bullet found in Mister Hunter was from the same weapon that killed a Steven Clarke in SW1 some weeks earlier. Mister Clarke, like Mister Hunter, was suspected to be less than squeaky clean in his affairs. There is also a third case outside of London where two known associates of Mister Costanza, twin brothers Maxwell and Jasper Calson, were shot and killed, along with a third man, a Mister Kingsley Fry. It looks like our shooter had company on this sojourn because the bullets that matched those which killed Damien Hunter and Steven Clarke were only found in one of the bodies in this case, that of Jasper Calson."

"That will be fine Chief Inspector, I'll show you to an office with a computer terminal where you can look up all the information you need. I'll send one of our younger officers in to show you how to access the data. I'll have any other documents that haven't been input into the computer brought in for you."

"Thank you, Inspector."

It turns out that the younger officer who Buckley said would help us is WPC Brown from the front desk, and she delights in only answering what we specifically ask, rather than telling us everything we need. We have to keep leaving the office to find her and ask for her to fill in the holes in what she's told us. She loves every second of it. Buckley and another officer appear shortly, each with a stack of folders and papers that they dump at either side of the computer. "Good luck gentlemen." This is all he says before leaving the room.

It's hard work. The paper and computer files are in no kind of order and it's a painstaking task to find what we need and cross reference all the different pieces of information. On the upside, Brighton isn't a big murder town so the number of individual cases is low, and most of the killings we do find are by heroin and crack addicts in botched robberies, which we quickly disregard. It's Lewisham who eventually strikes gold.

"Listen to this Sergeant. We have an unsolved shooting in a residential street in Brighton. The victim's name was Barry Carter. It doesn't match the modus operandi for the Hunter murder but it definitely matches that of Steven Clarke. The only difference is that the gun was left at the scene of

the crime, no prints found."

"Sounds good, any suspects?"

"None with any corroborating evidence, but the notes on the file say that Carter was rumoured to have been quite the ladies man, and that he chose the wrong lady. He supposedly slept with the daughter of a Stanley Costanza, and the word is that Mr. Costanza wasn't best pleased about it"

"This is exactly what we've been looking for, sir."

"You haven't heard the icing on the cake yet Sergeant. There is a list of all the residents in Mr. Carter's street, which seems to be about as far as Buckley's investigation has gone. The name of the next-door neighbour is a Mr. White, Mr. Thomas White. I think we're going to be down here for a little while. I hope your wife and children can survive without you."

"How long for sir?"

"As long as it takes."

Twenty-four

* * * * * * * * * * * * * * *

The friction of our initial meeting with Buckley has all but worn off. Buckley and Lewisham are never going to be best friends, but they seem to have reached a level of grudging mutual acceptance. Lewisham was furious that Buckley didn't mention the connection between the Carter murder and Stan Costanza at our first meeting, but said we needed Buckley's cooperation for now so he would have to put off berating him for his ineptitude until we had completed our enquiries.

I had expected our first move to be to question Tom White, but Lewisham insisted we needed to arm ourselves with as much information as possible before making White aware we were on his trail.

Lewisham and I are sitting in the office Buckley has lent us for the duration of our stay. Lewisham speaks. "We need a photograph of White to show to the shop assistant from 'Fancy That'. Mrs. Lewisham bought me one of those digital cameras for our wedding anniversary, I haven't been able to fathom the thing, I'm sure it's more up your street Sergeant."

"I'd be more than willing to show you how to use it sir." *I know full well what's coming.*

"You don't need to show me, Sergeant, you'll be the one using the camera."

"But I've only ever taken holiday snaps before sir."

"Could you see the faces of the people in your holiday snaps?"

"Of course sir."

"Well there you have it. That's all we need, a recognisable photo. You're the man for the job."

"But my holiday snaps were of my family, they were posing for the photos. How am I going to take White's picture without him knowing?"

"Sergeant, the Yard aren't going to free up one of their specialist photographers when all we've got to go on so far is a first name match, so it's down to us, well down to you really. You'll have to do the best you can. Get yourself over to Gravely Terrace and wait for White to appear."

"Shouldn't we run this past Inspector Buckley sir? He might get a little territorial if we start taking photographs of suspects on his patch without us telling him."

"Let me worry about that, Sergeant. We don't need to concern Buckley at this stage."

I sit in the unmarked car in Gravely Terrace, watching Tom White's house, armed only with five million megapixels and a four-time optical zoom. This is not a stakeout, I'm just after a decent headshot, but it's as tedious as the untold stakeouts I've been on. I've been here for two and a half hours and I've realised that if I don't go to the toilet soon then I'm going to split open like the liver of a foie gras goose, but I know full well if I do go and find a toilet now, that will be when Tom White decides to leave his house. It will be like waiting for the Gas Board to turn up, sitting expectantly by the front door for six hours then popping out for 2 minutes to get some milk and returning to find a card on the mat: "We're sorry, you were out."

I see movement, the door is opening and a man is leaving the premises. He has dark hair and fits the description given by the assistant at 'Fancy That'. I know this could be the breakthrough in our investigation. Whilst I've been sitting in the car waiting I haven't actually settled on a plan for when White appears. Now I have no idea what to do. He's on the pavement walking away from me and I have to decide what action to take. I leave the car and cross the road so I'm on the opposite pavement to White, and I walk past him. I move quickly but try to look casual.

If I had the right tools for the job, that is, a proper telephoto lens, I would have been able to get the shot as he left his house, but my inferior equipment wouldn't have captured more than a distant blur so I have to get close. I get to the end of the street and stop, pretending to be looking at houses and hoping I resemble an estate agent, although in my jeans and t-shirt I don't think I look the part. I stand as if I am taking a photo of the last house on the street, setting the zoom to maximum. White, who seems to be a considerate chap, stops short of the house so he doesn't obscure my picture. I take a picture of the house and thank him with a nod of my head. He starts moving again and I walk across the road to intercept him. My camera is still raised and I press the button as I get closer, he does me the huge favour of turning to look at me just as I do this, and I get a great close up of his face. I know he suspects I have taken his picture, so I continue walking forward, as if I have just been framing my next picture of the house. I can see him in the corner of the lens. He eyes me suspiciously but eventually seems to accept my unspoken cover story and continues on his way.

The door of the house I am in front of opens, and a middle aged woman appears. Her hair is in rollers and a pair of nylon slacks are pulled up almost to her chest. "Why are you taking pictures of my house?" I motion for her to be quiet, worrying that White is still within earshot. "So you're making gestures at me now? Explain yourself young man." I haven't been called 'young man' for longer than I can remember.

I hurry towards her, wanting to silence her as quickly as possible. "Police, madam." I speak as loudly as I think I can afford.

"Police?" Her voice is shrill.

"Please be quiet, just for a moment. I need you to be quiet."

Before I can show her my badge she runs inside the house and slams the door. I go to the door and see a sticker on the glass bearing the legend "Neighbourhood Watch Co-ordinator," and I realise I have a busybody on my hands. I knock softly on the door. There is silence so I knock again. I hear movement and talking inside, but she still doesn't come to the door. I knock again and see her shape move into the hallway through the frosted glass. "Go away, get away from my house."

"I just need to explain."

"I've called the police, they'll be here soon," she hisses through the

letterbox.

I squat down, wincing at the pressure on my full bladder, and attempt to open the flap of the letterbox but she pulls it shut, catching my fingers as she does so. There must be some string attached to the inside, this woman definitely fears the worst in people. "I am the police."

"Let me see your badge then. Put it through the letterbox, and don't try anything, I've got a beaker of acid ready." I believe her, in fact I feel lucky she doesn't have boiling oil to pour over me. Perhaps that's her next line of defence.

I take out my badge. "I'm taking out my badge," I say, trying to keep her from inflicting tremendous pain on my person. I lift the flap of the letterbox. "I'm lifting the flap of the letterbox."

"Don't try anything. This is my home, I can defend my home. I can use reasonable force."

"No force is required madam, please just let me do my job. I'm putting the badge through the letterbox now. There, I've dropped it. Please have a look at it then if you would be so kind as to open the door?"

There is silence then I hear her sigh as if she is disappointed that I am genuine, and that she no longer has a reason to shower me with acid. I hear bolts sliding and a safety chain being unlatched. As I wait, I see the sign to the left of the glass saying, 'No hawkers or canvassers, no circulars, no junk mail'. The door finally opens and she faces me, smiling. She has transformed into a different person. "My name is Eileen McCulloch." She returns my badge. "How can I help you Sergeant Milford?"

I don't want to start a panic but realise I have no choice but to tell her the truth. "Can I come in please Mrs. McCulloch?"

"Yes of course, would you like some tea?" I decline the offer and she shows me into the front room, which is immaculate but with thirty-year-old décor. "The reason I was outside, Mrs. McCulloch..."

"Call me Eileen."

"The reason I was outside, Eileen, was that I was taking a photograph to help an investigation we're conducting."

"Is it about that poor boy in number twenty-five?"

"It may well be."

"He was a nice boy, a little noisy, but he was friendly enough. I can't think why anybody would want to kill him. Do you have any leads?"

"I'm afraid I can't discuss that case with you Mrs. McCulloch, I'm not from the local constabulary."

"You're not one of Buckley's boys?"

"No, Mrs. McCulloch. I'm from Scotland Yard."

"Eileen," she corrects me once more, her face brightening at the mention of the Yard. "So tell me Sergeant, how does photographing my house help your investigation." The words of her question sound like she is suspicious, but her eyes suggest she is excited by the prospect of being involved. I've seen this before, she's been bored out of her mind for years and this is a big event for her.

"What I am telling you is out of courtesy and is under the strictest confidence, Eileen. You have to give me your word that you will not tell anybody what I am about to tell you, and that you will not act differently towards the person I am about to mention."

"You have my word, Sergeant, and that is a cast iron guarantee. These lips are like the gates to a high security prison."

I wonder when those cast iron gates were last penetrated. "We are trying to eliminate somebody from our enquiries, Eileen. Somebody who lives in this road. I had to get a photograph of him so we could check the statement of a witness in our case. That's why I was outside your house."

She thinks for a moment then remembers who was passing her house before she came out to confront me. "Tom White? The chap from number twenty-seven?" She puts her hand over her mouth in the archetypal shocked expression.

"Please, Mrs. McCulloch, Eileen, this is a delicate matter. Mr. White has not been accused of any crime, we are just trying to narrow down our investigation. The utmost discretion is called for. You have already given me your word that you will keep this between us and I trust you, so I won't say anything further. But please do not let me down on this."

"Of course, Sergeant Milford."

"You understand me?"

"Of course, Sergeant. You can count on me."

I am about to leave when there is a loud banging on the door and the face of a uniformed officer peering through the window. "It's alright Constable Robertson," shouts McCulloch. "It's a police officer, he's investigating Tom White from down the road whose neighbour was killed." She looks at me as I raise my eyes to the ceiling and puts her hand to her mouth once more. "Oops, I shouldn't be shouting that should I?"

"No, you shouldn't, Eileen, and I hope that this will be the last time you mention Mr. White in this context." I wonder if I can get away with my next question but realise I have no choice. "Do you think I could use your toilet?"

When I get back to the station an argument is already underway. Buckley is shouting at Chief Inspector Lewisham. "What on earth were you thinking of? You can't just go around taking pictures of people, especially people connected with my investigations."

"I'd like to see some evidence of your investigation Buckley, it seems to have stopped months ago. Tom White is no longer connected with your investigation. You wrote him off within an hour of the murder, if your report is anything to go by. Now I suggest you take a step back and let us big boys clean up your mess."

Buckley finally cracks. "Fuck you Lewisham," he screams. I never thought I'd see Lewisham get told where to stick it, and it's a moment I know I'll cherish forever. Unfortunately the moment is spoiled when Buckley stabs a finger in my direction. "And as for you, who the fuck do you think you are, telling residents of my town they have a murderer living in the neighbourhood? What are you trying to do, raise a lynch mob?"

"I didn't tell her that, but she saw me take his picture so I had to say something. If I hadn't she would probably have asked him herself, then he'd know we're onto him."

Lewisham comes to my aid. "Don't even bother answering him Sergeant, we have real police work to do." He turns back to Buckley. "Once our witness confirms this picture then you're going to realise you have a killer living next door to one of your unsolved murder scenes, a killer that talked his way out of your investigation with a few nods and smiles. You wouldn't last five minutes in a real city, Buckley."

Lewisham strides out of the station and I follow, remembering as I get through the door that we needed to make use of Buckley's computer to print out a copy of the picture from the digital camera. I wait until we have reached the car before pointing this out to Lewisham. "Well that's just fucking perfect isn't it?" I have never heard him swear before. "We'll have to go to a shop. We're going to be in the mall anyway."

We park the car at the shopping centre and look for a place with a photo-developing service. We eventually find one and I hand the camera to Lewisham as we walk in. "What are you giving it to me for?" He hands it back.

"Because it's yours, and I wouldn't know the first thing about what to do."

"Nor do I, I've already told you, it was an anniversary present, I didn't want it."

"What anniversary was it?"

"Thirty-first."

"Congratulations."

"Thank you. Now take the camera."

"Can I help you?" A girl behind the counter is looking over at us, ready to serve.

"Yes please," I say. "We'd like to get a picture printed."

"Analogue or digital?"

"Digital."

"Do you have a memory card?"

I turn to Lewisham. "Do we have a memory card?"

"What does it look like?" He is looking at me but I presume he's talking to her as I don't know what a memory card looks like.

"Is that the camera there?" She reaches for it and I give it to her. "Here it is, you just open this flap and look, it pops out." Lewisham and I stare, entranced by her magicianship. "Now, I'll show you how to operate

the machine."

"We have to do it ourselves?" Lewisham sounds shocked, like he has been told to wash his own dishes in a restaurant.

"Well, yes, normally, it's supposed to be more convenient for the customer, but I can go through it with you if you would prefer."

"Yes, I would prefer that," Lewisham reads her name badge, "Shelley."

She leads us to the machine and slides the memory card into a slot. The screen is divided into sixteen squares. My two pictures fill the two in the top left hand corner, leaving the rest barren. "You just have two pictures? I'm afraid there's a minimum charge of three pounds."

"That's outrageous," says Lewisham.

"I'm sorry sir, but it costs us a certain amount to maintain the machine, and if we allowed customers to pay for just one or two at a time then we wouldn't be breaking even. And besides, people normally have more pictures. Are these very important?"

"Yes, Shelley, these are very important. Very well, if we have to pay that astronomical sum then there's nothing we can do. Time is of the essence so please print those two out."

"Okay sir." She presses a button and the first picture enlarges. It is a perfectly framed shot of number two, Gravely Terrace and I can feel the heat of Lewisham's anger boring into me.

"I had to take that, it was my cover." I know I sound desperate.

The assistant enlarges the next image. I breathe out a sigh of relief as I realise it is a good, clear picture. "We just need that one, thank you. Sergeant, I hope you have some cash on you."

We go to 'Fancy That' and show the picture to the assistant who has no hesitation. "That's him, that's Elvis."

Lewisham speaks in his most patronising voice. "Thank you madam, you've been very helpful."

"Can you tell me what this is about?" This isn't the first time she has asked this question.

Lewisham gives the stock answer. "I'm afraid that's classified information madam," his voice is pompous, "but one thing I can say is that you have done a great service for your community."

She smiles politely but doesn't seem particularly impressed. "I've remembered something else since I spoke to the Sergeant by the way."

Lewisham becomes animated. "Go on."

"I told the Sergeant they were having an argument, that's why I remembered them so clearly, but I couldn't remember what it was about. It's come back to me now."

"Yes, yes?" Lewisham is trying to mask his impatience.

"They were arguing about the party, she wasn't invited at first, it was just going to be him, and she was upset. In the end he gave in and said she could go too. I heard them say where the party was going to be, it was in London."

"Did they say which part of London?"

"It's on the tip of my tongue, it's that trendy place, the one with all the sex shops."

I don't want to lead her to an answer but she's as good as said it. "Soho?"

"That's it, Soho."

We return to the station and Buckley, despite what Lewisham thinks of him, is a professional enough officer to put the earlier altercation behind him when he hears our news. In fact he's a little over-professional for Lewisham's liking. "We're doing this by the book Chief Inspector, I'm calling in an armed response unit. If White comes out shooting I want to be ready."

"How long for an ARU to arrive?" Lewisham's frustration is obvious.

"Up to two hours, we'll just have to sit tight until then. I'm sure White's not going anywhere, he doesn't even know we're on to him." Lewisham says nothing. He knows his hands are tied. Even though he is a senior rank, he's Buckley's guest, and it would be against protocol to make short cuts when making an arrest of a suspect who is known to be armed. Buckley turns his attention to WPC Brown who has been hanging around

like a spare part. "Katy, could you please make a dozen copies of this picture of White? I want to circulate it to all units making the arrest. Thank you."

"No problem sir."

Twenty-five

Laura didn't have a shift at the Pilgrim, so we had a relaxed afternoon and evening ahead of us. We were being decadent, having fish and chips with beer at three in the afternoon and loving it. Things took a turn for the worst when Laura's mobile rang. "Hi Shelley, how's it going?" Shelley was one of Laura's colleagues from the Pilgrim. Laura went silent while Shelley spoke, then spoke again. "Tom? What picture?" She looked at me, wide eyed.

"What's going on?"

Laura gestured for me to be quiet and continued her exchange with Shelley. "Are you sure he used that word exactly? He said 'Sergeant'?" She looked at me again and I wanted to tear the phone from her ear and talk to Shelley myself. Eventually she hung up. Her face was solemn. "Tom, I think the police are after you."

"What did she say?"

"She's just left work. She says two men came in about half an hour ago wanting a picture developed."

"They came into a pub and asked to have their photos done?"

"No, Shelley's rent is huge, she has to work two jobs, she works at that photo place in the mall during the day."

"Okay, so who were these men, and why do you think they were police?"

"Because one called the other 'Sergeant', and the one who

was a sergeant talked about not breaking his cover."

"What else did they say?"

"Nothing, but they only had two pictures on the camera, and one of them was of you."

"What was the other picture?"

"It was a house, Shelley said it looked like it might be around here but she wasn't sure. Anyway, they didn't want that one printed, only the one of you."

"Shit."

"Do you remember having your photo taken?"

"Yes, well no but yes. I went to get some milk earlier and there was a bloke taking pictures of Mrs. McCulloch's house, at least that's what I thought he was doing at the time, obviously I was wrong. He didn't look like a copper though, he was wearing a T-shirt.

"Coppers don't always wear helmets Tom."

"Shit, they must know where I live. It's only a matter of time before they get here. We've got to get out of here." Laura looked at her fish, clearly not wanting to leave it. "I'm sorry Laura but we've got to go. We'll get some more fish and chips later." I ran upstairs and packed a bag, making sure to take my passport in case I had to do something drastic. Laura joined me and collected any important things she had in my house and we went downstairs.

I sat Laura down and spoke to her carefully but quickly. "Laura, I'm sorry but I'm going to have to ask you to look away while I do something." Laura got the message and didn't argue, she turned her head to face the front window. I got a carrier bag and went to the Hi-Fi and opened up the back. I emptied the bundles of money into the bag along with Monica. I closed up the back of the Hi-Fi then went back upstairs and took the rest of the money from the bottom of my wardrobe, hidden by a stack of pillows. The money had been flowing in and I still hadn't found out about laundering it, so the space in the Hi-Fi casing had quickly run out.

I put Monica and the bag of money into a bigger case and then emptied the contents of my previously packed bag into it, pushing the incriminating items as far out of sight as possible. I got back downstairs and saw that Laura was still gazing out of the window. She held my arm as I came near. "What's this about Tom?"

"I have no idea."

"Is this about drugs, or is it about that bloke who died at the party?"

"Laura, I really don't know, can we go now?"

"Where are we going?"

"Your place."

She shook her head. "We can't stay at mine. The police might go there too. If this is about the murder at the party and they've found you, then they'll have found me too."

I wanted to tell her that it couldn't be about the murder at the party, there was no way they would have traced us back to here, but I couldn't very well tell Laura that it was most likely to be about another murder, probably my neighbour. I thought quickly. "We'll have to go to a hotel, or better a guest house where we can pay with cash. Actually, can I ask you to look away again please? I'm sorry." Laura did as I had asked and I opened up my bag and rummaged inside until I unearthed the bag of twenty pound notes. I managed to pry a handful out and stuffed them in my pocket before closing the holdall. "Right, thanks, let's go."

We left the house and locked the door behind us. As I opened the gate I saw Mrs. McCulloch walking towards us. She made a big show of turning up her nose and crossing the road to avoid me. I didn't know what her problem was, perhaps I'd put my bin bags out for the dustmen too early and she found them unsightly. We walked quickly out of the street and headed for a cab rank nearby. We asked to be dropped near the Palace Pier, not wanting to be dropped in front of any particular guest house in case the police had questions for our driver later. We travelled in silence.

We left the cab and started walking east, away from the pier and into an area that I knew had plenty of bed and breakfasts. Unfortunately, even though we were well into autumn, every window we saw said 'No vacancies'. I had almost reached the point of despair when I at last saw a 'Rooms Available' sign.

There was a reason it was vacant; it was disgusting. The owners hadn't made the slightest attempt to make it pleasant in any way, choosing instead to simply rely on weight of demand to see them through. They were happy to be the overflow, the place nobody visited on purpose, but because they had no other choice. It was called 'Peacock Lodge' and I swear I have seen cleaner dog turds.

A man sat behind the front desk. The desk was at a height that required a stool, but the man sat on a chair, the result of this being that we could only see the top half of his face. His eyes gazed vacantly between the top of the desk and the oil-slick of hair that was stuck to his head. There was a strange squelching noise and I realised he was repeatedly spooning food into his unseen mouth. I imagined he was feasting on the carcass of a slain guest from the previous night, the body lying in front of him, unseen to us, with its stomach gaping open, allowing him to scoop out the entrails. He showed a slight flicker of surprise at somebody checking in so early in the evening, or maybe at somebody checking in at all. "We'd like a double room please, with a bathroom if possible. We'll need to stay at least three nights."

"Credit card," said the flesh eater.

"I don't have a credit card I'm afraid. I've got plenty of cash though." I reached into my pocket.

"What about her?" It turned out he wasn't eating human flesh and sinew with a spoon, it was actually a fork, which was now in view and pointing at Laura's stunned face.

"She'll be staying too, we'll both be staying." I was trying to hurry this hideous transaction along.

"Has she got a credit card?"

"Why don't you ask her?" I was angry but then remembered we needed to be as inconspicuous as possible. "No, she doesn't, she's a student, she doesn't have any plastic." I counted some twenty-pound notes from the bundle in my pocket. "Look, here's some cash, a hundred and sixty quid."

"That's not enough. It's fifty-five a night for the one with a bog." The cannibal's fork returned to the fresh human meat. I tore another twenty out of my pocket, trying to mask my fury. "That's fifteen pound too much. I haven't got any change."

"That can go towards the fourth night if we stay that long and if we don't then you can keep the difference." On what we could see of his face there was no sign that he had yielded to my suggestion, but his fork-hand disappeared and was replaced by the same hand holding a room key. It was attached to a small wooden block with the number eleven written on it in marker pen. The wood was unstained and had splintered ends where it had been sawn from a longer piece but not been sanded. I didn't particularly trust The Golem's record keeping so I was about to ask for a receipt, so we wouldn't be asked to pay for the room again tomorrow night, but decided against it; I just wanted to be out of sight. The Golem returned to his feast of human offal, which signalled the end of the transaction. Laura was still staring, dumbstruck, at this objectionable creature and I had to gently ease her away and up the stairs.

It was one of those buildings where every inch of space had been used to cram in as many rooms as possible. This resulted in there being a maze of narrow walkways that went up and down stairs leading to rooms that really shouldn't be there. Even after the gloom of the front desk we didn't expect the sheer misery that faced us when we finally found our room. The wallpaper was the most striking feature, pasted seemingly with a mixture of snot and bile; it billowed like sailcloth from the walls. The carpet's pattern was no longer visible through the layers of dust that had doubled its thickness.

We had to push the door hard to get it to close behind us, as it had been poorly hung and was warped from all the damp. The bed was low and lumpy and covered with a harsh, itchy looking blanket in orange and black, and the teak headboard had bedside tables attached, suspended from the floor. This was probably the cutting edge of design in nineteen fifty-six. The curtains were not much more than rags and they fluttered in a draft that was having no trouble penetrating the closed windows.

Laura was standing just as far inside the room as she had to be to allow the door to close. She was staring at the room with the same expression she had exhibited for The Golem downstairs. "Oh my God."

"And we haven't seen the bathroom yet," I said, pulling the sliding door that would separate our sleeping from our ablutions. "Jesus Christ. Perhaps it would be best if you didn't see it."

Laura came and peered through the doorway at the one-foot square shower cubicle with a plastic curtain hanging from hooks on the ceiling and falling a foot or so short of the plastic ledge that separated the shower 'cubicle' from the rest of the floor. The shower's plumbing comprised of a plastic head and rubber hose with two nozzles that fitted over a pair of taps. The taps over which it fitted were in the sink outside of the 'cubicle'; the same sink we were meant to wash our faces and clean our teeth in. Looking into the toilet was like looking into the rectum of the devil himself. I smiled at Laura. "Well this is nice. I'm surprised I haven't read about this in any local guidebooks."

"This isn't funny Tom, this is horrible. What are we doing here?"

"I don't want to be here either, but we may as well make the best of it."

"There is no best to be made here Tom, it's the worst, and that's all that can be made of it."

"Okay, we'll make the worst of it." I was still trying to keep the situation as light as possible, but I knew I was failing miserably.

"Tom, this is crazy, we don't even know for sure if the police are after you. I was as panicked as you were when Shelley rang but now it's had time to sink in I'm thinking we overreacted. Shelley's not the most reliable source in the world, I like her but she's just a gossip at heart."

"There were two men developing a picture of me, they had no other pictures to print, just one of me. One was called 'Sergeant'. Doesn't that worry you?"

"Of course it worries me, but it might be a nickname, or even a surname."

"What about the Sergeant saying that stuff about his 'cover'?"

"Oh Tom, even if it is definitely the police, we don't know why they're after you. They might just want to talk to you. Perhaps they think you've seen something. The chances are you're not actually wanted for anything." I was sure that if Laura had any idea about the number of people I'd killed then she would realise that the 'chances' she mentioned were a lot slimmer than she thought.

"Laura, I'm a drug dealer, there's a high probability I'm

wanted for something."

"Perhaps, but they know where you live, seeing as they were in your road, so why didn't they arrest you before?"

"Maybe they don't want to let me know they're onto me until they've got all the evidence they need."

"It's not like you're a super criminal, Tom. What 'evidence' would they need to gather?"

"They took my photo. Why would they take my photo?"

"To identify you."

"Exactly, I bet they've got a witness and they're trying to match me to the person they've seen doing whatever crime it is they're after me for."

"What might you have been seen doing? I thought you did your business behind closed doors. You're not out in the street pushing bags of smack."

It was almost impossible carrying out a conversation as important as this one whilst having to keep up the deception of being a drug dealer and not a murderer. It meant I couldn't focus all my attention on the matter in hand, and that all of Laura's suggestions, however well intended, were doomed to be way off the mark. I needed to focus on the problem and I needed Laura's help, so I made a big decision.

I took a deep breath. "Laura, there's something I have to tell you."

* * * * * * * * * * * * * * * *

I'm completely off my trolley and so is Col. He shouts at me from the bar. "Katy, I mean Constable Brown. I'm getting shots as well as beers, what do you fancy, tequila or absinthe?"

"Tequila."

He comes back and bangs down two pints and two shots on the table, spilling beer everywhere. "Waste not want not." He starts licking the beer off the table.

"That's it, you've blown it. I'm not having your tongue in my mouth now, that's disgusting."

He waggles his tongue at me, he's having a laugh but it does get me going. "How about I put it somewhere else?" He looks down under the table between my legs.

"You'll have to wash your mouth out first."

"I'll tell you what, I'll sterilise it." He downs the beer in one then sinks his shot, swilling it around in his mouth before he swallows it. "There you go, clean as a whistle now." He looks at his empty glasses and grins at me. "It's your round."

"But I haven't touched these."

"You'd better hurry up then."

"Anyway, I didn't want to shout while you were at the bar but can you stop yelling that I'm a copper? A lot of people don't like it. I don't want any grief."

He leans forward and tries to lean his chin on his hand, but misses. He puts his finger to his lips. "Point taken, shhhh. Not a copper. Right, that's sorted. It's still your round."

"You're a feller, you're meant to drink fast. I'm a lady, I'm delicate."

"Yeah, you're a right little delicate flower you are. You could drink me under the table anytime. In fact, you have." He slides off his chair and lies under the table. I feel his hands pulling my knees apart. "It's okay, my mouth's clean now." His voice sounds muffled.

"Stop it, I'll piss myself!" People are starting to stare.

His hand appears and starts feeling around on the table. It closes around his empty pint glass and disappears beneath again. "Is this glass big enough?"

"What are you talking about?" I'm crying with laughter.

"To catch all your piss!" I feel him fall further to the floor and wrap his arms around my ankles, like he's hanging on for dear life. The glass rolls away and stops next to the foot of a chap at the next table.

After we get thrown out he suggests we go back to his. "I accept your kind invitation, gallant sir." I know I'm slurring, but not as badly as he is. We walk, arm in arm, to a cab rank, holding each other up. We take two steps to the side for every one forward so we're not making much progress.

Colin pulls me close to him and whispers in my ear. "Have you got your handcuffs?"

"No, but I hope you've got your truncheon."

We eventually get to the cab rank and I have to keep nudging Colin to stop him slagging off everyone in the queue. He whispers back but may as well be shouting, "It's okay Katy, you're a copper, nobody's allowed to start on us." I give up trying to shut him up.

* * * * * * * * * * * * * * *

I told Laura everything. I told her about my neighbour, and about how Frank and Cheese had turned up and offered me a job. I told her the truth about Stephanie, about Hunter and the Calsons and all the other murders. The one thing I did leave out was Colin. I didn't want to keep anything else from Laura, but I didn't have the right to confess on Colin's behalf.

The first feeling I had after telling her the truth was relief, but that didn't last long. Never has the term 'understandably upset' been so appropriate. After I told her, we sat in silence until it became unbearable, then we sat in silence some more. A million different platitudes shot into my head and I opened my mouth to voice them but rejected each one on the grounds that it wouldn't make the situation any better.

"Stop opening and closing your mouth Tom, you look like a goldfish."

I didn't know whether to laugh at this or not, so I compromised by smiling with my mouth whilst keeping my eyes sombre.

"Now you look like a vampire."

"Laura, throw me bone here, I'm trying to act appropriately and you keep making me laugh."

"You're the one pulling the funny faces." I had to be careful here, her words were light hearted, but I knew she must have been reeling from the shock of what I had told her. At that moment I didn't know what effect this piece of information, hanging between us like a landing craft for an alien invasion, would have on our lives, and I wished I hadn't blurted it all out. In all probability it would end our relationship, and it wasn't unthinkable that she would go to the police and tell them everything she knew. At this point I knew what thought was about to enter my head and I unsuccessfully tried to block it out: was I capable of killing Laura to stop her going to the police? The answer was taking shape in my head and I tried to distort it so I wouldn't see the truth about myself; a truth that I already knew. My mind was a Magic Eight Ball toy, the answer was drifting to the surface and there was nothing I could do to stop it: "Yes."

I started to tell myself that it wasn't true, that I wasn't capable of such desperate measures but I didn't want to risk losing the argument in my head and facing the awful truth, if indeed it was the truth. "What are you thinking?" I asked Laura, more to push the hideous thoughts out of my head than anything else.

"I'm not thinking anything Tom. There are a thousand thoughts in my head but I'm not thinking any of them, they're just there. I can't control them. I can't even make sense of them."

I had hoped she would say something more tangible. I wanted her to be angry so we could have a straight argument. That would be easier than this purgatory. I was walking over a carpet of eggshells with my hands snug inside a pair of kid gloves. "I want you to know that I only lied to you to protect you."

"I'm not going to let you boil this down into a row about

dishonesty, Tom, this is a row about you killing people, and it can never be anything else. I couldn't give a shit about you lying to me. Normally, yes, I'd be upset about being lied to, but this is so far from 'normally' that I may as well be flying on a magic carpet for all the sense it makes. Nothing you can say can make this acceptable, so it would be best if you just didn't speak."

I looked at her, and I knew I loved her more than I had ever imagined loving someone. I knew the answer to my recent unspoken question was no. I couldn't harm her, even if she was going to have me arrested and put in prison for the rest of my life. But I was sure I was going to lose her. I tried to think of a way of making it okay, but I knew it could never be okay. I had dragged Laura down to this; having her life turned upside down in a grotty little skank-hole. "I love you." I didn't mean to say it. It just came out.

"I know you do, and I bloody love you. That's the problem." She cupped my face with her hands, like she often did when she was messing around, but this time she was deadly serious. She literally didn't know what to do. She cocked her head slightly and stared into my eyes through a veil of tears. It was then that I realised that my own face was streaming with tears and soaking her fingers as they rested on my face. All the anguish and guilt that I had buried deep inside me came flooding out and I buckled into Laura's arms, sobbing uncontrollably.

"This won't win me over," Laura pulled me close and kissed the side of my head. "It won't win me over." The last one was a whisper. "You can't win me over." She kissed me over and over.

We hit an emotional stalemate and just held each other. Laura couldn't reconcile herself with what I had told her but the stress of the situation had highlighted the depth of our feelings for each other. Nothing could be said. So we said nothing.

* * * * * * * * * * * * * * * *

"Welcome to my humble abode." Col tries to get his key into the door, "And when I say humble I really mean humble. It's fucking humble." He starts giggling and I laugh too, but I don't know why. At last the key is in the lock. He opens the door and lets me in first.

I trip on something. "What's that?"

"That's a theodolite."

"The odder what?"

"It doesn't matter, it really doesn't matter."

"Where's your bog?"

"Christ, you're a real lady aren't you?" He opens a door to his left, "here you go, I'm afraid the bulb's gone so you'll have to leave the door slightly open, I promise not to look."

He goes into the lounge and I sit on the toilet. I'm glad there's no light in here because it smells bad. I don't bother washing my hands; I'd rather take my chances with my own germs than catch something off that sink. I go into the lounge. Col's sitting on the sofa, there's a whisky bottle and two glasses on the table. He's grinning. "You ready for some races?"

I sit down next to him. "I don't think I can manage any more, and I don't know how much more you can fit in either."

He puts his hand on my leg and kisses my neck. It feels good. "I'm sure you can fit something in." I'm too pissed to know if he's trying to be sexy or if he still wants me to drink with him.

"I've got to get some water," I say, hoping he'll go and get me some.

He flops away from me. "Okay, the kitchen's on your left as you go out of this room."

I go to the kitchen. There are plates, cutlery, glasses, mugs and bowls piled high in and around the sink. I open all the cupboards and find them empty; the pile around the sink is everything. I rinse a glass under the tap, hoping the hot water will kill any germs. I see a notice board on the wall with phone numbers, take away menus and club flyers stuck on it. There's also a picture of Colin holding a bottle of beer in the air. I wonder if he's always drunk. The person in the picture next to him looks familiar.

I go back into the lounge. Colin is rolling a joint. "You don't mind do you? I know you're a copper but it's almost legal these days."

"Who's the bloke in the picture in the kitchen?"

"Why that's me my dear."

"Who's the bloke next to you."

His face clouds over. "That's someone I used to be friends with."

"What's his name?"

"Why do you want to know?"

"What's his name?"

"Fucking hell Constable Brown. Don't interrogate me. You're not at work now."

I don't know why, but it seems really important to me that he tells me who's in the picture. I've got a feeling about it. I wish I hadn't drunk so much. "Who is it, Colin?" He doesn't answer but I suddenly remember who it is. It's the guy from Lewisham's photograph, the one I had to make copies of. The hitman. I'm suddenly sober. "How do you know Tom White, Colin?"

"I don't know anyone of that name. The bloke in the picture's called Brian." Colin might be a good liar when he's sober but he's obviously shit at it when he's hammered.

I can't deal with this in this state. I've got to get out. "I'm calling a cab." Colin doesn't try to stop me leaving.

* * * * * * * * * * * * * * *

My mobile broke the silence. I felt uncomfortable acknowledging it while Laura and I were in the middle of such a significant exchange, although it wasn't really an exchange anymore as neither of us had spoken for over ten minutes; we had just been holding each other without speaking.

"You'd better answer it."

I took out my mobile and saw that it was Colin. This was all

I needed. "Hello?"

"Tom, you're in trouble." He was slurring his words. "The police are after you."

"Shit, what do you know?"

"Do you remember Constable Brown?"

"No, should I?"

"When you - when your neighbour bought it - we had a visit from two coppers, remember? One of them was Constable Brown."

"I remember, I had to stop you asking her for her phone number."

"Not quite, but yes, her. I got talking to her tonight in a bar, she didn't remember me, and I didn't remind her who I was. She came back to mine and she was just about to shag me when she saw your picture in my kitchen, the one where you've just sank a yard of ale and you're about to puke your guts up."

"You were going to shag her in the kitchen?"

"When I said she was about to shag me I meant it was on the cards, not that I was about to chuck one up her that very second. Anyway, that doesn't matter, after she saw the picture, her whole mood changed. She kept asking what your name was, but I wouldn't tell her. Then she left pretty sharpish. You'd better lay low for a while."

"I already am mate."

"Where are you?"

"I can't say, not over the phone."

"If you knew the coppers were after you why didn't you tell me?"

"I didn't think you wanted to talk to me."

"I didn't, but if they're after you they might be after me too."

"If they were after you, that copper wouldn't have come back for a shag."

"If I had known they were after you I wouldn't have spent the evening with a copper. And what if it was all a set up? What if they know I'm involved so they sent her in to find out what she could?"

"Surely she would have stuck around and asked more questions rather than buggering off after seeing the picture."

"I can't handle this. I've got to get out of here. Tell me where you are."

Despite the advice I had given to the contrary, I was fairly sure that Colin was right; if the police were after me then they would probably end up at Colin's door, if not before, then definitely after seeing my picture on his kitchen wall. "Hold steady mate. I'll make a call then get right back to you. I'll sort something out."

I ended the call. "Laura, I know we haven't even got close to sorting this thing out between us but we're going to have to put it on hold for a while. Colin's just been with a copper, she's looking for me, and they may be after him too, I'll explain why later. I know you have no reason to stay with me but please bear with me on this. I've got to sort this out and there isn't time for us to talk about the situation, we've just got to grin and bear it for now. Is that okay?"

Laura nodded, there were still tears in her eyes.

I selected the name Monica in my telephone address book, the 'extreme emergency' number Stephanie had given me months ago. I was in no doubt this was an extreme emergency. I pressed the 'call' button.

"What's up Thomas?" Stephanie's voice.

"I'm in shit, and so is a friend of mine."

"Colin?"

"How do you know about Colin?"

"Let's not have this conversation again Thomas, you've told me you have a friend called Colin."

"No, I mean how do you know he's in shit?"

"You said 'a friend of mine' and you only have one friend that I know of."

"I might have other friends that I just haven't mentioned."

"Thomas, I presume this is an emergency, which is why you called the number I gave you for emergencies."

"It is an emergency."

"Then why are we talking about how many friends you've got?"

"Good point. Here's the thing. The police are after me."

"Surely that's an occupational risk for you. You must be used to it."

"No, I'm not used to it. I'm not really a hitman, well I am, but I wasn't, not until recently."

"Well you seem to have got very good at it very quickly."

"I know, it's weird, I seem to have a knack."

"Well thanks for calling, see you soon."

"No, Stephanie, you've got to help me. The police are after me, they know where I live. I'm hiding out with Laura. The police may be after Colin too."

"There are more dangerous people than the police after you Thomas."

"What do you mean?"

"I mean stay there and don't move. Tell me where you are."

"We're in a guest house, it's called the Peacock Lodge. It's in Torley Street near the Palace Pier."

"Right, stay there, it'll take a couple of hours to get down there."

"Are you coming to get us?"

"Not me, but I'll sort something out. Call your mate Colin and tell him to join you there."

"But the bloke at reception won't let him in unless he's staying here."

"Use your head Thomas. He'll just have to pay for a room, I'm sure you can afford it."

"Yes, that was stupid, sorry."

"Tell Colin to be careful getting across town, he's got to keep his head down."

Twenty-six

* * * * * * * * * * * * * * *

I hang up the phone. Stan doesn't speak, just waits for me to fill him in.
"That was the copper, Taylor on the phone, he had some big news."

"Spit it out then Andy."

"He says Chief Inspector Lewisham is crowing about having some big lead that will blow organised crime wide open."

"Is that us?"

"Who?"

"Organised crime."

"Yeah."

"It doesn't feel very organised, it feels like fucking chaos." He smiles, *more of a sneer really. "So who's this Chief Inspector Lewisham?"*

"He's Taylor's boss, the one who reckons he's going to take down organised crime."

"How many times have we heard that? Every few years another fucking copper thinks he's going to cure this disease when really he should be thanking us. If it wasn't for the likes of me there'd be more crime on the streets. But you know all this Andy, you don't need me telling you. So what's this Lewisham got?"

"He's got a suspect for the Hunter murder."

"Good, I hope they catch the fucker, if he's not already dead."

"That's exactly what I said Stan, but there's more. Lewisham thinks the same guy did the Clarke murder. The bullets were fired from the same gun."

Stan shrugs. "Clarke? Who's Clarke?"

"He was a fence for Barrett, you had his brains blown out a few months ago."

It dawns on Stan what I'm trying to say. "The same guy is working for me and Barrett?"

"And there's more. Lewisham found bullets from the same gun in one of the Calson twins, and in a dozen other corpses, some ours, some Barrett's."

"So who's our double agent?"

"Tom White."

"He's one of Frank's boys isn't he?"

"He's the one who killed Barry Carter." I realise Stan isn't going to remember Barry Carter. "You wanted Carter because of what he did with your daughter. White killed him on your birthday."

"White never did tell us who paid for that gift did he? "So do you think this was a set up from the start?"

"By White? It can't be, how would he have known that his next door neighbour had pissed you off, and that it was your birthday?"

"Inside knowledge? Frank and Cheese seemed to find him pretty quickly."

"You think Frank and Cheese are against you? That's a big thing to say Stan."

"They never forgave me for what I did to Tony Visconti. They were always his boys."

"They knew that was business Stan, they're both pros. They've been solid for us all these years."

"They've been waiting, Andy, waiting to make their move."

"It can't be Stan. Not those two, they're as straight as they come."

"It's all falling into place now. I haven't been able to understand why Barrett has been making these wild moves, and nor have you, Andy."

"Barrett's finally lost it, that's all Stan."

"No, Andy, that's not it. Well not all of it anyway. White's killing Joe's men as well as ours, so Joe must be as much in the dark about this as we were. From what I know of the fat fuck he's easy to influence, so there's *got to be someone upping the stakes between me and him. Someone's whispering in his ear like in that Shakespeare play with the darkie. There's no way he'd be going for me like he is unless someone's stirred him up."*

"For the record, Stan, I still don't believe Frank and Cheese would be fucking with you."

"We'll just have to find that out Andy. I want you to get talking to Joe Barrett's people, it's time me and that fat fuck had a sit down."

* * * * * * * * * * * * * * * *

After speaking to Stephanie, I called Colin back and passed on her instructions, adding that he should bring plenty of money in case he couldn't go home for a while. Saying this made me realise that I had no idea what we were going to do, and if I would ever be able to return to my home. He balked when I said to bring his passport but didn't waste time arguing. He seemed to have sobered up pretty quickly. I tried to put a positive spin on Stephanie's warning that parties other than the police could be on our tail. This didn't make him feel any better.

Laura and I had been deadlocked; trapped between deep affection and the irreconcilable fact that I was a professional killer, but now the spate of telephone calls had broken the silence. I took her hand and looked her in the eyes. We were used to joking around so it was difficult not to look like a parody of solemnity. "We need to make a decision."

Laura ignored my statement. "How is Colin involved in this?"

"I wasn't keeping that from you, I just hadn't got round to it yet."

"Well get round to it now."

I let out a long, slow breath. "Colin came on a few of the jobs with me, he helped me out."

"So you didn't mind telling him about it but you couldn't tell me."

"I didn't mean for him to find out, he just turned up in my house while I was next door with my neighbour. He heard the gunshot and then I appeared out of the attic wearing gloves and a balaclava."

"Why were you wearing a balaclava? It's not like you were going to see your neighbour again after you killed him."

"That's what Colin said."

"So he saw you with a smoking gun and he just couldn't resist but to get on board with your burgeoning business venture."

"I wasn't holding the gun, I dropped it next door."

"Like Michael Corleone when he killed the Police Captain in the Godfather?"

I smiled in spite of the situation. "Yes, just like that. Anyway, Colin and I fell out."

"I did wonder why you haven't seen each other for ages. What did he do, acquire a conscience?"

"Pretty much, yes."

"But now you're friends again."

"He doesn't have anywhere else to go."

Laura sighs, "What are we going to do?"

"That's what I was trying to say, we have to make a decision."

"What kind of decision?"

"Actually, it's your decision. You have to decide whether to stay or go."

"Why is it up to me?"

"Of course it's up to you, I have to run, there's no alternative, but you don't have to, you still have a choice."

"What do you think I should do?"

"I think you should go of course." She looked like I had just slapped her. "I don't mean I want you to go, I just mean it would be safest for you if you did. The police, and possibly some other people, dangerous people, are after me. You've not been involved in anything so you could just go home and carry on with your life."

"What if the police questioned me?"

"Tell them I said I was going away, and that you haven't seen me since."

"You seem to have things all planned out."

"We haven't got time for bullshit Laura. We've only got time for facts. Of course I don't want you to go. I want you to stay with me. I'm crazy about you. I don't ever want to leave you, but if you do stay with me you could be in danger, and I couldn't bear that."

"So you *do* want me to come?"

"Yes, Jesus, yes, how many times do I have to say it? Of course I want you to come. I just think you'll be in danger if you do."

"If I go will I ever see you again?"

"I don't know, maybe sometime, not for ages, or maybe never."

"I'm staying with you."

I held her arm and fixed her with my hopefully not too solemn gaze again. "Are you sure?"

"I'm sure."

At this point I expected her to throw her arms around me, like a soft focus ending on a slushy daytime soap. I wanted an eighties power ballad to start booming around us as we held each other and kissed.

She didn't throw her arms around me and we didn't kiss.

There was no eighties power ballad and no soft focus.

Laura just looked scared, like she was stuck between a rock and a hard place that was stuck between an even rockier rock and a doubly-hard hard place.

We sat in silence and waited.

It was like being on a tube that's stuck in a tunnel and just sits there with no announcements saying what the hold up is. It's not the delay that's so much the problem; it's the frustration of not knowing what's going on. And we didn't know anything.

Colin's arrival diluted our fear and frustration, but only with awkwardness. Memories of the last few times I had seen him swam into my mind, and probably his too. I was ashamed that I had punched him and even more ashamed that I'd threatened his life. I tried as hard as I could to force the image of him curled up and sobbing on his sofa, out of my head. He'd tried to sever all ties with the world into which I'd dragged him, but now it had caught up with him and here he was in this cesspit of a guest house waiting for whatever help Stephanie was sending. I hoped I hadn't ruined his life like I had Laura's.

We carried on sitting and we carried on waiting. I didn't know what Stephanie could really offer in the way of assistance, or why she should help me at all. All I could think of was that I was being chased by police and criminals alike. I was a unifying force between these two polarised groups. I was their common enemy, and I was dragging Colin and Laura along for the bumpy ride.

The cavalry arrived without any bugles blowing or flags waving. They came unseen, and they called when they arrived. It was Frank on the 'phone. "We're just round the corner, come and get in the car, be nice and relaxed and do it slow. We'll be out of here before you know it." I should have welcomed the familiar voice, the friendly voice, but I knew enough about the kind of people I was working for to know that if they thought I was about to spill my guts to the police then they wouldn't hesitate to spill my guts first. The other reason for not being happy to hear Frank's friendly voice was that Frank didn't have a friendly voice. Frank had a voice that was always laced with menace, regardless of his mood. If Frank was on the warpath his voice sounded menacing. If Frank was singing nursery rhymes his voice sounded menacing. In this climate his voice sounded downright evil, like he was the Grim Reaper himself come to drive us all to Hell.

I ended the call and stared into space, trying to think of what to do.

"Who was that?" Asked Colin.

"It was Frank."

Laura saw the fear on my face. "That's good though isn't it?"

"I hope so."

Colin took my shoulder. "Are you thinking he might be here for something else other than to help us?"

"Have you got Dave?"

"Who?"

"Yes, who's Dave?" Said Laura.

I rummaged in my bag and pulled out Monica, I checked she was loaded.

"Oh, Dave," said Colin, "I forgot I'd called it that." He opened his jacket to show his gun tucked into the pocket.

Laura looked disgusted. "Christ, look at the pair of you. This isn't High Noon, this is serious. If they wanted to kill us they would have done it by now, they wouldn't try and do it out in the street, and they're not going to drive the three of us off somewhere to do us in. This isn't a Scorcese film, there's no desert. Put those stupid things away and let's get out of here."

My phone rang again. It was Frank. "So, are you coming or what?"

We went outside.

Despite Laura's insistence that we should trust Frank and Cheese, which I think was due more to her wanting to get out of the unpleasant surroundings of Peacock Lodge than anything else, I still felt nervous to the point of nausea as the three of us piled into the back of Cheese's car and drove towards London. I sat in the middle with Colin to my left and Laura to my right. The radio was on and Frank, as is typical of people in the front seats, didn't realise how loud the music was in the back, and attempted conversation with us. Neither of us wanted to tell Cheese to turn down the radio, so we struggled to hear Frank, sometimes asking him to repeat what he was saying but mostly we just nodded and said, "Yeah."

Eventually Frank realised. "Is it really loud in the back?"

This time I heard him, but my answer was the same as it would have been if I hadn't. "Yeah."

"Cheese, turn it down, it's too loud, they can't hear me."

"What?"

"Turn the radio down." Cheese grudgingly reduced the volume. Frank was turned round in his seat to face us, hugging the headrest. His blonde hair was cut shorter than normal and didn't have the parting that I had grown used to. The dome of Cheese's bald head protruding above the driver's seat told me that he hadn't changed his hairstyle, or I perhaps I should say headstyle.

I decided to do some belated introductions. "Frank, Cheese, this is Laura, and this is Colin."

Frank shook Colin's hand. He couldn't reach Laura so they just smiled at each other, Laura's smile looking much more awkward than Frank's. It was obvious that Frank was trying to work out in the near-darkness whether Laura was good looking or not. Every time we went under a street light his eyes darted in her direction. I think he came to a conclusion fairly quickly because his glances were replaced with all out stares. I was still wary of him and this didn't help me relax.

"Where are we going?" I tried to take Frank's attention away from my delicious girlfriend.

"West London, hotel. I don't really know what we're going to do with you though."

A deathly chill struck me. "What do you mean?"

"What do *you* mean?"

"I mean, what do you mean by 'you don't know what you're going to do with us'?"

"I mean I don't know what we're going to do with you, the police are after you, Costanza's after you, Barrett will be too when he finds out."

"Who's Barrett? And what might he find out?"

"Joe Barrett, you've been working for him. You've been working for both of them."

"No I haven't."

Frank's smile was patronising, "Oh yes you have. Steph will explain it all, and she'll work something out, but I hope you've all brought a decent book. You're going to be sitting around for a few days. We've got some business to attend to." He turned in his seat to face forward and turned the radio back up.

Twenty-seven

Stephanie was in her element. I had always thought she exuded confidence but now she was flowing. Something was giving her extra poise, making her look more assured. I quickly realised the extra ingredient was power. Frank and Cheese had seen and done it all, or at least most of it, and yet it was obvious that it was Stephanie who was in charge here. The banter flew between the three of them, particularly from Frank, who exchanged mock insults with Stephanie, which thinly disguised his deference to her. It appeared to be disguising something else too; Frank's actions were like that of a young boy pulling the pigtails of the girl next door, not knowing how else to show his feelings, feelings that he finds confusing. After the impression Laura had made on Frank in the car it was good to see him focussing on Stephanie.

We had a family room in a hotel that overlooked Hammersmith flyover. Either Frank or Cheese knew the owner, which meant we could pay cash and no questions would be asked. It wasn't a palace but it was a thousand times better than Peacock Lodge which now seemed like a distant memory.

It was late, about two in the morning. Stephanie had come to the room about twenty minutes after we arrived. She was also staying in the hotel. She introduced herself to Colin and Laura, acknowledging the fact that she had briefly met Laura before, and that she knew who Colin was. Then she spoke at length to Frank and Cheese in the corner of the room while we sat and looked at each other uselessly. The conversation was heated and detailed, and like listening to a foreign language, punctuated with the occasional familiar word. The four words that we particularly recognised were 'Stan', 'Costanza', 'Joe' and 'Barrett'. Calls were being made. Something was being arranged.

Laura and I were sitting on one bed and Colin was on the other, facing us. We were aware that everything was out of our control, we were just waiting to be told what to do, how it would all be miraculously sorted. The three of us tried to shrink into the furniture. We felt grateful for being given this sanctuary and were conscious of being in the way, so we became the filling in a huge humble pie. Colin's eyes were fixed on Stephanie and I knew that in any other situation he would be sliming all over her, but thankfully he kept his moves to himself.

Stephanie broke off her machinations with Frank and Cheese and came and sat next to Colin; joining the group like a scoutmaster at a camp fire. "It's about time I told you what's been going on. You're going to hate me."

I couldn't think of anything to say. Colin just stared. Laura looked like she hadn't slept for days.

"My full name is Stephanie Marena Visconti. My father was a gang boss named Tony Visconti. Frank and Cheese worked for him. Also working for my father were two other men, Stan Costanza and Joe Barrett. Costanza was down in the pecking order and was something of a protégé of Barrett's. My father was a good boss, a fair one. I won't pretend he was a saint because that would be wrong. He was a criminal, a very powerful one, and his standards and code of ethics were of his world, a different world, one that he was powerful enough to shape to some extent. I won't try and sell him to you because it doesn't matter to me what you think of him, but he was a lot more than a gang boss. He was my father."

She stopped to let her words settle in. I wasn't sure how to react. It all seemed a bit over the top to me, and not what I would have expected from Stephanie, from what I knew of her. This was the first time I'd seen a sincere insight into her as a person. I was feeling rather embarrassed.

"I know I'm being a little mushy," Stephanie continued. "But I wanted to set the scene. This is something I feel very passionate about."

"Of course, he was your father," Laura surprisingly chipped in.

Stephanie smiled. "Thank you. As I have said, my father wasn't perfect, and one of his weaknesses was that he was a very trusting man, many in the business," she looked over towards Frank and Cheese who were standing together near the window, "including Frank, thought this would be his undoing. And those people were right." Frank shuffled uncomfortably. "It's too late to cut this long story short so I won't even try but the upshot is that Stan Costanza and Joe Barrett killed my father. They also killed my mother and thought they had killed me too. Then they took my father's empire and divided it between them, effectively forming two gangs, gangs that would quickly learn to distrust and despise each other."

"But surely they wouldn't have been able to get away with it. Wouldn't your father's men have taken revenge?" As I said this I hoped it wouldn't offend Frank and Cheese.

"You have to understand my father's world, Thomas. Frank and Cheese's world. None of the men were happy with what had happened, but in their eyes it was just business. Like a corporate takeover."

"Not to me it wasn't." Frank interjected. "I went along with it and I kept my head down, but I was always going to make amends for what happened to Tony."

"And the same goes for Cheese," Stephanie said. Cheese

nodded.

"Everybody thought I was dead. My parents were dead in the front seats and I should have been dead too, but I survived. Frank and Cheese made sure that nobody else knew I was alive and I left the country. I went to live in Texas with my uncle. I was eleven."

"And now you're back." Colin's tongue had loosened. He obviously wanted to get in on the big scene, or get in with Stephanie.

"Yes, I'm back," she said, a little too dramatically for my liking. "Now this is the bit you're not going to like, particularly you, Tom."

"I think I've got a rough idea already." Anger had leaked into my voice. "You've been playing Stan Costanza and Joe Barrett off against each other, using me somehow. You lied to me about working for the same boss as Frank and Cheese, you're not working for anyone. You've had me killing members of both gangs. I've been risking my life on your behalf."

"I said I'm sorry, but I'm not going to feel guilty about it if that's what you want."

"That *is* what I want." I sounded a little too petulant for everybody's liking.

"Well you're going to be disappointed. I didn't make you do anything you didn't want to do."

"You sent Frank and Cheese round with that whole birthday present story, what a load of shit that was."

"Watch your mouth Tom," Frank interrupted.

"Fuck you Frank, I'm not talking to you, I'm talking to her." Frank made a move towards me but Cheese, thankfully, held him back. Laura's face displayed her shock at the way I had just spoken to such an obviously hardened criminal as Frank. I glared at Stephanie.

"Calm down, Thomas. It wasn't like that. Stan Costanza did

send Frank and Cheese to find you so you could tell him who paid for his birthday present. That was genuine."

"Why should I believe you?"

"Because it's true, and I'd like to know too. Who did pay you to kill your neighbour?"

"Nobody."

"He killed him because he was too noisy," I was surprised to hear Laura's voice.

Frank looked at me, he was laughing. "Is that true? You bumped him off because his stereo was too loud? It was nothing to do with the old man's birthday?"

"I didn't know who the hell Stan Costanza was at the time. How would I know it was his birthday?"

"So you weren't bluffing when we came to see you?"

"I didn't have a clue what you were talking about, I was scared shitless. I wasn't a hitman. I was just fed up with my noisy neighbour."

"So you killed him?" Frank wasn't going to let this go.

"Well, yes. Then you two came round offering me loads of money and saying all this weird shit about it being some old man's birthday. I'd committed murder and now two gangsters were trying to thank me. I was completely freaked out."

Frank started laughing even harder than before. "We thought you were the real deal, you had all that Chinese gear on and you didn't have no furniture or nothing."

"I was having a new carpet fitted. All the furniture was in the kitchen. I was wearing my dressing gown."

This was too much for Frank. "Carpet? Dressing gown? So you're not, you're not, like, you're not a ninja?"

"No I'm not like a fucking ninja!" Frank collapsed at this.

"But you did that thing!" Cheese was also pissing himself.

"What thing?"

"That ninja thing!"

"The bouncing thing!" Frank could hardly speak through his tears.

I was completely confused. "What are you talking about?"

Frank calmed himself enough to speak. "That first time we came round, you came to the window then dived on the floor and sort of sprung yourself back up again, like you bounced."

"Like a breakdancer," said Cheese.

"Like a ninja!" Frank collapsed again.

"Ninjas don't wear dressing gowns!"

Stephanie interrupted. "I don't like to break up this trip down memory lane but can you lot give it a rest?" Frank and Cheese complied as best they could, but their shoulders continued to shake. Stephanie continued, "So as you can see, it wasn't a total set up. You were offered a job by Costanza fair and square, and in their capacity as Stan's employees, Frank and Cheese were your go-betweens."

"So when did you get involved?"

"Soon afterwards. I came back to England and met up with Cheese and we decided that you were just what we were looking for."

"And what were you looking for? A dumb-arse who you could manipulate easily? What do they call it in America, a pastie?"

"I think you mean patsy, but no, we wanted someone from the outside, someone who wasn't connected with Costanza or Barrett, someone who didn't know the politics of their relationship."

"Don't bullshit me, Stephanie."

"Okay, there was a level of manipulation, but you would have done it anyway. You signed on the dotted line, you joined the dark side and you did rather well out of it, so I don't think you have the right to feel too aggrieved."

"You put my life in danger."

"You chose to become a hitman."

"Whatever. So how come Costanza's after me? Has he got wise to your gunpowder plot?"

"He's got a good contact at Scotland Yard. Forensic science is amazing these days. They can tie a bullet to a certain gun."

"The same type of gun?"

"No, the same exact gun. It's something to do with the inside of the barrel making tiny grooves in the bullet casing as it spins. Each one has its own unique fingerprint apparently. It didn't take long to work out that the same weapon was being used on both sides and that you were the owner of that weapon."

"Just because it was the same gun it doesn't mean it was me who did the murders."

"Not in a court of law it doesn't, but in the world of Stan Costanza, Joe Barrett, Frank, Cheese, my father, it's more than enough for a conviction, and of course a death sentence."

"Thanks for putting it so delicately."

Stephanie smiled. "Hopefully it won't come to that."

"Is that supposed to make me feel any better?"

"No, it's the truth. Listen Tom, I'm sorry for the deception. You're right. I did use you, but please try and see it through my eyes. I was returning from a different country, back to my father's world, the world that killed him and my mother. All I had driving me was revenge, but things changed."

"How do you mean?"

"I'm still driven by revenge, that won't change until this is over. What has changed is that I don't see things in black and white anymore. To me you were just a killer, a utility I could use. You were expendable."

"Thanks very much."

"Let me finish. As time went on I got to know you," she pointed at Frank and Cheese who had finally stopped laughing, "and those two got to know you. We realised you weren't just a resource, you were something approaching a friend."

Under normal circumstances I would have been horribly embarrassed by this slushy comment. "But still you didn't tell me what was going on. You were happy to let me be an unwitting double agent. You're only telling me now because it's all come to head."

"Thomas, we didn't have to come and pick you up when you were stranded. We didn't have to babysit you and your little gang here while the police and Costanza are after you, but we did. You're safe for the moment, I don't expect gratitude but you can stop whining."

"I'm not whining, but please see this through my eyes. My life is fucked. I can't go home."

"I'll think of something, really I will."

Colin chipped in. "I'm sorry for dragging everyone back, but I'm a bit lost here, how exactly were you using him? I can see that you were taking orders from these two bosses, Barrett and Costanza, but I can't see what difference you made."

"She wasn't just taking orders from Barrett," I replied, "She was making some of her own. Isn't that right Stephanie?"

"My aim was to cause the maximum reaction on both sides. I knew from Frank and Cheese who Costanza valued most, and if Barrett hit them, then Costanza would retaliate as strongly as possible. I tried to persuade Joe to go for these targets, but if he didn't make the order then I made it myself."

"Directly to me."

"Exactly."

Colin still wasn't finished. "But didn't this bloke Joe Barrett find it a bit suspicious that people on the other side were being killed without him ordering it?"

"That wasn't a problem. He just thought he had some overzealous employees. We were careful not to do it the other way round though. Stan Costanza is a lot more savvy, and a lot more suspicious."

Colin had another question. "You said the police knew the bullets came from Tom's gun, was there any mention of a different gun with different bullets?"

Stephanie smiled. "You mean you're worried about your part in the murder of the Calsons?"

Colin looked terrified. "How do you know that?"

"I've been keeping an eye on things. I know you helped Thomas out for a while, and I know you were in the thick of it at that paintball party in Hampshire. There were a lot of people watching. By the way, in case you're interested, the other person you killed was called Kingsley Fry."

"Why didn't you say anything?" I said.

"Because it would have made it obvious I was checking up on you, and it wasn't really my concern, you were getting the jobs done, causing more and more retaliations, there was no need to change anything."

Colin was like a limpet, he wouldn't let go. "So what about the police? What about Costanza? Are they after me too?"

"The police don't have any strong leads but they know you're friends. I don't know about Costanza, he could well be after you, he's got eyes everywhere. If I were you I'd assume you were in as much trouble as Thomas. I don't mean to put the fear of God in you but it's better to be over-cautious than not cautious enough."

"Wait a minute," I said. "How did the police find out where I live? Why were they taking my photo?"

"I wondered when you'd ask that. After the Hunter murder," she turned to Laura, "the fancy-dress party that you were at, the police contacted all the costume rental outlets in the South East. Your big bird and Elvis outfits were tracked down to Brighton. The shop assistant remembered your names.

Then Scotland Yard found out that somebody was murdered who lived next door to someone called Thomas. They wanted a picture so they could get the shop girl from the fancy-dress place to identify you."

Laura was horrified. "So the police are after me too?"

"Probably, they would have done their homework on Thomas, and if they've found out he has a girlfriend called Laura then they're going to make the connection."

"Shit."

"So what now?" I said. "If Costanza's after me does that mean he's rumbled your game too?"

"He wants to have a sit-down with Joe Barrett."

Laura spoke softly. "What's a sit-down?"

Twenty-eight

* * * * * * * * * * * * * * *

Sit-downs are a bastard to set up, especially with players like Costanza and Barret. They hate each other, and what's more, they know each other really well so there's zero trust. Nightmare.

I met up with Crowley, Barrett's boy to arrange it all. It was like one of them United Nations things where they work through the night agreeing a treaty on how much money to give to Africa. We eventually settled on a place to hold it – a neutral ground, like for an FA Cup semi-final - a prefab hut on a piece of wasteland near White Hart Lane stadium in North London. The wasteland becomes a car park on match days and the prefab is the office for the wide boys charging top dollar for the service. It's a shithole but it's just right for us because the hut's exactly the right size and it's surrounded by open ground, which means there's nowhere for a shooter to hide. It's out of sight from the main roads, so we won't have anyone sticking their nose in. Me and Crowley have both told the coppers on our payrolls to make sure we aren't bothered by the filth tonight.

We got here earlier today, me and Crowley with three men each. We parked our vans just outside the gate. Everyone was right fucking jumpy, nobody took any chances. There's what you might call a 'strict protocol' to follow at times like these to stop it getting messy, well try and stop it anyway. Two from Barrett's side came into our van and two of ours went into theirs to check all was as it should be. After that we kept to those mixed groups, two of each, so everybody was always close to someone from the other side. Next came the pissy bit. We had to get undressed right down to our keks and let a bloke from the other side check we weren't stashing a piece. Then we all had to put on these blue jumpsuits. No pockets, tight fitting. Nowhere to hide nothing. We felt like dicks, but at least we knew we all felt like dicks. We unloaded the gear from the vans - Crowley and me had already agreed who should bring what. Everything from our van was checked by everyone in the group, as well as the containers it came in, and then the empty van too. We had to make sure there were no nasty surprises hidden anywhere. We locked the vans and me and Crowley swapped keys.

Keeping in our groups of four, two from each side, we checked the car park fence, and fixed any weak points with thick cable so you could only get in through the front. Then we put temporary fencing around the hut, leaving an opening where we put the metal detector, like at an airport, but portable, run off a generator. We checked the prefab to make sure there was only one usable entrance, put four folding chairs inside and pumped it full of tear gas to make sure nobody was hiding inside. This was a bit much to be honest, nobody could possibly have been hiding in that tiny space, but none of us was going to suggest breaking procedure. We left the hut open for a while to let the gas clear, then locked the door, twice, once with Crowley's padlock, then with mine.

We put halogen lights at each corner of the car park, hooked up to the generator too. And that was that. All we had to do then was to keep an eye on each other for the rest of the day to make sure nobody came into the compound or passed anything in. We ate the sandwiches we'd brought along, knowing we weren't going to leave this car park until the small hours, and then just sat and watched each other. I've had better days. We hardly said a word to each other. Maybe if Crowley and me hadn't have been there the others would have been more relaxed and chatted more, but none of them wanted to look like they were being too friendly to the other side in front of their boss's right hand man.

As it started getting dark we powered up the generator and turned on the lights.

It's nearly time now. It's quiet except for the generator rumbling.

We see two sets of headlights making their way towards us and we regroup back into our own sides. Everyone can feel the tension.

The cars stop next to each other right up against the entrance. There's no gap between them, and only a small space between the bumpers and the fence. The door behind the driver in the car on the left opens and Guy Salford, Stan's most notorious piece of muscle steps out, looking big, confident. Salford's the real deal, only brought out for the big jobs, the special occasions, like the fine china of muscle. The rear right passenger door on the right-hand car opens and I recognise Barrett's man Paolo, I don't know his surname. He's just as big and cocky-looking as Salford. We've all got opposite numbers. We're all matched, like twin towns. They stand and face each other over the cars then take a step back and pull the door open to let their bosses out. Two other men get out of each car and get close to their respective boss. Stan and Joe, shielded by their muscle, walk slowly down opposite sides of the two cars.

When they reach the fence, Stan and Joe leave the shadow of their minders and shuffle sideways along the small gap between the fence and the cars. This is where they're most exposed, they're on their own, they've got no human shield, but they've each got a minder who knows exactly where to look for a sign of trouble. They come through the gate together and step apart. The four of us inside the fence in our crew surround Stan real tight. Crowley and Joe's other boys do the same. We walk towards the hut. As we get to the metal detector Crowley and me leave our bosses and step through. The other three men on each boss close ranks to fill the gap in the shield. Barrett's first through and I run the detector over him. He's clean. Crowley does the same to Stan, then the other six men in jumpsuits come through - like me and Crowley, they've already been searched and scanned - and again we huddle round our bosses and lead them to the door of the prefab. Crowley and I unlock a padlock each and both go into the office, followed by Stan and Joe. The others in the jumpsuits stay outside. Stan and me sit down next to each other and Joe and Geoff sit opposite. This is it.

It's a sit down.

After years of luxury hotels and restaurants you might think these men would look out of place here, but they look right at home. Just like the old days before they reached the top; when they had to get their hands dirty. It feels strange for me, and probably Geoff Crowley too, we've worked together all afternoon and now we're back on opposite sides of the table at a council of war.

There are no handshakes and no Mafia-style embraces. These men are enemies and they don't try to hide it. Barrett speaks first, "So what's this about Stan?"

"We have a piggy in the middle Joe."

"Stan, there's some nervous armed men out there and there's a half dozen more who aren't armed but are dressed like these two," he waves his hand at me and Geoff with a sneer on his face, "who want to get this night over with as quickly as possible, so if you could drop the riddles that would help everyone."

I glance at Stan, expecting to see steam coming out of his ears but he's smiling. "Oh dear Joe. You always have to be the big man don't you? Okay, if you feel you've got to prove yourself in front of Geoff and Andy here, then you go ahead. I'm more interested in finding out who's fucking us both over."

Barrett must have felt that but he just returns the smile. "Well get to the point then."

"Someone's working for both sides. He's killing your men and mine. He killed the Calsons for you…"

Joe interrupts, "who said I killed the Calsons?"

"If you're so concerned about getting this night over with, then stop fucking around."

Joe waves his hand and leans back. "Go on."

"So, he did the Calsons for you, and others of mine, Damien Hunter for starters."

Joe leans forward. "And who did he do for you?" It's obvious Joe's trying to push Stan as far as he can.

Stan speaks slowly and carefully. "Clarke. Smith." He turns to me. "You're going to have to help me out here Andy."

"Kellis, Turner. I think that's enough examples." I look at Barrett. Barrett turns to Geoff. "Who did the Calsons and Hunter?"
"Tom White." Stan answers Barrett before Geoff Crowley can reply. Joe carries on looking at Crowley. "Is he right?"

Twenty-nine

* * * * * * * * * * * * * * *

I nod. "Yes, he's right Joe."

Joe's trying to keep up appearances, but I can see his reality collapse in his eyes. I'm sure his mind is racing with memories of our conversations in which I warned him about Stephanie. Now he knows that Tom White, the man Stephanie was so insistent on bringing aboard, has been, as Costanza so succinctly put it, 'fucking us over'. Andy and Stan exchange glances and it's obvious they've seen a chink in Joe's armour. In fact they've seen a gaping hole. It's hard to believe Joe was once Stan's superior under Tony Visconti, there's such a gulf in class between them.

"What's going on Joe?" Costanza asks. Joe is now in a desperate position, he can't let on to Costanza that he's been manipulated, especially by a woman, but in order to resolve the situation he needs to know what Stan knows, and to do that he's going to have to give him something. Joe makes a show of getting back on top but he's already paid the price for his slip. Stan and Andy can't possibly know why Joe is on the back foot, but in a world where appearance is everything, they know there's something lurking behind Joe's façade; they know they just have to lift some rocks. Andy looks smug, as if Joe's floundering reflects on me. I have every reason to look smug myself, because I know I'm going to have the last laugh, but I push my pride away and make an effort to look troubled, so Stan and Andy think they've got the upper hand. It's not easy but I can't give anything away yet.

It should be time now, I want to look at my watch but don't want to be seen doing it, so it becomes a major operation. My right arm is crossed over my left and covers the watch. I rotate my left arm beneath my right so the watch is upright but still obscured. I gradually slide my right arm away from the left, doing it so slowly as to be barely visible. I can feel my pulse racing in my wrists as I know the big moment is coming. The buzz I feel is amazing, I'm going to be part of something that will be talked about for generations, but it's laced with real fear; this is a big move, the biggest, and I can't control what goes on at this stage. I have to sit and act as I would if nothing was going on, rather than take direct action. The problem is that I can't remember how I'd act if nothing was going on. Every expression on my face feels magnified and distorted.

I return my attention to making my watch visible. My right arm is still moving away from the left, and soon the face of the watch will be in view. My arm moves further, slowly, carefully, and I know the watch is exposed but I can't look at it yet, in case somebody has noticed my movements. Clock watching is just not done in a situation like this, and it would certainly raise the already heightened suspicion in this shabby little hut if I were to be caught. I finally flicker my eye in the direction of my watch face and see the time. It's twenty past nine. Something's wrong, they're ten minutes late. I realise I haven't been following the conversation that has been going on around me while I've been lost in my thoughts. I feel wild panic and hope to God it doesn't show on my face, but I feel sure that it must be painfully obvious that something's up with me.

I wonder if Stan and Joe felt like this when they made their move on Visconti. I conclude that Joe probably did, but that Stan is immune to normal human emotions like fear and nerves. I become aware that I have once again drifted off into my own thoughts and I mentally kick myself. I have to focus. I'm sure somebody is going to speak to me in a moment and I'm not going to know what the fuck to say. The more I try and focus on the political exchanges around me, the more my mind drags me away. A mantra starts in my head: "cavalry's coming cavalry's coming cavalry's coming" but the cavalry's not fucking coming. The cavalry's late and I'm stuck here dressed like an extra from Star Trek, in a porta-cabin in North London with three men who, if they knew what I know, would have ripped me apart with their bare hands by now.

It's when I'm at my lowest ebb, shifting desperately in my chair like a schoolboy needing the toilet, that I hear the cavalry's fanfare: short sharp bursts of machine gun fire and some shouting which I don't catch properly. I act exactly as would be expected of me in this situation; I dive on top of Joe, shielding his prone body. Andy does the same with Stan. Joe shows no sign of trying to get up, but Stan shrugs Andy off and stands to look out of the window. I leave Joe on the floor and do the same. It feels strange to be standing next to the most powerful criminal in London at the moment of his downfall; like being a part of history. All we can see in the darkness beyond the floodlights is four sets of headlights, all stationary. Something much closer catches my eye and I see the six jump-suited men who were mine and Andy's co-workers this afternoon. They are lying in the dirt with their faces in the gravel and their hands clasped behind their heads, just outside the temporary fencing. At first I think they are dead, which I'm sure isn't part of the plan but then I see one of them move slightly, and realise that if Stephanie had had them killed, she wouldn't have arranged them in such a neat row.

Stephanie walks into the light with Frank and Cheese standing on either side of her. As soon as I see her I feel like I've been kicked in the guts. She looks like the star of her own movie. She's wearing a long flowing camel hair coat and a long black skirt that tapers into knee-length black boots with a razor-sharp heel. I forget the enormity of the situation, the dangerous men in the room with me, the dangerous men outside, I forget everything and just see Stephanie. I've been thinking about how quickly I accepted the proposal she made just a few days ago; I agreed almost instantly despite the danger of her plan, the sheer audacity of it. Seeing her now reminds me exactly why I came round to her way of thinking. She could have told me to exhume my mother and have sex with the body and I think I'd probably have done it. Stephanie breaks my reverie by calling out. "Stan, Joe, come out, your time is up." I look at Joe, knowing he's going to recognise that voice, and sure enough he reacts, standing up and coming to the window. Stephanie calls again, "Joe, Stan, it's time to pay the piper."

I can't resist speaking. I turn to Joe, who is still cowering on the floor. "I told you not to trust her Joe," I don't care how smug I sound, "But you wouldn't believe me would you? Instead you threatened to have me killed."

It's the first time I have seen Joe lost for words. He just stares at me.

Stan Costanza raises his eyes to the ceiling. "Fuck it. Fuck it." He turns to Andy who is now standing. "You fucking knew didn't you? All that shit about Frank and Cheese being trustworthy, you fucking knew, you fucking knew." He turns to Joe and gestures at me. "Looks like we've both got traitors."

Andy looks at me. "Are you in on this too?" The simplicity of the question throws me for a moment. Andy continues. "Did she come to you too?"

I just nod weakly. Andy looks as astonished as I do.

"Well isn't this a nice little surprise for you both?" Stan breaks our incredulous exchange. I consider for a moment that he might try and jump either me or Andy, but something tells me he wouldn't risk his dignity on a fist fight with a younger and fitter man. Joe doesn't seem to have taken in what's going on yet.

"Stan. Joe. Don't keep me waiting. Get out here now." Stephanie's voice again.

Andy speaks. "Looks like it's time for you two to go."

Stan makes his way to the door, kicking Joe on the way. "Get up you fat fuck. It's time to pay the fucking piper, cheap fucking shit fucking line." Andy has to back out of the way to allow Stan to pass but Stan stops and turns so their faces are within an inch of each other. He hocks up a mouthful of phlegm. It's obvious what's coming, and Andy could easily get out of the way, but he doesn't move a muscle. Stan unloads the contents of his mouth onto Andy's face, then turns and makes for the door. Andy doesn't flinch, it's like it's a penance that he accepts willingly. Only when Stan is out of sight does he take out a handkerchief and wipe the disgusting mucus off his face.

Joe follows Stan out of the porta-cabin. Andy joins me at the window but we don't speak, and there are no Hollywood-style high fives. We've been on opposite sides for too long. We stand in silence in our ringside position. The halogen lighting makes it look artificial, like we're watching from behind the director's chair.

Behind Stephanie, Frank and Cheese, there's a line of armed men, the four guards from each side and Guy and Paolo. They stand ready to do Stephanie's bidding. I see Andy's eyes widen in amazement and know he is mirroring my own expression. I knew Stephanie had recruited a few men, but not the whole fucking lot. The gunshots earlier must have just been a warning to the unarmed men inside the fence. The fact that they are still eating gravel tells me they weren't in on the plan.

Stan shows no sign of nerves. Stan's staring at Stephanie. "It's you isn't it? You're Visconti's girl. You're dead. Why aren't you dead?"

Joe is right behind Costanza and calls out. "Stephanie? Steph? What's going on?" *His voice sounds defeated, lost.*

Stan turns to Joe, whose face fills in the blanks. "You fat fuck Barrett, I knew someone was cranking your handle. That's Tony's daughter. What the fuck has she been telling you?" *Joe just stares. Stephanie answers for him.* "I told him I was your lover, Stan. I told him you kept me like a prisoner and that I needed someone to save me. Joe was my knight in shining armour. Sweet isn't it?"

Stan turns to Joe and slaps him hard across the face. He doesn't need any words. Joe recoils in pain and despair. He doesn't retaliate. In a stroke he's been reduced from a proud, fearsome man into nothing. Less than nothing. He's as far down as he was up before.

Stan's doing a better job of keeping up his image. "So you've got it all sewn up." *He fixes his eyes on each of the men lined up with Stephanie in turn and starts clapping,* "You've rounded up some traitors and you've caught me and this fucking moron with our pants down, bravo." *He stops clapping.* "Now what?"

"I think you know." *Stephanie's eyes sparkle under the lights.*

"There's no way you can kill two unarmed men, Visconti."

"My parents were unarmed when you killed them."

"You of course have my sympathy, but that was just business. Your father would have known that, and you should know that."

"I don't care about your business Stan. Actually, that's wrong, I do care. I care a lot, because it's now my business. I'm taking everything you've got, starting with your life. And you're next Joe."

"You can't do it, you won't pull that trigger." Joe's first words for a long time.

She points the gun at Joe. *"You've been watching too many crime thrillers Joe, those scenes where the goodie can't kill the baddie because they don't want to stoop to their level? That's not real. That argument doesn't wash in real life, only in fiction. I'd say 'just watch me' but you won't be able to watch, the bullet's going to move too fast. Goodbye Joe."* Joe's mouth gapes open. Stephanie squeezes the trigger and half of his face explodes. His body falls into the dust.

Stan doesn't bat an eyelid. *"So you've learnt to shoot. Aren't you a clever girl?"*

She points the gun at his head. She's about three yards away. *"Say you're sorry Stan."*

"Sorry for what? I've got nothing to be sorry for. Your old man had it coming. He should have seen the signs. Everyone I killed had it coming. They should have all seen the signs."

Stephanie smiles, *"You should have seen the signs Stan."*

Stan scratches his head. *"You're right. I should have seen the signs. Maybe it's time I gave up the reins."*

"You don't have the reins anymore Stan. You've lost everything. You're about to die."

Stan still won't crack for Stephanie. He knows what she's after and he's too stubborn to give her the satisfaction.

"One more chance Stan. All you have to do is say sorry, and it'll be over quickly."

Stan spits on the ground in front of Stephanie. *"Fuck you, you fucking whore, how many cocks did you have to suck to get these cunts to turn against me?"*

Stephanie blows Stan a kiss. She lowers her aim and fires, hitting him just below the waist. Like the commentators say, that's gotta hurt. He doubles over and starts howling. It's a horrific transformation. His violent nobility has become animal agony.

"Say sorry Stan."

"Fuck you."

She shoots him again, in the leg this time. He screams even louder.

Stephanie walks to his squirming body and puts her boot on his head, forcing it down onto the ground. The stiletto heel must have punctured the skin. "Say sorry."

"Bitch," he whimpers. Blood sprays from his lips.

Stephanie leans down and pushes the gun hard against the uppermost side of Stan's head. It's a tableau of deadly erotica; her perfect form, the curve of her thighs and shoulders, her face flushed with adrenaline as she pins this powerful man to the ground. I know that my erection is not alone. She speaks directly into his ear, loud enough for everyone to hear above his whimpering. "Say you're sorry you pathetic washed up old man."

Stan's whole body is shaking but she keeps his head steady with her heel. A look of satisfaction crosses her face. Stan must have said the magic word. She pulls the trigger, turning her head as she does so to avoid the spray of brain and tissue.

Thirty

We'd been confined to the hotel room for three days but it seemed more like a week. Stephanie, Frank and Cheese didn't visit often, but each time they did see us they reiterated that we should stay put. Frank and Cheese brought us provisions but only the basics and I quickly tired of cheese and pickle sandwiches. They also brought magazines and some books, but the literature available in the convenience store nearby didn't really catch my imagination. Colin seemed happy though, ravenously chewing up the chick-lit that Frank, showing a terrible lack of judgement, had bought for Laura.

We weren't even allowed to order takeaways unless either Frank, Cheese or Stephanie were there to take the delivery, and as they weren't there very often we had to go without for long periods.

We heard banging on the door of the hotel room at three in the morning on the fourth day, but by then we didn't really know if it was night or day. We were watching a film on the tiny television in the room. We had long given up trying to stop the picture from rolling up the screen every few minutes. I went to the door and saw Stephanie through the spy hole, flanked by Frank and Cheese. They all had huge smiles on their faces that were made even bigger by the fish-eye glass.

Before I had the door open fully they had barged inside. Frank and Cheese were both holding magnums, of Champagne that is.

Frank spoke first. "We fucking did it."

"He's right," said Stephanie, "we fucking did it. Ask me how Joe Barrett is."

"How's Joe Barrett?"

"He's dead. Ask me how Stan Costanza is."

"He's dead isn't he?"

"Ask me."

I went along with her. "How's Stan Costanza?"

"He's dead!" Stephanie snatched the champagne off Frank and took a swig. It fizzed out of her nose and she was nearly sick. That set Frank off. He was busy trying to open another bottle of bubbly but was too amused by Stephanie's mishap to complete the task.

They told us the story of what had happened that evening, that they had taken Costanza and Barrett down, that their careful planning had ensured that they had enough men from both sides on board to make their move. Then Cheese produced the biggest bag of coke I had ever seen and made a succession of thick, fat lines on one of the bedside tables. We got completely fucked. Frank kept shouting 'time to pay the piper' which made Cheese laugh and Stephanie cringe, but I never found out what it meant.

Our little soiree continued into the night. Stephanie came and sat beside me and I tried to avert my eyes from the glimpse of flesh that was revealed between the top of her boot and the split of her skirt. "I'm really sorry about lying to you Thomas, but I'm really grateful for all your help. I can let my father rest now."

"What are you going to do now?"

"Well first we've got to sort you three out. Obviously you don't have to worry about Costanza and Barrett anymore but the police will still be after you. It's okay, I've got a plan, and it seems that my plans work out just fine. Then I'm going to go away somewhere."

"You're not going to take over where your father left off?"

"I'm going to leave that to these two." She gestured at Frank and Cheese, having a one-sided piggy back fight with Colin and Laura.

Thirty-one

I'm woken by bright sunshine streaming onto my face. I open my eyes and see Laura opening the curtains. She is in a white t-shirt and silk boxer shorts. Her hair is wet from the shower and is combed back from her face. I thought yesterday that I couldn't love her any more than I did but realise that today I do. A coffee is on the table next to my side of the bed.

"I thought you were never going to wake up."

"I thought one day you'd let me sleep."

"I wanted some company." She jumps onto the bed and straddles me, poking at my chest and face. "You've gone hard!"

"Of course I have, I'm only human."

"Well don't get any ideas, I'm all clean now and you're in a puddle of your own sweat."

"You're so romantic."

"Come on, I've got to do the sheets, I want to get them out on the line before lunch while the sun's out."

"This is Texas, the sun's always out."

"Yes, but if I leave the washing out too late it'll get covered in bugs. Come on, get up." She lies next to me and pushes me with her hands and feet.

After I've had a shower, which lost pressure halfway through when Laura turned on the washing machine, I get dressed and go onto the front lawn to retrieve the newspaper flung by the paperboy in the general direction of the house. I stoop to pick it up and hear a voice, a strong southern accent.

"Good morning Peter." I turn to return to the house and hear the voice again. "Peter, are you going deaf?" I still haven't got used to my new name. I turn and see my neighbour, Todd Willis. He is a beefy, amiable man who seems to wear the same Texas Rangers baseball shirt every weekend.

I turn to face him, shielding my eyes from the sun with the tightly rolled newspaper. "Morning Todd, sorry, I'm still half asleep. How's it going?"

"Damn, I just love that crazy accent Peter. You're going to knock 'em dead at the barbecue tomorrow."

Todd has been keen to welcome us into the neighbourhood, which I'd really rather he didn't. I am still undecided as to what the American flag hanging outside his front porch represents. In my experience from back home, strong patriotism is often a front for xenophobia, or downright racism, but I have yet to understand whether Willis's fierce pride in the Land of the Free should be taken at face value or not. Laura has argued that by keeping my distance from him, I am myself being prejudiced, and shouldn't judge him without getting to know him. The bottom line is that I don't want to go to his barbecue because the idea of meeting his friends and neighbours appeals to me like an afternoon in a leper colony. It's not so much the tedium of small talk that puts me off, although that's obviously part of it, it's more the pressure of having to remember my fictional personal background.

"We're looking forward to it Todd."

"Is Dave bringing a lady friend?"

"I don't know Todd. He seems to be keeping his options open for the moment."

Dave, or Colin as I know him, has also found that his 'crazy' accent goes down a storm. He's picked up a different girl almost every night since we arrived, but I don't know if he even remembers their names, let alone thinks about bringing any of them to polite social functions. It would have seemed strange for two English best friends to buy houses next door to each other in this small American town, so to keep things simple Colin – Dave, is Laura's brother, or rather he's Monica's brother, for Monica is Laura's new moniker.

"He's got red blood in those veins of his for sure." Despite his frequent church-going, Todd seems impressed by Colin - Dave's Lothario lifestyle.

"You can say that again, Todd." I hope he doesn't say it again.

I go back into the house and find Laura – Monica in the kitchen. "Breakfast will be ready soon." She's cooking pancakes and bacon. She has been quick to embrace American-style eating despite my protestations.

"Pancakes are a sweet dish, bacon's savoury."

"Everything's sweet if you put enough maple syrup on it." Laura – Monica punctuates her point by squeezing half a bottle of syrup onto her sacrilegious plate. "I know you're deliberately rejecting our new culture so I've cut some bread for a bacon sandwich for you." She sits down and sets about demolishing her food. I finish making the sandwich and join her. "When are you working next?" She asks.

"Tuesday."

"They're keeping you busy aren't they?"

"Yeah, it's like they're clearing a backlog or something. I'm so jealous of you. I can't believe you've got another three weeks of sitting on that gorgeous arse of yours."

"You're always the charmer Peter, I prefer that name by the way. Anyway, I'm not sitting around, I've got loads of studying to do. I don't want to be the dumb English girl when I start my classes. I'm shit-scared they're all going to be miles ahead of me."

"You'll be fine. Colin starts his new job on Monday."

"You mean Dave."

"Sorry, Dave. He's looking forward to it." Colin – Dave has been given a job in a construction company, which is just another example of how far-reaching Stephanie's influence is. After bringing down Stan Costanza and Joe Barrett she was as good as her word and made arrangements to get the three of us out of the mess she had been more than partly responsible for getting us into. She conjured Laura's passport up from somewhere and escorted us on a flight to America, via Morocco. Nobody at customs challenged us at any part of our trip, despite the fact that I had nearly two hundred thousand pounds in my holdall. They just took a look at the name on Stephanie's passport and waved us through. We learnt to stop questioning Stephanie's seemingly magical powers.

She knew a senior official in the Texas State Government who put us onto the witness relocation programme, despite the fact that we weren't witnesses to anything but our own crimes. We went through strenuous training and instruction as part of the programme, and our case officers, unless they were very good actors, didn't seem to be in on our secret; to them it was normal not to know anything about the people they were relocating. They gave us new homes, new names, new life stories and they gave me a new job, one that makes good use of my talents and protects my anonymity.

Stephanie stayed at Colin's for the first week to make sure we settled in okay. She quickly despatched any hopes Colin had that she was interested in him when she pointed out that he would be on the sofa for the duration of her stay. We've all missed her since she left even though she's only a short drive away, in Dallas. I still can't think of that word without thinking of the TV show. It doesn't seem like home in this all-American small town and it probably never will, but none of us ever had any real connection with 'home' anyway. I look out of the front window and watch provincial America amble past. It seems so familiar in my memory that's been shaped by imported movies and television shows. I wonder how the barbecue will go tomorrow, and remind myself that my name is now Peter in case I accidentally ignore anybody. My fiancée is called Monica, her brother is called Dave.

I remember that I need to go to the store today. I need some new shoes for work. The State of Texas likes its executioners to look smart under that black hood.

FROM THE AUTHOR

I really hope you enjoyed it this book. If you did then please tell all your friends and leave a glowing review.

To check out other books I've written and to be updated on future releases then please go to my website and click on follow:

awwilson.com

If you want to get in touch, then please do:

contact@awwilson.com

Thanks!

Printed in Great Britain
by Amazon